PRAISE FOR HARPER ST. GEORGE

"A glittering ballroom romance bursting with the industry and wealth that so define Gilded Age heiresses."
—*Entertainment Weekly*

"*The Heiress Gets a Duke* is a charming, compulsively readable delight and I can't wait for the next book from Harper St. George's magical pen!"
—Evie Dunmore, *USA Today* bestselling author

"St. George marries classic elements from historical romance greats like Lisa Kleypas and Julia Quinn with subtle winks and nudges about the genre that would appeal to the more experienced romance reader."   —*Forbes*

"A sparkling jewel of a love story, full to the brim with Victorian wit, romance, and heart-stopping heat. Road trips in a carriage and four don't get much sexier than this."
—Mimi Matthews, *USA Today* bestselling author on *The Devil and the Heiress*

"A sexy, emotional, romantic tale . . . Harper St. George is a must-buy for me!"
—Terri Brisbin, *USA Today* bestselling author on *The Heiress Gets a Duke*

"Wit, seduction, and passion blend seamlessly to create this deeply emotional romance. St. George weaves an intriguing plot with complex characters to provide the perfect sensual escape. There's nothing I didn't love about *The Heiress Gets a Duke*, especially its lush, captivating glimpse into history."   —Anabelle Bryant, *USA Today* bestselling author

"With sizzling chemistry, brilliant banter, and an unapologetically strong, feminist heroine, Harper St. George sets the pages ablaze!"

—Christi Caldwell, *USA Today* bestselling author

"Fun, tender, and definitely sexy, *The Heiress Gets a Duke* is already at the top of my list for the best books of the year. Don't sleep on this refreshing and feminist romance."

—*BookPage* (starred review)

"Harper St. George just gets better and better with every book, penning the kind of page-turning stories that you will want to read again as soon as you finish each one."

—Lyssa Kay Adams, author of *Isn't It Bromantic?*

"A rich, compelling, and beautifully written romance. St. George brings us the story of Violet Crenshaw, an American heiress with distinctly modern ideas about love and marriage."

—Elizabeth Everett, author of *A Perfect Equation* on *The Devil and the Heiress*

"Luscious historical romance." —PopSugar

"Rich with period detail, *The Heiress Gets a Duke* brings to life the Gilded Age's dollar princesses in this smart, sexy, and oh-so-satisfying story."

—Laurie Benson, award-winning author of the Sommersby Brides series

"You'll sigh, you'll cry, and you'll grin yourself silly as this independent and cynical heiress finally gets her duke."

—Virginia Heath, author of *Never Fall for Your Fiancée*

TITLES BY HARPER ST. GEORGE

The Gilded Age Heiresses

THE HEIRESS GETS A DUKE
THE DEVIL AND THE HEIRESS
THE LADY TEMPTS AN HEIR
THE DUCHESS TAKES A HUSBAND

The
DUCHESS
TAKES A HUSBAND

HARPER ST. GEORGE

BERKLEY ROMANCE
New York

BERKLEY ROMANCE
Published by Berkley
An imprint of Penguin Random House LLC
penguinrandomhouse.com

Copyright © 2023 by Harper Nieh
Excerpt from *The Stranger I Wed* by Harper St. George copyright © 2023 by Harper Nieh
Penguin Random House supports copyright. Copyright fuels creativity, encourages
diverse voices, promotes free speech, and creates a vibrant culture. Thank you for buying
an authorized edition of this book and for complying with copyright laws by not
reproducing, scanning, or distributing any part of it in any form without permission.
You are supporting writers and allowing Penguin Random House to continue to
publish books for every reader.

BERKLEY and the BERKLEY & B colophon
are registered trademarks of Penguin Random House LLC.

ISBN: 9780593440988

First Edition: May 2023

Printed in the United States of America
1   3   5   7   9   10   8   6   4   2

Book design by George Towne

For all the readers who asked for Camille's happily ever after. This one's for you.

AUTHOR'S NOTE

Thank you so much for reading the Gilded Age Heiresses. I hope you enjoy the opulence and richness of this time period as much as I do. One of my favorite parts of the Gilded Age are the Dollar Princesses. These were real women from new money families who were often pressured into marriages with European nobility for the sole purpose of raising the status of their families in Society. There were over 350 of these marriages from 1870 to 1920. They were the inspiration for this series.

Sometimes the marriages were consensual, as in the case of Jennie Jerome, who accepted the proposal of Lord Randolph Churchill after knowing him for all of three days. (Their first child was Winston Churchill, who was born premature at nine pounds.) Some believe it was this love match that started the avalanche of heiresses into European society. Then there is the famous case of Consuelo Vanderbilt, who was forced by her parents to give up the man she loved to marry the 9th Duke of Marlborough. Accounts from the time indicate that she was crying as she walked down the aisle. This story in particular was the inspiration for Camille.

Camille has been somewhat of a cautionary tale for my Crenshaw heiresses throughout this series. They saw her forced marriage in the prologue of book one and decided to run from every marriage their parents tried to arrange for them. Camille's book was not planned when I first started writing the series, but I am so glad that readers wanted and asked for her story. She deserves her happily ever after.

There is no question that Camille was a victim of domestic violence. Please be aware that some of the abuse she suffered in her previous marriage is remembered in this book, in case that is a sensitive topic for you. It's not explicit, but it is discussed.

The National Domestic Violence Hotline defines domestic violence (also referred to as intimate partner violence, dating abuse, or relationship abuse) as a pattern of behaviors used by one partner to maintain power and control over another partner in an intimate relationship. No one deserves to have this happen to them. Anyone can be a victim. If you suspect this is happening to you or someone else, please call the National Domestic Violence Hotline at 1-800-799-7233 (SAFE) or 1-800-787-3224 (TTY) or text "START" to 88788 for anonymous and confidential information. Their website www.thehotline.org has information about the signs of abuse.

Victoria Woodhull was an outspoken proponent of women's rights. In particular, she was an advocate of Free Love. At this time in history, this movement meant that people should be free to enter into marriages and to leave marriages as they wished without hindrance from society or the government. She was a lecturer who traveled around the United States discussing her ideas, and she also ran a radical newspaper touting women's rights. The portion of the speech in this book is from Woodhull's 1874 speech "Tried as by Fire; or, the True and the False, Socially." By 1878, Woodhull had left New York for England, where she lived with her family until her death. I thought it possible she would attend the London Suffrage Society meeting (which is fictitious).

I took a few liberties with the origin of cabaret. Cabaret was started by Rodolphe Salis in the Montmartre district of Paris when he opened the nightclub Le Chat Noir in 1881.

The entertainment featured a platform surrounded by an audience, where various acts would perform poetry readings, song and dance sets, comedy routines, and shadow plays. Frequently, the entertainment turned toward political and social commentary. The different acts were all brought together by a master of ceremonies who entertained the audience. It wasn't until 1889 and the opening of Moulin Rouge, a dance hall that popularized the cabaret style, that the entertainments veered more toward seductive and sometimes bawdy.

Chapter 1

❖

Smile, but not too wide. Smiles in public are meant to be mysterious, not expressions of joy. Keep your shoulders squared at all times but always, always remain demure. Chin tilted downward the slightest bit, darling. It wouldn't do to appear too confident. A wise woman knows her place is one of support and encouragement. When a suitor gazes upon her he should see a prospective helpmate, someone who will assist in his life instead of forcing her own will. No one likes a headstrong woman.

Camille, Dowager Duchess of Hereford, closed her eyes, attempting to block out the words. No matter how she tried to ignore them, her mother's advice always seemed to play in the back of her mind when she least wanted to heed it. As the only child of Samuel and Martha Bridwell, she had been raised to the most exacting standards from birth. Her mother had been fastidious when it came to her grooming, comportment, and even her friends. Her education had centered around the intricacies of both running a large household and navigating the treacherous waters of Society. Nothing had been more important to her parents than seeing her married well, and Camille had all these speeches memorized, having heard them relentlessly.

Unfortunately, her parents' ideas of married well had been vastly different from Camille's. She had valued kindness and affection, while her parents had valued social status. That was it. That seemed to be their sole requirement.

She opened her eyes and smiled at her reflection in the mirror before her, the muscles in her face responding from memory, curving her lips upward in a cold imitation of happiness. She hated this practiced smile. It made her feel aloof and untouchable. While it had its uses in London ballrooms, it was not what she needed now. She was at Montague Club, not a mansion in Mayfair. The gaming club was for entertainment, not social climbing. Something a bit more sincere would probably be better for her purposes this evening, though she honestly didn't know. She'd never tried to seduce a man before. Her stomach fluttered in nerves and perhaps a tiny bit of anticipation as an image of Jacob Thorne came to mind.

She let the smile drop and leaned forward to get a better look as she rubbed her fingertips along the bracket lines left behind in the fair skin on either side of her mouth, hoping to make them disappear. At twenty-three she wasn't old, but recent years had given her face a maturity that her mother had warned her against when Camille last visited her in New York.

Haven't you been wearing the night cream I sent you?

Camille had lied and answered yes, but when she'd returned home to London, she had found another case of the fancy French jars waiting for her. At the time she'd been annoyed. She'd been in mourning for a dead husband whose loss she did not grieve and her mother was already stressing the importance of marrying again. Well, Camille did not want to marry again. *Ever.* But now she rather wished she had started applying the night cream. Men liked women who looked young and fresh. The cream might help that, but there was nothing she could do about her eyes.

Her eyes were sad, and she didn't really understand why. Hereford was dead and not around to control her life anymore. She did not miss him or his high-handedness. She was a wealthy widow with all the freedoms inherent in the position. Though the bulk of the money her father had transferred to Hereford upon their marriage had gone to his heir on his death, she had been provided a small pension and a London residence. Then, completely unprompted, her father had bought her an estate situated not far outside of London. She suspected he had been motivated by guilt but had never questioned him. So given that, she should be very happy, but there were her eyes, staring back at her and calling her a liar.

She smiled again, this time wider and with joy, revealing a row of mostly straight, white teeth, but her brown eyes did not brighten at all. Sighing, she sat back, thinking of all the women she had seen Thorne escort about the club with their easy smiles. It reaffirmed her instinct that he would like her better if she could smile more naturally, and she would have tried again, but the door to the ladies' retiring room swung open and a beautiful woman came sweeping in. She paused in surprise as soon as she set eyes on Camille. She appeared to be about the same age as Camille with dark eyes and hair and a golden complexion.

"Well, well, well, you do exist." The newcomer smiled and took a seat beside Camille on the elongated ottoman that was set before the mirror and vanity. "Lilian Greene," she introduced herself.

"Camille—" she began, but the woman took over.

"Duchess of Hereford, yes, I know." Lilian Greene's

smile had no trouble lighting her eyes as she turned toward the mirror and leaned forward to adjust a hairpin hiding near her temple in her raven tresses. She was elegantly dressed in a modestly cut chocolate-colored gown.

"Dowager now," Camille clarified.

"Of course, Dowager." She paused, her sympathetic eyes catching Camille's in the mirror. "I am sorry for your loss, Your Grace."

Camille gave a nod of acknowledgment. "Please call me Camille. I'd prefer to have one place where my title doesn't matter." She hated the title, actually. It had brought her nothing but pain and frustration.

"Then you must call me Lilian. When Jacob told me another woman had joined the club, I was happy, of course, but then I never saw you here and I wondered if he'd made you up simply to placate me. I am always on at him to bring on more female members and stop referring to it as a gentlemen's club." She chattered easily as she arranged other pins in her hair.

"You know Mr. Thorne well, then?" There was no reasonable explanation for why the fact that Lilian had called him by his first name made her feel so heavy inside. Lilian seemed unaware of this fact as she pulled out a small cosmetic tin from the handbag dangling on a strap looped around her wrist and dabbed a bit of scarlet rouge on the apples of each cheek and her lips.

"Would you like some?" she asked instead of answering the question, holding the little pot out to Camille.

"Oh, thank you." Perhaps a little color would brighten her face.

She put a dab of the cream on her fingertip and slicked it across her bottom lip. It was brighter against her lighter skin and blond hair, but she loved the effect. Usually, she wore only neutral shades meant to subtly enhance her peaches-and-cream coloring, but the scarlet was arresting, drawing the eye immediately to her lips. A tiny revolt against the social constraints of her life. She couldn't help wondering if Thorne would like it. Another swirl of anticipation swooped through her, prompting her other hand to press against her stomach.

"That color works well on you. And to answer your question, yes, Jacob and I know each other well. I'm a long-time member." Lilian winked and rose, adjusting her skirts.

It was absolutely none of her business, but she couldn't help but wonder if Lilian and Thorne were lovers. He had lovers. Camille knew that. She had been a member of the club for a few months, and in that time she had seen any number of women arrive by the ladies-only entrance and greet him very warmly. Sometimes he'd offer his arm, other times he'd slide his hand around their waist and disappear with them into parts unknown and she wouldn't see him again that night. She couldn't say with reasonable certainty that he slept with *all* of them, but it was a fair bet that he'd bedded a few.

"How many women members are there?" Camille hadn't thought to ask when she'd filled out her registration form and paid the rather expensive dues. She'd joined because Hereford would have been appalled, not because she'd been trying to prove a larger point about equality of the sexes.

"A dozen, give or take, not nearly enough. I have to hurry off, but I would love to chat more. Will you be here another evening this week?"

Camille opened and closed her mouth when she realized she didn't know what to say. If Thorne rejected her proposition, then she couldn't imagine showing her face here again, but she didn't want to miss the chance of making a new friend. She didn't have many of those. Since coming to London over three years ago, she'd become *that American* because she could never seem to live up to the expectations of being Hereford's duchess. It had become the done thing to invite her to events only to sneer at her behind her back. Fellow American heiresses the Crenshaw sisters, August and Violet, were her friends, but they were both happily married now and starting families of their own.

"Perhaps we could have tea one afternoon?" she offered.

Lilian's smile was genuine when she said, "I would like that very much."

They exchanged goodbyes and Camille was left alone. She didn't bother practicing her smile again because it could quickly become a procrastination tactic. Either he was attracted to her and he said yes, or he wasn't and he said no. Taking a deep breath and letting it out slowly, she rose and brushed out invisible wrinkles on her skirts. She wore an emerald-green gown cut the slightest bit lower than modest and in the natural shape that emphasized the flare of her hips, selected precisely because she thought it showed off her figure to the best advantage.

Pushing open the paneled mahogany door, she made her way down the wide corridor to the gaming room. It was nearly ten o'clock in the evening, which meant Thorne was probably there talking with patrons or dealing cards. He owned Montague Club along with his half brother, Christian Halston, Earl of Leigh, and their friend Evan Sterling, Duke of Rothschild. Both men were married to the Crenshaw sisters, so Camille had met him socially a handful of times. While she had always been charmed by his handsomeness in those social settings, it wasn't until she had joined Montague Club that she'd found herself viewing him differently . . . as someone she might want to get to know in an entirely more intimate way.

The double doors that led to the main gaming room were thrown wide open, revealing a dimly lit but richly appointed setting. Gilded sconces topped with frosted globes were set at regular intervals giving off flickering gaslight that was immediately absorbed by the dark wood paneling, creating playful shadows and an aura of intimacy. Aubusson rugs in dark reds, greens, and gold matched the sofas and overstuffed chairs set in small groupings near the fireplaces on either end of the space. Rosewood gaming tables topped with green baize were scattered throughout the middle of the room. It was a slow night, so only a few had men playing at them, while the rest sat empty.

As usual, the table where Jacob Thorne stood dealing cards was busy. He was well-liked and the club members seemed to gravitate toward him. He was as sinfully handsome as his half brother, Christian, but not nearly as forbidding. They were both tall and filled out a frock coat nicely, but where Christian's smile seemed to hold an edge of cynicism, Thorne's was more open and friendly. That was partly why she had decided to approach him with her indecent proposition. He was kind and trustworthy. She didn't think he would laugh at her or brag to his friends, but even more than that, he was the only man who had turned her head in a long time. Since her parents had introduced her to Hereford. Once she had met her future husband and reluctantly agreed to the marriage, she hadn't viewed men in the same way. She'd begun to despair that she ever would again, but something about Thorne had her looking twice.

She studied him as she made her way around the tables to reach him. He was dressed as well as the men he entertained with nothing about him to indicate he owned the club and they were customers. His clothing was bespoke like theirs and had probably come from the same tailor. He was the son of an earl after all, though born outside of wedlock. He had been raised by his father, and that aristocratic arrogance showed on his face and in his mannerisms, except he wore it more naturally than many. It wasn't conceit with him, so much as grace and charm.

His well-formed lips parted in a smile as he dealt another hand of vingt-un and made a joke she couldn't hear. The men at the table laughed as they added to their bets. Thorne picked up the deck of cards with a skill born from years of practice and tossed another card onto each stack.

His hands were strong but graceful with long fingers and clipped nails. If all went to plan, he could be touching her with those very hands soon. She paused as a flush warmed her face, but it was too late. He'd caught sight of her.

"Your Grace." He smiled as the other three men greeted her in turn. "Have you come to join us?" he asked, his voice rich and smooth.

She swallowed and willed the butterflies in her stomach to cease their antics. She'd talked to him many times since joining his club, and tonight didn't have to be any different. Only it was. Fighting past her nerves, she took the chair at the end of the crescent-shaped table. "Yes, but I'm afraid I've never played the game before."

"Not to worry, Your Grace. We'll teach you, won't we, gentlemen?"

They murmured their agreement. A footman came forward almost immediately, bearing a small tumbler of her favorite whisky on ice. The service here was remarkable. Accepting it with a smile, she spent the next several minutes watching the men play as Thorne went over the rules. The game seemed easy enough; one simply tried to get the sum of their cards to add up to twenty-one without going over. It wasn't complicated. Finally, Thorne dealt her in, and she promptly lost the first two hands.

"Too aggressive," he warned her with a shake of his head when she asked for another card on the third round. The gaslight played in his thick, black hair, and she wondered if it would be as soft as it looked.

"I'm not aggressive," she said.

"Stand on anything higher than fifteen," he instructed. "The risk is too high otherwise."

"Good God, Thorne, don't help her. You already win most hands; if you teach her to best us there will be no use in any of us playing."

She recognized the man who spoke as a young lord who had inherited his title a few years ago. Most men at the club had been a bit reticent with her presence; they accepted it but didn't embrace it. Their clubs had long been a refuge from female companionship. He'd been one of the few who had not been bothered by her.

"Come now, Verick, you can't be upset that a mere woman might best you?" she teased.

Verick grinned and said, "My male pride can only take so much, Your Grace, before it needs soothing."

She didn't miss the inuendo, but Verick wasn't who she wanted. She also didn't miss the way Thorne's eyes cut to him at the comment. A little wisp of pleasure flickered to life in her belly that Thorne would care.

"All right, I'll stand." Her cards added up to sixteen. The other men went over and she won by default. She smiled in satisfaction.

The game continued for a little while with her winning a few more hands before the men drifted away, leaving her alone at the table with Thorne. He handled the cards easily as he shuffled, his gaze flicking up to her from beneath a thick fringe of lashes. "Another hand?"

"Actually, I hoped we might talk a bit." She cleared her throat as it threatened to close. "In private." She forced the words out.

"Intriguing." He shuffled the cards and set them in the small tray on the table before placing his palms on the green baize and leaning toward her a bit. "It almost sounds as if you have a proposition for me."

She swallowed under the force of his gaze, letting her eyes take in the strong lines of his face to avoid meeting it. He had high cheekbones that any woman would kill for, and his nose was blade straight. "Of sorts."

"Shall we go to my office?" The inky slash of one brow rose in question.

No! That would be too intimate. What if he refused her and she was forced to sit there beneath the intensity of his stare? What if he said yes and expected to follow through tonight? It couldn't be tonight. She'd only concocted the scheme over the last week. If he agreed, she would need a couple of days to prepare herself.

"Perhaps semiprivate would be best. One of the lounges."

He nodded. "Follow me."

Taking one last fortifying sip of her drink, she left it there as she walked with him. He led her through the larger rooms, where a few groups of men congregated on leather chairs talking politics, to a smaller room in the back corner of the club. A modest fire roared in the hearth, and bookshelves lined one wall. The little nook faced a side street that was quiet at this time of night, and though it was adequately lit, the moonlight that came through the windows made it seem more intimate than she would have liked. The door was open to the nearby lounge, however, so they weren't completely alone.

"Will this do?" he asked, indicating she should take one of the chairs before the fire.

"This is fine." She had to walk by him to sit and caught the scent of his cologne, a very pleasing mix of sandalwood and vetiver. She had admired it before, but this time it made her thoughts swirl in her head, or maybe it was because she had to move so close to him. He was tall and broad, and the very indecent question she meant to ask him made her aware of how very large and solid he actually was. Her breath hitched in a strange mix of fear and anticipation.

He waited for her to settle herself before he sat down opposite her, his long legs stretching out before him as easily as if they were old friends convening for a visit. His gaze searched her face, the firelight casting a sable tint to his deep brown eyes.

"A drink for you both, sir?" A footman materialized in the doorway.

"No, thank you, Marcus."

The footman gave an abbreviated bow and left them alone.

"So, what is this proposition, Your Grace?" he asked.

"Camille," she said, but he didn't reply. He simply watched her with the corners of his mouth turned up in that easy way he had about him. That expression always seemed to say that he knew far more about you than you knew about him. "I've been having an issue . . ."

God, is that how she meant to ask him? To come to him as some sort of charity case in need of his help? To admit that something was wrong with her? Had she not once practiced what she might say in this moment? No, she'd been too focused on the goal to actually plot out a persuasive argument. Her heart pounded as her mind went blank.

How could she properly explain to him that she didn't understand why she never enjoyed sex? She was starting to believe that something was wrong with her, and he was her last hope. But she couldn't say that. Of course she couldn't.

He shifted back in a languid pose and clasped his hands across his stomach as he waited patiently. She had to say it now before she lost her courage. With tact not an option for her at the moment, she decided to be as straightforward as her pride would let her. Squaring her shoulders and raising her chin a notch for confidence, she met his gaze and said, "I would very much like to go to bed with you."

Chapter 2

✤

Jacob sat very still as every muscle in his body clenched in frustrated awareness of her. Each nerve ending, long trained to a forced compliance in her presence, bristled against its restraint, sending crackling heat along the surface of his skin. When Camille had asked to speak with him, he had expected her to request some sort of accommodation for the female members of the club, not this. He wasn't even certain he'd heard her correctly. Perhaps he'd been having so many sordid thoughts about her they had finally manifested themselves in a way that had turned a perfectly innocent request into something far more decadent.

He opened his mouth to speak, but his throat was too dry. He should have had Marcus bring him that drink, but he'd been too anxious to hear what she had to say to waste another second. She stared at him wide-eyed, as if she, too, were surprised by the words—or terrified by them. It was that edge of fear shadowing her face that gave him the wherewithal to grab on to his wilting restraint and drag it back to the forefront of his good sense where it belonged. Every inch of his body hissed its displeasure.

"Why?" It wasn't very eloquent, but it was all he could utter past the roaring in his ears that demanded he not question the gift of finally having her in his bed.

"B-because I find you handsome and I believe you are attracted to me." Her gaze drifted to the fire as if she couldn't say those things and look at him at the same time.

"I do find you beautiful, very much so," he said, warmth stealing over his chest when her cheeks tinted pink. "My query is more along the lines of why now? Why me? I don't bring every woman I find attractive into my bed." *Evidence to the contrary aside.*

"Oh!" She closed her eyes in embarrassment and sat back in the chair. "I didn't think . . . If you don't find me attractive in *that* way, then of course I understand."

"No." Christ, he hadn't meant that at all! He reached out to put a reassuring hand on her knee but reconsidered when his trousers got noticeably tighter at the prospect. He recalibrated and shifted his aim to her hand, but the hot throb of anticipation that darted through his groin told him that skin-to-skin contact was out of the question. Now that the subject of sex breathed between them like a tangible third presence, his body was waging a ferocious war with his mind, and he wasn't certain whose side he was on.

Crossing his legs to hide the unfortunate side effect of her request, he fisted his hands and kept them firmly on the arms of his chair where they would stay *not* touching her, *not* pulling her into his lap where he could kiss her properly, and *not* tugging her bodice down to finally get a look at what he suspected was the most perfect set of tits in London. No, he was not going to do any of that.

Taking in a serrated breath, he said, "I find you more than attractive . . . That isn't my point." What the bloody hell was his point? Rational thought was fast losing the battle. "Do you think our being together in"—he couldn't say the words; he'd be gone—"*that* particular manner would be wise? You are very close with Lady Leigh, who is married to my brother; her sister, with whom you are also close, is married to my business partner. It seems a bit—"

"But that's why I thought we might be perfect. I trust you." She stared at him with such perfect innocence compared to the havoc running rampant inside him, that he convinced himself with some difficulty that she hadn't said that to merely make it worse.

"I am not looking for any sort of permanent relationship, Your Grace—"

"Mr. Thorne . . ." She took in a breath, rallying herself for her next words. "Now I understand your hesitation. I don't think I made myself very clear, and I'm sorry for that. I've been married, and now I find that I very much enjoy *not* being married. Marriage isn't something I plan to do again for a long time, maybe never. When I said that I wanted to—" She paused to look past him, ascertaining that no one was about, before she added in a lowered voice, "To go to bed with you, I meant in a friendly way."

His brain had stopped working after the word *bed*, because all the blood in his body had rushed to the massive cockstand in his trousers. He could only manage to parrot, "In a friendly way?"

She nodded, a gentle smile curving her fantastically red lips. "Yes, friendly."

He had absolutely nothing to say to that. Several scenes played out in his head of the things he wanted to do to her in his bed, all of them depraved, some of them possibly illegal, none of them friendly.

He must have stared too long, because she added, "Like some of your friends who I've seen you meet at the women's entrance. I don't mean to be presumptuous, but once or twice it seemed as if you had an intimacy with a couple of them. I'd like us to have something similar . . . a friendly relationship that sometimes involves more."

It all sounded so reasonable when she said it, and that's how he knew that she'd never properly had a love affair, which helped him shore up his restraint once more, tattered as it was. There was one difference between Camille and those women. They never looked at him as she was doing now. Her whole heart was in her eyes, and it was bruised and vulnerable. Those women were looking for a fun and pleasant evening. Whether she knew it or not, Camille was looking for more. He couldn't give her more.

Clearing his throat, he said, "The difference is that I don't see those women socially. Our involvement could make things awkward when we see each other at my brother's home, for example, or at Charrington Manor. Imagine how you might feel when you're finished with me only to encounter me at some family event. Casual intimacies are best left to those who are casual acquaintances, don't you agree?"

Her brows came together as she considered his words. After a moment, she looked down to where she worried a seam on her gown with her fingers. "I suppose you're right. I didn't consider that. It seemed like a good idea because I knew you'd be discreet, and I wouldn't have to worry about damage to my reputation." Rallying, she stared back at him with earnest intensity. "Is there someone you might recommend I approach? Someone who would be equally as discreet?"

Over his dead body seemed an extreme reaction, particularly since he'd just told her that nothing was possible between them and it would make him the worst sort of hypocrite to deny her pleasure with someone else, but it was how he felt.

"You could procure a sexual aid. A dildo, perhaps. They are very effective at pleasure and discretion, I'm told."

The corner of her mouth quirked upward, and she reddened even more. "Thank you, but I'm looking for a man."

"I regret that I can't help you, Duchess."

Her eyes flashed at his impertinence in calling her that. It made the lustful beast inside him roar in outrage that he wouldn't unleash him.

"What a shame, but thank you, Mr. Thorne." She rose and brushed past him, leaving notes of vanilla and amber lingering in her wake.

He closed his eyes and imagined giving in to the baser impulses that urged him to go after her, toss her over his shoulder, and carry her through the club like a prize he had won on the way to his suite. He knew instinctively that's how bedding her would feel. Ever since he had first seen her—and wanted her—at Christian's wedding breakfast, he'd been uncomfortably aware of her and how unattainable she was to him. From that point forward he had avoided her as much as possible at the few social gatherings they both found themselves attending. Now even with her husband dead, her close friendship with his sister-in-law made her a risky choice for a lover. No, it was best that he continue to hold her at arm's length, no matter that a certain part of his anatomy might vehemently disagree.

He waited until his pulse settled and he was able to walk normally. Pulling out the gold watch he kept on a chain inside his waistcoat, he took note of the time. He had a half hour before his next meeting. Though it might be the most important meeting of his life, he'd need a detour to his bedroom to get a handle on his lust before taking it.

Jacob arrived at the midnight meeting without a moment to spare. The tall pocket doors leading to the salon in the private section of Montague Club that served as his home loomed ahead. He had entertained in this room hundreds of times over the years, but tonight a tremor of nervous energy threatened. Tonight's meeting would help determine his future.

The club was in an expansive white marble house that took up half a block on a prestigious street in Bloomsbury. The building had been Jacob's childhood home. His father, the late Earl of Leigh, had purchased it for his mother soon after getting her pregnant. His own marriage had precluded him from marrying her, so he had set her up as his mistress in a home larger than most in Mayfair. The late earl had kept a home in Belgravia, but he had rarely spent time there, preferring to live here. Jacob had always assumed that was because he could hardly tolerate his wife. It was commonly understood that she had arranged for them to be found in a compromising position so that he would be forced to marry her. Since her status as a daughter of the nobility had been higher than his own mother's, a merchant's daughter, she had won her husband. Jacob's mother had won his heart, however, prompting the purchase of this home and all the fine furnishings within. It was only later when his brother Christian, current Earl of Leigh, had come knocking on their door that Jacob understood his father had stripped the earldom of its liquid assets to finance their lavish lifestyle, leaving his heir destitute.

It hadn't been long after that he had also come to understand that his own finances weren't where he wanted them to be. After arranging the dowries of his two younger sisters, he'd been left comfortable, but only if he economized. He had needed an income greater than the modest investments his father had left him, and Christian had needed to keep up the estates he'd inherited, which is why they had conceived of the idea of Montague Club. It was also why he was considering a new business venture. Jacob had kept a portion of the home for his private residence, and this is where the men were meeting him. He'd learn tonight if his potential business partners were keen to move forward with their plans.

The hair at his nape was still damp, curling against his collar. He'd spent a quarter hour in his bathing chamber letting lukewarm water cascade over him, hoping the spray would banish the need for Camille from his fevered body. All he'd manage to do was give himself time alone to contemplate what they could have been doing at that moment if he'd only accepted her offer. Instead of forgetting her, he'd fixated on the memory of her pretty red lips and come in his own fist.

The release hadn't been enough to banish her. Even now, her memory pushed against him, causing a thread of yearning to pull through him, drawing his skin tight across the back of his neck. He knew that bedding her would make his life infinitely more complicated, but just once . . .

"Good evening, sir." Webb, his personal manservant, stood at the closed doors. "Your guests are comfortable and appreciated the Glenlivet you requested they be served."

Damn, the men had arrived a few minutes early. "Thank you, Webb." Fixing a smile in place, he nodded toward the salon, indicating that he was ready to go inside.

Webb opened the doors to reveal two men in deep discussion on the stylish divan in the center of the room. A selection of artwork his mother had curated over her lifetime hung on the walls of the elegant space, family portraits nestled amidst them. Three tumblers, two of them partially filled, and a bottle of Jacob's best scotch awaited on a low table before them.

"Good evening, gentlemen." Jacob walked in and the doors slid silently closed behind him.

"Thorne, how good it is to see you again." Gilbert Turner, club patron and businessman, rose to greet him. A cigar clamped in the corner of his mouth, he came forward to offer a handshake. In his fifties, he had the thick, solid body of a man who was accustomed to a good fight in a dark alley. His face was lined and craggy, indicating he may have spent his youth doing just that, but his kind eyes gentled his demeanor.

"And you as well, Turner." Turning to the other man, he said, "*Bonsoir*, Blanchet," in slightly accented French. His mother had insisted her children be fluent in the language, so they'd had a tutor for several years. "I see the two of you have met." He spoke in English because Turner did not speak French, to his knowledge.

"We met downstairs in the cardroom. I saw a man winning and thought, that is someone I want to meet. To my surprise, he was M. Blanchet."

"The cards were good to me," Blanchet said with false modesty.

Jacob had met Pierre Blanchet in Paris a couple of years ago. He managed a small club for gentlemen in the Montmartre district. Jacob had visited as a guest of a mutual friend, and they had started talking and found that they had several common interests. One of them was finding ways to manipulate card games so they won more than they lost. While Jacob was reasonably talented in deck observation so that after a few hands he could predict what would come next to a high degree of certainty, Blanchet's skill was uncanny. He had never seen someone calculate a game of vingt-un so accurately. They had struck up an easy friendship, and Jacob had last visited his Paris club back in the summer where they had begun to lay the foundation for the venture. When Blanchet had mentioned he would be in London for the night on his way to Scotland to sample the goods of a few distilleries, Jacob had arranged the meeting.

"I am pleased you both could join me tonight. Please have a seat." He indicated the sofa. "More scotch?" he asked, topping them off and pouring himself a finger of the deep amber liquid before taking one of the chairs opposite the divan.

Blanchet took a sip of his, letting it sit on his tongue briefly before swallowing. "The scotch is very good, my friend. I am happy to have added the distillery to my tour."

Turner agreed. "Are you visiting Scotland to procure a supplier for your club?"

"I am," Blanchet said. "With Thorne's expertise, I've arranged to tour several facilities."

"It will also serve as his wedding trip. He was married last week. Congratulations again," Jacob added, raising his glass in a toast. "I look forward to meeting your bride."

"Ah, married! Best of luck, old man. May your marriage be joyful and fruitful." Turner looked delighted, clinking his glass with the group before taking a healthy swallow.

"*Merci.*" Blanchet sat back, smiling fondly at the glass in his hand, no doubt lost in thoughts of his new wife. "We are very happy." To Jacob, he added, "Thank you again for your generous gift. Margot was pleased."

The wedding had been a small affair in the country church of the village where the bride's family lived in France. Jacob had sent the couple a silver tea service. "I am happy she liked it."

"I am pleased you are married. Relieved, to be honest," Turner said. "I have recently married myself." When Blanchet began to offer his congratulations, he added, "Several years back now, which means I was a bachelor for far too long. Since that time, I've come to appreciate the importance of marriage and family. She has changed me for the better. A woman and a home can be a stabilizing force. I'd highly recommend the state to every man." He gave a teasing and yet pointed look in Jacob's direction.

Jacob smiled inwardly. If his own mother hadn't been able to convince him of the positive attributes of marriage, Gilbert Turner didn't stand a chance in hell. But the fact that Blanchet's marriage *relieved* him set off warning bells. "Then we owe a debt of thanks to the remarkable Mrs. Turner."

They all laughed as they were meant to, and then Turner shifted to face him more fully. "I am intrigued by your invitation, Thorne. I've wanted to buy into Montague Club many times over the years and you've only put me off. What is this new venture you've teased me with? I assume the bloke here has something to do with it." Turner was a straightforward sort, so it was no surprise he was ready to do away with the pleasantries.

Smiling at the businessman's eagerness, Jacob explained how he and Blanchet had met. After Turner asked the man a few rudimentary questions about his club, Jacob continued, "Blanchet has developed a new form of entertainment at the club he manages that is performed one night a month. It has proven so popular we think it would make a good business venture on its own."

Turner looked to Blanchet, who smiled like a cat who had found the cream. "We fill every seat on that night. You say standing room only, no?"

"Indeed, we do." Turner dropped his still-burning cigar into the crystal dish on the table and leaned forward in full attention. "What is this new entertainment?"

"A bit of café mixed with a bit of music hall," Blanchet explained. "The venue is intimate, with the small tables and the candles and the chic decor. Excellent food and wine. People come and enjoy the dinner and the conversation with friends, while we provide the entertainment. Sometimes there is music, singing, dancing, opéra comique, or political humor."

"Interesting," Turner said. Jacob could see the gears churning as he tried to imagine it.

"It's really quite amusing," Jacob said. "The show consists of a variety of performances on any given night, so the audience doesn't quite know what to expect, although there are sure to be favorites that come back every night. There is a host who keeps the guests entertained between acts and provides a sort of continuity to the show."

Blanchet nodded emphatically. "Yes, the host is very important. My *directeur* and I agree that Monsieur Thorne possesses the necessary charm for such a position."

"Thorne?" Turner's eyebrows rose as he favorably considered this.

"I have seen him in the club below on previous visits," Blanchet said. "He has also entertained at my club on his visit in the summer. He is charming and well-liked."

"I don't know that I'd host every night, but I do enjoy the atmosphere," Jacob said. "Perhaps to start, or for a set engagement every year, but I can't live in Paris permanently." They had discussed this before. The condition of him opening the club with Blanchet was that he would split his time between London and Paris.

Blanchet smiled. "The name will be En Soirée, because it will be entertainment in the evening. The entertainment I will call cabaret."

"Cabaret?" Turner repeated. "Doesn't that mean a tavern or inn or some such?"

"Of sorts, yes. Lately, it describes a sort of music tavern," Jacob explained. "En Soirée will cater to the regular people, not aristocrats or politicians. We want the artist, the professional, the shopgirl."

"Shopgirl? You mean to cater to men and women?"

"*Bah oui!* Men and women enjoy being entertained together." Blanchet's smile widened. "That is part of the allure, yes?"

"This is a very important part of the business model," Jacob said. "We don't want to exclude anyone. Old, young, rich, poor, man, woman. All are welcome, thus drawing in the most customers possible. In fact, we believe the allure of the opposite sex will bring in more customers. It will be a place to meet and mingle."

"Sounds like it could lead to debauchery," Turner mused, but he didn't seem put off by the idea.

"A certain decadence will be part of the appeal." Jacob smiled.

Earlier that day, Blanchet had presented sketches to him of the costumes he wanted the cast of house dancing girls to wear. They were covered modestly enough except that the skirts of their gowns revealed their ankles and lower shins from the front to allow for ease of movement. That alone would fill seats for months.

"And you're investing in this, Thorne?" Turner asked.

"Yes, but we are looking for a third investor, a silent partner, if you will. Since you have been very interested in Montague Club, I wanted to give you the first chance."

The truth was that Turner had the most liquid assets available of anyone he knew outside of the Crenshaw family and Evan, who had recently inherited a gold mine. However, he wanted this venture to be independent of them. He needed to prove that he could do something on his own. His entire life had been charmed by the status and wealth of his father. Even the success of Montague Club had been a combined effort and not something Jacob had undertaken on his own. A part of him that was growing more insistent every day needed to prove himself capable of achieving success outside of his noble ties.

Turner nodded, retrieving his cigar to sit back for a minute as he pondered the idea. The next half hour was spent with him lobbing questions at them and either Jacob or Blanchet answering. Finally, he said, "I presume the entertainment will include female dancers and singers and such?" He waved the cigar around as he asked.

Blanchet answered before Jacob could. "We have found the female performers to be the most popular, particularly the singers."

"How will you draw these performers to you?"

"Blanchet has found a theater space with rooms in the back for a boardinghouse of sorts. They'll live there. We also plan to contract with a few boardinghouses in the area, as needed."

Turner turned his attention back to Jacob. "And you plan to move to Paris to help run this establishment?"

Unease moved through Jacob, but he didn't know why. "Yes, for a while. At least until it's up and running, then I'll split my time between there and here."

"And you plan to help recruit these female performers?"

Now he understood. "I fear that my reputation for dalliance has been drastically overstated," he teased.

Turner laughed, but something about it didn't reach his eyes. "Perhaps, but it's not so much your reputation that concerns me. It's your . . . impact, shall we say, on the fairer sex."

"My impact?"

"Answer me this, Thorne. How many young girls—women who are not members—have shown up at the women's entrance begging to have a word with you?"

Uncomfortable in the extreme, Jacob swirled the rich amber liquid in his glass. "What does that even mean?" But he knew what Turner was getting at. At one time, Christian had been sought out by women all across Europe as a sexual conquest. Diplomatic wives and ladies of the nobility had all vied for an hour alone with him. Jacob had a similar problem, but he hadn't thought his reputation was as notorious. "I am not my brother."

"No, you're not, but you haven't answered my question."

Jacob shrugged. The truth was that it was impossible to know, because he *did* have his own reputation. It wasn't uncommon for women to send letters to him and gifts unprovoked, or occasionally show up unannounced. He'd guess one or the other happened a couple times a week, but he wasn't going to admit to it. "I don't sleep with most of them."

"Of course not, but they do seek you out and hope for the best."

"What are you getting at, Turner?" He frowned.

"While I respect your acumen and stewardship with Montague, I have concerns about your involvement with something like En Soirée. Your presence could damage the harmony of such a sorority."

Angry now, he said, "I wouldn't bed the performers."

Turner held up a hand to call for peace. "No, I don't think you would. The problem isn't you, but rather your effect on these girls. It could lead to friction. The slightest bit of discord the first year could lead something like this to fail."

"Yes, I can see this," Blanchet said, nodding. "It is the same in Paris. He is a . . ." He paused, searching for the phrasing. "Man of the ladies. *Homme à femmes*."

"A ladies' man," Turner agreed. "It will cause problems whether you bed them or not."

"It's not as if I encourage the attention."

"You charm them, whether or not you do it purposefully." Turner raised a brow and shrugged one shoulder.

"This is preposterous. You make it seem as if I leach sexual innuendo. I can control myself." His words simmered with anger.

The feeling only worsened when Turner shrugged again.

"What are you saying? You don't want to invest because I'm a ladies' man?" It was the most ridiculous thing Jacob had ever heard.

"I would be daft to not consider the problems. At Montague, it's not such a problem because you don't employ female entertainers. En Soirée, however . . ." He shrugged again. "Women can be territorial and competitive if they think one of them stands a chance with you."

Blanchet met Jacob's gaze, panic starting to rise in his face. Jacob had explained in a letter that Turner was all but a sure thing. Blanchet was in no position to put together enough money to start. Jacob had savings from his investments and Montague earnings, but it wouldn't be sufficient to fund them long enough to get up and running, nor would he put up his portion of Montague Club to secure a loan. If Turner walked away it would be Jacob's fault. Their dream would die a quick death and he didn't want to bear that responsibility. Jacob couldn't let his friend's dream perish because of *his* reputation.

"What if I told you I was engaged to be married?" The words came out before he'd had time to really consider what they meant.

Both men smiled, and their identical expressions of relief were undeniable.

"When did this happen?" Turner asked at the same time Blanchet said, "Margot and I want to meet her."

Jacob swallowed, already rethinking the unfortunate question. "It's recent. I haven't told anyone yet, because . . ." He swallowed again. *Because it's a lie.*

As it turned out, he didn't need to come up with a reason. The next several minutes were taken up with well-wishes and endless toasts. Without Jacob even knowing how it happened, they all agreed to have dinner in a fortnight when Blanchet and his wife finished their trip to Scotland and came back through London on their way home.

Bloody fucking hell. He had to find a fiancée.

Chapter 3

❦

CHARRINGTON MANOR, HAMPSHIRE
TWO WEEKS LATER

Charrington Manor, the ancestral home of the Duke of Rothschild, was a sprawling stone building that Camille was certain dated back to medieval times. She had visited it once soon after August had married the duke but hadn't been back since. At the time, it had been crumbling and badly in need of repair, an indication of the duke's desperate need to take an heiress as his bride. In the nearly three years since their marriage, the couple had made it a priority to renovate the home to its former glory, and they had succeeded.

Camille paused at the top of the stairs to admire the renovations. She had arrived late last night and hadn't gotten a proper look, but in the morning light coming through the large, multipaned window over the front door, every surface gleamed with fresh polish. The entrance hall was a grand room that soared several stories up with a large, medieval-looking lighting fixture hanging down from the center of the ceiling. The moldings fairly sparkled with new varnish, and fresh wallpaper coated the walls in a creamy textured print that lent a rather luxurious feel to the space. There was no hint of the mildew and water damage she remembered, not even a musty smell. It had been replaced by lemon oil and beeswax.

Gorgeous works of art, tellingly absent on her previous visit, graced the wall adjacent to the staircase. One in particular—a portrait of Charles I that had been Hereford's favorite—sat in silent judgment of her as she descended to the ground floor. She had happily gifted it to the couple after her husband's death, a tiny sort of retribution for the pain he had caused her. She had been indulging in those tiny rebellions quite a bit the past two years. Being a good girl who wanted to please everyone hadn't gotten her anything but pain, so now she would do as she pleased.

The estate had seen an amazing transformation, but then so had August's life over the past several years. She had gone from driven businesswoman who eschewed marriage, to driven businesswoman who was a devoted wife and new mother. The couple's son, William Alexander David Sterling, had been born a few months ago, which was the reason for Camille's current visit to the country home. She along with several other close family members and friends had been invited to his christening, which would be happening soon in the village chapel.

Camille couldn't help but smile to herself. If anyone had told her that August and Evan would get along so well, she would have never believed them. It had taken a long time for her to accept that love in a marriage was possible. But the fact that August had found it with a man she had all but been forced to marry was extraordinary. If only Camille had been so fortunate.

No. She wouldn't let her thoughts wander in that

direction. Hereford was gone and her life was her own now to do with as she liked. Too bad that did *not* include doing very naughty things with Jacob Thorne, her latest attempt at rebellion. In the two weeks since she had last seen him, Camille had almost recovered from the embarrassment of his rejection. *Almost.* She didn't physically cringe at the thought of how she had propositioned him anymore. It was more of a mental squirm. She could even go hours without thinking of that night now, especially since she hadn't dared return to Montague Club.

She had considered herself well on her way to putting the whole thing behind her, when the deep, rich sound of his laughter stopped her descent, leaving her clutching the banister with a grip that turned her knuckles white. The sound floated away before she could grasp it fully and turn it over in her mind. Surely, it wasn't him. *He was not here.*

Still, she crept quietly down the stairs so that her heels wouldn't make a sound. The laugh had come from the reception room off the bottom of the stairs. Another masculine voice joined the first, this one too soft to belong to Thorne. The doors were partially open, leaving a space large enough to reveal a sliver of the room beyond. Bright sunlight flooded the chamber, revealing a fireplace with a marble hearth, white mantelpiece, and rose-colored wallpaper. She was trying to convince herself she had imagined the whole thing, when a man stepped into view.

He stood relaxed and handsome wearing a dove-gray suit that fit him to perfection. The coat was wide and snug across the shoulders, narrowing the slightest bit near the waist. He grinned at something the man standing with him said, his teeth flashing white against his bronze skin as his eyes crinkled in good humor. A tug of yearning twisted inside her, but it was followed almost immediately by a terrible feeling of foreboding. Jacob Thorne was here, and this would not end well for her.

She meant to back away quietly, but haste made her

sloppy so that her heel clicked on the hardwood floor. He glanced over in a casual way that might have gone unnoticed had she been someone else. But she wasn't, and they had an awkward history now, so when his gaze caught hers it held, refusing to release her. The smile melted from his face as something more powerful and indefinable replaced it. Wrenching herself away, she turned and headed toward the drawing room where she was supposed to meet the family before traveling over to the chapel with them.

Please don't let him be attending the christening. Please don't let him be attending the christening.

Even though the mantra repeated itself, she knew it was futile. Why else would he be here? *Please, God, let there be another reason.*

She held on to the slender thread of that hope as she swept into the drawing room perhaps the teeniest bit too desperately. Every eye turned toward her, the three Crenshaw siblings with their spouses, Evan's mother, Margaret, his two younger sisters, even Violet's young daughter paused in her babbling in her father's arms to stare.

"Good morning, everyone," Camille said, forcing a smile she hoped didn't appear feral as she stepped farther into the room. The previously unseen footman quietly closed the door behind her.

"Good morning, dear." Margaret smiled at her, and it seemed to be the cue everyone needed to resume their conversations.

"Camille." Lady Helena smiled as she approached. She had married Maxwell, the eldest Crenshaw, about two years ago and now lived in New York. She still sat on the board of the charity she had started before she moved, the London Home for Young Women. It was devoted to housing, educating, and providing job training to the many unwed mothers of London who would have been forced to give up their children otherwise. "I'm so glad to see you. I hope you'll be able to join me for tea soon. I'd like to talk to you more regarding the vegetable garden idea you wrote me about. I think it could be a great addition to the school."

Much like joining Montague Club, volunteering at the charity was another rebellion Camille had hurried to do after Hereford's death, knowing he wouldn't have approved. Fortunately, she had found that she quite enjoyed the work.

"Of course. I'm excited to talk more with you." If only the specter of Jacob Thorne wasn't darkening the morning. She couldn't help but look back at the door, expecting him to come through it at any moment. But perhaps he wouldn't. Perhaps he *was* here for some other reason, and she wouldn't be forced to endure his presence through the service, and the breakfast, and the inevitable dinner tonight. But no, that was stupid. He and Evan were friends and related by marriage. Of course he'd be at the christening of Evan's son. She closed her eyes for a moment to regain control. "I . . . um . . . I'd love to speak with you. I thought a garden would give the children—"

"Camille." Violet hurried over to join them. "How are you?"

The sight of her dearest friend's smiling face was almost her undoing. Before she could stop herself, she grabbed Violet's hands as her unfortunate desperation made a reappearance. "Did I see Jacob Thorne out there?" Camille whispered.

Violet's brow rose in surprise. "Probably."

"He was invited?"

"Of course he was. You know he and Evan are very close." Voice lowering to a familiar conspiratorial pitch, Violet asked, "Why? Don't you like him? I thought you were a member of Montague Club."

"No, it's not that." But she shouldn't have said that because Camille could not tell her what it was. Maybe later when she didn't squirm with embarrassment remembering his rejection, but not now.

"Then what is it?" Violet leaned in.

She had to get a hold of herself. Straightening, she pasted a smile on her face and tucked an errant strand of hair that had flopped down over her ear back into its pin. "Nothing, I was simply surprised. Excuse me, I must go say hello to August."

She had barely made it across the room to her friend, when the door opened with a click. She didn't have to turn around to know that it was Thorne. The energy in the room shifted as it always did when he entered, as if the very air became heated and malleable in his presence.

"Camille, I'm so happy you could come," August was saying. "William has grown so much since you last saw him." Camille had last seen him only a few weeks ago.

"He's at least doubled in size." Evan smiled like a proud father should.

August rolled her eyes. "Not that much."

He laughed quietly. "Well, he has a healthy appetite, which I assume he gets from my wi—Ouch!"

"Ugh." August nudged him playfully in the ribs, and he responded by gathering her close to his side and nuzzling her hair, whispering something for her ears alone. His eyes drifted closed for the barest second, as if overcome in equal amounts of relief, gratitude, and love. August smiled up at him, their gazes meeting in a moment of intimacy so profound that it momentarily shut out the rest of the world. Camille was gripped by an unexpected wave of loneliness. It swept through her all at once, picking her bare so that she felt exposed and vulnerable to every sharp edge and tongue that might come her way.

"Don't mind him," August said. "Fatherhood has made him positively beastly and droll."

Camille smiled because she knew she was meant to. Her armor had become a series of niceties that stood as layers between her and the rest of the world. She scrambled to put them back in place. "Don't worry. We all humor the dukes, but no one really listens to them."

They all laughed.

"Say you'll be able to stay a couple of extra days," August said. "I won't start back to work until next week when we return to London. We can visit. I feel as if I've hardly seen you since William was born."

"You've been busy." August had worked, running the London office of Crenshaw Iron Works, right up until going into labor. "Of course, I can stay an extra day or two." She had grown up with August and Violet back in New York. They were very close, and Camille had missed her the past several months. She wanted to stay . . . unless Thorne also stayed, then she'd definitely have to go.

She was attuned to his whereabouts in the room without even looking for him. The murmur of his voice was a constant melody she could instantly pick out from all the rest. The next few minutes passed slowly as she tried her best to ignore his presence. She could feel his eyes on her, however.

Finally, the baby was brought in by his nurse, swathed in a soft white gown made of cotton and lace. The room fell silent except for Mrs. Crenshaw, who gasped aloud, and after the nurse placed him in his mother's arms, she hurried over to coo and ogle him. He really had grown since she'd last seen him. His sweet little cheeks were full, and his eyes were bright as he stared at the woman making silly noises at him. Camille stepped back to give them space and meant to go resume her talk with Lady Helena, but Thorne intercepted her.

"Good morning, Your Grace."

She had to draw up short to keep from running right into him. The skin on the back of her neck prickled, the room growing warmer. Notes of sandalwood taunted her, threatening to draw her closer to him. "Good morning, Mr. Thorne."

"I have missed seeing you at Montague."

Her gaze flashed up to his from where she'd been very

studiously engaged in the crisp folds of his tie. There was no hint of impropriety on his face. "I've been busy."

The corner of his mouth quirked, or she might have imagined it. "I would like to speak with you today . . . privately."

He could not be propositioning her right here in the middle of the drawing room. Her breath caught, and her thoughts swirled so fast she couldn't grasp hold of any one of them. "I . . . I don't think that is a good idea. Perhaps we should simply forget that I—"

"It's not that." A quick glance to make sure no one was paying attention, and then he leaned slightly toward her, lowering his voice. "It's about another matter altogether. It is a private issue, however, so I would ask for your discretion."

What could he possibly want with her? Her question must have shown on her face, because he gave her a wink that made her body clench in ways she had never experienced.

"Nothing too untoward. I promise."

Before she could answer, Maxwell crossed to them. "Thorne, it's good to see you. I haven't made it to Montague Club, but I intend to before we return to New York."

Thorne shook his hand, all but forgetting her and leaving her wondering what the hell he could want with her.

Jacob had tried to ignore the enchanting duchess all through the christening to little avail. She had been as beautiful as always even in her demure white gown made of lace and silk. Only now her beauty was tempered by a vulnerability he hadn't remembered noticing before. Her wide brown eyes revealed a softness that made him want to hold her against him until everything in her world was perfect. Perhaps it was how she had reacted to his presence making him feel this way. She had been startled, but more

than that, afraid, and he didn't know what to do with that
fear.

The fact was he could do nothing with that but wait. He
waited through the christening as the vicar droned on endlessly through the service. He waited through the breakfast
that followed, where she again tried her best to ignore his
presence. Dinner wasn't any better, with her refusing to
look at him, so he excused himself from the cigars and
cognac that followed and went to find her. A suspicion had
begun tugging at him ever since the women had left, and he
realized why the second he popped his head into the drawing room where the ladies were enjoying sweets and sherry.
Camille was gone.

Violet, the minx, grinned and rose, hurrying over to
him. "It took you long enough."

She had been married to his half brother for less than
three years, but Jacob had developed a fondness for her and
her mischief. "Whatever do you mean, dear sister?"

She knew, somehow.

Her grin widened. "You just missed her, but if you hurry
up the back stairs you can probably catch her before she
gets to her room. I don't know what is going on between
you two, but she's been as jumpy as a dog on the Fourth of
July ever since she realized you were here. I advise you to
tread carefully."

"Point noted. Thank you." He turned away, ignoring her
gasp of mock outrage that he wouldn't explain anything
to her.

Following her advice, he took the back stairs two at a
time, hurrying past two maids who gave him surprised but
lingering glances. He was afraid he had missed her because
he wasn't entirely certain which bedroom she'd been given
on the guest hall. But he turned a dimly lit corner and saw
her standing before a door, her hand on the latch. Her eyes
widened in surprise when she saw him.

"Thorne." The soft gasp had him wondering how it

might feel to have her gasp his name for a much more plea-surable reason.

"Would now be a good time to talk? I have to leave first thing in the morning." And this conversation was best had immediately and in private.

A line appeared between her brows, and he was certain she meant to say no, but then she nodded. Resolved. "Come inside."

Chapter 4

❦

The rich and lovely scent of vanilla—*her* scent—welcomed Jacob into the room. The cloud moved over him like a caress, filling his body with the warmth of Camille's presence. He took a deep breath of her and had to look away so he wouldn't dwell on the fact that he was in this bedroom alone with her. The four-poster bed, delightfully turned down on the far wall, did not help. It was a simple but luxurious room filled with overstuffed furniture and trimmed in shades of cream and gold with touches of green. There was absolutely nothing personal about it because she had only occupied it for one night; yet his gaze quickly found her tiny bottles of cosmetics scattered across the vanity top, and her silk dressing gown was on display draped along the back of a chair.

"My maid should be here soon, but we have a few moments." She moved around in brisk and efficient movements—pushing the dressing room door closed even though it had only been open a crack, stoking the fire to make it burn brighter—all things that accomplished very little except to keep her attention directed elsewhere.

Only when she had run out of things to do did she seem to realize he was merely standing there with his hands in his pockets, watching her. She blushed, embarrassed, and her flitting from one thing to the next ceased as she held her hands fisted at her sides.

"Perhaps you would like to sit?" he offered.

She nodded as if she hadn't thought of that and hurried over to one of the chairs before the fire. She sat, but she didn't settle easily, her fingers restlessly playing at the folds in her skirts. "Please?" She indicated the one opposite her.

This was foolish. If she couldn't be in the same room as him, then how on earth would they convince Turner that they were betrothed. He had been hoping that they could ignore her earlier proposition, but it was clear now that it had to be addressed.

"Your Grace—"

"Don't call me that." Her voice was harsh, sharper than she'd apparently intended, because she appeared immediately contrite. "When I think of *Your Grace* I think of him and . . ."

And she'd rather not think of him. That much was clear. What had the miserable bellend done to her? The cinders of a long-simmering anger at the men who would treat those entrusted to their care badly began to stir. Early after Hereford's death there had been rumors that she might have poisoned him. They had mostly died out now, but he wouldn't blame her if she had, because even now thoughts of her dead husband had the power to make a shadow of fear flicker across her face.

"Duchess, then. I think a little impertinence suits us." He grinned to lighten the moment.

The corner of her mouth ticked upward and she relaxed,

her shoulders falling by the smallest of degrees. "Impertinence suits you."

He dropped into the chair. "Being the bastard son of a peer does have a few perks. I've been entitled to impertinence and deviousness since my birth."

Her grin widened, revealing the tiniest dimple in her cheek that he'd never noticed before. How had he missed it? It gave her an impish quality that warmed her beauty. He found himself shifting, all too aware that the bloody bed loomed behind them, that it was night, and that she had asked him only recently to go to bed with her. Why had he said no again?

"Mr. Thorne, I want to assure you that I completely understand your very proper refusal of my indecent request." She glanced away. "Any coldness you might perceive on my part is merely foolish embarrassment that I had the temerity to put you in such an uncomfortable position."

"It is quite all right. You have no need to explain."

"No, there is every need. I have been avoiding you today, and it isn't right. Not when I am the very reason this awkwardness exists. I'm sorry."

He shook his head, unable to believe that she was apologizing to him. "There is no need. I am the one who is sorry to have had to reject your tempting proposition."

Her lips parted on an inhale as her gaze dragged itself back to meet his.

"Believe me, it was not a rejection that was easy to give. Duchess, you must know that you are a very desirable woman. I want to say yes, but—"

"But the awkwardness we have so skillfully avoided would be too much?" She raised a perfectly arched brow. She was teasing him.

He couldn't help but laugh. "Precisely." She laughed, too, and he noticed the color on her lips tonight was a deep pink, not the red she had worn *that* night. The color made her mouth appear soft and full and infinitely kissable.

"Since you made it clear that you didn't want to talk to me about that regrettable night, what did you want to discuss?"

He took a breath, experiencing a rare moment of hesitation. "It strikes me that we have to stop negotiating in front of hearths stood apart from each other like adversaries." He rose and went to the small bureau near the window where he'd noticed a decanter of brandy had been left with a set of cut-crystal glasses. "Would you care for one?"

"Yes, please."

He poured hers first and held it out to her. She took it and he couldn't help but feel a bit of jealousy when her lips touched the crystal. Now that she'd opened that door between them a crack, he hadn't been able to stop thinking of her in that way. Before, there had been an invisible screen between them, keeping her safely out of his reach, but it seemed to have gone now. Thoughts of her and her request creeped into his mind in the odd moments he found himself alone, tempting him more than he would have thought possible.

He took a deep swallow of brandy and stared at the gravel drive outside illuminated by the light of a single gas lamp. "I find myself in a rather peculiar situation and I had hoped that you . . . well, to be honest, you are likely the only one in the unique position to help me. Perhaps I should start at the beginning and then you'll understand."

She nodded her agreement.

"The short of it is that I have a friend in Paris, Pierre Blanchet. He approached me because he has an idea for a new type of club he's calling a cabaret. Essentially, it means that women and men will come to the club to view a variety of entertainments over the course of an evening. There will be singers, actors, small performances, and live music. The allure will be that of the entire experience. Low lighting and candles, small tables with excellent food, wine, and conversation in a lavish atmosphere. The average person, be they factory employee or banker, can step off the streets of Paris and be transported to another world for a few hours, led along by a sort of master of ceremonies who provides humor and distraction between each performance."

She smiled. "That sounds lovely, but I don't understand how I can help you. I don't have any sort of experience that will lend itself to those sorts of entertainments."

He shook his head. "No, your help would come before. Blanchet and I have decided that we need to take on an investor who will own a third of the club. We have an investor. Gilbert Turner?" he asked on the off chance that she had heard of the moderately well-known businessman. She shook her head. "But he has a very peculiar request."

Her brow furrowed. "I don't understand. Why do you need this mysterious third party? Surely, Christian or Evan would be happy to invest with you."

He shrugged. This is where things got strange for him. He didn't actually like to explain why he needed Turner to invest. The reason hit too close to his own insecurities. Having been raised from birth and given almost everything he'd ever wanted, he needed to do this alone, without help from his brother or Evan. While Jacob considered Evan a close friend now, they had met through Christian. Jacob wanted to do this in part to prove to himself that he could manage without their money, and in part because he wanted something that was his alone.

"Yes, I am certain they would. However, Blanchet and I have agreed that a more neutral third party would be the most ideal investor."

She nodded slowly, seeming to accept this. "Then what is this very peculiar request?"

Jacob took a quick breath, steeling himself for her refusal. "He would feel more comfortable investing if I were . . . settled."

"Settled?"

There were all sorts of things that word could mean, but her gaze narrowed as it began to dawn on her which meaning applied. She was from a world that revolved around well-made marriages, after all. Social and business capital were fed by those unions.

"Married," she said in a small voice.

She stood, her grip so tight on the crystal that he thought it might be in danger of breaking.

He hurried to reassure her. "We wouldn't actually need to marry. There is a meeting later this week, and I simply need someone I can bring and introduce to him as my fiancée. You would meet him and set his mind at ease."

"Me? Isn't there some other woman you could take to meet him?"

Yes, there were several, and he had considered them all in the past fortnight and rejected them in turn. "The women I know well enough to attempt such a thing would not . . ."

"Would not be good enough to pretend to be your future wife?" Now she looked piqued, her free hand settling on her hip as she stared at him. "Good enough for your bed but not your arm?"

"No, that's not precisely what I mean." By God, the woman didn't mince her words. "They are fine women, and any one of them could make a fine wife." To someone actually looking for a wife. "However, I think he would be more appeased if the woman were someone like you . . . someone who could entertain with ease and flirt with grace and . . . be a lady. Someone whose social status could be a boon for this endeavor. Honestly, the whole thing is ridiculous. Believe me when I say I understand that, but it is the final hurdle it seems in gaining what I want. I want this club, and you will be easy for him to accept. You're beautiful and refined and not the least bit objectionable."

"Then it would only be the one meeting?" she asked, mollified.

He shrugged. "For now, but until the contract is signed,

I cannot make any promises. We will say that we plan a long betrothal. Perhaps we plan for your parents to attend the ceremony and must wait for their schedules to allow them to travel from New York."

"But there will be no engagement announcement in the *Times*. Won't he be suspicious?"

"He trusts me." He abandoned the empty tumbler and walked slowly to her. He needed her to understand that he didn't take this deception lightly. "It doesn't sit well with me that I have to play this game, but his condition is absurd. I've run Montague Club without settling down with a wife, and I don't expect this one to be any different."

"Then why is he so set on you being *settled*?"

"Because we'll hire house performers, many of them women. They'll be housed by us, and we'll have regular contact. He thinks if I'm married it will lead to less . . . distraction."

The corner of her mouth quirked at that.

"Turner is a private person, and he isn't known among the same social circles you are, so knowledge of us shouldn't be known outside of this meeting."

She scoffed and gave him a rueful smile. "I don't care if it is known. Those people spread rumors about me anyway. What's another one?" After a pause, she added, "Although, my parents did send me a lengthy letter discussing their displeasure that I joined Montague Club. I don't suppose this would go over any better with them were they to find out." The upward tilt of her lips suggested this wasn't a problem.

She wasn't wrong about the rumors. He'd once heard that Bertie had pursued her. The prince *was* known for his proclivity for American heiresses. Given the way she had approached him, Jacob doubted she had spent any time in bed with the prince. The man usually sought more worldly women.

"They won't find out. As long as we are discreet, it won't go beyond our small circle."

"How do you propose we eventually end things? We cannot be engaged forever, even if it's pretend."

"That's the easiest part." Though something told him it would not be easy to end any sort of claim to her, even a superficial one. "I'll be in Paris for months; you'll be here or in New York. Many relationships fold under the strain of distance. Why should ours be any different? I shall simply inform Turner that you've decided to move on."

"You certainly make it sound simple."

He could feel her on the cusp of agreeing. "Then you'll do it?"

She thought it over a lot quicker than he had anticipated she would. He was already mentally listing more arguments he could use to convince her, when she said, "Fine. I'll do it, but on one condition."

He swallowed, certain he knew what it would be.

"Say yes to my initial proposition."

"No!" The word was out before he could think of a more tactful reply.

Her lips tightened, revealing a stubborn streak he was only just beginning to suspect lurked beneath the surface. "Fine, then my answer is no." She marched to the door and would have yanked it open had he not followed and put his hand out to keep it closed.

"You don't know what you're asking."

"I'm a grown woman who has been married. I know exactly what I'm asking."

"I don't think you do. You might have been married, but you have never been to bed with me. You don't know what that might mean for you."

She laughed in his face, crossing her arms over her chest. "You have a rather high opinion of yourself, don't you?"

He shrugged. "Yes, but that does not mean my opinion is inaccurate."

She didn't quite know what to say to that level of

honesty. Her lips parted, but there were no words. Finally, she glanced away.

"What you're asking for is ludicrous. Think of how awkward today has been. Now think of how it might be ten times worse if we've slept together."

She flinched, closing her eyes, and a chill crept across his skin, drawing it tight.

"Duchess . . ." He reached for her but stopped short of crossing that last barrier between them. His fingertips savored the heat radiating from her cheek, before closing in on themselves as he dropped his hand back to his side. Something else was happening here. Something more than her desire for him. "Why does this mean so much to you?"

Her eyes were wide and sparkling when they met his, and he had to hold his breath so he wouldn't visibly react to the vulnerability he saw there. "It doesn't matter. I'll find someone else. Someone who doesn't think it's *ludicrous*."

He took the bridge of his nose between his thumb and forefinger. It turned out arguing with a desirable woman while simultaneously fighting an erection gave him a headache. "I'm sorry I said that. Help me understand. Tell me why you have asked this of me."

She stared at him, and he imagined an internal battle waging in her head. Finally, some of the tension drained away, softening the line of her mouth. Fixing her gaze straight ahead, somewhere at his collar, she said, "Fair enough. I . . . I have never liked . . . the . . . the act of intercourse. I'm not a fool. I know that women are capable of enjoying it. To hear Violet and August talk of such things . . ." She blushed. "Well, I suppose I shouldn't tell you what they say, but it's never been like that for me. You have something of a reputation, so I had hoped that you might be able to help me . . . to teach me how to enjoy it."

"I don't mean to speak ill of the dead, but I can assure you that no one would have enjoyed *that* with *him*." The whoreson.

She shook her head. When she spoke again her voice was so low, he had to move forward until he was so close to her that a sweet jasmine scent joined the vanilla. "He's not the only one I've tried things with. I haven't enjoyed it with any of them."

"*Any* of them?" He couldn't immediately get past the instant and unreasonable jealousy that gripped him. There were more men in her past than her husband.

She gave a firm nod and repeated it, finally meeting his eyes again. "Any of them."

"How many have there been?"

"That is none of your business, unless you plan to share the number of women you've taken to your bed." Before he could respond, she held up her hand. "Never mind. I don't want to know."

He actually didn't even know the number, but considering he'd bedded his first at the age of fifteen and he was now almost thirty, even accounting for a mere eight to ten women a year, the number amounted to a figure higher than he suspected would meet with her approval. Although, to be fair, the last several years had seen him settle into a comfortable routine of sex with the same handful of women. "I suppose it doesn't matter except that I wonder what sort of man might neglect to ensure your enjoyment."

She shrugged one shoulder. "Perhaps, in hindsight, I didn't choose wisely. I think I was so desperate to try someone else—*anyone* else—that I reacted impulsively."

Jacob could already feel himself being swayed to say yes. He absolutely did not want this to be true for her, but he had to ask. "Have you considered that perhaps the issue might be that you do not have sexual urges? It's fine if you don't. I've met one or two people over the years who simply do not have those needs."

Her brow furrowed as if she had not considered that at all. "Well . . . no. I assumed that I should."

"Shall we test the theory?" His body vibrated with the

need to touch her. Somewhere in the back of his mind lurked the suspicion that he had brought up this topic only to have a reason to touch her.

She nodded, and the final barrier came down. He lifted his hand, surprised to find that it trembled with his need for her. He brought it up to her face, the backs of his fingers stroking over the soft curve of her cheekbone before dropping down to her mouth. She took in a ragged breath as his fingertip touched a bit of moisture gathered on her plump bottom lip. He licked his own lips as the need to taste her urged him closer, but it would be too much too soon. This was only to test if she responded. Kissing her could very well make this a full-blown seduction, and this evening at Charrington Manor was neither the time nor the place.

Moving forward even more, he crowded her against the door, savoring the heat from her body. He dipped his head to take in more of that sweet jasmine scent he'd caught earlier. She sighed in delight when he followed it to the spot behind her earlobe where she must have dabbed it before dinner. He sniffed and then exhaled, letting his breath caress her ear and neck, making her skin prickle. So slowly that it very nearly killed him, he touched her with his lips. Not quite a kiss, but a gentle drag that caressed her from jaw to shoulder.

She instinctively turned into him, her face seeking his as her hand came up to grasp him and pull him closer. Unable to resist, his teeth grazed over her neck in a tender bite that would not leave a mark. He was rewarded by her quick inhale of breath and the tightening of her fingers in his hair.

Desire pounded through him, demanding that he take more now that she was all but his. Instead, he pulled back just enough to look down at her. Her wide brown eyes were glazed with passion and need. "I think it's safe to say the theory proved incorrect."

"Yes," she whispered.

Something told him he would regret this sooner rather

than later, but he was helpless to do anything but agree to her terms. It was the *any of them* that had done it. She deserved to be more than a quick fuck for some selfish bloke.

"After the meeting at Montague Club with Turner, we can discuss how to proceed with your . . ." What in hell did they even call this? "Lessons," he said for lack of a better term.

"No, I'll come by the day before the meeting." She took in a ragged breath that made her bottom lip quiver. "We can begin then."

"I won't renege on our agreement, if that's your fear."

"I know you won't. Don't you think it's best that we get to know each other a little better if we're pretending to be engaged?"

She had a point, though he still wasn't entirely certain the intimacy she had in mind was ideal. He nodded and pushed away from her.

"I'll send a note with details of the dinner. See you later this week."

Chapter 5

❦

Jacob . . . *Mr. Thorne* had left the next morning before Camille had gone downstairs for breakfast. A twinge of disappointment resonated at his absence. The kiss had been more than nice, and she was a little relieved to know that he could make her feel *something*. But it was that touch of his lips on her neck that had made her understand the strange and dangerous game she would be playing with him. Instinctively, she already knew that being with him wouldn't be like being with Henry or Frederick Kip, the two men besides Hereford she had attempted sex with. That difference was part of his allure, after all. It would be more pleasant, and that pleasure came with a downside she hadn't grasped, and still didn't fully. Apparently, tenderness and affection came parceled along with the pleasure. The trick would be to keep that affection managed and not let it get out of hand.

After a quiet breakfast passed in conversation with the

dowager, Camille answered August's summons and joined her and Violet in her private sitting room. There they oohed and aahed over adorable little William until he fell asleep in his mother's arms and the nursemaid came to take him to his crib. The three friends had hardly been left alone before Camille blurted out, "I've made a scandalous deal with Mr. Thorne."

"I *knew* something was happening between you two." Violet grinned, grabbing her hand and leading her to the sofa.

August hurried over and took a spot on her other side. "What sort of deal?" the older sister asked, her brow furrowed in concern.

"Is there sex involved?" Violet asked.

Camille stared at her friend, quite confounded that she had guessed. She laughed, but it only made her sound as uncomfortable as she was. What exactly had she hoped to gain from telling them? She didn't know. Confessing had been a compulsion with no real thought, except that she was tired of feeling like there was something wrong with her. Now that she was on her way to attempting to solve the issue, it seemed like the sort of thing one might share with her closest friends.

"Perhaps . . . well . . . it's very likely," Camille admitted, finding it extremely difficult to say so outright.

"Likely but not certain?" August asked, her analytical mind ready to pick apart every detail of their arrangement. Her eyes couldn't have pierced deeper had they been fixed with darts. Camille flinched and wondered if it was too late to change the subject.

Violet giggled, but her expression was much more subdued. "Why have you come to this arrangement, and what exactly are the details?"

"I suppose it's no secret that Hereford and I . . . well, that our time together is best forgotten. I want to know what it's like to be with a man and enjoy myself." She did not tell them about the other two men. Since those failed experiments had been disappointing, there was no reason to. She also did not tell them about her very real fear that there could be something wrong with her. That maybe she was broken and there was nothing anyone could do to fix her. "Mr. Thorne has agreed to tutor me, to show me how things should be, and in exchange . . ." Did she tell them about the pretend engagement? He hadn't sworn her to secrecy, but it seemed a delicate topic considering their husbands might not be aware of his business venture.

"And in exchange he gets a beautiful woman in his bed," Violet said with a wink. "Seems straightforward to me."

Camille smiled. "You both must think me very brazen."

The word *hussy* came to mind. Widows were given certain latitudes in their behavior. If one took a lover, people were likely to look away as long as it wasn't flaunted and the man was acceptable. Those rules generally applied to older widows who had already borne children and would not be expected to join the marriage market anytime soon. She did not think they would be applicable to her. She was young enough that everyone believed she should marry again, and soon. Joining Montague Club had made people in Society label her as rebellious. If joining the club had been a ripple in the pond, taking the owner as her lover would be a tidal wave, should it be known. She wanted to not care, and most of the time she didn't, but she couldn't hide that small part of her that longed for acceptance.

"No . . . well, maybe a little." Violet laughed but squeezed her hand. "I think this is something you deserve. Besides, you're hardly the first woman to find herself in such a position. I know several widows who enjoy the freedoms of their stations. You were in New York visiting your parents, but last summer Lady Montrose raised eyebrows when she was seen leaving Montague Club at an odd hour." Lady Montrose was one of the wealthiest women in England and well over the age of fifty.

"Not with Mr. Thorne?" It shouldn't matter if she was with Jacob or not, but it did.

Violet shook her head. "I believe the whispers were about the fabled room they have there and several gentlemen. I can confirm Jacob was in Paris at the time."

There was no accounting for the relief she felt that he hadn't been involved, because she had no claim to him whatsoever. In fact, it was only weeks ago that she had arrived at the club at the same time as a certain famous actress and watched them both disappear into parts unknown. He would have many lovers, and there was nothing she could do about it. There was nothing she wanted to do about it. *Right?*

"What do you mean by fabled?" she asked to change the subject from her bizarre and growing obsession with him. "You must know by now if it's real. You're there all the time redecorating."

"I can neither confirm nor deny it. I've made a solemn vow." Violet's deep blush, however, confirmed both the fact that it existed, and that Christian had likely demonstrated the finer points of the room to her.

August shook her head in amusement. "I agree with Violet. A dalliance couldn't hurt as long as you take appropriate precautions."

"You don't think it will make things extremely awkward in the future?" Camille asked.

"Those are the precautions I'm speaking of." August grinned. "You're both adults. As long as you're clear on the rules up front, that it's strictly physical, then you should be fine."

"Oh, but what if you *do* fall in love? We could be sisters." Violet's beaming smile was as off-putting as it was comforting.

"I don't think I'm ready for anything like that. I'm not even certain I know what I want out of a relationship with a man." Or if an emotionally close relationship was even possible. She couldn't imagine putting that sort of trust in anyone.

"Because of Hereford." Violet nodded in understanding, her smile softening into something mild and warm.

"I want to enjoy my freedom, not hand myself over to another man to control." She hastened to add, "Well, not any more control than his heir has now, at any rate." Scarbury, Hereford's heir, had proven himself to be rather overbearing at times, and he liked to withhold her allowance when it suited him.

"But it doesn't have to be that way," August said.

"I know. Evan and Christian are fine husbands, but I don't see myself being ready to take that leap for a long time." Maybe not ever. A husband had total control over his wife and it simply wasn't fair.

Hereford had treated her like an unwanted ward, sending her to her room without supper when she displeased him, and even to his dilapidated country estate twice when he'd thought she had flirted too much with dance partners. It never mattered that she hadn't actually meant to flirt—social teasing was expected at Society events—or that Hereford himself had kept his longtime mistress at his beck and call. All that had mattered was his displeasure. He had dressed her as he wanted and demanded final approval of her weekly schedule. She was not to even have one conversation or outing that didn't fall within his control. He had even limited her access to the Crenshaw sisters, her dearest friends, when he had deemed them too progressive for his comfort.

"Then you should proceed at your own pace," August said. "If you never want to remarry, then you don't have to."

"Thank you both for your understanding. I hadn't intended to tell you, but I think I needed to get it out in the open. My behavior yesterday had to be quite telling or possibly confusing."

Violet's brow raised. "It was a bit obvious that something had happened between you two."

"Well, nothing has happened yet." Though she could still feel where he had touched her. The sparks his fingertips had scattered across her skin had been unforeseen and utterly delightful. "Nothing besides discussion, that is."

"If you want to talk about it once things do start happening, you can come to us, you know? If there's anything unexpected or something you don't understand, we can help, or merely listen," Violet said.

Camille nodded but couldn't bring herself to go on. For some reason, the conversation was making her feel raw and exposed. If he could not help her, then she didn't know what she would do except give up because she was irrevocably broken, and that wasn't something she could consider right now.

The night of her assignation with Mr. Thorne arrived faster than Camille had anticipated. She had been beset by nerves all day, so that by the time she walked into Montague Club at ten o'clock, she wondered why she had insisted on doing this before the meeting with the investor. It was done now, however, so she had no choice but to persevere. Backing down was not an option.

The ladies' entrance of Montague Club was cool and dimly lit. Although it lacked the grandeur of the main entrance with its marble pillars that soared two floors above to a frescoed ceiling, it retained the same sense of style and opulence. Dark wood paneling shone in the flickering gaslight, and a large emerald-colored rug softened the marble floor. Tasteful art adorned the walls, and plush furniture invited conversation near the fireplace. It was very much like stepping into a lady's receiving room. Sometimes Camille used the main entrance, but she needed the quiet of this one tonight.

Thankfully, it was empty except for the young woman sitting behind the desk. She stood and smiled brightly at Camille the second the doorman closed the door behind her.

"Your Grace, how wonderful to see you again." Miss Davies hurried over to help Camille with her outerwear.

She was charged with seeing to the care of all of the female members of the club as a sort of valet. She was around Camille's own age and had come to the club at the recommendation of Lady Helena, whose charity had taken her in several years ago when she had been alone and unemployed after her factory job had fired her for becoming pregnant and her family had disowned her.

"Good evening, Miss Davies. It is good to see you again."

The woman draped Camille's cape over her arm and gathered her gloves and hat to put them away. "Would you care for a bit of supper this evening, Your Grace?"

"No, thank you. I've already dined." If pushing food around on her plate for a quarter hour because she was too anxious to eat it counted. "I am here to see—"

"Good evening, Duchess."

Thorne stood at the entrance to the corridor that led to parts unknown, the parts of the large house that he sometimes disappeared to with other women. He must have been waiting for her. Her stomach tumbled pleasantly at the thought. He was half in shadow with the gaslight sconce on that side of the room only partially revealing his face. His full lips were curved in an almost-smile, but the upper part of his face was nearly hidden. She could see only the glittering of his eyes, but not what expression they held. The corridor behind him and the rooms to which they might lead remained in heavy shadow. A shiver of both fear and anticipation shook through her, and she honestly did not know which one might win out.

"Good evening, Mr. Thorne." In an effort to regain her

equilibrium, she turned her attention back to Miss Davies only to realize the girl had gone. She was probably only taking Camille's things to the space off the entryway where they kept the coats, but her absence seemed calculated somehow. As if she knew what they were about and meant to give them privacy.

"Shall we?" He turned slightly and offered his arm.

She nodded, switching into some sort of automatic form where her body did things while her mind began to slowly unravel. He didn't put his arm around her like she had seen him do with the other women. Instead, he waited for her to take his arm and then led her down the corridor. It was dimly lit with sconces that flickered ominously as they walked, casting a pale, yellow light over their path.

"I'm glad to see you," he said. He had probably thought she wouldn't come.

She nodded and murmured some reply she forgot as soon as she uttered it. He said something, but she couldn't pay attention over the growing hum in her ears. There were several doors along the hallway. As they approached each one, she wondered if that was the room where he meant to do the deed. Or if he meant to take her to *that* room, the infamous one. She didn't want to go to that room. Perhaps she should tell him, but her throat seemed to close, and she couldn't make the words come out.

"Duchess?" They had come to a stop without her noticing, and he stared down at her. This time the sconce ahead of them perfectly illuminated his face. His brow furrowed with slight concern, but that almost-smile stayed on his lips, setting her at ease.

"Yes?"

"You seem distracted. Are you feeling well?"

"I'm fine." She replied a bit too quickly, making his eyebrow quirk upward.

"I asked about your travel home. How was the journey? I hope you didn't get caught in the rain that came through."

"No, the weather was gray, but no rain."

His gaze took a moment to roam over her face, as if ascertaining that she was indeed fine. She managed a weak smile and it seemed to reassure him. "Good." He resumed their pace, and the corridor ended in a small, marble-floored gallery. An elaborately carved door inlaid with brass and ivory led outside, framed by two narrow windows. A curving staircase rose above them to the first floor. He closed the door behind them and turned the lock, indicating that this was a private area. This must be the entrance to his home, where he lived and Christian and Evan kept a suite of rooms for when they were working at the club.

Is this where he took the other women? Did it even matter?

"I thought you might feel more comfortable in my private quarters." He nodded toward the stairs but paused before leading her up, and she realized he was asking her permission.

His consideration mollified her anxiety considerably. "Yes, thank you."

Being rebellious meant stepping outside the normal boundaries of her life. It meant taking chances that were both scary and enticing. It meant taking control of her life. She didn't know what tonight would bring, but she was glad that she had him at her side. She trusted him, and she hoped that was enough.

Chapter 6

❧

Jacob smiled, his teeth flashing white against the olive tone of his skin. He was always handsome, but his smile enhanced his looks to a degree that made her stomach flutter in excitement. Camille could hardly believe that this was happening. He would take her up those stairs and she would know what it was like to lie with him. She would know the pressure of his mouth on hers, the weight of his body above her, and the length and breadth of his cock. Her face heated at the naughty thoughts. The situation hardly seemed real, yet he put his hand over her fingers where they rested on his arm and led her up the stairs. Tingles of anticipation whispered down her spine.

A rich carpet the most beautiful shade of scarlet muffled their steps on the marble stairs and continued down the wide corridor once they reached the top. This floor was tastefully decorated with art and spindly tables and weightier bureaus set at intervals. They were mostly topped with flowers and statuary of garden sprites, indicating an unexpectedly feminine touch.

She must have stared too long, because he said, "My mother always kept fresh flowers when she was alive, and I haven't been able to bring myself to stop the tradition."

His mother. Knowing that he still held her dear soothed her even more. Most men she had known barely seemed to notice the women in their lives except to control them. The fact that he would honor his dead mother in such a way touched her. "That's very sweet that you'd continue her habits."

"It makes me feel as if she's still here in some small way," he said, as if it was nothing at all to admit that he missed his mother. And it shouldn't be, but in her experience anything that could be considered a vulnerability was to be squashed and smothered, not spoken of openly.

She didn't know what to say, so she smiled and wondered at the depths that might be hidden in this man as he led her down the wide corridor.

He paused in front of a grand doorway that was almost as tall as the high ceiling. The room behind it was nothing short of opulent. It was decorated in a subtle but obvious rococo style, with gilt-edged moldings around the fireplace and ceiling, and inlaid in the walls. The furniture was a mix of creams and red, with rich scarlet drapes held back with thick gold cords at the windows. It was as lovely as the grandest London drawing room she had ever seen.

"Please have a seat," he said, closing the door behind them.

She suspected a butler or footman usually saw to the task, but Thorne must have dismissed his servants for the evening because the room was vacant, and the rooms that swept off to either side were dark and still. The only sounds were the crackling of the fire in the hearth and the ticking of a tall, longcase clock. Apprehension returned to churn in her stomach, but she ignored it and walked to the sofa, an elegant piece of furniture that was cream colored with garnet and rose details. A tray of sweets and brandy had been laid out on the low table before it.

"Brandy?" he asked, as he approached.

She was sorry she had sat, because he loomed over her, seeming taller and more powerful than she remembered. Now that she was here, and they were alone, tiny fissures were beginning to appear in her anticipation. But it was only her mind playing tricks on her. She knew that, so she nodded as she should and fought back the fear that was quickly edging out any sense of excitement. "Please join me."

He poured them both a drink and sat on the sofa next to her. He was close enough that she could feel his body heat, and the scent of sandalwood drifted over to her, bringing with it a sense of comfort and familiarity. He took a sip of the brandy, partially closing his eyes to savor it. She couldn't look away from the slight bit of moisture left behind when he licked his lips, or the strength in his long and graceful fingers as he twirled the drink. He was so beautiful. That smolder from the other night ignited in her belly, sending liquid relaxation through her body. If only she could hold on to these good feelings.

"How long has your mother been gone?" she asked to cover her distraction.

"About eight years. We've missed her every one of them."

She vaguely remembered that he had two younger sisters. "You're close with your sisters?"

He nodded. "Mama made certain of it. Whenever Maura and I would argue, she would give us a day to calm down and then make us spend time together. We fought often because she is only two years younger than me, and the story Mama told is that I didn't take it well when she was born. I didn't like her temerity in taking up so much of Mama's attention. Maura thought I was a bully, and perhaps I was." He laughed. "I'm happy to report we settled our differences when Lilian was born. I was seven and Maura was five, so we joined together against the little invader. It wasn't long before Lilian had us wrapped around her chubby little finger and stealing chocolates from the kitchen for her."

"Lilian?" Could he mean the same woman she had met in the ladies' retiring room? "Do you mean Lilian Greene?"

He grinned. "Yes, she's my sister. I assume you've met her here at the club?"

"A few weeks ago. We plan to meet for tea soon." Only Camille hadn't followed up because she'd been too embarrassed that she had approached Thorne only to be rejected and had tried to forget everything about that night.

He let out a huff of air, a laugh, and shook his head.

"What?" she asked.

"Neither of my sisters have ever had tea with a woman I've taken to my bed."

He said *taken to my bed* so casually while it sparked an image in her mind that she couldn't quickly erase. In fact, it lingered there . . . the idea of his skin touching hers, his breath on the parts of her body that air never touched, made her feel hot and swollen somehow.

"I-is that a problem?" She forced the question out to cover how unsettled she was.

He grinned, his eyes going partially hooded, making her think that the phrase might have affected him after all. "Only in that it creates potential for more awkwardness."

"I promise not to tell her your secrets, Mr. Thorne, if that's your concern."

"Thank you." His gaze slid over her face. "You two are more alike than I initially realized. You should get along well. She knows her own mind and has never cared what people think of her."

"Is that what you believe of me?"

"Am I wrong?" he asked.

"There was a time I cared. That's why I ended up married. I wanted to do what my parents asked of me. Now I realize how misguided that intention is. It's possible to care so much about what others think of you that you forget to take into account what you think of yourself. Then one day you realize that you don't think very much of yourself at all." Her voice died away as she finished. What had possessed her to spill so much of herself all over him? He probably thought she was silly.

His eyes didn't seem to be expressing that. He watched her quietly, somehow making her think he saw more than she wanted him to. His body moved by slow degrees as he carefully set his glass on the table and then narrowed the gap between them until the heat from his body penetrated through her gown. Her pulse quickened under his perusal, not daring to look him head-on, but taking shallow breaths beneath his study of her. What did he see when he looked at her that way?

His hand moved very slowly, nearly touching her arm as he reached up to trace the backs of his fingers over her jawline and then the nape of her neck, much like he had at Charrington Manor. A delicious shiver moved through her, though she kept herself still to not break the spell. This was very nice.

"You are far more than you show the world, Duchess. Beneath your fashionable exterior and devil-may-care smile, I believe you may harbor the soul of someone who feels much more than they let on." His voice was soft and raspy, thick with meaning.

Not for the first time, she thought that maybe he did, too.

"It's what I have become," she whispered.

She had not always been this solemn, injured thing. There had been a time when she had been girlish, laughing at life and whatever the future held. She had fallen asleep easily and not been awakened by a squeeze of pressure in her chest so tight that she had to force herself to breathe. Sometimes she hated that she could not get back to that foolish and winsome girl. Hereford had changed her, and even though he was gone, she could not rid herself of him or his influence. Their time together had extinguished that fire within her, and no matter how much she missed it, she couldn't seem to get it back. Another failure on top of her many.

"I like who you've become," he said.

She blinked at that, not quite sure what to make of it. Men admired her for her beauty or sneered at her for her lowborn blood, but she didn't know one who had bothered to know her enough to form an opinion about her personality. Even Christian and Evan knew her as a friend of their wives, not her.

"What do you like about me?" She spoke softly, almost afraid to hear the answer.

He didn't hesitate. "I like that you don't back down from challenges. How you sought me out and were bold enough to proposition me . . . twice. How you haven't let your troubles turn you away from living your life."

She was absurdly thrilled by the compliments. "I didn't know you could see so much of me."

"The more I know of you the more fascinated I am."

He caressed her leisurely as if they had all night, his palm curving around the back of her neck and his thumb stroking her cheek, leaving tiny sparks on her skin. His other hand took her tumbler and set it on the table before closing around her fingers. Her eyes fell shut as she attempted to control the pounding of her heart. The night was starting.

He brought her fingers to his mouth and pressed a gentle kiss to the backs. His lips were soft and warm, promising pleasure without ever saying a word. Every moment was languid but somehow calculated. He turned her hand over and kissed her palm before dragging his mouth to the inside of her wrist.

"You smell of jasmine and vanilla," he murmured, a slight moan in his voice as if the scent put him in a sort of agony.

"You smell of sandalwood and vetiver."

He smiled at that. She still didn't open her eyes, but she could feel the shape of his lips against her skin. "Do you like it?" he asked.

"Yes, very much so." Just the hint of his smell now had her stomach swirling in anticipation.

"I want you to tell me what you like." The tip of his tongue touched the pulse point in her wrist. "And what you don't like."

Her gaze met his. Would she be able to tell him if she didn't like something? The prospect already had her feeling embarrassed.

As if he sensed her thoughts, he said, "You can tell me and I won't take offense. We all have different things we enjoy, parts of our bodies that are more sensitive than others. Sex should bring you pleasure."

His mouth continued its way up the inside of her arm, weaving a trail of heat through the fabric of her gown. It wasn't all that intimate because of the barrier between them, but her breath came faster and the muscles deep inside her clenched. Then he was at her neck, continuing the touch from the night in her room at Charrington Manor. His breath touched her with moist heat as the tip of his nose brushed her skin, followed by the softness of his lips. The kisses were light, but they hinted at so much more that she could feel her blood rushing in excitement beneath her skin.

"Mr. Thorne—"

"Jacob." He corrected her immediately. The word was hot against her ear.

She shivered at how much she liked the sensation, and then his teeth scraped over the tender flesh of her earlobe, and she let out a soft sound that could only be described as a moan. He laughed quietly and did it again.

"Jacob," she whispered.

He sobered, his body tightening ever so slightly as he pulled back enough to look down at her. His eyes were darker than she had ever seen them, dilated with need and desire. She didn't know what she had meant to say, only that saying his name made her feel grounded and connected to him in a way that she needed.

"Say my name again."

The strength of the command coupled with the delightfully wicked curve of his lips had her whispering his name. She felt nearly euphoric, like they were adolescents who had only just discovered the joys of something forbidden. She couldn't say who moved first, but his lips were on hers and she was opening to him in an eager hunger that she had never experienced before. His tongue stroked hers, sliding against hers in a way that felt foreign but so good. It stopped just short of being too much. He seemed to understand what she needed, pulling back only to take more from her again. He cupped the back of her head, bending her to him as he feasted on her as if he'd never get enough. She wanted the euphoria and oblivion his kisses promised her.

Her fingers crept up his chest, seeking the solid reassurance of him. She pushed beneath the lapels of his coat, finding the smooth silk of his waistcoat. His heart beat with the steady rhythm of a drum beneath her palm.

"Camille," he whispered, pulling back to catch his breath.

She kissed his chin and then his neck, unwilling to stop now that she'd had a taste of him. The salt of his skin was heady. He tugged at the pins in her hair. They fell in an unsteady rhythm, the seed pearls clinking like raindrops against the table and falling to the floor. Her hair fell in a cascade down her back only to be picked up by his hands and brought to his face where he inhaled like a man denied her scent for too long. She couldn't help but stop kissing him to stare in awe at the sight. Her other times with men had either been cold or hurried and frenzied. No one had ever paused to appreciate her the way he did. It was as if he were savoring every part of her.

This is why so many women sought him out, she realized. He was intoxicating, consumed in his want for her in such a way that she would have believed she was the only woman he had ever wanted in his life if she didn't know better. Which she did. She knew that he probably looked at every woman he had bedded as he looked at her now, as if she were the only one. As if he might expire if he wasn't able to kiss her, hold her . . . join his body with hers.

The image that evoked brought with it the unsettling feelings from earlier. She never liked that part. Something always happened on the way from the pleasant beginnings to the painful end . . . a male body rising over her, using her ceaselessly in his single-minded purpose to reach fulfillment. She became an object and no longer herself.

She shifted and turned her face into the warm skin of Jacob's neck, breathing him in as she sought to rekindle the need he was awakening inside her. The exotic and sweet scent of sandalwood soothed her. It wasn't the heavier and sharp bay rum she always expected in these moments. This was Jacob and he wanted to make her feel good. He cared about her pleasure; that was the whole point of this exercise. She took a deeper breath, breathing him in, and a flicker of heat reignited within her.

She squeezed his hard shoulders and pressed herself into the wide, flat plains of his chest. She had admired the width of his shoulders often and had wondered what it might be like to touch them. He felt as strong as she had thought he would, the muscles only slightly giving beneath her fingers, promising strength and beauty. His arms came around her, holding her against him, and something warm fluttered through her. An ache started deep between her thighs. She sought him with her lips, delighting in the salty taste of him when the tip of her tongue touched his neck.

He groaned softly and buried his face in her hair again. His hands roamed her back and sides, coming up gently between them to test the weight of her breasts. The corset and layers of clothing did much to muffle the sensation, but she could still feel the pressure of his fingers, and her nipples beaded in response as she instinctively pressed closer to him. She wanted this. This was good.

She repeated that to herself as he gently guided her to lie on her back on the sofa. He rose over her, backlit and in shadow, but she could feel the weight of his gaze as he ate her up with his eyes. Part of her loved the intensity with which he looked at her; part of her trembled in a very real fear she couldn't control. The ache between her legs had her body clenching, longing for his fingers, his cock, anything that might fill her; but a light wave of dread turned her stomach, because she knew what would follow. With that intensity came a selfish and inevitable need in him that would overpower whatever desire she felt. He would use her, and she would be left trying to hold the shreds of her dignity together.

He reached for her gently, touching her cheek with a tenderness that made her throat close. "Are you afraid?" he whispered.

She could only nod, mortified that he had noticed. He settled beside her on the sofa and gathered her close to his side, tenderly cradling her head against his chest. His other hand moved languidly in a slow repetitive stroke up and down her side.

"Nothing will happen here that you don't want to happen." His lips moved against her temple as he spoke.

"I want this," she whispered.

He didn't reply right away. Had she put him off? Had he decided that she was too much trouble, and he would be better off slaking his lust elsewhere? Her heart pounded in every part of her body as she thought of the other women he'd been with, women who enjoyed everything he did to them, women who could please him and not shrink from him, women who were worthy of him. What if he was lying so still because he wanted her to leave?

She shifted to move away, but her wrist touched something very hard and very large between them. He didn't move, but his breath caught. So did hers. At least now she knew that he still wanted her, physically anyway.

It was better to stay than to make things more awkward by running, surely. If she could simply close her eyes, she could endure it. Besides, this was Jacob; it wouldn't be that terrible. He smelled nice, and he looked even nicer. With that in mind, she turned toward him and pressed kisses into his neck. He was so warm and felt so good that she could have stayed just like this all night in his arms without doing anything more, but that wasn't why she was here. He had never agreed to all night.

Taking her cue, his hands roamed up and down her back, soothing her with gentle strokes. Without noticing her intention, she somehow made her way to his mouth. He kissed her like she was the very last chocolate tart on earth and he was savoring every bite. Her blood turned to warm honey, sliding through her veins in a slow and lazy path that melted her inside. She pressed against him, and before she realized it had happened, she was on her back and he lay half on top of her. She didn't even care this time, because he was still kissing her, and this was heaven. Heaven was being kissed by Jacob Thorne.

He groaned, a deep, husky sound in the back of his throat that sent tremors of longing through her. His lips and the faint scrape of teeth found her neck, and she arched toward him, needing more. This was good. His hand was back to roaming, first her waist and then up to her breast. She wanted the clothing between them gone so she could feel his skin on hers. Her fingers pushed at his shirt, sliding between the buttons to reach him and then tugging at the ends tucked into his trousers. His hands moved freely now, no longer restrained, and grasped her skirt. She didn't realize what he was doing until the cool air hit her legs through her silk stockings. His hand seemed large as it roamed up her calf, gently massaging the muscle as he moved upward. His fingers touched her naked thigh. A gasp left her as her eyes flew open in shock. He'd gone up beneath her drawers.

She stiffened instinctively, though she immediately tried to force herself to relax. She wanted this. She did. But the need turned to a strange sort of anxiety again that chased away the ache that longed for him. She startled when his hand found its way between her legs. His groan of pleasure at the dampness he found there made her desire swirl with nausea. This is when it would start. He would lose control and she would become nothing but a receptacle. In her mind's eye, she saw him on top of her. His eyes clenched tightly closed as he thrust into her with a need so mindless that she ceased to exist except as a way to quench his desire.

For one heartbeat she lay there willing herself to accept his touch as she had accepted all the ones that had come before him. This was when she was supposed to lie still and receive him. Usually, she could make her mind think of something else . . . except for near the end when the movements would become such that she could not think of anything but the pressure and sometimes pain and how she wanted to be anywhere else. In some other body, in some other place. She could not bear to experience that with him . . . not Jacob. She didn't want to look at him and remember that. And that quickly, panic took hold. She had to get away from him.

She sat up so fast that she pushed him off of her, leaving him off-balance. Using that to her advantage, she put one foot on the ground and levered herself off the sofa anticipating that he might grab her and make her stay. As soon as she whirled to look at him, she realized her mistake. He stared at her in bewilderment and concern. There was not a shred of the anger she had expected. Frustration could make men harsh and unyielding. His expression was distressed but tender.

Her face warmed as the full extent of her overreaction became clear. He had done nothing more than enjoy their kisses and caresses as he was meant to do. He had touched her because that was why she was here, and a part of her was sad that she had stopped him. That was why this was so frustrating. She *did* want him. *She did*. Her throat closed against the ache building there.

"Camille—"

She held up her hand to stop whatever he meant to say. Any kindness he showed her would only make her burst into tears. Tears would bring on his pity and she could not withstand that. She had been a fool to think that sex with him would miraculously solve her problems. She was irrevocably broken.

"I'm sorry, Jacob." The backs of her legs touched the seat of the chair behind her, nearly sending her toppling over.

He rose quickly to help, but she managed to grasp the back of the chair and right herself.

"Don't leave," he said. "I went too fast. I can go slower."

She shook her head and swallowed against the lump in her throat. He could move as slowly as he wanted, but she was starting to think it wouldn't matter. He was kind and gentle and the most attractive man she had ever laid eyes on, and that was saying a lot because Christian was devilishly handsome. Jacob had all of Christian's good looks, but with a charm and ease that was like sunshine to his brother's moonlight. It was a combination she vastly preferred and it hadn't been enough. God, she still ached for him between her legs, and her knees trembled as she started to walk away, but it wasn't enough to overcome this confusing mix of emotions swarming her.

"I have to go. I'm sorry. You did nothing wrong. It's me."

She wanted to explain, but everything inside her rebelled in shame. Besides, what could she say? *I want you, but I can't bear your touch*. It was best to go and never speak of it again. She did just that, leaving her hairpins scattered across the floor and never looking back once as she hurried downstairs to collect her cape.

Chapter 7

❖

Jacob had not been able to sleep last night. After Camille had left looking terrified and wounded, he'd been too startled to follow her immediately. Once he'd been able to gather himself and run down the stairs to find her, Miss Davies had told him she'd left. He had gone outside in time to watch her carriage turning the corner. He'd considered going to her home but rejected the idea. It was clear she was afraid, and stalking her like prey wouldn't help that.

Instead, he'd lain awake remembering what had led to the terror on her face. He'd pushed too hard and too fast. He should have taken more care. She'd told him she didn't enjoy sex. He knew that her previous experience had been with bloody Hereford and had assumed that meant that she simply had never had a man concerned with her pleasure. Now he suspected that her issue was deeper than that. *She feared it.*

He should have realized sooner what being forced to lie with Hereford might mean, but he hadn't because he'd been intoxicated by her. She had responded to him and, fool that he was, he'd let it go to his head. He had assumed that all she needed was someone who knew what he was doing and spent time touching her in all the right ways. Now she was hurting, and he didn't know what to do about it.

That morning he had written a note, discarded it, then written a new one. He had felt like an ass sending it over, so he had gone himself to her home on Upper Brook Street, weighing the risk to her reputation if someone should see him there with the anguish she might be feeling on his account. In the end, it hadn't mattered because her butler had told him that she wasn't at home. Whether she was actually home or not, he hadn't been able to tell. He had left the note for her. It had seemed woefully inadequate, but he made it clear that he did not expect her to come to dinner with Turner and Blanchet tonight. God knows she deserved not to have to see him. Yet, he stood pacing before the doors to one of the club's private dining rooms, hoping that she might show even as somewhere deep in the house a clock chimed the hour that meant he should go inside.

There was no hope for it. He sighed, accepting his due. He would have to go into that room and admit his lie to Turner and Blanchet.

"Sir!"

He paused, afraid to hope as Webb rushed to him.

"Sir, there is a . . ." The servant hurried down the corridor and, realizing his voice was loud, looked around as if someone might shush him. His lips were pursed with an urgency that made it appear as if the words might burst out of him without his permission if he wasn't careful.

"Does Cavell need assistance?" Jacob asked, referring to Simon Cavell, the club's manager who had been left in charge.

Webb shook his head as he closed the distance.

"What is it?" But Jacob already knew. He *knew* she had come, and everything in him stilled, awaiting confirmation.

Only a few feet away now, Webb said, "Her Grace, Camille the Dowager Duchess of Hereford is here."

Jacob stood still for the length of a heartbeat as he pondered what this might mean. Had she forgiven him? He could hardly countenance it, but unless she had come to vent her rage before an audience, he could think of no other reason for her appearance. "She's here now?"

"She said you might want to know before your dinner." Webb nodded. "Forgive me, but I ran ahead to catch you before you went inside."

Jacob rushed to the corridor only to almost run into Camille as her slender form came around the corner. He took hold of her arms when they would have crashed into each other. She made a startled exhale and looked up at him with her wide eyes, a strand of silky blond hair falling from its hairpin. "Jacob!"

The muscles of his stomach tightened in remembrance of how she had looked tousled and more beautiful for it last night. Her use of his given name put a fine edge on the sensation. "Camille." He couldn't help but smile at her and glanced pointedly at Webb who gave an abbreviated bow. "Thank you, Webb. That will be all." Waiting until the sound of his steps had faded, Jacob said, "I didn't expect you to come. Didn't you get my note?"

She surprised him by smiling. "Yes, thank you for sending it. I wouldn't leave you in such a situation, however. We made a deal and I intend to honor my side of it."

Her smile wasn't one of joy. It was born from years of rigor and tutelage because it did not meet her eyes. His heart fell a little. "But I haven't honored my side of it." He realized he was still holding her arms, so he gave them a gentle squeeze before letting her go. "I made you afraid and for that I am deeply sorry—"

"It was nothing you did. Not really." She gave a dismissive wave of her hand and set about tucking the strand of hair back in place. "The problem is with me, and I realized that instead of forcing myself to continue that I didn't want to mar our friendship with such . . . sour memories. *I* should apologize to *you*. I left you in quite a . . . a state."

She meant to walk past him, and his first instinct was to step in her path, a move he regretted as soon as uncertainty crossed her beautiful face. If she was afraid of him, the last thing she needed was him to bully her. He took a step back to put some much-needed space between them. "Never apologize for being afraid. Not to me or anyone else."

"I wasn't afraid." Her chin lifted a notch, which indicated that her pride had come into play. She had been on her own for so long, cast adrift in a world that wasn't hers, that she didn't know how to be vulnerable. There was no reason that she should be comfortable being vulnerable with him. The need to protect her from those who would harm her nudged at him.

"All right, then let me rephrase. Never apologize for leaving a man unfulfilled. You don't owe him—*me*— anything. You have the sole right to your person."

Her gaze flickered, a crack in her well-mannered facade. "I'm afraid there's an entire legal history that would disagree." Then she shook her head, and the polite smile was back. "Let us not speak of last night again. It was an unfortunate incident that I hope we can both forget. Tonight, we have our roles, and we should go and play them, yes?"

When he didn't answer immediately, she hurried past him. "Are they in here?" she asked, pointing toward the closed dining room door.

He wanted to talk more. They were not finished, and whether it made him a bully or not, he couldn't let this rest. He could see the secret pain she tried to hide, and an impotent and unreasonable rage was taking over. What had that man done to her? He wanted to kill Hereford with his bare hands even though the man was already dead.

Now wasn't the time, however, and she didn't deserve to

have to deal with his anger on top of everything else. He took a few deep breaths as he approached her. By God, she was lovely tonight. Her hair shined in an intricate series of coils pinned to her head with several curls left free to lie on her shoulder. She was dressed in a garnet-colored gown that shimmered in the light. It was tasteful but what some— not him—might describe as a bit low-cut. She was beautiful. A single ruby on a gold chain lay nestled just above the deep V of her flawless cleavage. The plump swell of her breasts reminded him of how perfectly she had filled his hands last night. The sudden and harsh constriction of his abdominal muscles caused a tingling near the base of his spine.

Christ, he still wanted her. Badly. With her fear so prominently evident, he didn't know if that made him a cad or a fool.

He cleared his throat to fight against the sudden tightness, but even so, there was a husk in his voice when he spoke. "We will speak on this later, Camille." And they would. Doubt clouded her eyes when she looked at him, but he didn't give her a chance to respond as he opened the door and escorted her inside. "Good evening, everyone."

The group of four—the two men and their wives—stood near the fireplace, conversing amicably and sipping on sherry a footman had poured for them a few minutes earlier.

"Thorne!" Gilbert Turner was the first to turn and address him. His exuberance filled the room almost as much as his large voice did. "You *did* come. I don't mind telling you that I half expected you to call off. Didn't I say that, Ruthie?" he asked the middle-aged woman at his side, presumably his wife. She nodded along. "I thought you might be pulling my leg with your talk of this charming woman. Blanchet here assured me that you were indeed serious."

"I did," the Frenchman confirmed. "I said to him that

our Jacob Thorne is an honorable man." The sly smile in his eyes confirmed that he, too, had been wondering if Camille existed.

"As you can see, she is very much real."

Jacob managed to keep his voice level even though the whole thing was ridiculous. Blanchet would know the truth soon enough. The moment Turner signed the contract and sent over his investment funds Jacob planned to leave for Paris. Jacob would tell Blanchet the truth then, and he didn't expect the man to mind. Marriage had never been one of his conditions when they had first conceived of the idea back during the summer. It would be abundantly clear to Blanchet anyway when Camille never bothered to visit and there was no wedding. Jacob didn't like to handle his business affairs in this way, but Turner had left him little choice. Investments should be handled and evaluated based on the competence of those involved. Not the existence of spouses.

"May I present Camille, Dowager Duchess of Hereford?"

Turner's mouth dropped open a suitable amount. Not enough to be too obvious, but enough to imply he was both shocked and impressed.

To Camille, Jacob said, "These are my business partners, Mr. Gilbert Turner and M. Pierre Blanchet."

Fully embracing her role of his betrothed and host, she said, "It is my pleasure to meet you and welcome you to Montague Club. I hope we can now put to rest any discussion of my existence." Turning to Blanchet and his wife, she said, *"Bonsoir. C'est ravi de vous rencontrer tous les deux. Félicitations pour votre mariage."*

For a moment, no one spoke. "You speak French?" Jacob asked before he could think better of it. As her fiancé, this was probably information that he should already know.

"Oui." She smiled at him with a hint of mischief in her eyes.

"You never said."

"You never asked." She shrugged.

Turner laughed, and the next several moments were taken up with introductions all around. Turner's wife, Ruth, possessed a coarse sort of attractiveness that indicated she, like her husband, had seen more than her fair share of life. She nearly matched Turner in both size and demeanor. When she laughed, which was often, her voice filled the room, and she was quick to take control of the conversation. Blanchet's wife, Margot, was quiet, though that may have been due to the language barrier. It quickly became apparent that she spoke minimal English. Jacob, like Camille, addressed her in French, and she smiled at him in relief. She was young with a strong frame that indicated she performed physical labor on her family's farm. It was clear that Blanchet was smitten with her in the way he constantly deferred to her as they spoke of their trip.

"Tell us, Thorne, how did you come to be betrothed to this lovely woman?" Turner asked.

It wasn't an unexpected question, and Jacob was prepared to answer it. "As you may recall, my brother married recently and Camille is close friends with his wife. The first time I saw her I knew she was very special." That much was the truth. She blushed prettily at the compliment and glanced away. His hand found its way to the small of her back, needing to touch her.

"Don't be coy. Tell us how you met." Turner smiled as if he knew he was prodding beyond Jacob's level of comfort.

He could remember the first time he had ever seen her as vividly as if it were yesterday. "We were both attending my brother's wedding breakfast. I was at Christian's side greeting guests, and Her Grace was across the room with Violet."

Jacob looked at Camille as he spoke, wondering if she

had noticed him that day. In truth, she might not have. Violet had been upset to be forced into the marriage, and Camille had likely been completely occupied with consoling her friend. Jacob himself had taken up a position of support beside his half brother who had been experiencing the extreme emotions of joy and heartache all at the same time; joy because he had married the love of his life, heartache because his bride despised him. Tending to the quagmire of emotions hadn't left much room to focus on anything else.

Camille looked at him in question and a small bit of wonder. Jacob held her gaze as he continued, "The crowd parted in a rare lull to reveal the most beautiful woman I had ever seen." He didn't need to fabricate any of this because it was the absolute truth. "I immediately asked my brother who she was."

Hereford's duchess, Christian had replied. Those two words should have been enough to suppress his interest— he did not pursue married women—and yet they hadn't completely snuffed it out. Her presence had entertained the shadowed corners of his mind ever since.

"Is that how you remember it, Your Grace?" Turner asked.

Belatedly, Jacob realized that he had probably revealed something too intimate. Even if she had taken note of him, she couldn't very well say so in front of everyone. She had been a married woman at the time and to acknowledge she had any interest in him at all would be unseemly.

"No, I should say not," Jacob added with a self-deprecating laugh he hoped didn't sound completely forced. "I'm afraid she barely took note of me at all when we were introduced later that day. My admiration was doomed to go unrequited."

"Never fear, he charmed me completely when I joined Montague Club several months ago," Camille offered, turning into him slightly to complete the ruse of the infatuated couple. "He taught me to gamble and I knew he was special. But then he asked me to marry him, and I knew I was lost to him completely." The way she looked at him had Jacob forcing himself to remember this wasn't real.

Everyone laughed and Turner mused in wonder, "So you're a patron of the club?"

"I am."

"You're a very forward-thinking woman, then." Turner looked at her appraisingly.

Jacob didn't know if that was a good thing in Turner's estimation or not, but before he could reply, Mrs. Turner said, "Don't worry, lamb—er, Your Grace. He likes forward-thinking lasses," and nudged her husband in the ribs.

Turner opened his mouth to offer a rejoinder, but before he could, Camille turned to Blanchet. "M. Blanchet, I would love to hear about your wedding. I've never been to a wedding in France."

Jacob smiled at how skillfully she had taken control of the conversation and directed it away from their deception. "Shall we dine as we chat?" Jacob asked.

The group agreed and settled themselves at the round table in the center of the room set with a small centerpiece of roses and lavender and the club's best silver and china. They sat in order of alternating sex as was the custom, but Turner made certain to settle himself next to Camille. Jacob nearly rolled his eyes at the man's obvious fascination with her. Whether that stemmed from her beauty, title, or both, he couldn't say.

As soon as they were seated, Webb, assisted by a second footman, brought in the soupe à la Reine. They settled into a pleasant discussion about the Blanchets' wedding. Jacob fervently hoped the night would be enough to put Turner's mind at ease.

* * *

W hen did you learn French?" Jacob asked, later that night.

The other couples had left moments ago, so it was only him and Camille in one of the private drawing rooms off the dining room where they had retired for drinks and dessert after dinner. Jacob had refilled Camille's glass subtly so that she might be inclined to linger and talk with him. Their earlier conversation had not been far from his thoughts all night.

"My parents insisted upon it. They thought a future husband might appreciate the fact that his wife was cultured." She took a sip of her drink as if there was nothing off about what she had said. "It didn't occur to them until I was nearly fifteen and one of their friends suggested it. From that day on I had lessons almost every afternoon. I don't speak it as well as you do, though."

He'd been happy and a little proud, truth be told, when Camille had engaged Blanchet and Margot in conversation in French throughout dinner. However, the reason she gave left him feeling cold and ill at ease.

"It was for the benefit of a future husband and not for yourself?" he asked.

She smiled at him ruefully over the rim of her glass. "What benefits my future husband, benefits me. Or so they believed." Setting her wine down, she raised a brow at his harsh expression. "Come now, you sound as if you aren't aware that's how the world works for girls. I believe you've met the Crenshaw sisters." She teased. "You know the great lengths their parents went to in order to secure titled matches for them. Their use as a commodity in marriage is something most girls of our class understand by the time they reach thirteen. What's a few French lessons?"

"Yes, despite their attempt at an olive branch, I don't get the feeling Violet has completely forgiven her parents. I simply didn't think that mercenary philosophy was so prevalent."

"I find that difficult to believe. The aristocracy is similar. Your father was an earl. You have younger sisters who are both married. Did you or your mother not"—she shook her head—"groom them, for lack of a better word, to make the best matches possible?"

"No, not as such. Mama saw to our education, of course, and refused to send me to boarding school. She thought they were elitist and rife with immorality." He grinned in memory of how she had won that particular battle with his father.

"You find that amusing?" She raised a brow in question at the smile on his face.

He shook his head. "No, not that. It was a subject of contention between them. My father insisted that I must go, and he had even made arrangements for me to attend one in Scotland. Mama was livid when he told her. It was one of the very few times I can remember her being angry with him. They shared a bedroom, and she had his clothing relocated to another room downstairs. I didn't understand the significance at the time, but he relinquished his position that very day."

She smiled. "I'm glad he saw reason on the matter."

"We had tutors instead," Jacob added. "My sisters received the same education as I. That included the sciences, mathematics, literature, and several languages, though French is the one she made certain we mastered."

"But you knew they would marry someday and that marriage would secure their futures?"

"Marriage was never discussed with any seriousness. Mama had married for love—married in her heart, at least—and she firmly believed any marriages in our futures should be our decisions to make."

A speculative look came over her face. "Your mother seems like she was a woman ahead of her time. I'm sorry to have never met her."

His immediate response to that was that he was also

sorry she had never met Camille. He squashed it, however, because it had no place here. This deal with the duchess would prove tricky. He could already feel himself wanting to get closer to her. The Halston men were historically bad at love, and he wanted no part of that legacy.

When he didn't respond, she continued, "Then you're saying that your mother did not aspire to titled husbands for your sisters?" An attractive pink colored her cheeks. "I am aware of your particular circumstances," she added, alluding to their illegitimacy. "But you live well, and I assume the legalities of one's birth can be overcome with such . . . grandness."

"You are not wrong. Money can overcome much. No, Mama never aimed for titled husbands. I suspect her own relationship had something to do with that." She had loved his father, and God knows his father had loved her to madness, but theirs was not a relationship that should be repeated. His father's title and all that was inherent with it had come between them often. As a result, their relationship, though filled with love, had been unhealthy and was the primary reason Jacob had decided that marriage was not something he wanted, or at least not for a long time.

She wanted to ask about his parents' relationship. Her gaze narrowed and a line appeared between her brows, but when she opened her mouth, she asked, "If not titled husbands, what sorts of husbands did she want for them?"

He smiled. "Kind husbands who are good providers and who care for them. Maura married a man who owns several shops in Manchester. I only see her a few times a year, but she's happy there helping him run his businesses and raising their children. Lilian met her husband at a suffrage convention, although Mama was already gone by then. I admit I wasn't happy with her choice, at first. A radical isn't the sort of husband that can provide a stable life. However, he was also an apprentice in an accountant's office and only occasionally attends radical events. With her dowry, I made certain that he purchased a small house, enough to see them comfortable for some time."

"I can imagine you as the overbearing brother-in-law." Her eyes were sparkling with humor as she swirled the wine in her glass.

He shrugged, but his grin widened. "I'm certain Anthony would agree, but she is settled, and I stay out of their lives as much as possible."

He liked this ease they had found together. Talking with her was comfortable, and she seemed content with him, despite what had happened last night. He was hesitant to bring it up, but there was no way around it. The terror and shame on her face was too vivid in his memory. He could not accept never speaking of it again.

"Camille—"

She must have sensed what he was about because she set down her drink again and stood. "It's getting very late, so I'm afraid I have to go home. I had a shift at the London Home for Young Women this afternoon, and I am meeting with Lady Helena in the morning."

She had every intention of running out of here and never looking back. If he didn't talk to her now, he might not ever see her again with the way she was being guarded with him.

"What do you do there?" he asked, grasping at the threads of their short-lived harmony.

She paused but managed to find something very interesting about the hem of her sleeve rather than look at him. "It's not very glamorous, I'm afraid. Sometimes I teach comportment and French, but today they were shorthanded, so I helped in the kitchen."

"You cook?"

She shrugged, looking toward the hearth, her voice a little bit lower. "Not really. I have tried, but only at the London Home. I do enjoy it, but I'm not very good at it. As one might imagine, being a duchess doesn't lend itself to learning the finer points of food preparation. I was baking.

We celebrate birthdays of the residents one day a month, so I prepared a simple sponge with a whipped cream topping. It's really the only thing I can make well."

In the time she spoke, he had crossed to her, drawn to her in that way he had noticed lately. He had always found her fascinating and beautiful, but the barrier of her marriage and title followed by the simple fact that she was a close friend of Violet, who had become a sister to him, had kept him at a distance. Now that their deal was coming dangerously close to splintering that last barrier, he found himself peering over the top of it even though it was a risky game. One wrong move could send it toppling. It had taken all of his willpower to keep from touching her at dinner. Even though they were masquerading as an engaged couple and he should have had the right. It took all he could now to keep his hands to himself.

"Why don't you learn more pastries?"

She finally looked at him. "I'm a duchess. Everyone knows duchesses don't cook."

"Your husband's dead, Duchess. He can't tell you what to do. Unless I'm wrong, you live in that house of yours all alone with an army of servants. You can do what you want."

She laughed but it lacked humor. "They would look at me as if I were daft and probably have me carted off to Bedlam."

"You don't have to live by their rules anymore."

Her gaze fixed on his. A breath passed between them as she started to speak, but then she changed her mind.

"I have to go," she finally said.

This time he did reach out. Her arm was warm and soft beneath his palm. "We need to discuss last night."

She glanced at his hand but didn't try to back away. "As I said, I know it was unfair of me to leave like that."

"No, it was not unfair." He let her go and ran his hands through his hair as he fought back frustration. "You do not owe me anything, not even this conversation, honestly, but I hope you'll humor me. I want to understand what happened. I want to understand *you*, if you will help me to do so."

"Why?" Her chin rose a notch, and that flash of fire he admired about her had come back.

"You asked me for help. I want to help, but I find myself hindered if I do not understand what happened."

"There isn't much to understand." She gave a mirthless laugh and turned toward the window, finding something outside to occupy her as she put space between them. "After my marriage . . . I find it difficult to . . ." She dropped her gaze and whispered, "I feel so ashamed talking about this."

"I do not think any less of you, Camille. You are beautiful and brave, and nothing you can say will change that in my eyes."

She shook her head as if she didn't believe him, but she continued, gathering resolve as she spoke. "What happened wasn't your fault. I enjoyed it . . . up to a point, and then I didn't. It's as simple as that, and it doesn't seem to be something I can control." Turning to face him, she said, "I know from other women that the process can be enjoyable, so there is simply something not right with me. It will take time, but I am now determined that I must accept it."

A tightness squeezed his chest. "There is nothing wrong with you."

"Then perhaps I am one of those women who cannot—"

"I didn't mean it quite like that. I believe that given time we can overcome what happened to you. You like my touch." He reached out gradually, and she watched him until his fingertips touched her shoulder. Then they both watched as he dragged them down her arm in a slow stroke that made her shiver in pleasure. In a quiet voice, he added, "You were wet when I touched you last night."

"Yes," she whispered so softly that he almost didn't hear it.

"Come to me again. Let us try once more."

She stiffened immediately and pulled away. Before she

could deny him, he added, "You will stay fully clothed, and I promise not to touch you."

Her wide gaze swung back to him, confused as to his intention. "Then how?"

"There are other things we can do that can help you become more comfortable with me. Rest assured, Camille, you'll retain your power."

She shook her head, but the wheels were turning in her mind. He could tell that she was intrigued despite herself. "I'll have to think about it."

"Take all the time you need. I will be here when you are ready."

She moved to walk past him but paused, drawing in a quivering breath. Her lips parted as she met his gaze, but she couldn't say the words.

"Yes?" he prodded gently.

"It's stupid." She shook her head and slight color rose in her cheeks. He wanted so badly to take her in his arms. Some instinct told him she would have to come to him. He couldn't force this. So, he waited, and she finally asked, "Did that really happen?" Her fingertips pressed into the sleeve of his coat as she rested her hand there. He dared not move for fear that she'd remove her touch. "Did you really first notice me at the wedding breakfast?"

"Yes, everything I said was true." He breathed the word. "You were wearing champagne silk and pearls."

She smiled. "I noticed you that day, too." Her fingers clenched his arm briefly before she walked away, leaving her vanilla scent to linger. "Before, actually, to be completely honest."

Something trembled inside him, warning him that it was too late to save himself from her.

Chapter 8

✦

What do you think, Your Grace?" The woman Camille was training as a lady's maid stepped back from the dressing table and gave an appropriately restrained but hopeful smile as they both regarded her handiwork in the mirror.

Camille shifted in her seat, turning her head from side to side to view her pinned-up hair at all angles with the help of her hand mirror. The sheen of it shifted in the light, aided by the jasmine-scented bandoline Ingram had applied. "It's perfect. You are progressing nicely in your lessons," she said.

Ingram gave a subtle laugh at the compliment and clapped her hands once before remembering that such displays were inappropriate. She had been living at the London Home for Young Women for the past year and had decided that she wanted to go into service. Camille had brought her on as a lady's maid to help her prepare. "Thank you, Ingram. You deserve to celebrate."

Ingram blushed in pleasure as she straightened the vanity surface. "Will there be anything else, Your Grace?"

"No, I think I'm ready. You may go."

Ingram nodded and hurried out of the room. Camille was expecting Lilian Greene to arrive soon for afternoon tea. Prompted by the knowledge that she was Jacob's sister—and the certainty that he wouldn't have told her about their failed experiment—she had invited her for tea at long last. It was time for her to make new friends that were not among Hereford's Society if she was planning to stay in London.

It had been several days since Jacob had invited her back to see him, and Camille still had not managed to conquer her nerves to take him up on his offer. She wasn't afraid of him. She was afraid to get there and find out that no matter what they tried, nothing helped. What would she do then?

It was really a very silly problem to have. Sex wasn't important. At least according to the women in her mother's social group. Camille could remember overhearing several of their conversations when they thought no one was listening. The discussion would inevitably involve a sigh of disdain followed by a declaration that it was best to simply lie there until the whole thing was over. This would be followed by another woman agreeing that such an act was regrettably necessary, in a tone that implied she meant that it was shameful and degrading. Soft, uncomfortable laughter would soon follow, and the conversation would travel to less vulgar territory.

Camille had always been confused by these attitudes. Sex was a necessary part of life if one wanted children. She had been raised her entire life to believe that her one purpose was to marry well and produce children. Why was the one act that was necessary for the fulfillment of her supposed single purpose in life shameful? These beliefs had always seemed shortsighted and small-minded. If she embraced it, it meant that she would inevitably descend into shameful and degrading behavior. This led to the natural conclusion that should she marry well and produce children as everyone meant her to do, her triumphs would be marred by shame.

She refused to be that sort of woman and had not embraced those attitudes. She had flirted at parties and allowed several kisses with boys her own age, and she had enjoyed them all. Then her parents had foisted Hereford upon her. At fifty-six years of age, he'd been three times her own age, and not the husband she had ever imagined for herself. She had imagined someone like Maxwell Crenshaw. Someone fine and dignified who would perhaps love her or respect her at the very least.

Hereford had looked upon her with disdain from their very first meeting, and that had not changed after their marriage. To him, wedding her—a woman without blue blood and the breeding that implied—had been several steps down the social ladder for him. He had deigned to do it because his estates were near bankruptcy, and he'd had no choice. But he had never let her forget how she was unworthy of the title of duchess, and how he had resented having to lower himself to her.

Her dread of their wedding night had been something awful, though thankfully she could not remember much of the actual night. Champagne had always been doled out to her in careful servings, enough to enjoy but not to overindulge. That night she must have drunk an entire bottle of the stuff, perhaps more. She could remember him coming to her bed in his nightshirt and his sneer as he had shoved back the blankets. Even drunk, she had clung to them to cover herself, but what happened next was lost in a fog. She awoke the next morning with a cottony feeling in her mouth and her virgin's blood on the sheets. The worst of it, though, was that terrible feeling of being used, of knowing that he could—and would—use her again, and there was nothing she could do about it.

It was a sad sort of irony that she had become just like those women her mother called friends, despite her best intentions. Perhaps she had been the one who was wrong all along.

The ring of the doorbell sounded downstairs. Camille hurried to grab a handkerchief from a drawer in the dressing table. The telltale glaze of tears made her eyes shiny in the reflection, so she dabbed at the corner of her eyes. Self-pity would get her nowhere, and she'd been wallowing in it a bit too much lately. Mrs. Greene was exactly the distraction she needed.

A few moments later she joined Jacob's sister in the drawing room. "Good afternoon, Mrs. Greene, it is good to see you."

Lilian turned away from the glass cabinet that held seventy-four (Camille had counted them) shepherd and shepherdess figurines hand-selected by some nameless Hereford ancestor. The woman smiled, and Camille wasn't certain how she had missed the similarities between her and her brother. They had the same rich, black hair and olive skin, and there was a bit of good-natured mischief in her expression that perfectly matched Jacob's.

"Please call me Lilian. I was happy to receive your note. I worried when I didn't see you at the club again."

"My commitments have kept me away." She still didn't know if she could return. Dinner to honor her commitment had been one thing; to go on her own would be quite another. "I am glad you could call. Please sit down." She indicated the settee that faced the window.

"I brought this for you." The woman rifled in her handbag and pulled out a small cosmetic pot and presented it to her. "The same color as the one I shared with you."

Surprised at her thoughtfulness, Camille took it but didn't quite know what to say. "Thank you."

"You're welcome. It was a lovely color on you, so I thought you should have some of your own," she said, taking her seat.

Camille held the small container in her palm, touched

beyond words that she would remember how the rouge had looked on her. "I do love that color. I've never chosen red before." She immediately thought of Jacob and wearing it for him. His gaze had lingered on her lips that night.

"You should. It suits you."

Camille smiled, the feeling she'd had that night, as if she'd rediscovered a long-lost friend, making a reappearance. "Perhaps I'll wear it to the club next time I go."

Lilian agreed that she should, and they settled into a polite exchange of pleasantries. After a few minutes, Lilian let her gaze roam the room from the heavy wood paneling to the caramel wallpaper and the heavy furniture. "This room is rather dark. Do you ever find it . . . oppressive?"

Camille laughed, recalling how Jacob had indicated his sister was a bit outspoken. "The house belonged to my late mother-in-law. I never met her, but she seems to have had rather old-fashioned and dreary taste." She used the home that was part of her dower when she was in town but hadn't made significant changes to it yet.

"Ah, that makes more sense. It doesn't suit you at all. Have you considered redecorating?"

"I had planned to, and I have redone my bedroom and sitting room. After my husband's death, I spent some time in New York with my family. I only returned in the autumn, and I haven't had a chance to address the main floor." The truth was that she had lost her enthusiasm for the project. She didn't particularly like it here, and had considered leaving the dower house, but winter had set in.

"You didn't prefer to stay in New York with your family?" Seeming to realize that she was probing, Lilian smiled. "You don't have to answer my questions. Jacob claims that I talk too much and don't know how to mind my own business. Do not tell him, but he's sometimes correct."

"Your secret is safe with me." Camille laughed again, becoming more at ease with her with every passing moment.

There was a natural way about her that made Camille believe her questions came from a place of empathy. Certainly, any of her Society acquaintances would have been asking probing questions in an attempt to gain gossip to share with their friends later. "The truth is I'm not very close to my family, not like you are with Jacob and, I assume, your sister. I'm an only child and my parents and I see the world differently. I anticipated wanting to stay in New York, but I no longer felt at home there." Not that London felt like home, either. "At least here, I have freedom. My own home, no one to tell me what time I should be in every night, no one to remind me of what is proper and what isn't." Society matrons, the scandal sheets, and Scarbury did their own sort of policing as far as that went.

Mrs. Hartley, her housekeeper, walked in with a tea tray. Camille spent the next several moments pouring their tea and arranging the platter of sandwiches and pastries. Once they had both settled with a cup of tea, Lilian regarded her over the edge of her cup.

"I can tell you are a woman who enjoys her freedom. You're quite lucky in that way."

"In what way?" Camille asked.

"Only that many women don't have freedom."

"Yes, I know." Thinking of the times she had felt a prisoner in her own home, she added, "Once upon a time I was one of those women."

Lilian looked at her thoughtfully. As if she could intuit Camille's thoughts, she asked, "And then your husband died?"

Camille nodded, wary of this turning into another discussion of her marriage and all the things that had been done to her. Sometimes talking about it made her feel as if she were still helpless. "Is it that obvious? I don't plan to marry again for a long time, if ever."

"Husbands hold the keys to freedom or servitude."

Taking a cue from the forthright Lilian, she asked,

"You're a married woman. Have you found freedom in your marriage?"

Lilian's warm laughter filled the space, its pleasant sound easing any hesitation Camille might have still harbored about opening up to her. "Yes, but I am extraordinarily lucky. Mr. Greene is a unique man. He believes the same as I, that a marriage should not give a man complete ownership of a woman. We have our disagreements the same as any couple, but we are equals in our marriage."

An unexpected wave of jealousy caused her throat to close. It appeared that she was doomed to be surrounded by absurdly happy couples who espoused progressive ideals and shone new shades of light on just how inferior her own marriage had been. "How fortunate."

"Forgive me. I do not presume to know the particulars of your own situation."

"No, I am happy you have found someone who shares your ideals."

There was a slightly awkward pause as they sipped their tea. "Jacob tells me that you volunteer at the London Home for Young Women. Do you like it there?" Lilian clearly hoped to change their topic of conversation.

"Yes, it's a wonderful organization. They do such good work for people who have been otherwise left behind. You should come by sometime. There is always room for another person willing to help out."

"Thank you, I think I will. I have to admit that I was surprised when I read about it in the *Times*. It's a radical concept. A home for fallen women and their illegitimate children. I admire Lady Helena for conceiving of the idea."

"It was a charity born of the need she saw at the Bloomsbury Orphanage. Many women would be forced to leave their children there, not because they didn't want them, but because they had to work and had no family to help with childcare. Not to mention that many lost their jobs once they became pregnant."

Lilian nodded in understanding. "Yes, I can see the need for it. I only meant that ladies do not usually support radical causes."

"Yes, you're right. I suppose it upsets the balance of what is proper. Lady Helena is an unusual woman in the very best way."

"You don't seem to be bothered by *what is proper.*"

Camille smiled. "Neither do you, if your brother can be believed. He claimed you met your husband at a suffrage convention."

"Jacob talked to you about me?"

Camille shrugged off the question, not wanting to dwell on what came after in that conversation, and picked up her tea. "He did. I was a little surprised. In my experience most men aren't very progressive."

"Perhaps you've been associating with the wrong men."

"Touché."

"Universal suffrage is a passion I share with my husband." Lilian reached for a cucumber and dill sandwich. After taking a delicate bite, she asked, "Have you given much thought to women's suffrage?"

"No," Camille answered honestly. To be fair, her life had been very complicated until recently. "My friend August has recently joined the London Suffrage Society, but I'm afraid I've been preoccupied. I do believe it is a just and good cause."

"Yes, I am a member of that group. We were very happy when the duchess joined us. If your schedule permits, you must come to our next meeting. The American Victoria Woodhull will be speaking."

"Her name sounds familiar, but I'm afraid I cannot place her."

"She ran for president of the United States several years ago."

"That's right." Camille vaguely remembered the hubbub that had caused and that she had been arrested several times. "I remember her now."

"She's only recently relocated to England with her family and has graciously offered to speak to our group. She has peculiar views, which makes her an important voice in the cause. We believe that only with suffrage can *all* women truly find the sort of freedom that you've found."

She wasn't as free as most liked to believe, since she only had an allowance under her control. "You're right. Until women are able to vote on the laws and politicians who represent our interests, we will never have true equality."

"I'm glad we agree. It sounds like you're ready to join our cause."

Camille grinned. "Was this your way of recruiting me?"

Lilian shrugged. "It wasn't that difficult. You only needed a little nudge." They both laughed. "I would be happy to introduce you to a few women I believe you would like. I don't want to pressure you, but the cause could use someone in your position."

"I'm not altogether certain what I could do. I'd be happy to donate, of course."

"Your status alone could be a boon," the woman said. "We need names like yours to lend legitimacy to our fight. Unfortunately, many of the titled women as well as the heiresses from America have been reluctant to step into the suffrage movement. They stand with the queen in suggesting that a woman's place is firmly in the home and any talk of suffrage will upset this mystical balance."

"Why do you suppose they feel this way?" While Camille had been too self-absorbed in the past several years to give the situation much thought, she did believe that women deserved the right to see to their own livelihoods. Suffrage was a natural and just way to help achieve that. If she had been in charge of her own livelihood, she might have avoided Hereford altogether.

Lilian gave a shrug. "Sometimes it's easier to keep things the way they are, especially if you aren't the one suffering."

That was true. Even now, Camille was reluctant to join because it would mean changing things and chancing uncomfortable situations. One of the reasons she rebelled was that people would talk about her regardless, so she might as well give them something to talk about. This, however, would be worse than her petty rebellions, like joining Montague Club. Women's suffrage roused genuine feelings of anger and insecurity in those in power. It would lead to a different sort of backlash. "Could I think about it?"

"Of course." Then in a lower voice Lilian added, "With your help, we could stop other women from facing a similar fate."

Camille glanced at her, unsure what she knew about *her* fate.

"I don't mean to be presumptuous, but Hereford's reputation and age were no secret." Everyone knew that he had died in the bed of his mistress. They also whispered about Camille being his poisoner and executioner. "Every woman should be able to choose her own spouse."

"I agree completely." How much suffering could she have saved herself if she had chosen her own husband? It might not have been a happy marriage, given the pool of eligible bachelors her parents would have approved, but it might not have been so . . . damaging.

"Then help us make sure that can happen. With your assistance, we can make certain every woman has the freedom she deserves."

If joining the movement could help ensure another young woman didn't have to suffer, wouldn't it be worth the risk? She couldn't help but wonder what Jacob might think of such a bold decision, and she wanted to talk it over with him. He listened to her in a way no man ever had before. Almost immediately, she realized that he would applaud her instead of feeling threatened. He was strong and secure in himself and special in ways she was only just starting to understand.

Chapter 9

❧

Parliament sat beginning in January, but the Season didn't truly start until the families with country estátes came to town after Easter. Lord and Lady Ashcroft were óne of the few who held a ball every winter during this lull for those who were in Town. Since it naturally was more exclusive, it had become a veritable who's who of London insiders. Camille had learned that the term *insider* translated to the people who considered themselves most important to the running of the country. The pretentiousness was such that she generally tried to avoid the gathering, but Hereford's heir had been most insistent that she accompany him when he arrived on her doorstep the evening after her tea with Lilian.

"Did you not receive my note? I sent it to you along with the invitation last week." He addressed her very firmly in the middle of her own drawing room. Gloves in hand, pacing before the fireplace.

"Of course I did, Scarbury."

"Hereford. I will thank you to use my title." He interrupted her, speaking through gritted teeth.

She sighed. In her mind, Hereford would ever be the ogre she married, even though the title had transferred after his death. "Hereford," she said to appease him. "I simply do not understand the need for my presence." She was still catching up on correspondence after her trip to Charrington Manor and planning for a board meeting for the London Home for Young Women. A ball was not on her agenda for the evening. "Did you not receive my reply?"

He paused to give her a sharp look that could have pierced her very soul had she given a fig about his opinion of her. Luckily, she didn't. Nearing forty years old, he could have easily passed for fifty. It wasn't only his receding hairline and gangly build that sometimes made it seem as if he stooped that made him appear older. His aged look was also owed to his pinched features and sallow complexion. Or, perhaps, it was how he seemed to look down at everyone and everything as if he were far superior simply because of his birth.

Not bothering with a response to her question, he said, "I will return in precisely two hours, and you shall accompany me to the Ashcrofts."

Camille rose, only barely managing to restrain herself from stamping her foot like a recalcitrant child. This family brought out the worst in her. "Why must I go?"

"You are the dowager," he said, pulling the gloves on over his thin fingers. "It is what is required of you."

"You have a wife for these things."

"Eleanor is at the estate and not suitable for public appearance at any rate, as you well know."

While she knew Eleanor was pregnant, it had slipped her mind that the woman was so far into her pregnancy. They weren't exactly close. "She's due to deliver any day now, isn't she? Shouldn't you be there at her side instead of here in London?"

She thought of Christian and Violet. He had been an absolute wreck in the lead-up to the birth of their daughter two years ago and had hardly left her side, sometimes to her humorous displeasure. Then there was Evan, a duke as well, who had been emphatic about changing his schedule around to be with August and their son at Charrington Manor in the months after she had given birth. In fact, tonight was their first foray back into London life since William's birth.

Scarbury merely stared at her as if she had lost her mind. "Whatever for? The butler will wire me when the child is born, along with the pertinent details."

Memory was a strange thing. Sometimes it sat there in its corner of the mind perfectly content to exist in its allotted space. Sometimes it got restless and seeped into all the nooks and crannies surrounding it until it colored the present with its garish stain. His callous words reminded her of the first time her husband had left her at the estate in Sussex not long after they had arrived from America. He had gone to London to ready the house for her. (Now she suspected that he had gone to soothe the ruffled feathers of his mistress.) As he was leaving, she had overheard him instructing the housekeeper to send word should her courses not arrive on schedule because she was expecting. The exchange had made her feel violated all over again. As if what he did to her in her bed wasn't enough, he had to invade her privacy as well. The exchange had been so very impersonal and degrading that it had further solidified what she had suspected: she was an object who existed in his life for the sole purpose of playing her role of wife and giving him children. She wasn't a person anymore . . . if she ever had been in his eyes.

Without even meaning to, she felt alone and bereft, as if she were back there all over again; alone in a foreign country and with a man who hardly cared if she lived or died as long as he had her father's money. She hated this detached way of living where there was no room for intimacy, tenderness, or even hope.

"Are you ill?" Scarbury asked, and she realized she had been lost in her thoughts for too long.

"If I were, would you leave me alone?"

He let out a sigh and walked past her toward the door. "You are still a child in many ways, Camille. It is an unattractive feature for a woman of your age. My carriage will be round in precisely two hours. If you do not accompany me, we shall have to reevaluate your allowance and that refurbishment you were planning." He paused, glancing over his shoulder. "You still have duties as a dowager. Do not forget that."

He could take his duties and hang them. She didn't reply and he left. She had never seen the contract her father had signed with Hereford, so she didn't know if what he threatened could legally be accomplished. Scarbury had cut off her allowance once in the early days after Hereford's death when she hadn't presented herself as he felt befitted a widow. He had also instructed her butler to not allow any callers for a time, because he felt that her friends were visiting too often. Another reason she had pleaded to go home with her parents to New York. If only that had turned out to be the sanctuary she had craved.

In the end, she decided to accompany him to the ball because it was easier than involving the solicitors. Although she did write out a telegram to her parents demanding to see her marriage contract. The air in the carriage on the ride over was frostier than even the winter air would have suggested. They were late, which meant the music was already playing and several couples danced, but most looked on while in conversation. As she greeted Lady Ashcroft, she caught sight of Evan and August in the middle of the room. He was tall and elegantly dressed, his tawny hair mussed the right amount to make him appear rakish. August, always fashionable in the latest Worth creation, laughed at something he said as he led her into a turn. The gold trim of her gown shimmered under the gaslight. He pulled her a little too close and whispered near her ear. Camille envied their easy way of being together.

"You shall join me in the next dance," Scarbury said under his breath as he made a show of adjusting his cuffs.

The warm feeling she got from watching the happy couple receded at the chill in his voice. They had danced together before at the handful of events she had been obligated to attend with him. It should be routine, but the idea of touching him in any way tonight seemed unbearable. "No, I hardly think that's necessary."

He raised a brow and gave her a look of disdain. "For show only, my dear. Don't flatter yourself that I will enjoy it any more than you."

An acquaintance approached and greeted them both. She managed a nod as the music floated around them. She understood why she so despised attending balls with him. It was like being married to Hereford all over again, down to the nauseating churn in her stomach. The pressure that she might inadvertently do something gauche or unrefined and upset him had been almost overpowering. She refused to go through that again with his heir.

When the acquaintance moved on, she said, "Go to hell, Scarbury," with a smile pasted on her face. The same one she had practiced in front of the mirror so many times. She turned only to be brought up short by his hand taking her wrist in an attempt to stop her. Before she could look back at him, a newcomer said, "Good evening, Your Grace."

The familiar voice had her looking up, her breath caught in surprise. Jacob approached them and, though it wasn't immediately clear which of them he addressed, his eyes were focused on the hand on her wrist. Scarbury released her quickly, but the damage had been done. Her skin smarted under her glove, recoiling from his touch, and she was certain Jacob had seen.

"Thorne, what a surprise," said Scarbury, sounding bored. "I rarely see you at such events."

It was true. Camille could count on one hand with a finger or two left over the number of times she had seen him at Society functions not hosted by August or Violet over the three years she had been in London.

"Scarbury," Jacob said, not sparing the man a glance as his eyes met hers. She nearly smiled when Hereford's heir didn't bother to correct Jacob and insist his title be used. "Are you all right?" Jacob's gaze was intense, as if probing her face for secret wounds.

She didn't know how to respond to the vigor of his concern. She shook her head. "Fine."

He inspected her for a heartbeat longer. "A man in your position would do well to know his own power."

Scarbury sniffed and muttered, "The same could be said for a by-blow."

Jacob's gaze cut to him, and she couldn't help but smile when Scarbury took a step back in very real fear. "You will touch her only when she gives you leave to do so."

Instead of answering, the man looked away.

"Dance with me, Camille." Jacob's voice was full of that warm husk that raked pleasantly across her skin and curled in her stomach.

She nodded, noticing the music had faded during the exchange to change songs and was starting up again. A quadrille. Scarbury's quick intake of breath meant that he had likely noticed Jacob's impertinent use of her name, but she didn't care. Offering him her arm, she walked with him to the middle of the floor as other couples took their places.

"Do you think it's wise to provoke him?" she whispered. "He could make life difficult for you if he chose."

"He shouldn't touch you." His calm voice gave way to suppressed anger. A glance confirmed that a muscle twitched in his jaw.

"That was nothing." She meant it to be reassuring, but

the way he looked at her, assessing her for more hidden damage, told her that he suspected it went far worse than a mere touch to her wrist. Placing a hand on his upper arm, she smiled. "I hardly ever see him. His particular power is over my allowance, not my person."

"Can he do that?" he asked, drawing her into place across from Evan and August. Christian and Violet took up a spot to their right.

She smiled at her friends and gave a little wave, waiting for Jacob to greet his brother before she whispered, "I don't actually know."

It was embarrassing to admit that she had never seen the contract. To be honest, it was humiliating always being the one who needed saving. Violet had once intervened at a ball when Hereford had overreacted, and August had frequently asked her if she was being mistreated. She wanted to be normal for once, especially with Jacob. If he saw her as some poor creature in need of saving, she wouldn't be able to stand the humiliation.

"But no need to worry," she hurried to add. "I have sent a message to my father for the contract so that I may find out."

"Good. Scarbury is an entitled ass who believes only men like him should have any rights."

"I don't want to talk about him. Why are you here?"

"Entertainment," he said vaguely. Mollified, he relaxed his arm under her hand. "You look very beautiful tonight."

Her stomach fluttered. Despite the fact that many gentlemen entertained a polite flirtation with her, none of them had ever told her that. Her husband had never said that to her. And this was Jacob, the man who had kissed her so gently. She remembered the heat in his gaze that night, and her whole body warmed. "Thank you," she whispered as the song truly began.

They passed through the couple across from them and August leaned over and whispered, "I see things are going well." When she passed, Camille caught her gaze as it went toward Jacob. He was watching her with thinly veiled admiration.

Things hadn't gone well at all. His offer to try again had been more for his own vanity, or so she had assumed. But the way he looked at her made her think she had been mistaken. Perhaps he did want to try again. Perhaps he did desire her for her and not the way a man would desire any attractive woman who offered herself to him.

What did that mean? She wasn't certain, but the thought made her head feel warm and fizzy, like she had been filled up with champagne. She laughed at the image and enjoyed the rest of the dance. For once her troubles fell away and she was glad she had come to a ball even if it meant tolerating Scarbury.

The second the dance was over a woman approached Jacob. She was older than Camille, perhaps in her thirties, pretty and well put together in a gorgeous gown of ice-blue silk. Her fingertips rested lightly on his forearm and her smile was full of suggestion. The strains of a polka began, and Camille felt a moment of panic that if she did not claim him then some other woman would. She made to step in his direction, but Violet put her arm around her waist.

"You must tell me everything," Violet whispered, leading her away from the dance floor.

Camille's gaze caught Jacob's, and he appeared regretful as he accepted the woman's request to dance. She could not look away from him as he and the woman hurried around to the fast pace of the music. His broad shoulders only appeared more solid beneath the well-cut drape of his coat, reminding her that she had only recently held those shoulders. She knew how it felt to hold herself against him. She had touched the flat tautness of his stomach and knew the warmth of his skin beneath her touch. A warmth in her belly reminded her of how magical that night had felt . . . until it hadn't.

"Well?"

Camille glanced back at Violet. How could she explain to her friend what had happened when she still wasn't certain herself? "I can't tell you here."

"So something *did* happen?"

"Not a lot." Though he had touched her intimately. Didn't that count for something? "We kissed," she offered.

Violet nodded, seeming to accept that this was all she was getting for the time being. "The kiss must have made an impression. He seems charmed by you to put it mildly."

"What do you mean?" She tried to sound nonchalant, but her heart pounded at the prospect.

"The way he looks at you. I can tell. I've met a few of the women he keeps company with and I have never seen him look at them like he does you." Violet watched the couple move around the other people on the dance floor.

Camille followed her gaze and tried not to enjoy it quite so much when his eyes caught hers across the distance. "What do you suppose that means?"

"I don't know, but I hope you find out." Violet laughed.

Camille smiled, feeling very much like a girl with her first infatuation. It didn't help that his torrid offer kept coming to mind. *There are other things we can do that can help you become more comfortable with me.* What were those things? After that dance another woman approached him and then another. Thankfully, Scarbury had disappeared into the cardroom, so she was left to dance with Evan and then Lord Devonworth, a very attractive man who she knew was prominent in Parliament.

Devonworth was a bit reserved for her taste. The few times his name had appeared in the scandal sheets he was always referred to with the adjectives *cold*, *aloof*, or *frozen*. It was almost always in reference to some debutante having her heart broken by him. He was rumored to be almost penniless, but that didn't stop the young women from wanting him. When she had first arrived in London, there had been chatter about some greater scandal in his past, but she hadn't ever heard the details.

Finally, she was able to claim Jacob for a waltz, but not before yet another matron tried to make her move. The movement of the woman's skirts in the corner of her eye prompted her to hurry. She reached him at the same time as the other woman and blurted out, "Mr. Thorne, I have you on my dance card for the next waltz."

The woman frowned in displeasure but gracefully stepped away.

He grinned and pulled her into his arms with possibly a bit too much familiarity, but he appeared as happy as she was to be with her again.

"Thank you for saving me," he teased her, keeping his voice low.

"Is it always like this?"

"Like what?"

"You're quite the belle of the ball," she teased.

He smiled. "Some have to avoid the maneuvers of the matchmaking mamas, but I have to avoid the formidable women themselves. They would never want me for their daughters, as I have no title, but an assignation for themselves is entirely different."

"How hunted you must feel."

He shrugged, leading her into a turn. "It's one reason I usually avoid these things."

"Then why are you here?"

He was quiet for a moment, his magnetic gaze taking in her features as she twirled. "You," he finally said when they came together again.

The very real joy that brought her was almost palpable. "How did you know I would be here?"

"I didn't know for certain. You were worth the risk."

She didn't know how to respond to that. He had come to an event he admitted he didn't like on the off chance that she might be there. There were no words to describe how absurdly pleased that made her. "I'm glad you came."

He smiled and they didn't talk anymore as he led her in the waltz. She was almost certain that she would have allowed him to lead her anywhere. Perhaps even into trying once more.

Chapter 10

❦

Jacob left his home before midday the next morning. It was a little too early for calling hours, but this task could not wait. He should have come to Violet the morning after Camille had run from him in fear. He hadn't because he hadn't wanted to invade her privacy. However, after last night and what he had seen between her and Scarbury, he could no longer wait to find out the truth of what had happened to her. Violet would know and be able to shed some light on the details of her marriage. Jacob had a terrible feeling that Camille was dealing with something more than simply an unfortunate history of inept lovers.

As soon as he rang the bell at the elegant white stucco and stone home on Upper Belgrave Street, a child's delighted squeal met his ears. Their butler rushed to open the door before the precocious nearly-two-year-old beat him to it.

"Good morning, Mr. Thorne," Winston said, standing back to hold the door.

"Good morning, Winston." Jacob didn't even have a chance to take off his hat before little Rosie was throwing herself against his legs.

"Uncle Jacob," she yelled at the top of her lungs, though a passerby would be forgiven for not understanding her.

"What is this?" he asked, tossing her up and then settling her against his chest. "You're a proper beastie, little one, attacking me before I am even inside the house."

She laughed her full-throated chuckle that always had him laughing with her. "Sweets," she demanded, rifling with the ferocity of a bill collector through his coat pockets for the boiled sweets he always brought her.

"Looking for this?"

He withdrew the tin of sweets from his pocket, and she grasped it with her pudgy fingers before wiggling to get down. The moment her stockinged feet touched the floor she grabbed his finger. "Come!" She dragged him farther into the house with a string of babble that he only partially understood.

"Wait a moment. Let me hand off my coat." She gave him precisely two seconds to hand over his coat, hat, and gloves before reclaiming his hand. "After you, Lady Rose," he said as she pulled him along again. They didn't get very far before Violet stepped out of the sitting room holding two wallpaper swatches.

"Jacob, I thought it must be you." She smiled and hurried over to give him a hug. "She never gets this excited about anyone else, not even Uncle Evan, but don't tell him I told you that."

"Good morning." He kissed her cheek and continued to allow himself to be pulled by the toddler into the room.

This was the family's private sitting room where they entertained family and close friends. "Morning," Christian drawled from the sofa, where he was currently covered in fabrics and swatches.

"Busy morning?" Jacob asked.

"We're redecorating," Christian said. There was a smile in his voice when he added, "Again."

Violet had given the whole house a renovation when they had married to rid the place of the specter of their father's ghost. Rosie didn't give Jacob time to question it as she took him directly to her toy chest and presented him with a miniature train engine painted emerald green. It was obviously her new prized possession. After admiring it for a suitable length of time and allowing her to demonstrate how it could glide around the floor, he sat on the sofa facing the couple, not quite certain how to begin his inquiry.

"I've never seen you up before noon, brother. Don't tell me Montague has burned down. You look entirely too fresh for that."

Violet smacked her husband's arm playfully and began divesting him of the layers of fabric. "Don't give him trouble. He knows he's welcome here anytime, day or night."

"What am I looking at?" Jacob asked. His brother resembled a beast domesticated and tamed by layers of taffeta and lace.

"I am decorating one of the bedrooms for Rosie. We have the space and she's outgrowing the nursery."

"She's not even two yet." Jacob raised his brow as suspicion took hold.

Violet shrugged, a happy blush staining her cheeks. "Two at the end of the month. By the way, you will be here for the dinner, right? My mother is in town and, honestly, the more people who attend the better."

"Yes, I will be here."

"Good. It will be only close friends and family. Lilian and Anthony are coming, but Maura sent her regrets along with the most adorable rocking pony. I'll show you later." Pausing in her folding, she looked at him with meaning and said, "Camille will be here as well."

Just her name had a flicker of anticipation coming to life inside him. He hoped that she would come back to him for another try. That thought was immediately followed by another darker one and the reason for his visit. What the hell did Violet know about him and Camille? Perhaps he'd been too obvious last night. She had avoided Montague Club and he could think of no reasonable way to see her again aside from the ball.

Violet's expression told him that she knew something, but Christian continued unaware, holding his arms out for her to lay a freshly folded piece of fabric over. He didn't want to ask her about it in front of his brother. Their deal was between him and Camille, and telling Christian seemed like a betrayal on top of the one he was about to commit with the new club.

"I am looking forward to the celebration," he said. To steer the conversation back to safer topics, he asked, "Is there a reason the nursery should be free?"

She smiled and glanced at Christian. The affection that passed between them was almost too intimate to witness. "We plan to announce it at the dinner party, so please don't ruin the surprise, but we are expecting again."

Christian had thrown his whole heart into the small family he had created after a childhood that had been bereft of almost all affection, mostly due to their father. They had grown up not knowing the other existed, only to form a bond of brotherhood that Jacob hoped would last a lifetime. He could be nothing but happy at the news and was touched they wanted to include him in their joy. "Congratulations! I'm very happy for you both."

Free of the drapery encumbrances after Violet took them away to set the folded stack on the sofa, Christian rose and said, "Thank you," ready to intercept Rosie as she ran by. "It was a bit of a surprise but I'm getting accustomed to the idea."

Violet rolled her eyes. "He worries excessively. He'd be happy with only one birth experience to contend with." She put her arms around Jacob in a warm hug and he placed a kiss on her smooth cheek.

As she looked up at him beaming with joy, he couldn't help but compare her with Camille. They were around the same age, but there was a bright-eyed youthfulness about his sister-in-law that had been taken from Camille. Or perhaps Camille had never possessed it, although he thought he had seen glimpses of carefree joy in the small moments of delight he'd witnessed her experience. The time she had held baby William at the christening and he had cooed at her. The first time she had won at cards at Montague. The way she had watched Jacob so intently and with wonder their night together before the fear had taken over.

"You will be fine." To his brother, he said, "Rosie's birth was easy, and Violet is strong. There is no reason to think this one won't be the same."

"Yes, I'm certain you're right." Christian nodded, but his eyes gave away his worry. Jacob couldn't help but wonder what it would feel like to love someone so much your very existence depended on theirs. It was too much to consider. He loved his family, but he liked living his life for himself, with no one to worry about.

"You both can hug. There is no law against it," Violet said.

"I'm certain there is a decree or some such forbidding it," Christian answered with a smile.

"Perhaps they teach you that at Eton," Jacob teased and draped an arm around his shoulder since he still held Rosie. Then he rubbed noses with the little girl, sending her into a fit of giggles that had her throwing herself into his arms and hiding her face against his chest. He held her for a moment, marveling at her slight weight in his arms and the protective wave of affection that came over him. He hadn't considered a future with children in his life, but the toddler and her cousins had carved out a place for themselves in his heart.

"We'll celebrate properly at the club later. I've a bottle of aged Glenlivet I've been saving."

Christian agreed, then said, "Is the club what brings you here so early today? I hope it's not trouble with Cavell again."

The club's manager had grown up on the streets of Whitechapel before coming to fight as one of the first bareknuckle brawlers the club sponsored. He had proven himself intelligent, loyal, and ambitious and had quickly worked his way into other jobs. The only problem was that his past found him at the club from time to time.

"No, Cavell's troubles seem to be behind him for now. I have come to speak with Violet on a sensitive matter."

Violet looked at him with concern, while Christian grinned. "Women troubles?"

"Something like that," Jacob said.

"I know when I've been dismissed. Come, little one, let us go give your purple pony one of your boiled sweets." Christian set the girl on her feet, and she happily led him from the room.

Jacob closed the door behind them and turned to see Violet looking at him with a raised brow. "I assume this is about Camille?" she asked, sitting on the sofa he had recently vacated.

He joined her there. "Yes, but first, what do you know about us?"

She smiled a little, the beginning of a blush staining her cheeks. "Only that you've made some deal to tutor her in the . . . um, bedroom arts."

He laughed at that. "That is one way to describe it. I'm a little shocked she told you as much."

Violet shrugged, her gaze drifting away from him in guilt. "She's only told us that much. No details."

"Us?" Christ. This was exactly why he'd been reluctant to enter into this arrangement, but no way in hell was he backing out now.

"August knows, too, but I promise the only detail Camille gave is that you kissed." She hurried to add, "I think she only confided in us because she wanted reassurance. This is a big deal to her."

He nodded. He couldn't deprive her of the support of her friends when she so desperately needed them. "I know it is."

"Is it . . . going well, the tutoring?"

He paused, torn between revealing enough to find out what he needed to know and not invading Camille's privacy. "Well enough. I simply wondered . . ." He could not tell her about Camille's fear. It would be a step too far. Instead, he asked, "What can you tell me about her marriage with Hereford?"

"Her marriage?" Twin lines appeared between her brows. "The less said about that the better. He was an ass and I am glad he is gone."

"He was harsh with her?"

"Harsh? I'd say so, yes. Once—the very night I spoke with Christian alone for the first time—Hereford had escorted her from the ballroom because he thought she was flirting. I did not see her flirting any more than any other married woman does at those things. She smiled and danced and enjoyed herself. Enjoying herself was a step too far, apparently. I came upon them alone and he was berating her. He then sent her home."

Jacob could feel heat rise into his face, but he held back his anger. It would be useless now at any rate. "Was there anything else?"

"Countless things if you're asking about all the ways he mistreated her. She was only allowed to entertain visitors with the doors open, not in private. There was a period of time he refused to allow her to see August and me, because he thought we were bad influences. Of course, that changed once August became a duchess. She was forbidden sweets because he thought she had gained weight. I'm almost certain her correspondence was monitored. I sent her more than one letter that she never received. He planned her social outings to his benefit. Honestly, he treated her like an unwanted ward who had been foisted upon him, but I don't think those things were the worst of it."

He didn't want to know while at the same time needing to soak up every detail of her life before he had entered it. "What was worse than that?"

"The way he spoke to her. That night at the ball, for example. He criticized and disparaged her constantly. I don't know that I ever heard him say a kind word to her. In his eyes, she was not good enough. He had married her for the Bridwell money and her blood simply wasn't blue enough for him. He never wanted her to forget it." She shook her head and gave an empty laugh. "When he forbade her from having sweets, he said terrible things to her about her appearance."

Jacob rose and paced to the window that overlooked the garden. It was fallow now in the dead of winter, a light sprinkling of snow covering the rhododendrons. An ache squeezed his chest, forcing him to take several deep breaths. He despised this dead man whom he had never met. He had known him by sight, however, and spent a moment imagining what it would feel like to put his fist through his face.

"He undermined her confidence. If there was ever a time he was kind to her, I didn't see it. If there was ever something she wanted, he refused it. If she so much as stuttered in public, he would scold her in private. She tried to warn me about marriage to a man for money. Even though I saw it with my own eyes, I don't think I was able to comprehend the absolute hell her life must have been. Now that I have Christian, who would sooner cut off his right hand than see me hurt, I understand better what she missed out on." Her voice was tinged with guilt. "That night at the ball, I asked her to run away with me. She refused and I let it go. I ran away without her. I can't help but think that I should have tried harder."

She closed her eyes and her shoulders stooped in dejection. Jacob went back to sit beside her and put a hand on her back. His other he rubbed up and down her arm. "It's very difficult to help someone who doesn't want your help." But Camille had asked for his help, and he couldn't figure out how to actually give it. "Did he physically harm her?"

She shook her head. "That night of the ball he held her arm harshly and left a red mark, but she never mentioned that he was physically violent with her." Then her voice lowered. "We never spoke of the marriage bed, though. Perhaps he was. Why?"

"She has a reticence of men and I simply hoped to understand her better." He already felt as if he was delving too far into her privacy with this conversation, but he had to know what she experienced. He couldn't share the details of her fear with Violet even though he very much wanted to understand her.

"Oh . . ." She looked down at her hands clasped in her lap. "I suppose I never considered that. I hate that she was ever given to a man like him. Camille is kind and loving. She didn't deserve that. No woman does."

"I know. He's gone now. I wish to help her through her recovery."

"Recovery?"

"Camille lived with abuse. It will take time and patience for her to recover from such trauma." He didn't know very much about abuse, except for the little he had learned when Lilian had a friend she had helped run away from a husband who drank to excess.

"Of course," Violet said. "I didn't think of it that way. We have women come to us at the London Home frequently now that our operation is well-known. They're no longer only unwed mothers. Some of them are looking for a safe haven for themselves and their children. Unofficially, that's not what we do, but we cannot turn them away. We hide them for a bit until we can make arrangements for them to leave the city. Most of them come with bruises and broken bones, but a few have other wounds. Unseen injuries."

She rose as if to do something but stopped because there was nothing to be done. "I should have realized. I failed her."

Jacob stood and took her into his arms. "Not all abuse can be seen. He made her afraid, and he manipulated her. He stole her confidence. That's its own special form of abuse."

"What can we do?" Violet looked up at him with glassy eyes.

"Lilian mentioned that she visited with Camille and invited her to a women's suffrage meeting. Perhaps you can encourage her to go. I think if she has a cause that she feels is her own, it could help her feel that she can take control of her life. That seemed to help Lilian's friend."

"That's a good idea. I'll speak to her about it." Her face brightened momentarily, only to darken again. "Unfortunately, she still has a Hereford in her life to contend with."

"Scarbury." He remembered the way the whoreson had touched her last night. It had taken every ounce of his self-control not to lay him flat. Scarbury's antiquated opinions on women's rights were well-known since he was often quoted in the papers. He was an unbearable wretch.

"He doesn't wield as much control, but he manipulates her. He withholds her allowance if she displeases him."

"Why does she live in the dower house, then? Can she not afford to move out?"

"I don't know. Her father bought her a cottage not far outside London but I don't know her finances."

Jacob frowned. He had several weeks yet before he would leave for Paris. One way or another he would see her protected before he left. Even if he had to pay Scarbury a visit himself to put the fear of God in him, he would not see her manipulated anymore. She had been through too much and come too far to have another Hereford trying to control her.

Chapter 11

❦

I commend Your Grace for the thoroughness of your plan. You see, I myself have long touted the benefits of embracing a natural education along with the rote and tedious subjects of arithmetic and language. Children do better when they can connect to the natural world. I have always said so." Mrs. Peabody nodded vigorously and took another long drink from her cognac, nearly empty now. She settled her slight body back into the deep sofa cushions.

Camille met Helena's gaze over the older woman's white-plumed hair and held back a smile. Mrs. Peabody was the last holdout on the board who had not immediately embraced Camille's idea that the children should be allowed to learn gardening as part of their curriculum. She and Helena had worked together that night to persuade her over a long dinner in Camille's dining room and several glasses of her best wine. She hadn't meant to ply her with drink to gain her agreement, but Mrs. Peabody had demanded more until it was almost comical, and it was hardly past nine o'clock.

"I am thrilled we are in agreement," Helena said, reaching out to tactfully take the drink from the woman's hand before it could dribble on the folds of her skirt.

"I am happy you feel that way, Mrs. Peabody. We can start immediately," Camille said, walking to the bureau near the window.

She had written out a brief outline of lesson plans after consulting with the cook who oversaw the kitchen gardens and the school's primary teacher. She wanted Mrs. Peabody's agreement on the plans before she left here tonight so they could put everything in motion tomorrow on the off chance the woman didn't remember a thing come morning. Retrieving the folder, she started back to the sofa when Sampson appeared at the drawing room door. He cleared his throat delicately and gave her a pointed look as if he needed her. Her stomach tumbled in delightful anticipation. Was it so late in the evening already?

"If you please?" She handed the papers off to Helena.

"Of course," Helena said, her brow raised slightly in concern.

Camille gave her a reassuring smile before following Sampson out into the corridor. He maneuvered them so that they were out of the line of the sight of the room's occupants. "Yes, Sampson?"

"There is a message, Your Grace." He offered her a folded piece of paper and glanced toward the entryway.

For the first time she noticed a boy standing there looking very formal, if slightly uncomfortable. Opening the note, she read:

The carriage is waiting around the corner.

Jacob hadn't signed it but there was no need for him to. She recognized his handwriting from the note he had sent her that morning. Turner had asked for him to demonstrate the cabaret so that he would have a better idea of how the club might function before he made his decision. Jacob had gathered a quick array of street performers from Covent Garden, and they would put on an ad hoc performance tonight at Turner's home before a group of his friends and associates. Jacob had asked if she would be interested in attending as his fiancée, and she had readily agreed even though she was busy tonight. Since it was so late in the evening, he couldn't very well show up on her doorstep himself without courting scandal, so he had sent a carriage.

She hadn't seen him in the days since he'd made the surprise appearance at the ball. She had been too busy arranging this meeting and volunteering, though to be honest, much of it was because she had been avoiding Montague Club because she was afraid to have another try with him. She was afraid of failing again. But this would be different. This would be an evening out together, perhaps another dinner, with other people around, and she would get to see him and talk to him without worrying about what it might lead to.

"I'm afraid I'll be late."

"Pardon me, Your Grace?" The butler's eyebrows shot up his forehead.

Forcing her voice to be calm instead of alarmed, she said, "Please tell the boy I may be a little late and give him a coin for his trouble."

"As you wish." He offered a cursory bow and she composed herself as she returned to her guests.

Her mind immediately started to race. What should she wear? Would she even have time to change? The clock struck ten. It was later than she realized. No, there was no time for a change of clothing. She needed to leave as soon as possible. She stroked her fingers over the hair at her temples, hoping to smooth back any flyaways.

Helena looked up as she approached, her eyes silently asking if there was a problem. Camille realized that she would need to usher her and Mrs. Peabody out as quickly and politely as possible. Those two did not always go hand in hand.

"A small matter has come up," Camille said gently.

"Of course, say no more." Helena stood and said, "Why don't you allow me to walk you out, Mrs. Peabody? I'm afraid that I need to get home for the night. It's been a rather tedious day at the Home."

"Thank you, my lady." The woman rose and looked at Camille with pursed lips, the closest thing that passed for a smile with her. "Your Grace, it has been a lovely evening." They spent the next several minutes maneuvering the woman to the door, where Sampson handed both women their outerwear. The boy was nowhere to be seen.

Sampson retreated quietly after the door closed behind Mrs. Peabody. Helena let out a yelp of excitement. "We did it! I can't be certain if it was the brandy, but she agreed and that is all that matters."

Camille laughed. "Yes, we must get started tomorrow before she changes her mind."

"Let's meet after luncheon at the Home. Mrs. Peabody never goes out before three in the afternoon."

Camille hugged her in happiness, then she hurried upstairs and had Ingram run a few fingertips of bandoline over her hair to tame it. She did not have time to reset the entire hairstyle. She glanced longingly at her wardrobe, wishing she had enough time to change into something more appealing, perhaps with cleavage. Her dinner dress of wine-colored silk covered her arms and shoulders, and was accented in pink satin trim and white lace with twin rows of buttons down the front. It was perfectly serviceable for the occasion, but she had noticed Jacob admired her bosom and she liked how he looked at her in more revealing gowns.

Hurrying downstairs she gathered her cape and gloves from the stand, hoping to avoid Sampson, but he came around the corner as she was securing the ties.

"Your Grace?" He stood stunned. "If you are going out I can send for the carriage. It will only take a moment . . . a quarter hour perhaps."

"No, thank you." Once she would have floundered over her answer, come up with some excuse to put him off, but not now. Scarbury had not said so much as a peep since her exchange with him at the ball. She was finished letting anyone run her life, and she would not justify her actions to a servant. Not anymore. "I have a carriage waiting. Good night, Sampson. Do not wait up for me."

She didn't know if he stood there gawking as she hurried out because she didn't bother to look behind her. She barely kept herself from running around the corner to find the unmarked carriage waiting for her, the driver standing by the door. "Your Grace," he said.

Camille arrived at Turner's residence in Marylebone soon after. The four-bay brownstone, one of the largest on the residential street, had a cheerful gas lamp flickering by the front door. She had no idea what she might discover inside, but she was excited to find out.

The door opened before she could reach the top of the steps, and a butler in livery greeted her. "Good evening, Your Grace. We've been expecting you." Delightful piano music drifted out from the open door.

"Good evening." She stepped inside, noting the gleaming dark wood paneling and floors covered in thick Persian rugs. A heavy staircase rose high toward the back of the entryway. The hum of voices from several conversations at once came from deeper in the house. "Thank you," she said as he took her outerwear. She was excited, not only to see Jacob, but she really had no idea what to expect. "I hope I'm not too late."

The man, who appeared to be in his thirties, younger than most men in his profession, merely smiled as he handed her apparel off to a maid who had materialized behind him. "Not at all, Your Grace. Please, follow me."

He led her toward the back of the house to a room that might have been a ballroom. It was difficult to say for certain because instead of leaving the floor empty, with chairs along the perimeter, the floor space had been filled with small tea tables, meant for seating no more than four people. Two would have been more comfortable, particularly if dinner were to be served. The tables were draped in luxurious cloths that nearly touched the floor, maroon to match the patterned wallpaper, and sparkling place settings. Gas sconces flickered on the walls, but each table was set with a single candle inside a glass globe, leaving the room with more shadow than light. Tiny stars made of tin had been strung across the ceiling, reflecting what little light there was and giving the room an almost magical feel, as if they were outside beneath the night sky.

There were probably at least thirty people in the room. Some sat at the tables while others stood about in small groups of two or three. Jacob was not among them. They were all dressed extravagantly in silks and satins and formal blacks. She smoothed her hand over her skirt and lamented the fact that she hadn't had time to change into one of her Worth gowns. She could have worn one of her old ones; she recognized no one in the group, which meant they hadn't seen her in one of them before.

"Your Grace!" Turner's booming voice found her through the crowd, drawing the eyes of nearly everyone, as he hurried away from the group he had been chatting with and came to her side.

"Mr. Turner, I apologize if I'm late." She actually wasn't certain if she was. This wasn't a proper dinner party or tea or ball. She didn't know the protocol.

"You are right on time. Thorne will be happy to know that you've arrived. We were about to start."

"Good evening, Your Grace." Mrs. Turner hurried over to them. "Welcome to our home."

"Thank you for inviting me."

"You shall sit with us." She indicated the table at the front of the room and guided her around the other tables to reach it.

A heavy black curtain was draped from the ceiling to the floor several yards away and she realized that must be where the stage had been set up. Jacob slipped through the part, smiling as he saw her. He was dressed in formal black attire.

"I'm glad you're here," he said, taking her hands and brushing his lips to her cheek.

She couldn't quite explain the way she came alive at the mere sight of him. "I'm intrigued. I wouldn't dare miss it."

"Good. Then we can start. I was waiting for you."

She was too pleased by that to respond right away. His obvious joy at her presence made something more precious than happiness well inside her.

When he let her go and disappeared behind the curtain, Camille settled herself at the table while a footman brought her a glass of champagne. A moment later a young woman dressed in a strange but lovely white dress striped with black scrollwork stepped out from behind the curtain.

"Ah, here we are," Mr. Turner said, still standing behind her.

The young woman held a brass triangle aloft and played a soft but effective triangle roll. The talking quickly died away and the unseen piano music stopped. There was shuffling as people looked for their seats. Mrs. Turner smiled at her in excitement as she settled herself to Camille's left.

"Thank you all for coming." Mr. Turner joined the peculiarly dressed woman at the head of the room. "You are very dear friends, which is why I have invited you to this unusual demonstration. I know several of you have been beside yourselves with curiosity because I have refused to answer your queries." There was a pause here and a few chuckles in the audience. "I am happy to inform you that the wait is over. If you could kindly take your seats, we shall begin.

"I hope you enjoy this special evening Mr. Thorne and I have planned. I guarantee you have never seen anything like it." He gave a short bow and joined them at the table, sitting on Camille's right.

Everyone clapped, though it was clear from the hesitation that no one knew what this was about. The room darkened as the gas that fed the sconces was turned down very low, leaving the candles on the tables as the main source of light. The people gathered began to murmur in excitement. A small army of footmen hurried out with trays of food, little plates of escargot and pots of butter.

The hidden pianist played a dramatic glissando, fingers sliding across the instrument from low to high keys, and the curtain swirled back to reveal a makeshift stage. Twin lamps sat at opposite ends of the floor space, glinting off the sleek ebony piano. A beautiful woman smiled out at them from behind the instrument as she played another glissando. The audience clapped in response and Jacob walked out. He smiled and Camille was stunned anew by how handsome he was. She gave him a small wave and he winked at her, causing her heart to trip over itself.

Everyone applauded again, a few in apparent recognition as this time the cheers were louder.

"Good evening. For those of you who do not know me I am Jacob Thorne, a friend of the Turners. I recognize a few of you from Montague Club." He nodded at a man in the back of the room who called out a greeting, and several more gentlemen joined in. Once everyone had settled again, he said, "Thank you for joining us tonight in an evening that I am certain will be unlike any you have ever experienced. Your only goal tonight is to enjoy your meal as you let the entertainers we have assembled amuse you."

There was a whisper of conversation as the pianist played a soft melody and the first of the entertainers entered the stage area. Jacob introduced her as Zelda the contortionist. She was dressed in a scandalous one-piece costume of ruby silk that clung to her curves and covered her legs like pantaloons. She wore black ballet slippers on her feet. As the music turned low and dramatic, it quickly became apparent why she would need such a costume. Somewhere behind the curtain a drum had started a low beat. Her body moved in rhythm to the music, seeming to be almost fluid as she slid to the floor and into a contortion that brought her ankles over her head but only for a moment as she twisted out with the next beat of the drum. The woman quickly moved into another contortion, her tempo changing as the music became faster.

The crowd exclaimed softly in wonder as she dipped down again until her chest was almost on the floor, her body twisting in ways that made her seem boneless. The silk shimmered in the light like flowing water. All too soon, the music came to a stop and the woman curtsied before disappearing behind the curtain. Jacob walked back to the center of the makeshift stage and the pianist started playing a soft tinkling melody in the background that wouldn't overpower his voice.

He commended the contortionist, ending with, "That was the most graceful bit of maneuvering I've seen since Turner tried to talk himself out of his loss in a game of dice last week."

Everyone laughed since they all appeared to know Mr. Turner. The man himself laughed the loudest, his voice rising over the others in the room. "And it would have worked had I looked like Miss Zelda there," Turner called out much to everyone's enjoyment.

"No one would mistake you for a contortionist, Turner," a man in the back called out.

Jacob's attention was drawn to the other man, whom he playfully called out for his own debt owed to Montague Club. Turner leaned toward her. "What are your thoughts so far, Your Grace?" he asked in a low voice. "I believe people are enjoying themselves."

"Yes, I believe so." A footman whisked away her barely touched snails, and a plate of smoked salmon was set before her. "Mr. Thorne has a wonderful way with people. I've admired that about him at Montague Club."

"You know, we never had a chance to talk about what his moving to Paris might mean for your relationship." As he spoke, he used the blunt edge of a knife to spread the salmon on a piece of crusty bread.

"What do you mean?" She tried to keep her tone light to cover the fact that she didn't have a ready answer. They hadn't discussed this part of the ruse in much detail.

"Will you marry before he leaves?"

"No, my parents won't be able to attend until later and I'd like them to be present at the ceremony." There was no way to avoid his question, so she said the only thing that would make sense, especially if Jacob intended to extend the ruse past his leaving London.

He nodded and popped the food into his mouth. The curtain shifted as another performer seemed to be getting ready behind it. "So then you intend that he go to Paris alone?"

She hadn't really thought about the fact that he would be leaving soon. She would miss him terribly. "It does seem to be the most proper alternative," she said vaguely.

Turner nodded, his attention going back to the stage where Jacob stood engaging another member of the audience with a joke. "He's very good at this and I believe he enjoys it. I know he indicated that he intended to be the master of ceremony only until he could procure an adequate replacement, but he might well stay in Paris longer than we think."

She nodded and a pit of dread opened in her stomach. What if he did stay in Paris? She could very easily see him enjoying the lifestyle. It would be like attending a party every night. There would be laughter and women. "I'm certain we'll muddle through." Then because she wanted to play her part well, she added, "I am not opposed to living in Paris after we're married. It's where the House of Worth is, after all."

Turner chuckled. "Glad to hear it, Your Grace."

The curtain parted to allow in the next set of entertainers, a man and a woman who sang sad love songs in Italian. Camille found that she could barely pay attention. Her gaze kept finding Jacob, who was observing the shenanigans from several yards away in the darkened corner of the room where the stage lights didn't quite penetrate.

Despite the fact that she could hardly see more than his outline, her stomach gave a little swoop every time she set eyes on him. Perhaps she was being foolish not trying again with him. A very large part of her clearly wanted to. Only now, she worried that it might make her even more attached to him. She had never properly considered before what his leaving for Paris might mean. She hadn't realized that somehow she had come to care for him . . . at least a little bit.

The light glinted off his eyes and she realized that he was staring at her. Heat rushed to her face even though he likely couldn't see her clearly. He smiled and she smiled back and tried to force herself to pay attention. Yet, even through the other acts—a pantomime group, a comedian who poked fun at mesmerists, and a group of fire-eaters— Jacob held her attention the most. It thrilled her that he also kept looking at her.

Finally, the evening came to an end and he started toward her table only to be intercepted by a gentleman at the table next to her. She rose in anticipation of talking to him, downing the last of her champagne. Somehow she had managed to finish several glasses without noticing.

She wobbled a little, feeling a bit off-balance, but thankfully Jacob was finished saying hello to the other table and his hands at her waist steadied her.

"Hello," she whispered.

He smiled, leaning in and greeting her with a kiss to her temple that probably appeared proper and bland but felt anything but. His lips were warm and soft, his breath hot on her skin. She remembered how it had felt to kiss him while sitting on his sofa. Just the hint of his scent made her want to touch him in ways that were entirely unsuitable.

"What do you think?" he asked, looking very much like the happiest man in the room. His eyes tried to devour her.

"I thought I understood what you meant by cabaret, but this is extraordinary. It exceeds anything I could imagine. You have *me* wanting to invest." His hand had gone around her waist exactly as she had seen him walk away with those other women at Montague Club. Even through the layers of her clothing, she could feel the drag of his fingertips across her skin. Her pulse thumped between her legs. The champagne was causing her to feel things she shouldn't, not in public, at least.

He laughed. "As you know, I am seeking investors—"

Before he could continue, Turner cut in. "You're not giving away my opportunity, are you?"

Jacob smiled. "There's nothing wrong with a little healthy competition."

Turner laughed. "Indeed. Come join me? There are a couple of gentlemen I'd like you both to meet."

"Of course," Jacob agreed.

The room had gone slightly fuzzy around the edges, giving everything a soft sheen of enchantment. Something must have tipped Jacob off, because he leaned down slightly to whisper, "How many glasses of champagne have you had?"

"A few," she whispered back. This was probably her penance for Mrs. Peabody. She wasn't quite drunk, since she had already eaten her supper and forced in a few bites of the food Turner had served, but she felt very nice.

His mouth tightened at the corners as if he were trying not to smile as his gaze settled on her.

"What?" she asked when he merely continued to look at her, an odd but pleasant look on his face. She noted with a great deal of pleasure that he hadn't let her go yet. The hard muscles of his body pressed against her, making her feel warm and soft.

"Your cheeks are flushed, but you're still the most beautiful thing in the room."

Her mouth opened at that but not one word came to mind.

"We can leave if you want," he said.

"No, I want to stay."

"Are you certain?" he asked, a smile curving his lips.

She did her best to ignore how that made the room tilt. "I'm certain."

When he led her to the group that included Mr. Turner, she couldn't feel her feet moving across the floor. It wasn't because of the drink . . . not *only* because of the drink. It was because of him and how happy she felt on his arm. These people thought they were engaged. They thought she was to be his wife, and something about that made her feel elated. She didn't mind belonging to him for the night, because it meant that he belonged to her.

Mr. Turner introduced them to the men in the group. She managed to hold herself together and comment when it was appropriate, but the entire time she was nearly overcome by Jacob's touch, the smell of his cologne, and the deep timbre of his voice. Everything he did seemed to be amplified.

After that he whispered in her ear again, his breath sending warm embers skittering across her skin. "We should get you out of here. It won't do to have you meet more people as my fiancée who you might run into at Montague Club."

In her eagerness to see him tonight, she had forgotten the game they were planning had the potential to become dangerous. "Should I pretend to swoon?" she teased.

"I could carry you out, if so." His grin left no doubt that they might both enjoy that.

Before either of them could do anything, Mrs. Turner came over and pressed a cool hand to her warm cheek. "You poor lamb. You are flushed."

"I should see her home," Jacob said.

Camille looked away. Her flush was only marginally from the champagne.

Mrs. Turner walked them to the front hall and the butler hurried to collect their outerwear.

"Don't you need to stay?" she asked when they were alone. "You did so well. You should stay and enjoy the accolades."

He chuckled, his husky voice filling her ear. "I'd rather spend my time with you. You can shower me with praise if you'd like."

The image her mind conjured up for how she might do that was shocking. It involved him in the nude and her kissing every inch of his body. That thrum between her legs happened again. But that was most definitely not what he meant and not what she should be thinking about in public. It made her giggle just knowing her own thoughts were so naughty in the midst of everything.

"You were the most perfect host, dear Jacob," she teased. "The most handsome and charming and desirable host in the entire world. Your sheer mastery of the room was a sight to behold. If you weren't already otherwise engaged in your hosting duties, I would engage your services until the end of time."

He let out a bark of laughter. "These are the sort of accolades I prefer. I'm glad you understand me."

The butler returned and helped her with her cape and then he was opening the door, the cool wind hitting her face. It felt marvelous. Once they were on the pavement, Jacob's arm at her waist guided her along. Before she knew it, they were in the delicious darkness of the carriage. She sat far closer to him than was necessary. She told herself that it was the champagne making her behave this way, but the very fact that she was cognizant enough to grasp at the excuse made her realize the lie.

"I haven't had this much champagne in a long time." Not since the early days of her marriage at any rate. Then, she had wanted its muting effects. Now, she liked how it helped her be bold. She pressed her thigh against the hard length of his.

He didn't move away. Instead, his arm went around her shoulders, holding her closer, as if sitting like this were the most natural thing in the world for them.

She let her head fall to his chest. He was the only solid presence in her life at the moment. Maybe at all. Before she could debate the thought, her mind focused on the way his fingers rubbed small circles on her arm.

"I had fun tonight. I can't remember the last time I had fun," she said.

He took a wavering breath. "I'm glad." His lips touched the top of her head.

She closed her eyes, imagining how his hand might feel with no clothing between them. Her breasts tightened and that wonderful fluttery feeling happened in her lower belly. The smell of sandalwood filled her nose. She rubbed her thighs together to relieve the strange pressure growing there.

"Shh . . ." He misunderstood her restlessness. "I'll have you home soon."

"No." She grabbed a handful of his coat and he startled a bit. "I don't want to go home. I want to be with you."

His lips pressed together and she had the disturbing feeling that he was trying not to smile. "It's the champagne." One hand covered hers and gave a gentle squeeze, while the other tightened at her waist.

"No, it's not." But that wasn't completely true. "Maybe, but only a little. Haven't you ever . . . had sex"—God, she'd actually said it!—"under the effects of champagne?"

He grinned. "Of course, among other things."

"Then we should try again. Now . . ." Er, maybe not in the carriage. "We could go to your house."

"Camille . . ." He cupped her head and dragged the pad of his thumb across her lips. "I want you more than you will ever know, but not tonight. Not like this." Before she could process that, he pulled her into his lap, where it was readily apparent to her that he was telling the truth. He did want her very much, because he was hard and thick beneath her bottom. Staring into her eyes, he said, "I will be inside you one day soon, and when I am I want you to remember it well."

She wanted that, too, more than anything she had wanted in a very long time. His mouth covered hers and made her feel hot and overly sensitive. His tongue stroked against hers and her bones melted into him. Her breath became a part of him, so that when the carriage came to a stop and he pulled back, she felt as if he took a piece of her with him.

"Good night," he whispered.

She bade him a good evening, even though she was disappointed, and he helped her out of the carriage. As she turned away, he called her back.

"Hereford's heir . . . has he bothered you since the Ashcroft ball?" His brow furrowed in concern.

"No, I haven't heard from him." Thankfully, Scarbury seemed content to leave her be.

"Good. You know you can come to me if you need assistance with him."

She smiled. She had no idea what Jacob thought he might do about the man, but she loved that he cared. "Good night, Jacob."

She floated down the block and up the steps to her front door. Her key turned the lock and she glanced toward his carriage waiting at the corner. It was too dark to see inside the windows, but she knew he was watching her. Giving a little wave, she hurried inside and up the stairs, not wanting anyone to see her in such a state. After she had undressed and lay in bed, she kept hearing him promise that he would be inside her soon, and she kept remembering how magnetic he had been onstage and how athletic he had appeared in the exhibition matches she had seen him fight at Montague Club. Then she imagined that it was his hands that touched her as she fell asleep in a peculiar state of bliss and frustration.

Chapter 12

❦

Jacob had been in a foul mood ever since turning Camille down a few days ago. He couldn't stop thinking of her and wondering if she planned to give them another chance. Perhaps she had changed her mind. It didn't help that every time Webb approached him during the evenings, he'd automatically think it was because she had come. She hadn't yet. For all he knew, she might choose not to. He had already decided the choice would have to be hers. He couldn't help her unless she led the way.

Unfortunately, his poor disposition meant he was in short temper and with almost no concentration. He had stared at the column of numbers in front of him for so long the figures were starting to blur. He closed his eyes and squeezed the bridge of his nose. Bloody Turner and his insistence on playing coy. If the man would only agree to invest, then Jacob wouldn't be sitting here hammering out the details on yet another proposal for En Soirée. The demonstration had gone well. Turner had visited him the next afternoon full of ideas and questions about the cabaret club. Then the notes had begun. They had been exchanging ideas ranging from design to entertainment options to add to the proposal. Not one of the letters had included confirmation that he was definitely planning to invest.

The lack of firm commitment wasn't a surprise. He knew Turner well enough to understand that the man took his time when evaluating a potential investment opportunity, and he had expected nothing less. Still, it was an exercise in frustration running new numbers every time he sent over an idea. Jacob could have his accountant handle the legwork, but the idea was too precious to allow anyone access to it just yet. No one except for Blanchet and Jacob knew everything. Simon Cavell knew the basics, though not the details. Evan and Christian would find out only after Jacob had secured funding and knew for certain the club would proceed. They would likely have mixed feelings, since neither of them were very fond of Turner. The man had made himself a nuisance trying to invest in Montague Club. Which was why he was working so late this evening. He'd had to wait until Christian went home to bring out the ledgers associated with En Soirée.

A brief knock at his study door interrupted his ruminations. Webb looked around the door, and Jacob's heart leaped as it always did, hoping the man would tell him Camille was here. "Cavell requires your assistance, sir."

He sighed, torn between disappointment that she hadn't come and relief that he had an excuse to put the numbers aside for a bit. He went with relief. "Thank Christ," he muttered, pushing himself back from the desk. Any interruption from the infernal number tallying was welcome.

Webb's brow quirked up only the slightest bit in surprise. "He's belowstairs, sir."

"*Belowstairs*?" The only reason he'd be down there was either because a new stock of liquor had come in that needed to be put away in the stone cellar or there was a brawl scheduled. Neither of those was marked on the calendar for this evening. The liquor had come in yesterday. "There's no fight tonight."

Webb cleared his throat a bit awkwardly. "There was none scheduled, sir."

"Fucking hell!" Grabbing his coat from the rack inside the door, he was stalking down the corridor before he had properly shrugged into it. Webb was right behind him.

"One of the stock boys alleges that several of Brody's men attempted an attack on Cavell back in the mews."

"Then who's in the dungeon?" They were at the back stairwell. Jacob took them two at the time, half running to get there before the whole place was a literal bloody mess.

"It appears that he caught one of them, sir."

"He caught one and brought him to the dungeon?"

"Correct, sir," answered Webb.

Jacob muttered a series of expletives and sped up.

Montague Club was known for hosting bare-knuckle brawling matches. Many of the club's patrons participated in what was typically a sparring match between gentlemen. Those were held in the fighting ring in the club's gymnasium. The dungeon's fighting ring was a different matter altogether. That was where they held the matches that really mattered, the matches fought for notoriety and outrageous amounts of money. Sometimes, however, the matches were fought for honor and retribution. He figured the current match it hosted fell into the latter category. The idea caught flight when Evan had come into the dukedom and realized how bare his coffers really were, and he'd had to fight for prize money to keep his family afloat. Jacob had gone along with the plan because it had been good business for the club.

A gust of cold air raised the hair on his arms when he opened the door to the cellar. The thumps of fists hitting flesh interspersed with grunts met his ears as he hurried down the stone steps. He turned the corner to the room that housed the fight ring, not surprised to see it full of men watching the entertainment. Eight metal rods had been driven into the ground with twin lines of thick rope stretched tight between them to form a square of fifteen feet on each side. Cavell and another man were in the midst of what looked like a fight to the death.

"What the bloody hell is going on here?" Jacob yelled.

Cavell dodged a blow aimed at his chin by ducking down and charging his opponent, a man who was smaller by at least a stone but had the look of someone who had seen more than his fair share of scrapes. The other man growled in frustration and brought his knee up to land a blow to Cavell's stomach that had to have knocked the breath out of him. Jacob winced and glanced to the others in the room. Three of the club's hired security along with several of the kitchen staff, men off the street he didn't recognize, and the stock boy, who had probably seen the whole thing, lounged nearby on crates and chairs.

"Did you bloody well charge admission?" he asked Cox, their head of security.

The older man shrugged, raking a hand over his balding head in a rare display of nerves. "Only a bit of fun."

"Break this up," Jacob ordered.

"Right away, sir." Dunn and Sanford, the other two security men, jumped to their feet and quickly breached the fight ring.

"Did you at least relieve him of his weapons?" Jacob asked as he watched the two grapple with Cavell, who wasn't taking too kindly to having his fight ended early.

Cox scoffed as if the question was an insult. To be fair, the man did his job well, so Jacob already knew the answer. He was simply annoyed the fight had been allowed to happen. Cox indicated a crudely made clasp-knife on the floor at his feet. "That's all he had. We meant to let him go, but he exchanged words with Cavell and then this happened."

"Do you think Brody sent them?"

James Brody had been a thorn in their side ever since they had conceived of the prizefighting events. Brody had his own brawling club in a seedier area of London, but his operation was known far and wide, so he was able to draw large crowds. When Montague had started holding matches, and especially when Evan had quickly gained notoriety as one of their best fighters, Brody had taken exception to the business they took from him. It hadn't helped when Evan had beat one of Brody's best fighters.

Cox shook his head. "It appears they know each other."

It did seem the fight was personal. Cavell never fought angry, and he was spitting mad if the rage on his face could be believed. Jacob's security had the other man in hand now, but he wiggled out of their hold and lunged at Cavell again. Cavell had given up the fight, having reached for his coat, which hung over one of the ropes, so he wasn't prepared when the man landed a fist to his temple. A gash split open and Cavell's balance faltered, nearly sending him to the ground, but he caught himself with a knee.

Jacob cursed under his breath and bounded over the ropes. He took the man down with a right hook that left him stunned long enough for the security men to drag him out of the ring and toward the stairs without resistance. "Throw him in the alley and tell him if he comes back here he'll stay the night in our dungeon."

He glanced at Cox to show his displeasure. The older man dipped his head in guilt as he pocketed the weapon and began herding the spectators out of the cellar.

"Back to work," Jacob said to the kitchen staff who still lingered. They scurried up the stairs behind the others. By that time, Cavell was shrugging into his coat, effectively hiding the ripped seam in his shirtsleeves, but not the blood that had dribbled crimson stains at his collar. Withdrawing a handkerchief from his pocket, Jacob held it out to him. Cavell accepted it and pressed it to the open wound above his brow line.

"It's going to scar," said Jacob, nodding toward the wound. "The ladies aren't going to appreciate that."

"Ladies like to shag danger." He grinned.

He wasn't wrong. Now that Cavell had taken over Evan's place as their best fighter, his fights were swarmed by women hoping for a night with him.

"Care to explain what the fight was about?"

Cavell's jaw clenched and unclenched, his eyes still bright with unresolved anger.

"An old friend sent his regards." His tone dripped with bitterness.

"Do you mean Brody?"

He nodded as he brought the cotton square down. It was soaked in blood, so he folded it over and pressed it back to the cut. Head abrasions bled profusely, but they weren't generally dangerous as long as there was no concussion.

"Tell me what happened." Jacob walked over to check Cavell's pupils, guiding him out of the ring and toward the gas sconce on the wall. They were nearly the same height, and though he had filled out from the skinny runt he'd been with steady meals over the years, there was still a hunger about his face, a wariness, as if he was always on edge.

Cavell swallowed several times, clearly reluctant to talk. It had been this way ever since he'd appeared at the club's back door years ago. With a few cracked ribs, a broken jaw, and severely concussed, he hadn't been able to say very much for days. Thanks to his fevered ravings and the little he did say afterward, they had been able to piece together that he'd run afoul of Brody and had nearly been killed for it. He had been little more than a boy then and had disappeared as soon as he'd recovered enough to run, only to return in a similar condition months later. It had taken a couple of years, but Jacob had gained his trust. Now Cavell lived at Montague Club and had shown himself to be smart and capable, so that he ran the club when Jacob and Christian were away.

"I was on my way back from . . . visiting a friend." Cavell's hesitation likely meant that he had been with a woman. He was dressed in his more casual clothing of dark brown trousers and a wool coat. Not the fine fabric of the suits they wore when working at the club. "I first noticed them following me in Clerkenwell around King's Cross Road. Thought I'd lost them between there and here, but they knew where I was going and waited for me in the alley. There were three of them. Two ran off when Cox came running out, but the last one stayed."

Assured that his pupils were dilating as they should, Jacob stepped back. "What's his name?"

Cavell hesitated again. "Butcher."

"Butcher?" Jacob laughed. "Charming."

Cavell grinned, cracking the scab that had started to form over his bottom lip. "He's a charming bloke."

Jacob wasn't surprised by the name. He was no expert on the underbelly of London, but he did know that the gangs that ran the seedier parts of the city were vicious bastards. The fact that Cavell had been one of them and had dared to leave had upset their sense of loyalty and fair play. They wanted him back or they wanted him dead.

"This is the first time they've come so close to Montague. Do we need to be concerned?" Jacob asked.

"They know the club is secure. They wouldn't try to break in, and assaulting any of the patrons would have the police sweeping every mews and warren in the city. They want me."

"Might be a good idea to not go out visiting any *friends* for a while."

Hurt mixed with fury passed across Cavell's face. "She's not a friend anymore. She must have tipped them off I was visiting. It's the only way I can think they found me to follow me."

"Probably for the best." Jacob had been subtly guiding him away from the friends he'd known before working at the club. They were not good for him. More than once his prize winnings from fighting had disappeared because he'd given them away to people who only wanted to use him.

Cavell nodded. "I need a few minutes to clean up, but I'll be down soon."

"No, you're not working tonight." When Cavell looked stricken, he added, "Take tonight to recover. You'll scare the club members with that bruiser."

Cavell opened and closed his mouth a couple of times, before he finally said, "I'd rather not be alone tonight."

It was only in that moment that Jacob understood how Butcher's betrayal along with that of his female friend had wounded him far deeper than a mere fight ever could. He wanted to refuse him. That forehead would swell and no doubt his eye would soon be discolored. He couldn't walk through the club like that. However, Jacob understood from Christian how isolating it could be when left alone to deal with trauma. Their father had not been good to his half brother, and from what Jacob had gathered, Christian's childhood of loneliness had only contributed to his pain. Camille came to mind, and he wondered if he should call on her unprompted. Perhaps she was simply afraid to reach out to him.

"All right, you can deal cards in the Gold Room. I'll send Murphy to the main floor." The Gold Room was a private room where only their most daring and wealthy members played cards and shot dice. Like the women Cavell attracted, they, too, sought danger. Seeing him like this would likely only whet their appetites for his next fight.

Cavell nodded and hurried up the stairs to his room. Jacob was already tired, but it looked like he would have to spend a couple of hours on the floor tonight. Without Cavell there to oversee things as scheduled and Christian already gone home, it was left to him. He took the stairs much slower than he'd descended them, becoming aware of the pain in his hand. He flexed his fingers, grimacing at the stiffness already developing and the cut on his knuckles. He'd been reacting too fast and had been sloppy with the way he'd punched the whoreson. At least he hadn't ripped his coat sleeve.

Straightening his lapels and thinking he needed to go get ice for his hand, he opened the door into the corridor just off the main entrance when a familiar female voice found him. "Mr. Thorne, how good to see you, lovey."

Chapter 13

❦

The longer Camille sat at the card table, the more she became convinced that she had made a mistake coming to Montague Club tonight. She didn't even know why she had come, except that she hadn't been able to stop thinking about Jacob. She was very embarrassed by her behavior in the carriage the night he had seen her home. She had shamelessly thrown herself at him and ended up kissing on his lap only to be gently rebuffed. Was he disgusted by her? Did he pity her? It was finally the not knowing how he felt that brought her here, only now she was having second thoughts.

"Apologies, Your Grace." The young man who dealt the cards had turned over a jack of hearts, which meant she had lost. This was not a surprise since she could hardly concentrate. She kept looking for Jacob, who was not to be found.

"No need to apologize. I'm not very good at this game." He smiled. "Another game?"

"No, I'm finished for the night." She downed her

scotch—another rebellion against convention; everyone knew proper ladies did not drink scotch—and stood. "Good evening."

A commotion from the other side of the room had her glancing up from straightening her skirts. Mr. Cavell had just arrived. She had encountered him a few times when he dealt cards or managed the gaming floor. He wasn't conventionally handsome, but there was a character to his face that made her like him despite his sometimes intimidating demeanor. Tonight he was dressed in evening black with his dark hair brushed back to a shine with pomade. He walked with purpose, as if he had every intention of sticking to the perimeter of the room and passing through, but the crowd of patrons welcomed him with calls and greetings. He paused awkwardly to nod or say a word or two, but he kept a hand near his left eye in a strange gesture that had her angling her head to get a better look. Someone asked if there had been a fight tonight and she realized he must have a black eye. Her suspicion was confirmed a moment later as he walked toward her table and the better angle allowed her to see the swelling on that side of his face.

Jacob must have been downstairs overseeing the fight. A flutter of excitement had her glancing toward the archway hoping to see him following, but it was empty. What were the odds? The one night she had managed to corral her nerves enough to come here and he wasn't working. Perhaps it was for the best. She still didn't know if she could go through another attempt at sex with him. She walked around a group of men who were yelling at the cards at a baccarat table and turned toward the lounge to have a glass of wine before going home.

As she approached the lounge, two figures came into view. The room was separated into various seating areas for conversation, with each of them being dimly lit to foster a feel of intimacy. In the far corner a man and woman stood together much too closely for what was proper. She paused

within the arched opening, unsure if she should intrude or
find another lounge for her drink. The choice was taken
from her, however, when she recognized the set of Jacob's
broad shoulders. She gasped before she could stop herself
and then pressed closer against the wall and hoped she
stayed hidden. She couldn't move otherwise, not even
knowing that she should turn and leave them to their
privacy.

His back was to her, nearly hiding the woman, but the
dress gave her away. It was a green so dark that it was
nearly black. The woman was Eugenia Godwin, a widow
whom Camille had met not an hour ago. In her late thirties
or early forties, she was one of those attractive women who
exuded sexuality and style. She was all curves and confidence, and it very much appeared that she was well acquainted with Jacob. She leaned upward—*indecently
close*—and set her palm upon his chest. He put a hand to
her waist and Camille felt a pang of jealousy. It was clear
they were intimately acquainted with each other.

They were going to kiss. Camille's heart shuddered to a
stop, and everything fell away but the couple in front of her.
She had waited too long and he was with someone else. Or
maybe he had never stopped sleeping with other women.
He was beautiful. Of course other women would want him.
She had seen as much at the ball and then again at the
cabaret. The women in the audience had smiled fondly at
him. That knowledge didn't stop the gasp of outrage when
Mrs. Godwin's hand wandered up to toy in the thick, dark
hair that curled over his collar. Her own fingers clenched in
a pale approximation of the touch, bereft at the hollow feel
of the satin of her skirts. Why hadn't she caressed him like
that when she'd had the chance? She could have him if only
she would go to him. In that moment she determined that
she wanted him more than she was afraid of the conse-
quences.

His jaw clenched, and he looked away from the woman

as if he was impatient and not entirely enjoying her attentions. That propelled her into motion. Despite the tiny voice in her head that told her she had no right to be jealous, she found herself walking toward them. The movement caught his eye and he looked back, meeting her gaze. A slow smile of greeting curved his lips.

"Camille." His voice was low and so welcome that she had to take a breath as it seeped inside her, warming places she didn't have names for.

Mrs. Godwin had stepped away, putting a respectable distance between her and the man she had been trying to seduce.

"You're late for our meeting, Mr. Thorne, but I trust you have a good reason," she said and hoped he would take the bait.

His smile widened. He *was* happy to see her. "My sincerest apologies. There was an issue belowstairs that needed my attention. Perhaps we could talk now?" To Mrs. Godwin he extended his regrets that he couldn't continue their conversation.

She accepted the excuse with ease and bade them both good night before she left.

"You're here." He said it as if it were a relief to him, as if he had been waiting for her all this time.

Her heart took flight, sending her pulse skipping. She wanted to forget what had happened in front of her, but she was smarting from a jealousy she didn't understand and had never felt before. He was not hers in any way. Their one failed attempt at sex had ended abruptly and unhappily for both of them. He had never promised her anything more than his bed. One of the very important reasons she sought him out was *because* of his reputation gained from his experience with partners like Mrs. Godwin. It would be hypocritical of her to judge him or the woman or to harbor any sort of ill feelings. She knew that. Knew it with every logical bone in her body, but she could not make herself feel that. No, her feelings were very much in the primal part of her brain, which urged her to claim him for herself.

She forced her expression into something she hoped was neutral, calling on her early training. "I saw your . . . chat."

A corner of his mouth quirked upward in that way he had that never failed to make her admire his lips. A barely-there quiver thrummed in her stomach. "Ginny is a dear friend who recently returned from a tour of Italy."

Ginny? "Yes, we spoke earlier." She flinched inwardly at her tone, because it wasn't fair. Wasn't Camille here because she herself was eager to explore their friendship?

"She mentioned that," he said, his eyes hooded with knowledge of her jealousy.

"I came to tell you that I . . . I accept your offer," she blurted out before she could lose her nerve.

His eyes rounded in faint surprise. "My offer?"

Lowering her voice, she said, "T-to try again. Tonight."

"Camille . . ."

He glanced back as if assuring himself that no one had come into the lounge. Muffled cries of excitement from the gaming room confirmed that they were alone and everyone else was occupied. "Are you certain?" he whispered. His magnetic gaze came back to her, revealing a stark need on his face that took her breath away.

She nodded. The thought of him with someone else while she was too afraid to reach out for him was more than she could bear.

"Wait in my suite." He took a key from his pocket and pressed it into her palm, closing her fingers around it and holding her hand longer than necessary. "I have to finish up down here, but I'll join you soon."

She had barely nodded before he moved past her, leaving her alone. It was for the best because she couldn't find her voice. She had agreed to another night with him, and there were no words to describe the anticipation and fear that warred inside her.

* * *

The gaming tables operated at their usual brisk pace, but there was no crush tonight. It was midweek and Parliament hadn't long been in session, which meant the usual House of Commons crowd was preoccupied with meetings in the private dining rooms. The atmosphere was subdued, leaving Jacob too much time to think as he moved throughout the room. He was entirely too tense and distracted to deal cards tonight. His body was strung as tight as a bow as he thought of Camille upstairs waiting for him. He had counted in his head the steps it would have taken her to reach his suite. Had estimated the precise moment she sat down on the sofa they had recently occupied. Had imagined her restless roaming around his inner sanctum.

The truth was, he could have retired to his rooms earlier. Cavell was there, if out of sight, should there be a problem. The club saw to itself on nights like this. The problem was that Jacob was battling a strange case of fear. Had Ginny awaited him, he would have gone to her in a rush, the way she liked it. They would have fucked in that decadent all-or-nothing way of hers and she would have been long gone by now. It was the same for any of the women he usually took to his bed. He knew what they wanted, but more importantly, he knew what they required of him.

Camille was dangerous. She demanded too much, though she had no idea she was asking it of him. Sex with her by its very nature was intimate. He had to be open with her so that she would trust him enough to let herself go with him, to watch her and know what she needed because she couldn't or didn't know how to ask for it. This put him in danger of her creeping beneath the walls he had built to keep women at a safe distance. Knowing the danger existed, however, didn't stop him from wanting her. It sweetened the temptation of her. Thank Christ he would be leaving for Paris as soon as Turner signed the bloody contract.

The distance would effectively repair any of the cracks she made.

Still, he waited until half the patrons had left and the clock had long since ticked past midnight to make his way upstairs. Just knowing that she was waiting for him in his rooms had him half-rigid in anticipation. He couldn't remember the last time he had anticipated sex so enthusiastically. He opened the door, expecting to see her on the sofa, possibly asleep since he'd kept her waiting, but she wasn't there. A quick glance assured him that the room was empty. Perhaps she had gone.

Frowning, he made his way through the attached salon and then the small library near his bedroom. Though a lamp was lit and a book lay discarded on the table indicating that she had been there, she was not present. He couldn't resist walking over and picking up the brown leather-bound book. It was his newly acquired copy of *The American* by Henry James. Did she think of herself as the morally upright Newman, the American in the title; self-sacrificing Claire, the young widow who had been forced to marry her abusive husband; or perhaps the social-climbing Noémie, the only one who attained what she wanted in the end? Placing it back on the table, he walked to his bedroom.

The metal latch was cool beneath his hand as he pushed his door open. Satisfaction thrummed within him when he saw her on the bed. She had fallen asleep on her side, one hand curled beneath her cheek, while the other rested where he would lie beside her. She looked beautiful lying there atop the crimson counterpane, her bronze evening gown a perfect complement to the color. Swallowing against a wave of longing mixed with desire, he hurried through to his dressing room where he quickly disrobed and donned a dressing gown that closed in the front. His half interest had gone to full interest by the time he returned to his bedroom. That part of his anatomy would have to wait a little longer. He needed to make certain she agreed to what he had in mind first. Adding more coal to the fire, he turned out all the lamps in the room except for the one near the bed, which he turned down to a low flicker. In the soft glow, he climbed onto the bed to join her.

That odd cloak of intimacy that had graced them on the sofa returned to settle over the bed as he lay beside her. The club below, Turner and Blanchet, everything fell into the shadows around their cocoon where they both simply existed. She breathed in low, even breaths, her eyelids flickering with her dreams. He might have felt slighted had she been anyone else, but the fact that she felt secure enough to fall asleep in his bed made him feel full in a way he didn't want to think about, so he allowed himself a moment to take in her beauty. She was younger than the women he was usually with, preferring older and more experienced bed partners. Asleep, she appeared even younger. How truly young she must have been when she had become Hereford's bride. An intense ache swelled in his throat trailed by the familiar helpless rage that he couldn't have protected her from that. From *him*.

Her hair was silk beneath his fingers, lightly roughened by the dry texture of the styling tonic she used. It smelled like jasmine. He laid the wavy length to rest on her shoulder, exchanging it for her hand, which he brought to his lips. Her wrist smelled of vanilla. He wanted to lick the decadent taste from her skin and find the salty musk of her. It didn't help that he vividly recalled her unique and intimate scent on his fingers. Just once he wanted to taste her before this was over. He consoled himself by pressing his lips to her palm, allowing the tip of his tongue to taste the damp salt there.

She stirred, but instead of pulling away, her hand instinctively curved around his face. When she made a soft sound in the back of her throat, he couldn't help but smile. No, she wasn't one of those people who could do without sex. She was sensual and enjoyed touch. She'd simply been abused by the one man who was supposed to care for her. A black cloud of rage hovered in the back of his mind threatening to unleash its fury. She was so small and fragile, sweet and good, that he wanted to wrap his body around her, to protect her with his very being. Even though his body throbbed with need for her, somewhere lurking in the dark spaces he never thought to check was the knowledge that he could happily pass the rest of the night with her lying asleep in his arms. But he really hoped she wanted to do more than sleep.

Chapter 14

❦

Camille opened her eyes to see Jacob lying beside her. His eyes were heavy and dark as he kissed her palm, sending excitement swirling through her.

"Good evening," he said, his voice quiet in the near darkness.

"I didn't mean to fall asleep." She had been lying in his bed, luxuriating in his scent and the comforting feeling of having gained access to this private part of him, when she had drifted off. She went to sit up, but he kept hold of her hand and seemed in no hurry to let her go as he absently stroked her knuckles over his jaw. The beginnings of an evening shadow along the lower half of his face rasped pleasantly against her skin.

"I took longer than anticipated. It is perfectly fine."

She allowed herself to sink back into the fluffy pillows, her body relaxing. "How long have you been here watching me?"

That one corner of his mouth ticked upward again, and

she couldn't stop her thumb from touching the soft fullness of his bottom lip. "A few minutes. You don't mind that I decided to wake you instead of letting you sleep?"

"No, not at all. I would never presume to sleep here."

He slowly moved forward, and this effectively put him over her, except his weight was supported by an elbow and he wasn't touching her body. They were in bed and this proximity should have caused her a modicum of distress, but it didn't. A flicker of hope sparked to life in her chest.

"You can sleep here," he whispered.

Her heart took that far more seriously than he probably meant it. He was charming and undoubtedly talked to all the women in his bed in this kind and loving manner. It's why she had chosen him. "Your bed is comfortable," she offered, rather lamely.

He toyed with her fingers, the slightly rough pad of his thumb sending tingles skittering across her skin as it ran a lazy circle around her palm. "I told you I wouldn't touch you the next time we were together, but it appears I can't stop."

"I like your touch." Even as he violated his oath, she could do nothing but trust him. "Have we officially begun?" she teased.

He leaned toward her a fraction, and she felt the hard press of his desire against her hip. A thrill leaped through her. "I take that as a yes," she said.

He grinned and answered her with his mouth, gently nipping the meat of her palm with his teeth. He wore only a dressing gown of navy brocaded silk with gold trim. The buttons were unfastened, leaving a flimsy belt to hold it closed, exposing his calves, feet, and an expansive portion of his chest. His skin was that same lovely hue of golden brown everywhere, even where the sun never touched. His chest was covered in a sprinkling of dark hair. She wanted to feel it under her fingers. Usually by this point she didn't want to savor things; she simply wanted them to be finished.

"Are you all right?"

She nodded even though she wasn't sure that she was. Even thinking of how Hereford had made her feel had an echo of those feelings coming back. Jacob kept hold of her hand but leaned back, resting more on his side than his elbow. She couldn't resist a peek down at his impressive cockstand hidden within the decadent folds of silk. Mrs. Godwin would have had him in hand by now, she knew. She hated that she could not match that enthusiasm. She hated that—

"Camille." She hadn't realized that her thoughts had made her gaze wander to the fireplace until he called her back. "Tell me what you're thinking."

She opened her mouth to say nothing, which is exactly what she always did—she minimized herself to make things easier, but something else came out. It was a version of the truth. "I was thinking about the other times I've tried this with men."

She didn't know what she expected from him after that. Censure, perhaps? Disappointment? But this was Jacob and he didn't expect *anything* of her. He didn't want a particular version of herself other than the one she gave him. She didn't have to be good, because he didn't expect that. In a strange and twisted way she still couldn't work out, it helped her to take a deep breath.

"Do you want to tell me about them?" he asked, his dark gaze holding hers with patience.

She hadn't, but as soon as he asked, she was able to take another breath. "I don't want to talk about my husband." God no, even mentioning his name could ruin the entire night. She rushed forward instead. "There were two others. First there was Henry. Henry was a footman here at the duke's townhome in London. He was young and handsome, and I could tell he had a fondness for me right from the start. I snuck out one night with August soon after she arrived from New York and took him with us because I knew he would keep the secret. It's actually the first time I saw you. I didn't know who you were, but I thought you were very handsome."

He smiled and his brow rose with interest. "When was this?"

"In Whitechapel. The bare-knuckle brawling match where the man had spikes in his shoes and injured Evan."

"Ah yes. The man was Wilkes. I remember that night well."

"Somehow my husband found out about that adventure and that Henry had accompanied us. Henry was dismissed and I didn't hear from him again . . . that is until the duke died and I sought him out." She still didn't know why she had gone looking for him, except that she had hoped— *needed* what he had felt for her to have been real.

"He had told me once that he was from a small town in Sussex and that his mother had called in a favor from an uncle to get him into service with Hereford. I found him in his village and . . . I am ashamed to admit that I was so happy to see him that I didn't question anything. Not why he was sitting in a pub in the middle of the day or why he insisted we leave out the back entrance. He took me to his room and I thought we might . . ." She blushed and looked away. God, this was more difficult than she thought.

"You thought that you would make love?" he asked.

She shrugged. "I thought that we would spend the day together. Talking. Finding out that maybe what he felt for me was real and that I might return his feelings. I didn't even know my feelings for him, only that it felt good to be admired and cared for. But when we got to his room, he was in such a hurry to sleep with me. In fact, I even thought that maybe . . . maybe being with him was what I needed, that it would make me feel better. But it didn't . . ."

It had felt too similar to the way Hereford was with her. His touch had been tinged with desperation and a selfish need to possess. She had quickly begun to feel used.

"Someone knocked on the door before we got very far, and I was so relieved. It was Henry's fiancée. Someone at the pub had seen us leave together and gone to find her."

"Tell me that was the last you saw of Henry."

The plea in his voice made her laugh and gave her the courage to meet his gaze. No censure toward her was present, only disgust at Henry's actions. "That was the last I saw of him. I took the first train back to London."

"And the other man?"

She didn't miss the ardent curiosity in his tone. "No one important. He's a man named Frederick from New York. At one time our families thought we might marry, but that was many years ago, before my parents met the duke and thought he would be the better choice. We met again when I returned to visit my parents after Hereford's death. The experience was similar to Henry . . . the physical experience, that is."

"In what way was it similar? What is it precisely?"

She shrugged and said out loud what she should have said earlier. "I feel as if I become an object to be used. As if I cease to be a person." Her throat threatened to close in shame, so she sat up abruptly. This was too difficult. She didn't expect him to understand, but she couldn't stop talking. "I feel as if I am only there to submit."

He didn't move except to stroke a hand down her back. "What if we could make certain you do not feel used or forced to submit?"

She glanced over her shoulder, surprised to see him pensive and calm. "How?"

"You keep the control."

The silk tie had loosened so that his robe opened even more to reveal his stomach all the way to his navel. She had felt the power contained there but seeing the contour of muscle and sinew was entirely something else. The plains and valleys were evidence of the time he spent in the club's gymnasium. Each apparatus was designed to develop a different set of muscles, to help a man achieve his full potential and enhance performance. It had said so in the membership pamphlet. Apparently, the pamphlet hadn't lied.

His hand dropped from her back, drawing her attention to it. Even that part of him was strong. His fingers were long and tapered, graceful in their strength, but broad across the palms. The club sometimes hosted exposition bare-knuckle brawling matches in the gymnasium. She had seen those hands turn to fists and punch men twice his size and knew the damage they wrought. There was even a small cut and redness along one knuckle. Had he been fighting tonight?

"What control could I possibly retain when you are so very powerful?" she asked.

"You are more powerful than you think." His touch on her cheek was feather soft as he pushed back a strand of her hair. "More beautiful than you know. Stronger than you feel. You have all the control you want at your fingertips if you would only reach out and take it."

So she did. Her fingers trembled as she reached toward the valley between his pectoral muscles. The sprinkling of crisp, dark hair felt foreign beneath her fingertips. She had never touched this part of a man before, not with intent. His skin was soft over the firm brawny strength beneath. She squeezed a little, delighting in the tautness of his strength. Her palm moved over the mound in a slow glide that pushed the robe further apart, revealing his nipple. It was brown and rigid and she couldn't resist trailing her fingertip across the tight bud. His eyes seemed darker, dilated with a need that had become more potent in the last few seconds.

"Like this?" she asked.

"However you like." A husky texture roughened his voice. This tangible proof of how she affected him was indeed powerful.

She turned to sit more comfortably on the edge of the

bed, keeping one foot firmly on the floor to stabilize her. With both hands, she pushed his robe open until it fell off his shoulders. They were as broad and powerful as the rest of him. The few times she had attended the illegal warehouse fights, the men were usually shirtless. She assumed this prevented anyone from bringing weapons into the fray. She had only ever seen Jacob brawl in the exhibitions at the club where the fights were more civilized and the men wore shirtsleeves. The only skin revealed was their forearms, as they usually rolled up their sleeves.

"You're beautiful, Jacob."

The light played peekaboo with his physique. It highlighted the bulges and enticed her to feel where the sinew gave way to tendon and bone. She explored him with her fingers as if there was no light with which to see him. She delighted in the way his breath would hitch as he watched her. She traced the line of his shoulder down to his palm. On the way back up, she moved to his stomach. He flinched under the weightless touch of her fingers.

"You're ticklish." She didn't know why the knowledge charmed her so, but it did.

He leaned back farther against the pillows to allow her better access. A smile tipped his lips as he said, "I bet you are, too." His eyes left no mistake that he meant to find out one day. She was surprised that she very much wanted him to. His fingertips moved in a light touch against her hip, promising there could be more but demanding nothing.

"Perhaps," was all she said, reluctant to be distracted from her exploration.

His belly was flat, and when she pressed, she could trace the ridged muscle beneath his skin. He was so warm that she wondered what it would be like to lie next to him with no clothes between them, flesh to flesh, and have his body warm hers. She wanted to feel his firmness melding with her softness. Dimly, she was aware of her growing arousal. The way her breath came faster, propelled by the speed of her heartbeat. The way her nipples drew tight and made her breasts feel heavier. That pleasant ache had returned between her thighs, wanting his touch. But she also knew that the anxiety and nausea would be fresh on the heels of those good feelings if she pushed things too far. The moment she gave way to that goodness, the bitterness would flood in, so she didn't allow them to take her over. They stayed at the periphery of her mind, taunting her senses and leaving her nerves tingling with suspended anticipation.

"Do you want to touch more of me?" His voice was a hoarse whisper.

He was asking if she wanted to touch him even more intimately. She swallowed, caught in the very indecency of the question and her own desire to say yes. She had certainly never touched a man there before. He stood proud and ready behind the curtain of the robe that shielded him.

When she didn't answer immediately, he moved. She stiffened as he reached for what she thought would be her wrist. She expected he would take charge now and show her how to touch him. He didn't. He pulled the fabric tight so that the shape of his aroused length was clearly visible beneath it. She couldn't breathe as she watched him trace a line from his bollocks to the tip, which was only just hidden behind the part of the fabric. He was long and broad even there. Powerful.

Her hand dropped from his chest to rest on his thigh, the fabric soft and cool beneath her. She couldn't take her eyes from his fingertips lightly playing up and down his length. More than anything, she wanted to do that to him. She wanted to watch his face as he took pleasure in her touch.

Somehow, she found the nerve to ask him. "May I do that?" Her voice was barely a whisper.

"You have the control tonight, Camille. You can do whatever you want to me."

A thrill of exhilaration accompanied those words. She believed him. Following his lead, Camille touched the head of his erection with the tip of her index finger. He didn't move; even his breathing stilled as his eyes fixed on that point of contact. Her fingertip slid down his length as she marveled at how rigid and solid he felt. "Does it hurt you when you're hard like this?"

"It can, a bit." His voice did have the hesitation of someone in pain, as if he had to measure his breath to allow for sentences. "Similar to the ache in your cunny, when you're wanting to be touched . . . or filled."

His crude words had her looking at him before she could control her reaction.

"Do you know that ache?" The sheer magnetism on his face fed that yearning. He looked at her as if no one else existed.

She nodded and jerked her gaze away from his, back to the very real proof of his desire between them. His hands closed into tight fists when she made a little cove with her hand, palming him while keeping the pressure gentle. He felt foreign but not scary. Her gaze kept moving from his hard length to his hard torso, tracing the ridges and valleys of his chest and stomach. Just looking at him made her body feel heavy and tingly. She wanted to lie on top of him and feel him as many places at once as she could. And she *really* wanted to know what he looked like beneath the fabric.

"Do you want something?" he whispered. He searched her face, looking for any hint of what she might desire.

She wanted to see him, but it seemed as if it could be considered vulgar to say as much. Would it? There was so much about this she didn't know. It seemed there were rules to everything in life, so why would this be different? Instead of answering, she leaned forward and pressed a kiss to his bare shoulder. His skin was warm and soft beneath her lips. She inhaled smoky hints of sandalwood as she moved lower, trailing kisses until her chin brushed against his nipple. The urge to feel it under her tongue came over her. She licked him hesitantly, uncertain if he would like it. The moment her tongue touched him the heavy length of him jerked against her palm. *That part of him could move on its own.* A tiny spot of wetness appeared on the silk near the tip. She looked from the circle of darkened silk to his face only to find his eyes wide and fathomless as if he wanted to devour her with them.

"Did you . . . ?"

"No, a little can leak out." He grinned, but then continued seriously. "It is why you should never allow a man inside you unsheathed or without a sponge, even if he claims to be able to withdraw."

"A sponge?" She knew about sheaths. Violet had brought her one and they had giggled over its shape. Later, she had taken a tin with her when she had gone to see Henry, anticipating what might happen. Thank God they hadn't had to use it. But she had never heard of a sponge in this context.

He leaned toward the table beside the bed, and she was forced to move her hand away, making her realize that she didn't want to. She wanted to keep touching him. Opening the drawer, he retrieved an apothecary jar and reached inside with two fingers. He pulled out a small round material that looked like a sponge with a string attached to it.

"This goes inside you before sex. It's soaked in a vinegar mixture which prevents the sperm from taking root."

She stared at it, wondering how she was supposed to possibly put that where it was meant to go, then she looked at him and wondered how she felt so comfortable having this conversation with him. "I didn't know that such a thing existed."

He handed it to her before replacing the jar's lid and returning it to his drawer. "Sometimes they're preferable over sheaths, which can dull sensation. There is also the option of having a cervical cap made for you."

"Oh." She had never heard of a cervical cap, either. "I

suppose there's much I don't know," she said, turning the sponge over in her hand.

His fingertips touched her face, brushing a strand of hair back. "I can teach you. Is there something else you want to know?"

She shook her head and placed the contraceptive on the table, all the while considering how to ask him. "Well . . . perhaps . . ."

"Say it, Camille."

"I wonder if I could touch you without the fabric between us."

"Of course." Eagerness lit his face, making his eyes bright as he untied the belt and pushed the dressing gown back. It clung to his arms but left the rest of him fantastically bare. From the wide expanse of his shoulders to the ridged muscles of his torso, he was so beautiful. She wanted to savor the sight of him fully, but she couldn't because she was too curious about his newly exposed erection.

It rose between them, almost resting against his stomach, rigid and thick. Powerful just as she'd thought. A moment of anxiety stilled her hand.

"I won't hurt you," he whispered.

She believed him. Taking a deep breath to settle herself, she gripped his thigh. His muscle flexed beneath her, reminding her of how his strength was attractive to her. It could be the same with that part of him.

"I want to touch you."

He nodded his encouragement and went still. She reveled in the sharp intake of his breath as they both watched her hand slide up his thigh to his cock. She took him in hand again, only this time there was nothing between his flesh and her palm. With gentle exploration, she exerted a slight pressure as she gripped him. He let out a harsh breath and she looked at him for signs of pain.

"Do that again," he whispered.

So she did, and the pleasure that crossed his face was unmistakable. A pearl of moisture gathered on the tip, and she touched it before she could talk herself out of it, gliding the pad of her thumb over his satiny skin. She squeezed him again, and he took her hand in his. She watched, unable to react in any other way, as he brought her palm to his mouth and placed a kiss there. She gasped when he licked her, making her stomach quicken in pleasure. Then he brought her hand back to his cock and showed her how to pleasure him.

"Like this," he whispered, wrapping his hand around hers. Their fingers moved together up and down his length, gripping him in long, slow caresses with a slight twisting toward the end before going back to the base and starting again. When he was confident she had the movement right, he let go.

"Is this right?" she asked, checking his face, but too fascinated to look away for long.

He groaned, nodding. Under the power of her hand, his body became taut and firm, his breathing heavy as his head fell back into the pillow and his eyes found her face. He watched her through the fog of his pleasure, causing her own body to tremble with longing under the weight of it. Fisting the blanket beneath him, he thrust up and into her touch. "Camille," he groaned.

Her name was hardly more than a rumble in his voice, but it was heady, filling her with satisfaction. His skin moved like silk over the hard-muscled heat beneath. Every compression of her grip elicited a reaction from him. He wasn't using her, but rather she was guiding his pleasure. If she slowed, his hips slowed; if she increased her pace, his muscles tightened. He followed her lead, accepting whatever she was willing to give him. The control was intoxicating until he let out a particularly harsh sound, and she didn't know what it meant.

"Did I hurt you?" she asked, unsure of herself and him.

While she knew that when a man sought his pleasure it sometimes looked like pain and sounded like pain, she had never done *this*, and she didn't want to do it poorly.

"God no," he said through clenched teeth, his breath as heavy now as if he'd run up several sets of stairs. His eyes shut tightly as his hips rose to meet her. "Don't stop. Please."

A tiny sliver of foreboding found its way inside her. If he wasn't in pain, then he was close to finding his release. She knew the signs well. Harsh breath. Hard hands. Eyes scrunched tight. This was when she couldn't hide herself away. This is the point when all the previous times she could no longer pretend that this thing wasn't happening to her. The intensity brought her back to herself and she endured. Even though she knew that this was Jacob and not her husband, her shoulders stiffened, anticipating the moment when he would grab her.

She let him go and his eyes flew open, questioning. "I . . ." She rose and stepped away from the bed, aware that she was overreacting but unable to stop. "I'm sorry."

Chapter 15

❦

Y ou're all right, Camille. Nothing will happen that you don't want."

Jacob's voice was husky and raw, his eyes wide with alarm. Every muscle in his body seemed to be taut, primed for a release that she had denied him. Even though he had been mere seconds away from fulfillment, he wanted her to feel comfortable, even if it meant not reaching his own gratification, and that relaxed her more than anything could have.

"We can stop," he added, moving to tie the robe closed.

The rising wave of panic began to ebb almost as quickly as it had come on. He was still hard and the idea of him hiding himself away from her was so repugnant that she moved to the bed again, unable to tear her eyes away from the sight of him. "Will you . . . show me?" She gestured toward his arousal.

"Are you certain?" He paused in the act of covering himself, transfixed on her face.

"I've never been more certain of anything in my life." The fact that he was willing to stop when he was so close to release soothed her more than he would ever know. "Please," she added when he didn't move. "Let's continue."

Finally, he settled back against the pillows again and took himself in hand. The fact that his eyes never left her face somehow made the whole thing more intimate. It was an acknowledgment that he did this for her . . . for her pleasure . . . more than his own. He wanted to see her reaction. Her whole body felt suffused with light and heat, and she tore her eyes away from his to watch. He was very adept at handling himself. The head disappeared behind his big palm as he squeezed before showing itself again in long and languid strokes. It was quite possibly the most erotic sight she had ever seen.

"Are you imagining that it's me?" she whispered. Or had she ruined that?

"Yes." His voice was rougher than she had ever heard it. Everything in her trembled at the sound, but in the very best way. "But not your hand."

"Yes." The word was hardly more than a breath. Her whole body reacted to that, aching and tightening with need. Heat pooled between her thighs, where she suddenly longed to receive him. He held himself as she had except perhaps a bit rougher. She pressed closer to the bed, until the mattress bit into her thighs. His nostrils flared at her nearness, and though his free hand flexed in the blanket inches from her, he didn't reach for her. The intensity changed. She could feel it, smell his arousal in the air around them. He was close again.

His eyes fell shut only to slit open again and stay fixed on her face. Strong, masculine grunts filled the room, punctuated by the wet sound of his palm moving on his cock. All the tendons of his neck drew tight as he pushed against his hand, searching. And then he gasped, his cock jerking against his hold as his release painted across his stomach.

After a moment, he relaxed against the pillows, completely sated, the hint of a smile touching his face as he looked up at her.

She couldn't look away from him, lying there tattered and vulnerable in the aftermath of pleasure. He was the most beautiful thing she had ever seen. A nearly over-whelming sense of gratitude overcame her. He hadn't made her stay, even at the potential cost of his own pleasure. He had allowed her to leave him unfulfilled instead of grab-bing her as she had anticipated (even though she *knew* he wouldn't have). The irrational fear had taken over, and it hadn't made him angry or impatient with her.

Then something happened to her that had never hap-pened before. She felt genuine regret that she hadn't been more a part of what he had experienced. She was angry at herself for stepping away. He had fallen apart with pleasure and it hadn't been because of her. She wanted to do that for him. She placed a hand on his thigh, noting the slight tremble.

"That was . . . incredible." Not scary . . . well, not anymore . . . and not shameful.

"Thank you for that," he said.

"Thank you for the demonstration." She tried teasing to cover how truly vulnerable and awestruck she felt. Her cheeks flushed. "I didn't do anything."

He took her hand, lightly lacing his fingers with hers. "No? Was that someone else, then?"

"No . . ." She smiled at his attempt at levity. "But I stopped."

"Doesn't matter. I still came harder because you were here. You did that to me."

Harder? Did he mean the way his body tightened and shook? The way he had looked so intense and focused?

If her cheeks had flushed before, they burned now. She would never get accustomed to the easy way he spoke with her about sex. "Shall I go so that you can see to that?" She glanced to the semen on his stomach, wondering how it would feel . . . and taste. Did people do that? What had gotten into her?

"You can go whenever you want, but it isn't necessary," he said, releasing her hand.

She stepped back to give him space and watched as he rose from the bed. The long robe still fell off his shoulders to trail behind him. Her greedy eyes took in the broad expanse of his shoulders, the quick glimpse of a single buttock as it flexed and the silk flared out behind him. She desperately hoped the robe would fall away, but he disappeared into the bathing chamber before it could.

She felt strange in her own body. Inflamed and achy in a way that she knew would be relieved by his touch. She wanted to strip out of her clothes and lay there with him in bed all night, feeling his hard plains and soft skin pressed against every inch of her. It would be a strange request to say the least, and she didn't think she could actually manage to give voice to it. Besides, he'd found his pleasure. He'd probably want her gone.

A long, awkward moment passed as she considered if he would prefer that she not be here when he returned. Perhaps he was too kind to tell her to leave outright. Why would he want her to stay? In her experience, men left quickly after the deed was done. Also, she still felt raw from her own idiocy in pushing him away. She should wait near the door, so that he would see she wasn't planning to stay and bother him when he came back.

"Going so soon?" he asked a moment later when he came out to find her inside the door.

The buttons were fastened on his dressing gown and she nursed a moment of regret that the V wasn't nearly as deep as she would have preferred and the fabric fell nearly to his ankles, covering his muscular legs. Despite the awkwardness, she couldn't get enough of looking at him, it seemed.

"I thought it best."

He didn't stop, walking right up to her with that familiar, soft smile on his face. "Best for you?" Black hair fell over his forehead, curling a little now that it had been brushed free of the pomade he used. He gently wiped her palms with a warm, wet cloth.

"You, mostly. I've taken up enough of your evening." And hadn't even given him sex, not really. A swell of sadness mixed with the lingering arousal, leaving her feeling confused and weak.

"Shouldn't I get to decide that?" He raised a brow. "Unless you really have to go."

"I can stay for a bit, if you want." When what she truly wanted was all night, she groped at the chance for a few more minutes.

The pad of his thumb came up to trace her bottom lip. The same hand that had brought him pleasure; the same one that she suspected would be able to do amazing things to her. She thought he might kiss her, but he said, "I do want you to stay." Tossing the cloth away, he said with a smile, "Come have a drink with me."

She nodded. Despite her earlier fear, her arousal was constant, lying there in wait for him. She bit her bottom lip to stop it tingling where he had touched her when he took her hand as easily as if they had held hands a thousand times and led her through the library to the adjoining salon. He indicated that she should take a seat on the sofa and went to pour them both a drink.

The room, like every other one in his home, was elegant and sophisticated. Scarlet was the dominant color here but mixed with touches of royal blue, cream, and gold. Artwork graced the walls with several paintings and photographs she thought might be of his family. Instead of sitting, she walked closer to a section of wall covered with painted miniatures, curiosity about him and his family overcoming her.

One was of three children, a boy and two girls that she felt certain were Jacob and his sisters. The boy had a smile so full of mischief that it made her smile just looking at it. The girls sat on either side of him, the older one appearing more mature than her years would suggest, and the younger one peering up at the artist with wide and innocent eyes as Jacob held her against his side. Next to that was a miniature of a young girl who looked similar to Lilian, but the style of clothing she wore was older. Their mother, perhaps?

She moved on to a larger portrait of an attractive couple. The man stood facing the artist, but his body angled a bit toward the woman who was seated off to his side and in the forefront. There was something a bit regal about them both. She knew at once they were Jacob's parents. The man appeared almost fierce in his expression. From all she had heard, the late earl had not been a kind person, and his expression reflected such here. But the woman's mouth held the hint of a smile, and her eyes were kind. Jacob was a perfect blend of the two of them. He was handsome like his father and had his build, but he had inherited his coloring from his mother.

Seeing the couple now, she couldn't understand how Jacob had seemed to have had a happy childhood when she knew Christian had not. Violet had told her a little about her husband's lonely past. Abandoned by his mother when his father banished her to the Continent for her infidelity, he had grown up largely alone either at school or on his country estate. She had also mentioned that his father was responsible for his limp in a terrible accident.

"Your parents?" she asked when he approached her with the drink. Brandy, she amended, when she took a sip of the rich liquid.

"Yes, this was painted not long after Maura was born. Right here as a matter of fact." He pointed toward the window, and she could make out the exact arrangement of glass panes behind them and the archway that bisected the room, although the curtains were different. They were red in the portrait, but the current ones were gold.

"Were they very happy?" She surprised herself by asking the probing question.

He shrugged, drawing her gaze to that charming little cove where his neck met his shoulder. She had the oddest impulse to kiss him there. Instead, she settled for placing her hand on his upper arm, needing to touch him in some way. He didn't seem to notice or mind.

"I don't know that my father ever knew what happiness was. He loved Mama, but I doubt he ever had a day of true contentment. She was happy, I think. She loved it here, and being a mother seemed to bring her joy and fulfillment. Still . . . sometimes I wonder."

"What do you wonder?" He was easy to talk to, and that was because he was usually equipped with a thick layer of charm. Now, she realized that he wielded it to keep others at a distance. There was no armor now, just him and the stark truth on his face.

"How they worked together. She was warm and he was cold." He shook his head. "I loved him and he cared for us children, but I think he only had a certain amount of love to give and he used it all up on her."

"How sad to think that."

This caught his attention, and he looked from the painting to her. "You don't think there's a limit to someone's ability to love?"

"I suppose I never thought about it. You weren't very close to him, then?"

"Our relationship was difficult. To hear Christian tell it, we lived the charmed life with our father that he never had, but it wasn't how he likes to believe. Father was here, but often distant. He was a man of his class. He would send for us when it was convenient, usually after dinner, and then we might not see him again for several days. He lauded our accomplishments and didn't acknowledge when we failed. He was always good to Mama, though. You could sense the change in him when she walked into the room. She soothed him in some way I have yet to comprehend."

"I think I understand what you mean. Perhaps it's more that love is rarely a pure emotion. It has to filter through the other emotions and experiences of the person who feels it. Love can be warped by that. Poisoned or twisted, to an extent."

"Possibly. The one thing I know is that love is notoriously unreliable and can fade with no warning."

She startled at that. "You don't believe in it, then?"

He took a sip of brandy, rolling it across his tongue before he shifted his gaze from the painting to her. She was gratified to see that his eyes weren't shuttered. "I believe it exists, but it isn't a healthy emotion for some." Staring back at the painting, he added, "My father's love ruined several lives."

"Not ruined, surely. Impaired, definitely. But Christian has now found Violet, despite the rough start in life." She didn't know why, but this conversation was making her melancholy. "I've heard his mother even has a family and is living in Italy, or somewhere far away, at least. Life isn't over until the end."

"He ruined Christian's mother and her relationship with her family, and my own mother had a strained relationship with her parents because she chose him over a respectable marriage. That all happened because of his obsession with Mama."

"Love isn't obsession."

His smile was rueful. "You have to understand, for the Halston men love *is* obsession. Look at how Christian is with Violet. He didn't know he loved her at the time, but he did and he practically kidnapped her to have her. Even now, if anything happened to her, it would destroy him. Love isn't healthy for us. So to answer your question—yes, love exists, but it's not for everyone. It's certainly not for me."

"How do you know love would be the same for you? Have you ever been in love?"

"That's a very good question, Camille. I haven't been in love, but I respect the emotion and the experiences of those I have known who have fallen into its clutches. Even if it weren't that way for me, it requires too much. More than I can devote to it for now. I value my freedom too much."

She stared back at the couple, afraid to do anything else lest he know how he rattled her when he shouldn't. She did not love him, and she held no expectations that he would fall in love with her. She let her hand drop from his arm and took a swallow of brandy as she made her way farther down. In fact, if she thought there was a chance of him falling in love with her, she would end things now. She wasn't ready for love. And yet the thought of him alone in this big house years into the future left her sad, as did the thought that one day they might pass each other at a ball and be nearly strangers. It was a confusing mix of emotions.

"Perhaps we should make a pact," she said.

"Another proposition so soon?"

She could hear the smile in her voice, even though she still dared not look at him. It might make her admit things she wasn't ready to acknowledge. "If we aren't married by fifty, we can marry each other. No one should grow old alone."

A soft guffaw met her words. "Make it sixty and you have yourself a deal."

She smiled against the lip of her snifter, but the humor didn't cut through her inexplicable grief. "Deal."

He held out his hand and she was forced to look at him, all the while hoping he didn't read anything on her face. "You Americans shake hands on your deals, do you not?" he asked.

Transferring the drink to her left hand, she took his hand. "We didn't shake on our first deal."

"No, we didn't." His gaze turned pensive, and he kept

hold of her hand, which she did not mind at all. She quite liked the feeling of his big hand wrapped around hers. "We kissed on it, if I recall correctly."

His eyes flicked to her lips, which still tingled from his touch. She wanted to kiss him again, which made her jerk her gaze away to get herself under control. Her body had yet to cool from the confusing mix of emotions that had been coursing through her all evening, and she couldn't stop herself from remembering how he looked under the power of her touch.

He brought her hand to his mouth where he placed a very gentlemanly kiss to the backs of her fingers. Only it didn't feel very chaste the way her body responded to him. Tiny sparks of pleasure dashed up her arm to nourish the ache that continued to throb deep within her. He felt it, too, if the heat in his eyes was any indication.

"Come sit with me," he said.

Helpless to do anything else, even though a clock some-where deep in the apartments had chimed the late hour, she nodded, and he led her by the hand to the sofa. He kept hold of it after they sat, and she didn't mind. In fact, she savored the feel of his fingers entwined with hers. She was so close to losing her heart to him that it felt foolish to stay, but a stampede of wild horses could not have driven her away from him.

"I frightened you again," he said, his voice lowered.

"No, of course not."

He stared at her, unconvinced. "Earlier . . . in bed, when you would have brought me to release."

Her cheeks flamed at the memory. "It was stupid of me—"

"Shh . . ." The fingers of his other hand came up to touch her lips. Then he caught her chin between his thumb and forefinger. "It wasn't stupid at all."

"Rest assured it wasn't you. You did nothing wrong. It was me . . . again."

He seemed to mull this over, his gaze studying her face. "It sounds as if you believe *you* did something wrong."

He was right. She kept apologizing because she felt wrong. Swallowing past the growing lump in her throat, she said, "Well . . . I did. You wouldn't hurt me or force me, I *know* that you wouldn't, but I can't seem to make my fear understand that."

"That's because fear has no reason or logic."

"I know it doesn't. I simply want to be normal." She was so disgusted with herself that she wasn't.

He watched her with infinite patience, and his thumb continued to stroke her cheek. "But you are normal. I would think what is happening to you is a typical reaction to abuse that anyone would experience."

"Abuse?"

His jaw hardened slightly as he said, "Hereford abused his power over you. He was a cruel man who tried to control and manipulate you physically, mentally, and emotionally. It will take time to heal from such wounds."

"I don't know that it could be called abuse. He never hit me." She remembered the woman who had arrived at the London Home at dawn one morning a while back with a broken arm and two black eyes asking for help because the man in her life had done that to her. That was abuse.

His hand dropped from her face to her lap where he covered hers with both of his. "Abuse comes in different forms," he said, as if he could read her mind. "He made you submit to him in a hundred different ways. He made you feel less about yourself."

Had it been so obvious? Did everyone know and pity her the tyrant of a husband she'd had? Did Jacob pity her? Is that why he was being so kind? Wave after wave of confusing emotion moved through her: anger, fear, betrayal, resentment. She didn't know who to focus them on, so they swirled endlessly with no source or place to land.

Cruelty? Manipulation? The few bruises she'd sported

because of Hereford's handling hardly seemed to compare to broken bones, but did his angry tirades and hurtful accusations all add up to abuse? Her mind churned with memories, small moments that had left wounds she hadn't even noticed at the time. The way his anger made her cringe internally. The way a look from him could make her feel small and insignificant.

God, that monster was still controlling her from the grave. How had she allowed herself to be so thoroughly brought down by him?

She didn't realize tears wet her face until she felt them drop on their hands and Jacob was pulling her into his arms and onto his lap. She meant to remove herself immediately, but it felt so good and warm to be held by him that she gave herself a moment to relish the feeling. Belatedly, she realized that the brandy had fallen to the floor and would probably ruin the expensive rug, but he was cuddling her and making soothing sounds and she couldn't stop herself from burying her face in his neck and holding him.

Her breath came in hiccupping sighs as she tried not to cry. She would not cry one more time over her fate. Enough was enough. After a few minutes, she was able to hold the tears back and simply rest against him. After a few minutes more, she pulled back enough to look up at him. Where she had expected pity, there was only affection, tenderness, and something she didn't quite understand in his eyes, but it was good. No one had ever looked at her in that particular way. It felt so lovely and nourishing that she never wanted him to stop.

"You deserve good things, Camille." His voice was low and deep as if he were sharing a secret with her.

The lump in her throat swelled to nearly bursting. She had to swallow several times and clench her molars to keep fresh tears from falling. Thankfully, the clock saved her when it chimed the half hour. "I should go."

"You could stay." His voice sounded raw and intimate.

If she stayed he could hold her all night. She could lie with him with no clothes between them. They might even make love. *Make love.* She was too far gone for mere sex. If something happened between them tonight she would never recover herself. She would be his completely.

Whether he wanted her to be or not.

He didn't want love. He had said as much not even a half hour ago. No, she needed to leave and shore up her defenses again. He was leaving for Paris soon anyway.

"I told my driver to return. He's probably waiting. I think it would be too difficult to sneak out in the morning."

He nodded, accepting this logic, and helped her to her feet. "Then let me walk you out."

Taking her hand, he led her through the drawing room and out into the wide corridor. She savored the feel of his fingers laced with hers, giving his hand a gentle squeeze. He squeezed her back as he walked with her down the stairs. He didn't speak until they were at the front door where he paused, keeping hold of her.

He hesitated as he reached for the lock, and his gaze went to hers, full of questions and wonder. Before she could think better of it, she rose up on her toes and took hold of him, threading her fingers through his hair as she pulled him down for a kiss. His lips were soft, lightly tracing hers in a tease of a kiss that had her opening to him in an attempt to entice him to more. He made a growl in the back of his throat that set her heart racing. Tightening her fingers, she pulled him closer and delighted in the feel of the full length of his arousal against her stomach as she came up against him. Her body clenched in response. He plundered her mouth then like a desperate man on the verge of losing control.

When he finally set her away from him, she was breathing fast and could hardly see through the haze of her arousal and the sea of emotions that surrounded them. He appeared just as confused and lost as she was, until finally he shook himself from the strange cloud of yearning and opened the door. Peeking outside, he kept the door cracked as he said, "He's there."

She nodded but neither of them moved.

"Will you come back?" he asked softly, his breath still labored.

"Yes." There was no question in her mind that she would return to him.

"I have an idea of what we can try next."

Her heart leaped in anticipation. "What?"

"You'll see." He gave her that hint of a mischievous smile. Then he opened the door for her, hiding himself behind it in case someone happened to come along on the pavement to see him in his dressing gown. "Good night, Camille."

Chapter 16

❦

T o Christian and Violet and the many healthy and happy children they will have." Evan lifted his snifter of Glenlivet in a toast.

"To Christian and Violet," Jacob echoed. "May all go smoothly with the birth," he added, knowing his brother's concern.

It wasn't yet the evening of his niece's birthday, but the three men were all settled in Jacob's study several nights after his evening with Camille, when Christian had decided to tell Evan the news. The words had practically burst out of him as soon as they were all together, an indication of how happy he was to be a father again. They had decided that now was the perfect opportunity to break out the whisky.

Christian smiled as they clinked their glasses together and took a drink. "Violet claims to want five children. I pray to God that this one is a boy so that she can be satisfied," he joked. "She's determined we have an heir, but my heart won't survive many more births."

"You don't actually have to be there in the room with her while it's happening," Jacob pointed out, quite helpfully, he thought. In fact, most men were not.

"How could I not? I couldn't leave her to face such a task alone," Christian said, tossing back the rest of his glass as if reliving the memory required fortification.

"He doesn't understand." Evan shook his head at Christian who raised his eyebrows and nodded in agreement. To Jacob he said, "Once it's the woman you love, you'll understand how helpless you feel being able to do absolutely nothing to help. We men set up our lives so that it feels as if we're in control of things, but in this there is no control."

"Then I suppose I'm destined to not understand. I don't plan to ever fall in love."

"You're still going on with that?" Christian shook his head. "As I have proven, you don't get to choose when you fall in love. It finds you when it's ready for its next victim."

"Victim?" Jacob chuckled. "Don't let your wife hear you talk like that."

They both laughed. Jacob's laugh, however, was hollow. What had happened between him and Camille haunted him. Its grip had tightened rather than loosened in the ensuing days. He wanted to see her again, *needed* to see her almost like he needed air to breathe. It was a palpable feeling. He had never experienced this magnetism she held over him. Whatever had happened between them that night, it was powerful. As much as it scared him and made him want to set her away, it also made him crave her.

"I'd never," Christian said, which made them all laugh harder.

It was no secret that August and Violet could be strong-willed at the best of times.

"But in seriousness, you're nearly thirty now. Don't you plan to marry one day?" Evan asked.

Christian shook his head and answered for him. "Christ,

don't get him started. He's convinced that our father has set us up to be cursed in love."

"Not cursed," Jacob clarified. "I simply do not appreciate the sort of love in which the Halston men find themselves. Many would say that *obsessed* was a mild word for how our father felt about my mother. Christian himself kidnapped his wife."

"I take issue with the word *kidnapped*. She left with me of her own free will. I admit to not being completely clear on my intentions. Also—and this is pertinent to our discussion—I did not kidnap her due to love but because of the sizable fortune attached to her," Christian said.

"That defense sounds no better than what I said," Jacob pointed out.

"The love came later while I was nursing her back to health," Christian clarified.

"Nonsense," said Jacob, shaking his head. "You loved her already or you wouldn't have been able to entertain the idea of marriage. You can lie to yourself, but you cannot lie to me, brother."

Evan chuckled. "Thorne has the right of this one. You were obsessed with Violet from the first. I saw how you panted after her at the balls."

Jacob grinned and raised his eyebrows at his brother. "See? Balls you never attended before she came around."

Christian rolled his eyes. "Be that as it may, my point is that one day you, too, will feel that way, dear brother, and if what you say is true and it's a family trait, then you cannot dodge it."

"Perhaps not, but I can avoid the hell out of it for as long as I'm able." This elicited another round of laughter. Too bad he wasn't nearly as confident as he sounded. Camille had power over him, and he was starting to get the feeling that it might be too late to avoid her. "It is clear, however, that fatherhood suits you. I am happy for you."

"Thank you." Christian smiled. Despite the worries he professed to having, he was genuinely happy.

The conversation continued for a bit until there was a brusque knock on the door. It opened quickly and Cavell half stood in the room, his eyes bright with contained eagerness. He clutched a thick envelope. Jacob's heart stopped for a moment at the sight. He knew that Turner had sent it.

"Good evening, gentlemen," he said casually. Evan and Christian greeted him. "Could I speak with you for a moment, Thorne?"

Jacob nodded and made his excuses, following Cavell back into the hallway. Closing the door behind him, he walked around the corner to give him some space from his partners. He hadn't told them about the club yet because he'd been waiting for just this moment first.

"It's from Turner."

It wasn't a question, but Cavell proudly held it out to him and said, "It is. The courier said it's a contract and you needed to see it immediately."

Jacob untied the string holding the binding and pulled out the thin sheaf of papers. His fingertips tingled with the importance of what he held in his hands as he skimmed the first couple of pages. "He's investing. He's accepted the last scenario I sent over."

Cavell clapped him on the back. "Congratulations. I know this is something you've wanted for a while."

It was finally happening. Months of planning and now he would be in Paris in less than a fortnight. He'd have to leave after Rosie's birthday. Which meant that he would have to leave Camille. Christ. He hadn't properly considered what that would mean before now. He didn't want to leave her, not until they had accomplished the goal they had set. As soon as the thought crossed his mind, he knew that it wasn't true. He wouldn't want to leave her even then.

Fuck. Was it already too late for him?

The door to his study opened and closed, and he held the papers against his chest as Christian and Evan came into the corridor.

"Everything good?" Christian asked, correctly interpreting the conflicted look Jacob was certain was reflected on his face.

He nodded. "Fine." He'd have to tell them now. It wasn't a task he'd been looking forward to with any sort of joy. They were likely to feel left out or even hurt, so tonight wasn't the time. Christian deserved a night to celebrate without complications. "Let's go downstairs to throw some dice." He left the contract on his desk and followed them.

Unfortunately, he hadn't anticipated Turner's arrival later that evening. He was walking back to join the small group after seeing to an issue with the kitchen, when Christian and Evan met him in the corridor outside the main gaming room. He could tell from their closed expressions that something was wrong.

"What happened?" he asked.

"Turner's in there. The braggart came over and started talking about how he finally got in on an investment with you. He regretted that we hadn't joined you, but he figured it was for the best," Evan said.

Christian raked a hand through his hair. "What the bloody hell is he talking about?"

Jacob held up his hands in a call for calm. "Let's go to my office and discuss this. Turner was supposed to keep his mouth shut." The contract wasn't even signed yet. Though as soon as he said that he realized he made the situation worse.

Christian walked beside him stiffly and Evan took up the rear, neither of them talking.

Opening the door, he invited them to sit while he leaned on the corner of his desk and picked up the contract. As he spoke, he held it out to them. Evan was the first to take it. "I am planning to open a club in Paris with Pierre Blanchet." They had both met the Frenchman when he had come to London on an earlier visit.

"Paris?" Evan asked, his brow raised and his voice measured. Though his expression was stern, he seemed more inquisitive than Christian. "This is sudden."

"No, it's not. We've been discussing it since the summer." A muscle in Christian's jaw worked, and Jacob cursed himself for his word choice. For someone who generally always knew what to say, he was doing a poor job of it now. "Blanchet has an idea for a new type of club, and I believe it's a good one." He went through the basic idea of what a cabaret club was and how it would be different from the typical offerings found in Paris. Evan asked several pointed questions about the details before Jacob added, "I plan to go in as a partner with him."

"There's no doubt it's an interesting concept," said Evan. "What sort of partnership will you have? Not fifty-fifty?"

"No, we found it necessary to take on a third investor. It isn't feasible for me to take out my assets in Montague Club, and I don't intend to drain my liquid assets completely for the venture. We will each hold an equal one-third share."

"With Turner being the third." This was the first thing Christian had said since they walked into the room. His voice was low and tinged with an edge of bitterness.

"This sounds like you'll be in Paris for the foreseeable future," Evan added.

"If all goes to plan, I'll be in Paris for much of the next several months. We hope to open in April. Blanchet will see to the day-to-day of things once we get it running. I will hire and oversee the entertainment."

"You'll be moving to Paris." It wasn't a question and was filled with his brother's displeasure. "What about Montague?"

Montague wasn't the problem. Although Evan had sold most of his shares back to them after getting married, he was still nominally involved. Christian spent much of his time there, and Cavell had proven himself capable of running the daily activities.

"For a time, but not permanently. Montague will continue to be my primary focus and home. I'd never give it up. If all goes well, I will stay in Paris for a few weeks at a time throughout the year."

"I don't understand the impetus for this. It seems as if it could require a lot of your time and it's a huge risk," Evan said. His tone continued to be measured as he handed the contract to Christian, who accepted it but didn't glance down at it.

"So was this in the beginning." Jacob raised his hands, indicating Montague Club. "We didn't know if we'd earn enough in the ensuing years to support ourselves, but we have earned more than enough. I am comfortable and I wanted a new challenge."

"A new challenge? What's wrong with enjoying what we have here?" Christian asked.

"There's nothing wrong with it, but I wanted something new, something I had achieved on my own."

"What does that mean?" Christian asked.

"It means that my whole life I've had my father's money to live on. I have had both of your titles"—he indicated Evan—"to lend influence to Montague Club. I want to prove that I can make something on my own." This wasn't going quite as well as he had hoped.

"Is this why you went to an investor instead of coming to me?" Evan asked with a fair bit of hurt in his voice. As the owner of a newly inherited mine in Montana Territory, he had access to more cash than anyone Jacob knew. He would have been an ideal investor except for the fact that Jacob wanted to do this without him.

"Yes. It's not that I do not want you involved. It's more that I need to do this for myself."

"You could have told me." Christian's voice was rough

with anger or frustration or some blend of the two. "You could have come to me—to us—back in the summer when you started this and let us know, but we had to find out from Turner."

Turner and his brother weren't enemies by any stretch of the imagination, but the businessman's crude nature rubbed Christian the wrong way while Jacob rather thought his cunning would aid in the business venture. While not enemies, they would never be friends. It was likely why Turner had gone to him the second the final contract had been produced, to arrogantly proclaim that he had finally obtained his prize despite Christian believing he wasn't good enough.

"You're right. I could have. Perhaps I should have, but I am telling you now. I only received the final contract earlier tonight."

That didn't help, either. Christian's jaw clenched as he realized that was what Cavell had brought to him. "I didn't want to tell you then because I knew you'd react this way and I didn't want to spoil the evening."

"You mean you knew I wouldn't appreciate your betrayal?"

Jacob took a breath in through his nose to keep at bay the anger that was beginning to stir in him. "It's not a betrayal."

"You could have told me."

"Yes, I could have, and perhaps I should have, but it's not a betrayal to want something for myself."

Christian sat back, digesting the bit of news.

"Christian, I know you see me as some sort of favored son, but that's not how it was." Whenever there was friction between them it always went back to his brother's idealized view of Jacob's life.

Christian gave a bitter laugh. "That's exactly how it was."

"No. Father tolerated me because he wanted my mother.

Like you, my birth wasn't arranged. I was a mistake. He wanted my mother *despite* me. They had more children because Mama wanted more children. He knew that to keep her, he had to give her the family *she* wanted. Our family life was never like what you and Violet have created."

"What does that bloody well have to do with any of this?"

Jacob shook his head, angry that his own brother wasn't understanding. "I've spent my entire life living in the shadows. I was never the heir."

"You never wanted the earldom." Christian said it in such an accusatory way that he was momentarily taken aback.

"No, I didn't want that. I don't want that, but that doesn't mean there wasn't a cost to being the bastard. People know you, but they usually only whisper my name. They might disapprove of your mother, but they look upon mine as a literal whore. She was the best woman I have ever known but she doesn't get any credit for that. People whisper that I only have this"—he again raised his hand to encompass the entirety of Montague Club—"because of my association with you. If ever they want to besmirch my name, I get called the by-blow in public." He still regretted not laying Scarbury low because of that one.

"Is that why you're doing this? Because people talk and you need to prove them wrong?" Christian raised a brow.

Jacob stood. "Don't reduce this to some misplaced sense of inferiority. I have lived my life knowing what people say about me and my family. It's that, but it's more. My entire life has taken place within the walls of this building. I want to see what more is out there."

Evan stood slowly and held out his hands palms up. "Let's step away for a moment."

"Good idea. I need some air, anyway."

Jacob left the room filled with a frustrated anger he hadn't felt in a very long time. He had known they wouldn't be pleased, but he thought they would at least find a way to be happy for him. Christian knew his weakness and knew where to strike to make it hurt the most.

Damn him!

In fact, Christian knew him better than anyone. Even better than his sisters, because as they had grown up and found their own lives, his brother had been here with him. Their business venture along with how Christian had found his way to his wife had drawn them together. He should have understood Jacob's need to find his own way.

Sticking to the corridors, he found Webb discussing the finer points of serving a whisky with one of the footmen in the servants' dining room. "Inform Cavell I'll be in the gymnasium for the next couple of hours." Pounding out his frustrations on sandbags would be better than pounding on his brother, which is what he really wanted to do.

Camille smoothed down the lapel of her coat as she hurried inside the open front doors of the Hanover Square house. A large banner had been stretched across the front of the building with the words *London Suffrage Society Meeting* written on it. Even though the meeting should be starting now, carriages were still lined up outside to drop off their passengers. Victoria Woodhull was scheduled to speak tonight, and she could only assume that was the reason for the excitement. She was a celebrity of sorts. Lilian had assured her they only had around one hundred people attend their regular meetings. Yet, the hall was already packed.

Camille was despairing of ever finding Lilian in the crowd or even a place to sit when she heard her name being called.

"Camille!" Lilian's high and pleasant voice cut through the group of people to Camille's right.

"I am so happy you came. I wasn't sure you would." Her smile lit her entire face as she took Camille's hands.

"I admit I dithered a bit, but here I am."

"You won't regret coming." Lilian took her arm and led her down the aisle between the rows of seats toward the front of the large space. A high stage dominated the head of the room with a single podium and several chairs set off to the side of it. "I saved us seats in the first row just in case you came."

The front row was filled except for two seats near the aisle where pamphlets had been placed and Lilian's coat had been draped over one of the chairs. Several women who were already seated rose at their approach.

Smiling proudly, Lilian said, "I would like you to meet several women important to our organization."

Over the next couple of minutes she was introduced to the officers who oversaw the LSS. The women greeted her warmly and welcomed her to the meeting amidst comments like, "Mrs. Greene tells us you have a special interest in women's suffrage" and "Let's arrange a meeting to discuss your unique insight."

Camille nodded and murmured her assent, but the truth was she didn't think she had any particular insight to offer them. She still wasn't certain she agreed with Jacob's assessment of her situation and the term *abuse*, but she was certain that she wasn't ready to share her experience with anyone, particularly strangers, even if it was for a good cause. It was too intimate, and she felt like such a fool having not been able to change her circumstances.

Finally, a chime sounded and a familiar-looking woman with a regal bearing walked up the steps to the stage. Her hair was threaded with silver and she walked with purpose. Standing behind the podium, she introduced herself as Lady Anna Gore-Langton. Then she spoke a bit about how much women's suffrage meant to her and her husband, who was a member of Parliament. Camille had met her only once but hadn't realized her level of involvement in the cause. She was the rare daughter of a duke who would lend her name to women's suffrage. At the end of her short speech, she introduced Mrs. Woodhull to much applause.

Mrs. Woodhull was a handsome woman in her forties with dark hair and a calm manner. She stood tall and confident as she looked over the audience before gesturing for quiet. When she spoke, her voice rang out loud and clear, as she went through her time running for president and her address to Congress. But it was when she talked about her peculiar ideas regarding marriage that Camille truly began to pay attention, as did the rest of the hall. Silence descended as she spoke.

"The marriage law is the most damnable Social Evil bill—the most consummate outrage on women—that was ever conceived. Those who are called prostitutes, whom these bills assume to regulate, are free women, sexually, when compared to the slavery of the poor wife. They are at liberty, at least to refuse; but she knows no such escape. 'Wives, submit yourselves to your husbands' is the spirit and the universal practice of marriage.

"Of all the horrid brutalities of this age, I know of none so horrid as those that are sanctioned and defended by marriage. Night after night there are thousands of rapes committed, under cover of this accursed license; and millions—yes, I say it boldly, knowing whereof I speak— millions of poor, heartbroken, suffering wives are compelled to minister to the lechery of insatiable husbands, when every instinct of body and sentiment of soul revolts in loathing and disgust. All married persons know this is truth, although they may feign to shut their eyes and ears to the horrid thing, and pretend to believe it is not. The world has got to be startled from this pretense into realizing that there is nothing else now existing among pretendedly enlightened nations, except marriage, that invests men with the right to debauch women sexually against their wills. Yet marriage is held to be synonymous with morality! I say, eternal damnation sink such morality!"

Mrs. Woodhull paused only long enough to catch her breath before she launched into her ideas of marriage agreements and how they should be free from involvement and influence of all parties except the two people entering into the marriage. Camille couldn't help but think how that statement was grossly at odds with her own parents and all of Society who believed it was their mission to arrange alliances through marriage.

She tried to listen to the rest of the speech, but her mind kept returning to Mrs. Woodhull's earlier words.

Anger, cold and hot, prickled its way down her spine, making her skin feel tight against her bones and uncomfortable. And just like that night with Jacob, she didn't know with whom she was angry. The emotion was simply there. She was *not* Hereford's victim. She could *not* be a victim. It was such a diminishing word.

And yet, as the woman's melodious voice spoke about the importance of voting and power, Camille could not help but remember how powerless he had made her feel. That feeling was so strong that she wanted to get up and leave rather than remember it. But she couldn't leave without drawing attention to herself, so she made herself listen to the woman speak. Camille had noticed that when she felt overwhelmed with her memories, she could take a deep breath and force her mind to whatever was happening in the present. That meant she noticed the brown coil of Mrs. Woodhull's hair, shining and tinged with yellow under the gaslight. She took in the smell of wool from the winter coats around her and the light scent of Lilian's perfume, something floral she couldn't place. It was enough to settle her until an enthusiastic round of applause brought her attention to the sounds in the room.

Lilian rose, and Camille thought it would be for a standing ovation, but she left her seat, hurrying toward the stage. A man there in the shadows offered his hand to help her up the stairs, and a tender look crossed Lilian's face. That must be Mr. Greene. She craned her neck, trying to get a better look at him, but she saw only his gloved hand guiding Lilian up the steps. After, he faded into the standing-room-only crowd and Lilian moved to the front of the stage.

"Good evening. Many of you know me, but for those new to our meeting, I am Mrs. Lilian Greene." She didn't introduce herself as Mrs. Anthony Greene, Camille noticed. A round of applause followed. "On behalf of the London Suffrage Society I thank Mrs. Woodhull for speaking with us tonight. Her experience in women's rights and her persecution for her beliefs should be an inspiration to all of us. Change is never easy, and it is usually uncomfortable, but it is always necessary to make ourselves better. We cannot afford to be comfortable when there are young women in our society who do not have security, who cannot see their homes as a safe place, because those who are charged with their care abuse their power. As women, we are human. We are citizens. We deserve the right and the opportunity to take charge of our own lives." Her gaze met Camille's before passing on.

"Please donate if you can, but if you cannot we value the donation of your time as much. We need people to join our demonstrations, to pass out pamphlets, and to talk to those who can be influenced to our cause. Every woman deserves the right to have her voice counted by those in power. Every woman deserves the right to run for office. They cannot silence us if we all stand together. Help us get to that glorious future."

Applause made her pause. "Our next crucial step in this mission is to pass the Married Women's Property Act to ensure that marriage no longer steals the assets of women. It is vital to our ability to secure suffrage for women, and it won't come easy. Every woman should retain her voice and personhood in marriage. We will be meeting outside Parliament in a fortnight. Join us there so we can make certain they hear our voices."

Applause filled the room again. Camille clapped along with them. She would not allow herself to ever feel powerless again. The only real way to ensure that was to make certain women had a say in their government. As the crowd moved around her, standing to speak to friends, hurrying forward to talk to Lilian as her husband helped her from the stage, lining up to have a word with Mrs. Woodhull, Camille sat and let the words of the night move over her. For the first time in a long time the heaviness inside her eased. Where before the idea of women's suffrage had seemed important but out of the sphere of her reality, she now understood how important it was as a stepping-stone in gaining control of her life. Jacob had been right when he had approached their lessons with the idea of giving her control. It was the only way she could truly feel comfortable and in her own power. It wasn't about domination or submission; it was about equality. That was the one thing Jacob had given her that life never had. Suddenly, she wished he was here, because she wanted to share this night—this realization—with him.

Chapter 17

❦

Jacob's mother had loved to host grand balls to celebrate special moments in their lives. High Society never attended them, but those outside of proper Society—the mistresses of lords, businessmen, entertainers, and those eager to rub elbows with the earl—were always keen to attend. There was always a winter ball around Christmastime and, occasionally, a second one held later in the year. Perhaps their infrequency is what made them special. The first ball he attended was in honor of his father's birthday. Mama had deemed him old enough to participate, but only for the first half hour. Jacob hadn't cared that he'd had to leave before the dancing started. It had been long enough for him to see his parents in all their finery and to experience the magic that was the lit grand chandelier that hung in the center of the room. The crystals had sparkled as if each one contained a fairy. When he had relayed the information to Lilian, she had insisted they find out for sure and free them. Very early the next morning they had snuck into the room to discover the chandelier dark with all the candles removed. She had been disappointed, and so had Jacob although he hadn't dared admit he actually *thought* fairies could exist.

There hadn't been a ball here since his father had died. Mama had closed the room and never expressed interest in entertaining again. When Jacob, Christian, and Evan had decided to add a gymnasium to the club's offerings, the ballroom had seemed the perfect place. It was large and the high ceilings could accommodate the various apparatuses needed for exercise. They had installed many pieces of equipment, each with a focus on developing the muscular structure of a different body part. For the legs, there were several machines that allowed for leg lifts and repetitions. For the abdominal area, there was a machine for rowing as well as one that featured an incline with cables and pulleys. For the arms, there were standing machines with straps for pulling, which lifted weights from the floor, and a wall hung with slats and bars for climbing. Near the roped-off area that housed the exhibition fights, there was an area with burlap sacks stuffed with varying amounts of sand hanging from the ceiling.

The original crystal chandelier overlooked it all, because he hadn't been able to part with it or have it moved to another area of the house, even though he had no interest in hosting elaborate balls here. They only lit it on fight nights, so the candles were dark now, the room lit with gaslight sconces as Jacob swung at the heaviest sandbag, needing to feel the solid resistance against his fists. Anger and frustration drove each and every punch, vibrating the bag. He was only just starting to work up a sweat, which meant he'd be here for a while longer, at least until the urge to replace the bag with Christian faded. He still couldn't believe how terribly the conversation with them had gone. Thankfully, they hadn't followed him to the gymnasium.

"Jacob!"

He swung around to see Camille hurrying into the room from a side door that led to a corridor. It was an entrance usually only used by servants, as members generally came and went through the tall double doors that were the main entrance.

"Camille? What are you doing here?" Through the fog of his lingering frustration, he noticed that her face was very nearly euphoric. Her smile was brighter than he had ever seen it, and her eyes were lit with what might be joy. The anger raging within him smoldered, dampened the tiniest bit by her happiness.

He hadn't seen her in days, and the effect she had on him was palpable. He felt her arrival in the tightening of his muscles, every sinew primed toward her presence. A wave of tenderness threatened to overwhelm him as he focused on her joy.

"I had the most amazing evening and so I came straight over to tell you about it."

The shock of her arrival stemming somewhat, he glanced around the room to make certain no one else had come in since he'd last noticed. They were alone, which made sense because it was late. "Women aren't allowed here."

"I know." But she smiled proudly and skirted the rowing apparatus before coming to a stop before him. "Mr. Kostas very helpfully informed me of that as I attempted to use the main entrance. That's why I had to come in through the side door."

He chuckled despite himself. "You should go."

"You should allow women the opportunity to better themselves through physical activity." She tossed the words out with a playful confidence that had them landing softly.

"We have a gymnasium for women."

"True, but it's rather small and doesn't have half of this equipment nor does it contain a fighting ring." She indicated the roped-off section that took up almost a quarter of the room.

"Have you come to tell me that my female members want to take up bare-knuckle brawling?" he asked, wiping his wrist across the beads of sweat gathered at his hairline and turning back to the sandbag.

"No," she said easily, walking to stand on the other side of the bag to keep her gaze on his face. "Actually, I have no idea. They very well might want that, but separate quarters isn't equality, and I thought it was worth mentioning."

Her smile lingered as he took a swing, a rush of energy coursing through him when her attention dropped to his shoulders and then lower. He had taken off everything except his trousers in order to avoid rips and the inevitable sweat stains on his shirtsleeves. While the impropriety of the situation should someone come in played a warning in the back of his mind, he quite liked her attention on him.

"Noted. However, I already received a nasty letter from the Society Against Women's Suffrage when we allowed female members. This might just push them over the edge and lead to picketing outside."

She chuckled and a little more tension released from his shoulders. "Doing the right thing will never meet with full approval. It's a lesson I'm learning, which is why I'm here."

"Is that why you're so happy?" he asked, hitting the bag in a swift double punch. "That someone will find fault with you no matter what you do? Thank you for sharing, but I am well aware of that." Enough frustration lingered that he still imagined the bag to be his brother. He should have demanded they fight things out in the ring like they had done in the past.

"I'm getting to the good news, but your surliness is putting a damper on things. What's the matter?" A little furrow emerged on her forehead.

He shook his head, disappointed that he had made it appear when before she had been so pleased with whatever it was that had sent her here. "Never mind," he said, taking another swing.

"Something has happened to upset you." She stepped forward and gingerly took the bag between her hands, forcing him to stand back. "Tell me. Please?"

"I finalized the contract with Turner." It was only as he was saying those words to her, as he watched the emotions play across her face—happiness, uncertainty, melancholy, and then happiness again—that he understood some of his terrible mood was because of that. Because a contract meant stopping this arrangement with her and leaving her behind. The momentary sadness on her face meant that she realized that, too.

"I thought that was a happy occasion. Shouldn't I tell you congratulations?"

His chest felt tight, so he forced a breath and nodded. "It will take a few days yet to arrange the financing and everything here at the club, but yes."

"Congratulations. Now tell me why that is a problem."

Her prodding smile was nearly his undoing, and he found himself opening up without even meaning to. "Unfortunately, Turner told Christian and Evan about it before I could and they didn't take the news well."

"Why not? It's a grand idea for a club. I even plan to attend myself."

He couldn't bear the way she was looking at him. Her eyes were wide and concerned, the liquid brown shimmering with amber, like deep pools of gold. They had the power to turn the anger he felt into something raw and aching, forcing him to look away from them to catch his breath.

"Evan was upset I didn't come to him for the investment. Christian doesn't understand why I want to do this. Why I *need* to do this. They both saw it as some sort of disloyalty to Montague Club or disloyalty to them."

She put her hand on his arm, and he was so wound up from battling his anger, frustration, and the sandbag that the feeling was amplified by what felt like a hundred percent. His muscle rippled under the effect, prompting her to smooth her palm over his bicep and squeeze him gently. When she spoke, his gaze went to her mouth, his body craving an entirely different sort of comfort from her.

"Did you tell them why you need to do this?"

"Yes, but they don't understand how I could feel as if I've lived my life in the shadows. According to Christian, my life is charmed and I should enjoy it, never wanting anything more." He couldn't keep the bitter edge from his voice.

"I am certain it's more that they're hurt than that they cannot understand you. For years it's been you and them against everyone else, hasn't it? I'd wager not many people believed Montague Club stood a chance against so many alternatives in London. You can't turn a corner in this city without some pompous entertainment or bawdy establishment trying to part a man from his coin."

He laughed despite the ache in his chest, then he said, "You would win that particular wager. We did it because we needed the income, in spite of the many who believed we would fail."

"Of course you did. It's only natural that the three of you would become a single unit working together. Now you are trying to break it all apart and they are resistant to it." Her words were very reasonable, but he still felt frustrated that they were not more supportive.

"It is not my intention to break anything. I want Montague Club to continue. I *want* to continue our partnership. I simply want this for myself. I'm almost thirty. I need to prove to myself that I can do successful things without them." He didn't like the way that desire made him feel like a child.

"I know that you do, and it's a perfectly understandable need. You want to be seen as your own person and step out from under the shadow of your late father and your brother the earl."

He stared down at her in awe. "How can you understand

me so well when they cannot? I've known them for the majority of my life."

She shrugged and gave him a shy smile. Her hand dropped to his forearm, and he noticed she made no move to stop touching him. He liked that very much and found himself turning toward her touch. "You're not difficult to understand, Jacob. Not to me. Besides, in many ways I feel the same. I don't want to be Camille of Hereford. I want to be known for myself, not the poor rich girl who was married off because her family wanted stature more than they cared for her." She paused and breathed in through her nose, gathering herself before she spoke again. "I don't want to be pitied as the girl who suffered abuse."

There was that word. He had witnessed her response to it during their talk. It was accurate but it didn't sit right with her.

Her statement was said lightly, but that couldn't disguise the very real pain laced within its words. He couldn't have stopped himself from taking her into his arms if he had wanted to. He took her head between his hands wrapped in cotton batting and let his thumb stroke her cheek. "You are very much not that to me, Camille. I see who you really are."

She smiled. "I know that you do. That's why I came to tell you my good news first."

He returned her smile without even trying. "Then what is this happy news? I apologize for making you listen to my grumbling."

"I don't mind." She stared into his eyes, and the current that moved between them was so powerful he had trouble taking a breath. "I came to tell you that I went to the suffrage meeting that Lilian invited me to attend, and I heard Victoria Woodhull speak. She's the woman who ran for president in America. I was very much inspired by what she said, what they all said, really, and I intend to participate."

The enthusiasm in her eyes was unmistakable. "I am glad you went."

"This is the first thing I've felt excited about in a very long time. I believe that I could help make a real difference in the lives of women."

"You already do that with your work at the London Home, but I agree, this could be another way to help."

She smiled and his thumb drifted to the corner of her mouth, loath to stop touching her. "You're right, and I enjoy my work there." She took a breath and her bottom lip quivered ever so lightly. "But with this I feel as if I can stop other matches like mine. I can make certain that women aren't sold for status or money or the million other reasons families arrange marriages. If women are allowed to vote, then they'll be allowed to work, to divorce, to *not* marry for financial support, and with that comes freedom. True freedom. It means they can walk away from marriages that aren't working more easily."

Pain had crept in to mar her happiness, and he couldn't take the way it crushed her smile. It made the ache in his chest and throat almost too much to bear. Closing his eyes, he kissed her forehead. It was supposed to be a gentle thing of encouragement and support. A perfectly chaste symbol of his affection, but somehow he found his way to her mouth, and she was kissing him back and clinging to him with her fingers in his hair.

He released her as soon as he realized what was happening. This was not the time for sex. Yet, he couldn't bring himself to actually step away from her. His hand lingered on her waist. "I'm happy you have found something that is yours."

"Like you," she whispered.

He wasn't prepared for the way his heart leaped at her words or the way he loved how they sounded. Her need for him was a balm to a wound he didn't know he had. She easily filled all the tiny crevices in his heart. By God, he could fall in love with her so easily.

The thought went through him like the blast from a gun

and propelled him backward. His hand slid from her hip. This was becoming too real. He had felt it the other night when he had very stupidly tried to tempt her to spend the entire night with him. This could so easily traverse the ground from friendship to something more that he was momentarily breathless. It didn't help that she only followed him, stepping forward to close the distance between them as if unaware of the crisis taking place inside him. Even his heart seemed to stop when she pressed her hand to his chest.

"I like kissing you." There was no artifice about her. This was less a flirtation than an honest statement of fact. "Could we do that some more?"

God, yes. He wanted to devour her. His good sense took over and he forced himself to check the room again to make certain no one had crept in while he'd been occupied with her. It also gave him time to manage the emotions she evoked without even trying. "Someone may come in here, and we must have a care for your reputation. In fact, you should leave before that happens."

She didn't seem dissuaded. "Not here, then. Somewhere private. I'd like to try again." Her eyes were hesitant but hopeful.

He immediately went rigid with desire. Every good reason he had for turning her away fled and he was left with nothing but need. She had too much power over him. Even as he told himself this, he knew he would not turn her away. A single touch of her finger was enough to have him abandoning all self-preservation. All except for one minor thing.

"We can't go to my room tonight." Having her there would make whatever he was feeling for her even worse. He couldn't afford to have a repeat of the other night, and that would happen if she was in his space. She frowned in response, but he hurried on. "There is another room."

Her eyes widened as understanding dawned. *"The* room?"

"Remember how I told you that I have an idea? I believe it might help you step out of your head, but it will only work if you trust me."

"I trust you, Jacob." She agreed so fast that it took his breath away.

He watched almost as if he was outside his body as she reached for his hand. With slow and gentle movements, she unwrapped the cotton batting from his fingers and then his palm. The length of fabric fell to the floor unnoticed. She traced the lines on his palm, making the fine hairs on his body stand on end in pleasure.

"If there is anything I know, it's that you won't hurt me," she said, her eyes threatening to swallow him whole.

Christ, he hoped that was true.

Chapter 18

❦

Camille's heart pounded a fierce rhythm as Jacob led her through the back corridors of Montague Club. He was still in his fighting outfit, trousers and boots, but he had donned a black robe. It wasn't attire that he could be seen wearing wandering around the club, which is why she assumed they were taking the servants' route. They passed a footman and a woman wearing the apron of kitchen staff, but the twists and turns of the corridor were otherwise empty.

He made certain not to touch her, however. He had reached for her hand the second they had entered the hallway only to stop himself before making contact. She assumed it was because he was attempting to preserve her reputation, as if both servants they passed weren't aware they were alone together or the reason. Still, she humored him and made no move to get closer to him, even though she wanted to touch him. She did trust him, but she also needed the reassurance of his arms.

Something was different about him tonight. She had only ever seen him with his charming exterior firmly in place. She had long suspected that it was a shield of some sort to keep people at length, and a very large part of her was glad to get a glimpse behind it to the real man beneath. But a very tiny part of her, one that she was trying to overcome, was a bit apprehensive.

Each twist of the corridor seemed to make her heart beat faster. She hadn't intended sex tonight. She had simply been so overcome with excitement that she had wanted to share it with someone and he was the first person who came to mind. He would understand how she felt and why it was important for her. The idea of sex had seemed like a natural extension of that celebration, which was odd because sex had never been that for her. It had never been anything but an obligation before Jacob had showed her what was possible. Taking their joyfulness to something more intimate had seemed natural.

Now her heart was pounding in her ears when he stopped before a plain, white-lacquered door. There was nothing remarkable about it, except that it was at the end of the hall. He gave her a measured look that seemed to gauge for resistance, before turning the key in the lock and pushing it open.

The room beyond was dimly lit with a single sconce throwing pale yellow light over half the room. A large piece of furniture that appeared to be a round bed took up the center of the room. It was so large that she could have easily curled herself into the lush cushions for a night of sleep, although Jacob's feet might hang off the side. She really didn't think it was used for sleeping, however. It was covered with a simple white sheet, with a pile of pillows in the middle. Aside from that the room was mostly bare. There was no window and each of the four walls held a large gilt-framed mirror.

"This is *that* room?"

"Yes."

"Really? I admit I'm disappointed. I had expected . . ." What had she expected? She didn't know enough to anticipate the various apparatuses that one might need for adventurous sexual encounters, but she had imagined there would be more than a bed and mirrors.

"There are other items available if one chooses to use them, but I thought we might hold off on those." A smile was in his voice, as his hand on her back gently guided her into the room.

She was only dimly aware of the click of the door closing behind her and the turn of the lock. He put the key in the pocket of his robe. Intrigued by the *other items*, she took a tour of the room in search of what he meant. Now that her eyes had adjusted to the lighting, she could see the walls were covered in a blue velvet so dark that it was very nearly black. It appeared soft and luxurious, drawing her hand as she made her way around the room. There were other details she had originally missed. Leather cuffs hung from a knob near the ceiling on the far side of the room, while another wall was empty save for a series of pegs where she assumed various accoutrements were supposed to go.

It wasn't until one wall gave way to her prodding that she realized it was drapery. Perhaps there was more to this room than met the eye. She shivered as she let her hand guide her to the center parting where she peered inside. It was another room roughly the same size as the one with the bed, but the light barely penetrated enough for her to be certain. There were various pieces of furniture outlined in shadow and looking nothing like typical furniture. The one nearest her could best be described as an upholstered wedge—too high and too narrow for sitting upon—perhaps best meant for leaning. She turned her head to the side, wondering if a different angle would give it proper perspective. A person could be leaned over it with someone else behind them, she realized.

"Why are we here?" She drew the curtains back together and her entire body tightened, stuck in a strange place between preparing to run and anticipation. She focused on the latter. He had said they would not be using the other items.

He was right behind her when he spoke, having followed her journey around the space. "Nothing will happen here that you don't want." He waited for her to nod in acknowledgment before he continued. "We are here because the mirrors could be of use to us."

The mirrors were close to the bed, less than a few feet away, so that anyone lying there could reach out and touch them. There would be no way to avoid seeing what was happening on that bed. Her face warmed as she realized what that meant. "You mean to watch us?"

He shook his head and slowly traversed the few feet that separated them as if he anticipated that she might run. It made her feel like prey, like maybe she *should* run. Except, the fact that *he* was the one who would be chasing her sent a delicious shiver running through her. Wanting him was very confusing. She forced herself to stand still, and when he was close enough she took in a deep breath, pulling in the scent of his cologne and clean male sweat. How did he manage to smell so good?

"No, Camille, I mean for *you* to watch." His breath tickled the hair at her temple.

Her instinct was to say absolutely not. It would certainly be an indignity. But then she thought of how she had felt in the seconds after she had entered the gymnasium but before he had noticed her. Watching him move, his muscles shifting and bunching beneath the silk of his skin, had made her feel both warm and soft inside. A feeling she was coming to associate with being alone with him. Mirrors meant that she would have an unrestricted view of his beauty. Perhaps mirrors would be acceptable.

She stepped forward the half step it took to reach him and pressed herself against his chest. His arms immediately came up around her, calming the disquiet inside her. She closed her eyes as his palm moved up and down her spine in a soothing caress.

"Do you believe that will help?" she asked.

"Yes. I've been thinking of what we could try next," he said.

"You've been thinking about us?" Had he been thinking about them as much as she had? He was in her thoughts almost constantly. She closed her eyes as she imagined him going about his day all the while contemplating what he could do to help her overcome her reticence. She could hardly breathe past the tenderness that settled in her throat.

"Of course," he whispered. "I decided that I needed to find a way to get you out of your own head. Watching will accomplish that."

She turned in his arms and stared at their reflection in one of the mirrors. He towered over her by almost a head, and his wide shoulders were broader than her own slender frame. He was the most physically powerful man she had ever been intimate with, but he was also the most gentle and caring. She trusted him implicitly, but even more than that, she genuinely liked him. How could he be leaving so soon? She would miss him so much.

Despite the sad thought, she smiled. Had it only been weeks ago that she had wondered if she'd ever allow herself to be open with any man? But now? In this room with him looking at her as if he couldn't get enough of her? Now her growing feelings for him seemed right and inevitable.

Her gaze caught on the tilt of her lips, moving upward to her eyes. They glittered with joy despite the dredges of her lingering fear, almost sparkling in a way she hadn't seen in years. Gone was the dull glaze she detested. Jacob had helped to bring about that change in her and she would be forever grateful to him for that. If he wanted to try this because he believed it would help, then she would.

His hands moved up and down her arms in a lazy caress,

his fingers strong and tapered. He was giving her time to become accustomed to what was happening. Her heart twisted in gratitude. Noting the cut on the knuckle of his right hand, she took hold of it and brought it to her mouth. He let her kiss him there while his other hand worked slowly at the row of buttons down her back. Ingram, who had so diligently helped her fasten them, would wonder why she hadn't come home, but Camille couldn't bring herself to care that her servants might suspect anything.

The gown loosened in phases, the navy silk draping further from her shoulders as he made his way to her waist. She let his other hand go only when it was necessary for him to use it on the intricate buttons and clasps at her lower back. His eyes were afire when he looked up from the task and met her gaze in the mirror, his hands pushing the material down and off her arms to reveal her corset, chemise, and petticoats.

Anticipation leaped inside her. For the first time in her life she reveled in the idea that a man would see her nude. That he would like gazing upon her. She couldn't look away from him as he bent his head to the task of untying the bustle and skirt, letting it pool at her feet. She tried not to notice how adept he was at undressing her, but jealousy lingered at the perimeter of her consciousness, putting a fine edge on her arousal. Next, he unfastened her corset. The jerks and starts as he loosened it, the clink of metal as hook met eye, the swish of the silk-covered cord pulling free, made desire coil tight in her stomach.

He pushed the steel-lined contraption to the floor, and her body heaved a sigh of relief and freedom that he seemed to instinctively understand. His mouth found the side of her neck as his hands soothed her, moving up her hips and rib cage to palm her breasts. He grasped them in a gentle massage that had her pressing back into him. He was already very hard, and she wished that she was normal—that she could lean forward, kneel on the bed, and receive him all at once—but she wasn't. Even thinking of having him inside her twisted the arousal she felt into something scary. What if she could never feel the pleasure that she knew other women felt?

"Watch us," he whispered as if he sensed the tension in her, his breath hot on her ear.

Her eyes shot open. She had closed them without noticing. She found the mirror, his hands molding her breasts as if he knew exactly how to touch her, the dark of her nipples peeking between his fingers pressing against her thin, white chemise. He took the swollen nubs between his thumb and forefinger, plucking gently. She let out a soft cry and pushed her bottom into him. He nudged back, bending his knees enough that the rigid shaft found softness.

She wanted to close her eyes and savor the sensation, but she didn't dare. He was right. Watching helped take her outside of her head, where all her fears waited for her. As long as she watched, she could focus on him and how good he made her feel. She liked watching his hands on her. It was a heady sight, and she found herself leaning back on him, her body feeling heavier and her legs weak. He shifted, widening his stance to support her, as he continued to play with her in a way that was unhurried and slow.

"Do you see how beautiful you are?" His voice was smoke and honey.

She nodded because she wanted to please him, and he did make her feel beautiful. But her attention was solely for him, his hands on her, his hard thighs caging hers. She would stay here all night if he asked her—a week, a year, a lifetime. The ramifications of that knowledge vibrated through her like the charge of a cannon. If she simply watched them, she wouldn't have to think of what it meant. She didn't dare close her eyes.

His right hand strayed from her breast, roaming down over her stomach to the thatch of hair at the apex of her thighs. She sucked in a harsh breath as it came to a rest, his fingers skimming over the dark shadow veiled by her chemise and drawers. Had the linen not been between them, his fingertips would have played in her curls. She had never been so disappointed at being clothed.

"Is this what you want, Camille? Do you want me to touch you here?"

She hadn't known that talking would be part of the watching. Surely he didn't mean for her to answer him, but his raised brow when she met his gaze in the mirror suggested he did.

"Yes," she whispered.

His teeth flashed in the low light as he flattened his palm against her, his fingers delving into the crevice between her thighs. She didn't dare breath as the pressure of his fingertips parted her lips, giving the pad of his longest finger access to her. She jerked a bit at the jolt of sensation that zipped through her as he worked that place in a gentle rhythm. She felt hot on the inside, melting for him. Her knees felt like jelly, forcing her to rely on him to keep her upright. His thighs braced hers, solid and hard in their strength. She loved how strong he was.

A few more soft strokes of his finger and he withdrew, his hand drifting to her hips, where he gathered the skirt of her chemise and began to pull it upward. Anticipating his intention, she held her breath when he pulled it up over her head and covered her breasts with her crossed arms. He tossed the linen garment behind him and smiled at her modesty.

"Do you not want me to see you?"

She shrugged, but so slightly that nothing came loose. Her reflection turned pink before her eyes. "You first."

He chuckled and untied the robe, letting it fall off his shoulders and to the floor. She would never get enough of looking at him. Taking hold of her hips, he encouraged her to step out of her skirts. The moment she did, while still keeping her arms across her chest, he pushed the pile of clothing aside with his foot. Then he stepped around her to take a seat on the edge of the bed before pulling her to stand between his knees. He still wore his trousers, which she supposed was only fair since she still had on her drawers. She couldn't help but feel let down, though, that he hadn't undressed completely.

"You can cover yourself all you want," he whispered, his hot breath sending goose bumps over her skin. "But I can't properly taste your nipple until you feed me one."

She didn't know what to say to that. It turned out he didn't expect an answer. Instead, he set about kissing her chest. The hot, openmouthed caresses had her gaze finding them in the mirror directly across from them. His broad shoulders hid most of her, so she watched the muscle ripple under his skin as his hands moved around her body to fill themselves with the flesh of her bottom. She still wore her drawers, their only adornment a sapphire-colored ribbon tied below each knee. They were thin and she knew he could see the dark blond patch of hair in the shadow of her thighs, but he didn't seem to be looking at her there. He was entirely focused on her breasts. Releasing her breath, she let her hands fall to his shoulders, revealing herself to him. He wasted no time in taking a puckered nipple between his lips, sucking deep before grazing it gently with his teeth and moving to her other one. She watched this happen in the mirror off to the side, which gave her a perfect view of him in profile. It was as if there was a direct link between his mouth, her nipple, and the pulse beating between her thighs. She closed her eyes to savor the pull of longing.

"Watch." It was an order, spoken after he let her go with a loud smacking sound.

Her eyes flew open and a sound of regret issued from her lips as he rose. She reached for him, but he shook his head.

"On the bed," he said, his voice still gentle but commanding. She loved the way he said that, as if he knew she would obey. Of course she would, but first . . .

"Only if you take off your trousers." She grinned, not bothering to cover her breasts. Her poor nipples were obscenely swollen and nearly red from his sucking, but her reticence was leaving her. Her body was his for the night and she rather liked the idea of him witnessing the evidence of all the wonderful things he did to her.

The corner of his lips quirked upward. He moved slowly, teasing her, as he worked the fastenings. He left them gaping as he leaned down and unfastened his boots, kicking them off before standing to his full height and pushing the trousers and drawers down his hips and thighs and stepping out of them. He was fully aroused, the head of his erection glistening with the fluid of his desire for her as it rose up toward his navel.

She had done that to him. God, that felt powerful.

The trail of black hair leading up to his belly gave way to a light sprinkling that became denser on his chest. He was so strong he could hold her down and do whatever he wanted, but she had never felt more safe or in control. He watched her, patiently waiting for her. Stepping toward him, she wanted to grasp his cock but touched his stomach instead. His muscles tightened beneath her. The short hairs on his chest tickled her palm, and then she was grasping the back of his neck. Standing on her toes, she pulled him down for a kiss. His mouth took hers softly at first, his hands coming down around her hips to pull her to him so thoroughly that his arousal was wedged against her stomach. She gasped at the way her body responded to that. Every limb felt weighted, and heat suffused her, making her feel swollen and overly sensitive. He took advantage of her parted lips and deepened the kiss, resulting in a fierce duel of tongues that left her breathless.

He was breathing heavily when he let her go, stepping

away to put a hand on her hip, guiding her to the bed. "On your side," he said when she would have lain on her back. The mirror on that side of the bed was only a few feet from her, so she couldn't help but look. She almost didn't recognize herself. Her face was flushed, and her eyes were dark with arousal. She saw everything through a haze of lust; her whole world had become the pounding of arousal that whooshed through her body, making every part of her ache and crave his touch.

He moved onto the bed, settling down behind her and supporting himself on an elbow. His fingertips skimmed her shoulder, her arm, her hip, leaving goose bumps in their wake. She appreciated that he was taking things slowly, but she felt restless in her need. This feeling of oversensitivity and want was new to her, and she yearned to follow it to its natural conclusion before it went away. However, she couldn't very well put voice to her needs, not yet. She took hold of the back of his hand and brought it up over her hip to cup her breast, showing him where she wanted to be touched. He squeezed gently, watching her face in the mirror for her reaction. The sight of his hand covering her in such an intimate way was almost as powerful as the tug that tightened inside her when he pinched her nipple. Satisfied with what he saw on her face, he dipped his head to kiss her neck. She loved his mouth on her and almost closed her eyes to enjoy the heady sensation but opened them again at the last second.

She hadn't released her grip on his wrist, so she guided his hand farther down her body to where he had touched her before. Leaving him there, she untied the ribbon holding her drawers closed. "Here," she whispered.

"Beneath your drawers?" His heavy gaze met hers in the mirror.

"Yes." Her voice was hardly more than a breath.

She couldn't breathe as she watched his hand disappear beneath the white linen. His fingertips dipped between her lips so much deeper than before when they were standing and he found her wet. The easy glide of his finger over her flesh told her as much. She stiffened at the first touch, but kept her eyes glued to the sight as his fingers moved in a gentle rhythm, playing peekaboo with the slit in her drawers. He found the place that was most swollen and pressed two fingers against it, rubbing in a small circle that had her hips jerking.

Just when she was settling into his rhythm he pulled away. "Don't stop."

It was no use. He had sat up and was pulling the undergarments down her legs. She shimmied out of them to help, and he tossed them off the side of the bed. His attention was focused completely on that part of her as he knelt at her feet. One hand held her calf, while the other moved up her leg to her thigh. He paused at the triangle of hair and met her gaze. The teasing and charming Jacob she knew had been replaced by this man filled with a need so great she could see how he was restraining himself. His eyes were dark and hooded with an arousal so intense it very nearly consumed him. She shivered. The tangible proof of how badly he wanted her only made her want this even more. This was when she should become afraid, and the fear was there, lurking around a corner, but God, she wanted him.

"Jacob," she said when his gaze drifted back down to the dark blond curls. "Do you want to see me?"

His eyes widened, as if he hadn't thought such a wish could be granted. "Yes." His voice was a low rumble that seemed to take an extraordinary effort.

Lying on her back, she shifted so that her other leg moved to his side. He was now kneeling between her legs. His hand tightened on her calf, maybe in a way that was almost painful, but she was so far gone in her desire for him that every touch felt as if it was sending her careening higher and higher toward some unknown precipice. The hand on her thigh slid inward, his fingertips parting her lips, touching her core. The wet sound of his touch sliding over her might have been embarrassing if she had possessed any hold over herself anymore. But she didn't, and he didn't seem to mind it. The tip of one finger dipped inside her, and it felt both foreign and exquisite at the same time, but it was gone way too soon. He brought the finger to his mouth where he licked the wetness off, his eyes closing briefly at her taste.

Too stunned to say anything, she watched as he leaned forward. Her breath stopped completely as she instinctively knew what he meant to do. He let go of her calf and rested over her, his hands holding him up on either side and his face mere inches above her hips. His eyes met hers, asking permission. He couldn't possibly mean what she thought he meant, but she rather hoped he did. She nodded and he dipped his head, inhaling audibly. He was smelling her scent and she could not be bothered to care except that it made her entire body thrum with anticipation, and then his tongue found her, dipping between her exposed folds and lapping at her.

She meant to watch but closed her eyes as the sensation became too intense. He moaned and she whimpered at the way it made her want, at the sound of his tongue slicking over her. She was a creature of want and he had made her that way. "Please."

His response was to lick her again. Then she realized she was missing the best part and turned her head to watch him in the mirror. There were no words for how he looked bent over her, lapping at her need for him. It almost looked as if he were worshipping her, and maybe he was. She certainly felt treasured.

All too soon, he moved back to his previous position, his fingers dragging down her legs as if he hated to leave her. His face was drawn and intense, almost that of a stranger's, but it only made her want him more, to know that she had changed him into this creature of need. She took in a breath, trying to find some measure of control, and forced her eyes back to the mirror as he settled behind her again, this time bringing her leg over his. The strange position opened her so that the reflection of how he touched her was clear to see. He dipped his fingertip into her and then rubbed the newly slick pad over and around her clitoris. Her hips bucked at the pleasure, arching to get more of it. He repeated the gesture several more times until she was coated with her own need, easing the rhythm of his fingers and drawing her close to an orgasm. And she had *never* felt like this, as if she might die if he didn't give her what she needed.

She groaned aloud in a way that was decidedly unattractive, but he didn't seem to mind. His lips against her ear, he said, "Watch yourself come all over my fingers."

Her eyes flew open. When had they fallen shut? She was stretched out like a wanton. His knees were between hers, holding her open, and she half lay on top of him, her head supported on his arm. One hand gripped his forearm so hard she left half-moons in his skin with her fingernails. The other held his hip as she pressed herself very rudely back against him, her hips arching and writhing as she chased his touch. She realized she was seeking his arousal. Her hips moved, trying to get her closer to the length of his shaft, which was pressed against her buttock.

She didn't want to come on his fingers. She wanted to come on *him*. She wanted him inside her, easing the ache with his size. A flicker rippled through her belly, tightening that coil of need and promising the end was near. She needed him right now. If she angled herself, she could almost reach him.

She sighed aloud when the shift of position freed him, the hot length of him pressed against her inner thigh. On the next sway of her hips, his hardness rubbed against her core making her groan as it almost but not quite assuaged her need. Her body clenched desperately.

"Not your fingers." She covered his hand with hers, her hips shifting of their own volition, seeking him.

He let out a groan that sounded like it had been pulled from deep in his chest. "Camille." His hands tightened on her hips and he buried his face in her hair, pressing his lips to her cheek. He was nearly as gone as she was.

"I want you, Jacob."

Another harsh sound escaped his chest. "This is about you, not me." The words were uneven and tinged with a plea she didn't understand.

Turning her head, she took his mouth. The kiss was messy and frenzied and quite possibly the most honest one she had ever given. "I want you inside me."

He moved his hips, thrusting against her. She watched in the mirror, mesmerized by the sight of his cock sliding over her. His breath was harsh against her cheek, and his body shuddered against her back. He was trembling. His powerful body was actually trembling with his desire for her.

"Guide me in," he ordered, his voice harsh and guttural in her ear. His hand wrapped tighter around her thigh just above her knee, holding her open to him.

She reached between them and touched him, marveling at how smooth he was. She couldn't breathe as she watched him playing with her, teasing her with the satiny, blunt end. It was so easy as he worked his hips against her to guide him to her entrance. The rhythm pulled him away and she exhaled a groan of frustration; her hips followed, needing him to assuage the ache he had started. Finally, she whined, "Jacob."

He responded by thrusting against her again, and this time she canted her hips more to receive him. She watched in the mirror as the head of his cock disappeared inside her. The fullness when he pressed forward was welcome in a way she had never experienced. Stretched, but with an achiness that only wanted more of him. Disappointment nearly undid her when he withdrew, but he was back quickly, sinking in even deeper this time. She grasped his buttock and pulled him closer. His arms went around her, holding her against him so that not even a whisper of air was between them.

"Good?" His voice was so serrated and rough against her hair, she could hardly make out the word.

She hadn't fared much better. Her *yes* came out breathy and broken. She could only lie there with the weight of him inside her and marvel at how wonderful he felt. This time when he pulled his hips back, he didn't leave her; when he pressed forward he nudged up against something inside her that had her crying his name.

She wanted to close her eyes to savor the sensation, but the angle was such that she could see everything. She couldn't have looked away had she tried. The sight of his thick length disappearing within her was mesmerizing. She could barely move in this position, but she needn't have worried; he took care of that. Staying firmly where she wanted him, he pushed forward a bit only to draw back before settling into a slow rhythm that saw him penetrate her only halfway due to the angle before withdrawing again.

He was inside her and she wanted it, needed him to be even more inside her. His lips touched her neck and then her ear. His harsh breath rasping against her was its own caress. "Jacob," she urged him. Her body clamped down on him as if to hold him.

"Touch yourself. Come." His hot gaze over her shoulder met hers in the mirror. He wanted to see it as much as she wanted to feel it. Her pleasure was his just as his belonged to her. That knowledge was intoxicating.

She reached down to where they were joined. Her fingertips brushed the thick head of his cock before it disappeared into her again. Then she found her clitoris, swollen and achy. *This* was the most erotic thing she had ever seen. He must have thought so, too, because his gaze caught on her fingers, watching her mimic how he had touched her earlier. It was a poor imitation, but it was enough to heighten the pleasure, drawing it taut to that single part of her body, higher and higher until release crested through her in waves and her body clamped around him, squeezing him in spasms. She cried out, not caring if anyone heard her.

He responded by increasing his pace, which served to draw out her pleasure. His grip on her hips tightened as he held her in place, his thrusts becoming more measured and hard.

"Yes," she whispered over and over again.

This was what she wanted. His pleasure, his complete devastation as he lost his carefully structured control. Something about his harsh breath behind her indicating he felt this as much as she did made her whole body tremble with a heady mix of joy and pleasure. Then his rhythm faltered. His masculine grunts rumbled through her a second before he painted her sex and fingers in his own release.

She had done this to him. He hadn't used her for his pleasure, but they had found it together somehow. She met his half-lidded gaze in the mirror. His hands still held her tight and not in a way that was stifling or controlling. They made her feel wanted. They made her feel beloved and safe.

They lay there for several minutes, gasping for air and trying to piece themselves back together after what had happened. It had been unexpected to say the least. She was almost certain that he hadn't believed that he would do more than bring her to orgasm. He hadn't expected his own, not in that way. But it had been so right and good that she was overcome with a feeling of victory followed by relief.

She needed to feel closer to him, which made no sense considering they had just been as close as it was possible for two people to be. She turned in his arms to face him, her thighs falling down around his larger one as he gathered her close to him. His own breath was harsh from exertion near her ear, and she loved that she had made it that way.

When before she had only felt used and discarded afterward, now she felt cherished and valued in a way she couldn't appropriately explain. It was more than a good sexual experience, though it was definitely that. It was that they had shared something so special that she didn't think it could ever be replicated with anyone else.

She chanced a glance at his face to see if he felt an inkling of her own gratification. His eyes were still impossibly dark and intense as he stared down at her. Indeed, he was still half-rigid against her hip, which seemed impossible when she had only just witnessed his release. Renewed interest stirred low down in her body, that now-familiar coil of yearning tightening. Could they do it again in a little while? She didn't know if that was appropriate or if her body would let her, but she liked thinking about it. She also very much liked lying here in his arms, and she never wanted to leave. She had never felt so emotionally close to another person in her life. The way he looked at her, with awe and affection, she could tell that things had changed for both of them. There was no going back from this point forward.

"That was beautiful," she whispered.

His eyes shifted in an instant from warm and soft to something that she could best describe as hunted. Wary. Then they shuttered altogether. But his thumb stroked her cheek and he said, "*You're* beautiful, Camille."

Somehow, she had taken them off track. She stroked his jaw, and he turned his head to kiss her palm. "Thank you for this . . . for sharing this with me."

His hand moved in a slow caress down her back, but the earlier vulnerability didn't come back to his eyes. He swallowed audibly and took in a deep breath through his nose before he brushed her temple with his lips and gently shifted her to slide out from under her. He disappeared through the curtained-off area, and she faintly heard the sound of water running into a sink.

A cloud of disappointment swept in to take the edge off of her happiness. Lying with him in the aftermath had been pleasant. Did couples not do that for longer? Violet and August had spoken about the pleasure to be had in the marriage bed, but they had never discussed what came after. Was cuddling not something couples did? Having never been intimate with a man in quite this way, she didn't know.

But then, they weren't a couple. She kept forgetting that. Floating in her haze of astonished contentment, she had imagined that he had made love to her.

But that wasn't what this was at all. It was sex, not making love. No wonder he had run from her. She had stupidly forgotten the only true rule of their arrangement.

Chapter 19

✤

B*loody hell!*

The words were the only coherent thought bouncing around in Jacob's brain, which was reeling from what had just happened. He could barely focus, and it took a long while of staring at himself in the small mirror above the sink in the bathing chamber to make out his expression. His face looked positively ravaged by whatever the hell it was that had happened on that bed. It most certainly had not been fucking. He was familiar with the many pleasant and tender emotions that accompanied that particular activity. This panic mixed with extreme affection, inexplicable longing, and confusion was not generally on that list. He felt stripped raw.

It wasn't helped by the fact that he had taken her bare. There had been no sheath between them. He hadn't stopped to retrieve a sponge. She had asked for his cock and, God help him, he had been too far gone to think. Never in his entire life had he been so careless. There was no excuse for it. Thank Christ he hadn't come inside her. It had taken every ounce of self-control he possessed to withdraw, but what if it hadn't been soon enough? What if she was made to bear the burden of his selfish mistake?

Aware in some dark corner of his consciousness that the water was running, he forced his attention away from his reflection to the water swirling against the porcelain before disappearing down the drain. His fingers trembled as he splashed some on his face, but no amount of cold water could make him forget how goddamned good it had felt to be inside her. She had taken nearly all of him by the end without fear or restraint, and by God that had felt powerful and perfect. He closed his eyes and relived the sweet clasp of her cunt around him, fluttering and gripping him as she came. He'd given her that, and in return she'd given him . . .

What precisely? An orgasm was an orgasm.

Even as he tried to convince himself of that, he recognized that this was different. This felt more complex and, heaven help him, wholesome. He might have laughed at that had he been capable of it. Wholesome sex. It sounded like something a religious sect might propagate. Not sex involving a round bed and mirrors and a woman splayed on top of him with her sex on display, begging him to take her. But it was the only way he could think to describe the completeness coupled with the intense affection that had come over him when it was finished. He could have stayed in that bed with her. Taken her again. Slept with her curled against him. Held her the whole night through. Even now, all he wanted to do was take her to his bedroom where she belonged.

It was because of their deal. Her past. It had to be. No one else had made her come like that before, and he was just enough of a beast to let it go to his head. He wasn't one to usually feel territorial or possessive, but those were definitely the emotions pounding their way through him now. No one else had ever made that happen for her. The fact that he felt these things was because of that. She was not his.

For fuck's sake! He gripped the edge of the sink so hard, he half feared he was in danger of ripping it off the wall. She was not his. He did *not* want her to be. Except that he did. The spark of affection he felt for her was on the verge of becoming an encompassing blaze that would incinerate him. That's when he understood that sex with her again would only bind them together inexorably and that wasn't what he wanted. He did not want to want her in any way that went beyond physical.

That was beautiful.

She had been completely unaware of the love shining in her eyes as she said that to him. She had to be unaware. He couldn't accept what he had to do if she admitted how she felt to herself. He couldn't hurt her, but neither could he encourage this emotional connection that had developed between them despite his best effort. He was going to Paris. She was staying here. He was not going to fall in love. He would not be held captive by his emotions in that way.

His stubborn cock saw things differently as he washed and grabbed a fresh washcloth for her. It stood tall and proud, thoroughly undeterred by the cold water or the panic infusing his blood. He couldn't have been gone for more than a few of minutes, but it felt like he'd spent a lifetime in that cold room wondering how to extricate himself from the mess he had made. It didn't matter how long it had been. As soon as he saw her lounging on the bed, a pleasant smile on her face, her eyes so full of love that it physically hurt to look at her, he knew that it hadn't been enough. It would never have been enough.

She glanced down at his eager erection, her cheeks flush with bashfulness and interest, before moving to sit on her knees, her gaze returning to his. "Everything okay?" she asked, concern evident on her face. He suspected she knew that he had run from her.

He gritted his teeth to force himself not to join her there when the only thing he wanted to do was hold her in his arms and reassure her. However, he couldn't look away from her. He'd been right. She did have the most perfect breasts in all of England. They were round and high with taut nipples and they filled his hands perfectly. It would be so easy to push her back onto the bed, notch himself at her entrance, and tease her until she begged him to push inside her again. She'd welcome him. He knew that she would still be wet. Her nipples were still beaded, her chest flushed, and her eyes dilated with need. They could spend the next several hours exploring all the ways their bodies fit together so perfectly. But afterward he would be so completely and utterly lost in her that it would be terrifying.

It already was.

"Yes," he said, a belated answer to her question. "Here." He handed her the wet cloth and watched her blush darken. Turning to give her a measure of privacy, he retrieved his dressing gown from the floor and put it on. "How do you feel?"

After a moment, she set the cloth aside and sat on the bed with her knees against her chest. It was probably supposed to be for modesty, but while her breasts were now hidden, he had an unobstructed view of her glistening sex. She was pink and slightly swollen from his cock, and by God he wanted her again. He wanted to kiss her there, to make her feel good in a hundred different ways.

"Not very sore, if that's what you mean." She gave him a shy smile.

"Good."

He wanted to make them both sore. He wanted to fuck her until the sun came up and neither of them could move. Or if she wasn't ready for that, he wanted to hold her against him all night and whisper soft and naughty things to her as he licked her to endless climaxes. And then he wanted to fall asleep curled around her. It was that last one that terrified him.

"Camille, I owe you an apology," he said, pushing those

other thoughts from his mind. "I didn't protect you like I should have. I've never been with a woman without contraceptive before. I . . . I don't know what came over me."

"Oh." She blushed, her gaze dropping to the bed. "I . . . I didn't think, either. I suppose I shouldn't have asked you . . ."

"No." He hurried to sit on the bed at her side. "It's not your fault. Tonight was about you. I don't want you to regret any part of it. I withdrew and I believe we should be fine, but in the event you find out . . ." He couldn't say the word *child*. It had him imagining her with his child, and while that thought should induce a mild panic at the very least, it . . . didn't. "I want you to come to me."

She nodded. "I will."

He rose to combat the need to touch her. Distance was the only way to counteract that effectively, so he stepped over to her pile of clothes and fetched her chemise. Handing it to her, he said, "I am glad that we accomplished our goal."

He allowed himself one more unfettered view of her as she gathered up the linen and pulled it over her head. He'd never see her again like this. The thought literally hurt him as she tugged it down over her shapely thighs. He had to look away as he took in a breath. This had to be their last time or he would be too far gone to stop.

"Me, too," she said, rising to her feet. Touching his arm, she asked, "Did I do . . . something wrong—" A furrow had appeared in her forehead with twin lines between her brows.

"No," he said before she could finish. "Of course not."

She nodded, accepting but not understanding the change in his attitude. Christ, he was mucking this up and he didn't know how to *not* do that. Things were supposed to be over now. This had always been the plan.

"When I said it was beautiful," she continued, "I didn't mean anything more than a . . . a casual beauty."

He nearly laughed aloud at that. Her whole heart had

been in her face when she said that. She meant it exactly as he had taken it because it had been bloody beautiful. It had been the most intimate experience of his life.

"I know what you meant," he said, because he couldn't bear to lie to her about it. Instead, he took her in his arms. She pressed her face against his chest, and he couldn't stop himself from burying his nose in her hair. He wanted to remember the imprint of her body against his for years to come. Or at least while he was in Paris. Maybe when he returned things wouldn't feel so visceral and raw. Perhaps he could see her then and not feel this ache of longing that had taken root in his chest.

"I should go," she said when he released her, a suspicious rasp in her throat.

"I'll help you."

Over the next several minutes they repeated the ritual from earlier, only in reverse. He hooked her corset for her, and tied the tapes on her petticoats and bustle, then he pulled her gown over her head and fastened it up the back. Almost a proper lady's maid except for the raging erection that she must have noticed. To her credit, she did not mention it. Not even when he leaned forward at the door to place a chaste kiss on her lips.

It didn't stay very chaste. She parted beneath him, and before he realized it his tongue was brushing hers and he had to force himself to pull away. The liquid depths of her eyes threatened to drown him. He had to make certain she knew this couldn't happen again. There was no way he could resist her if she sought him out again.

"I'll be very busy finishing up things here now that the contract is final." *Too busy to fuck you.* It was the worst lie he had ever told. "Do not worry about Turner. I'll tell him that we have called off the engagement once I'm established in Paris."

Her eyes widened slightly in comprehension. "Will I see you at Violet's party?" she asked.

"Yes. If all goes well I leave for Paris soon after."

She nodded. "Thank you for . . ." She glanced back to the room. "This."

"Goodbye, Camille," he whispered.

Checking that the corridor was clear, he explained to her how to leave through the back entrance so no one would see her except for a stray servant. Then he closed the door behind her and vowed to lose himself in a bottle of scotch until he drowned the urge to go after her.

C amille sat at her writing desk late the next afternoon attempting to draft an essay for the LSS. She had spoken briefly with Lilian last night after the speeches, and Lilian had encouraged her to write about her own experiences. She had claimed that publishing personal stories had a real impact on people in power. Camille didn't intend to get into anything too personal with her marriage—she was still ruminating over the accusations Mrs. Woodhull had made in her speech and wondering if they applied to her situation—but she could discuss her powerlessness in drafting her own marriage contract, and the way that Hereford was still able to exert control over her property and finances through his heir. There were plenty of facts she could write in black and white without getting personal. Lilian would come over tomorrow to help her, but she wanted to have a first draft complete before then.

The problem was that her heart wasn't in the essay at the moment. She kept thinking about Jacob and the amazingly beautiful thing that had passed between them last night. She thought he had felt it, too, but then he had encouraged her to leave so fast that she wasn't certain anymore. And then he had made it clear that there wouldn't be another night between them. She was honestly confused. Did people experience what had happened between them and then go their separate ways? Did it always feel like that? Her instinct said no, but then she had never actually had such a positive experience with a man in bed before. What if her tender feelings were a natural extension of that and everyone else knew how to handle their feelings except for her?

Yet, as much as she tried to convince herself of that, she didn't quite believe it. She and Jacob had shared something special. Special enough that it had frightened him. She had never seen him like that before, closed off to her and disconcerted. If only she could talk to someone, but the emotions felt too raw and exceptional to speak of them yet, particularly since he had not returned her sentiments.

She was certainly very glad that she hadn't said anything more than *that was beautiful*. Although it made her wince every time she remembered it, it could have been worse. She might have said something very foolish about her growing affection for him. Thank God, she hadn't. Instead, he had sent her home and she had lain awake almost all night reliving what had happened.

It made her sad that it wouldn't happen again, and she couldn't properly decide why. She had known going in that this would not be any sort of permanent arrangement. He had made it clear that he wasn't looking for that, and she herself had proclaimed that a relationship was out of the question. Why, then, could she not stop wondering what he was doing now? She wanted to see him and kiss him and touch him, and those things did not mean she felt anything beyond extreme gratitude and tenderness toward him.

Right? Ugh! She was all over the place in her mind when it came to him.

She drew several lines through whatever it was she had been writing before tossing her pen aside and crumpling the paper. The doorbell rang as she was lobbing it into the bin beneath her desk.

"Perfect," she grumbled, glancing at the clock. Visiting hours were almost over, and when she had expected a rather uneventful day, someone had come calling.

She rose and reached for the bell to call for tea but froze as a high-pitched voice called to her from the foyer.

"Camille, hullo, darling. It's your mother."

It couldn't possibly be. No one had written or sent a wire to let her know of an impending visit. Impossibly, several pairs of heeled shoes were heading in her direction.

The door opened to reveal Sampson, her impassive and unflappable butler, as calm as ever. "Mrs. Bridwell has arrived, Your Grace."

"Don't be silly. She'll be thrilled that you're here." Her mother's voice, an octave lower, preceded her, but to whom was she speaking?

She didn't have long to wait. A moment later her mother appeared in the doorway, her slender frame swathed in a beautiful navy and cream traveling costume. "Surprise!" She smiled broadly, arms high in the air, as she scurried past Sampson. "It's only been since summer, but I feel as if I haven't seen you in forever." Grasping Camille's shoulders, she pressed a quick kiss to her cheek before pulling back. "You look tired, darling." Smiling again, she patted the same cheek she had kissed. "But beautiful as always."

"What are you doing here, Mama?"

"Surprising you, of course."

"Surprising me? How long will you stay?"

Mama laughed and narrowed her gaze in mock censure. "It sounds as if you don't want me here. Have I inconvenienced you?"

"No, of course not, you are quite welcome here. I'm only surprised." Surprised was a pale expression of her astonishment.

"Through Easter, darling." She glanced back over her shoulder at the empty doorway then turned back to Camille and lowered her voice conspiratorially. "However, I'm not the only surprise. You'll never guess who I brought with me."

At a loss, Camille guessed, "Father?"

"No, silly, he couldn't come, what with business taking a

downturn with the depression." She rolled her eyes at the terrible inconvenience, even though they were too wealthy to have felt the financial pinch directly. "I brought the next best thing. Frederick, dear, you may come in now."

No! She didn't dare believe it, but in walked the very last man she wanted to see, not counting Henry. Frederick Kip stood framed in the doorway, his handsome facade not the least bit rumpled by the two-week voyage from New York or the train from Liverpool. He was the man her parents had insinuated they wanted her to marry now that she was free to do so. He was also the man she had foolishly attempted to sleep with in New York before running back home to London.

God help her.

Chapter 20

❧

Dinner was an awkward affair that night. The few hours since her mother and Frederick had arrived had been taken up with quick refreshments, hastily exchanged tales of their experiences on the ship, and polite gossip from New York—marriages, births, and deaths—all while Camille's staff arranged appropriate bedrooms for their unexpected guests. Camille's gentle suggestion that a bachelor might be better suited to a hotel had been met with a quick rebuttal from her mother.

"Please, Camille, don't let him hear you. He is a very dear friend of this family." Then she had shaken her head. "A hotel?" As if the very suggestion were ridiculous.

"It is hardly proper that he stay here," Camille had pointed out, quite reasonably, she thought. As a young widow, she was still supposed to abide by the most basic of social protocols.

"Is your mother not a fit chaperone?" Then Mama had added with a raised eyebrow, "But I will say that I am glad you are finally concerned with what's proper."

Camille had sighed in frustration, though she had to agree it might be too late for her to play the concerned society matron. She had let the topic drop.

Thankfully, the servants were well trained and had no trouble accommodating the extra people for the evening meal on short notice. There was food and wine, but the conversation could be considered lacking.

Over a superbly roasted pheasant, Camille stared the man down across the table from her. "What brings you to London, Frederick? You never did say."

"It's the funniest thing," he said, setting his wine aside and dabbing at his mustache with the napkin in his lap. The mustache was new, but she had to admit that it suited him. His features tended toward square: a square face, square shoulders, even his nose formed a square at the end. The mustache softened the effect in a way his thin lips could not.

He was handsome, but differently than Jacob was handsome. Jacob's beauty was fascinating and could prompt an admirer to want to sit for hours to gaze at him from various angles. Frederick's was more conventional, though she supposed if she liked his personality more then she might see him differently. His brown hair was always stylishly kept, as was his clothing. He wasn't offensive in any way, except for in character. He had been unwilling to accept the fact that she didn't want to continue their intimate relationship.

"It has been some years since my last trip here," he continued, smiling first at her and then her mother. So far he had been very careful not to hint that there had ever been more than friendship to their relationship. She hoped he had forgotten all about that night they had taken the train back to New York together. "I was relaying my pleasant memories to your parents one evening at dinner around Christmastime. As luck would have it, Mae mentioned she was considering traveling here and that I might want to join her. We planned the trip over the next several weeks. I wanted to wire you, but she insisted on keeping it secret."

"Hilarious," Camille replied sarcastically, gaining an eyebrow raise from him. Interesting that he referred to her mother by her nickname now and not Mrs. Bridwell as he had for as long as she had known him.

"I welcomed the company." Mama smiled. "You know how I so despise traveling alone, darling."

"You travel with a maid, Mama." She knew she was being bratty, but she couldn't seem to stop.

She laughed. "That's hardly the same thing as traveling with a dear friend, now is it?"

It wasn't, but Camille was having a terrible time controlling her mood. She took another swallow of wine. "Will you be staying through Easter as well, Frederick? I hear Venice is beautiful this time of year. Perhaps you'd like your trip to expand farther into Europe?" What would she do with them in her house for six weeks?

"I haven't made any firm plans."

Mama glanced at her in warning, prompting her to bow out of the conversation as they discussed their sightseeing plans while in London. All was fine until the dessert course was brought out and her mother waved hers away. Stifling a yawn, she rose, stating, "Please forgive my discourtesy, but I must retire for the evening. The train ride was quite rough today, and I am feeling poorly." To Camille, she said, "Let's have breakfast tomorrow, darling." She squeezed her shoulder as she left the room.

"Good night, Mae." Frederick waited until she'd left the room before sitting back down. "Your mother is a kind and generous woman. Do you know I had to insist that I pay for my own passage?"

Given that Camille was inclined to believe this entire visit was an elaborate scheme to see her wed to Frederick, she was a little surprised he hadn't been delivered wrapped in a bow. So much for her mother as chaperone. She briefly considered escaping to Stonebridge Cottage, but they would only find her there and it wouldn't change things. She would have to approach this head-on.

"I am not surprised," she said, lifting a fragile meringue drop with her spoon. "My mother can be generous to a fault when she feels like it."

When husband-hunting, she mentally added. The dessert melted on her tongue, dispersing the pleasant and lightly sweetened taste of lemon. She wondered if Jacob liked meringues and the taste of lemon, which annoyed her and made her feel even more gloomy. It was only the hundredth such thought she'd had about him that evening, her most recent being which wine he might prefer and whether he was eating his supper now or dealing cards in one of the game rooms. She was starting to suspect that she had gone and fallen in love with him.

Oh, bother!

"Camille?" Frederick's concerned face materialized across the table.

"Yes?"

He indicated her plate. She looked down to see that she had eaten the meringues, and a footman patiently waited for her to place her spoon so that he could take everything away. Apparently, Frederick had been talking to her as well, but she had no idea what he might have said.

Dropping her spoon, she thanked the footman, who gave a gracious nod and swept her plate from the room. A few moments later they were left alone with their after-dinner sherries. Frederick wasted no time in moving around the table to take her mother's vacated spot.

"Tell me you are happy to see me, Camille." His hopeful gaze swept from her mouth to her eyes. "I could hardly contain myself when I saw you. You are even more beautiful than I remember, if that's possible."

"Frederick—"

He grasped her hand, which had been resting in her lap.

"I know that I should have written before I came, but your mother talked me out of it. She told me you would enjoy the surprise better. Tell me she wasn't wrong."

Camille stood, pushing her chair back and forcing him to release her. She did not want to have this conversation with him. They had already had a version of it in New York. "It's inappropriate for us to be alone. I'm going to retire for the night," she said and hurried out of the dining room. The corridor was empty, so she quickly made her way to the stairs, where he followed her up.

"That didn't seem to bother you in New York."

She grimaced at the reminder of her stupidity. In Newport they had engaged in a light flirtation for weeks. Camille had indulged it because it had felt good to be admired. She had known him and his family for years. In fact, he was the man her parents had intended she marry before they had gotten the idea that a duke would be better. The Kips were wealthy and well-connected, but they were not British nobility, and they did not have access to the Knickerbockers of New York Society. They were wealthy and respected in their own circles, but they were no better than the Bridwells, which had been the fatal flaw to the marriage plans. But seeing him again had brought back memories of the time before Hereford, when she had been more carefree and bold with men. She had indulged his interest because a part of her had thought that if she could like him, then she could come to love him, and her time with Hereford could be effectively erased.

It had been a stupid whimsy that had not worked. She had liked him well enough in the beginning. He'd hung on her every word and played the devoted suitor. What wasn't to like when he had made himself into such an agreeable version of himself? It was only toward the end when he had been pressing for more that the seams had started to show. When she had decided to return to New York, he had taken the train back with her, and then she had gone to his apartment.

"As I explained," she said, keeping her voice low as they walked up the stairs, "that was a mistake. I should have never gone home with you. I am sorry if I led you to believe that our evening together would lead to more."

She had been very clear with him in Newport that she didn't intend to marry again. It was not her fault that his bravado had convinced him that he could change her mind. Only Jacob had the power to do that. She frowned at the unwelcome reminder of how she had so quickly lost her head to a man who didn't even want her.

He stiffened beside her. "I did not accept that then and I do not accept it now."

"Frederick." She turned at the top of the stairs and he paused a couple of steps below so that they were of the same height. "You have no choice but to accept it. Our time together is over."

"I nearly bedded you, Camille." His voice was higher than either of them would have liked. He flushed and glanced around to make certain no one had heard him. "That must mean something to you," he added in a lowered voice.

"Frederick." She went to press a hand to his chest, but then thought better of it, not wanting to mislead him with the touch. "That night is in our past, where it shall stay. We have already spoken of this."

"But Camille—"

She whirled away from him, ashamed that she had allowed things to go so far with him. She hadn't even liked him by that point. It had been a poor decision based on her bad experiences with Hereford and then with Henry. Frederick was known to have had a mistress or two in his past. She had thought that surely he would know how to touch her and then she could be assured that nothing was truly wrong with her after all. It had been a terrible idea, not the least of which was because he had wanted more from her. She would have been better off choosing a stranger because she had ended up pushing away from his kisses when they had crossed the line from curious to demanding. That's when she had realized the problem was most definitely with her, and her only thoughts had been to get away from him and everyone else in New York. She had run away from him with her hair mussed and her clothing rumpled.

"Camille!" He called her from behind, his voice a harsh whisper.

"What happened between us doesn't give you any right to me," she said over her shoulder.

"No, you're right." He followed her down the hall and mercifully didn't say anything more until he caught up with her outside her bedroom door. In a whisper, he added, "But you must admit it gave me some ideas about the future of our relationship."

"Yes, I can see that, which is why when you came to my parents' home the next day, I told you in no uncertain terms that our relationship would not continue. I believe I even said it to you that night before I left."

"You didn't mean that, though. How could you mean that when we are so good together?"

"Of course I meant it. I wouldn't have said it if I hadn't."

His jaw tightened in frustration. "You are meant to be mine, Camille. You were meant to be my wife before Hereford came along. I can forgive your parents, because nothing had been decided, but I cannot forgive this. You are free to marry as you wish now. I know you said you don't wish to remarry, but reconsider. We could have a good life together if you would simply give me a chance."

Reining in her annoyance, she said as gently as she was able, "Even if I did plan to marry, Frederick, I would not choose you. My life is not in New York anymore. Now if you'll excuse me, I plan to retire for the evening." She turned away, but his hand on her waist stopped her. A frisson of unease crept down her spine as she became aware that he could do with her as he wanted. If he wished it, he could cover her mouth, push her inside the room, and have his way with her. She didn't think he would do that, but she didn't really know him, did she?

"Unhand me." He seemed to come to his senses and glanced down at her waist as if he was surprised to see his hand on her, and let her go.

His eyes were hard and furious when she met them. "Do you tease men so easily, Camille?"

"I'm going to pretend you did not say that, and in the morning you will never attempt to speak privately with me again."

He looked momentarily stricken and then he nodded, aware that he had pushed too far. She fled inside her room, locking the door behind her for good measure. She paced her room for the next several minutes, uncertain of how to react to what had transpired. Camille would have to speak with her mother over breakfast and make it perfectly clear that marriage between them was out of the question. The conversation would be challenging because her mother never wanted to talk about difficult topics. She preferred to smile and make jests and gloss over anything that couldn't be solved easily.

Ingram arrived a few minutes later and helped her dress for bed. Thankfully, Frederick was not out there when she opened the door. Afterward, Camille climbed into bed alone and closed her eyes, trying to reclaim the warm feeling she had had last night after coming home from Jacob. She had lain there savoring the phantom imprint of his warmth on her body and the smell of him on her skin. Some of the sensation had faded, but it was still there if she closed her eyes and imagined hard enough.

Unfortunately, other darker thoughts began to intrude. The imprint of Frederick's hand on her waist. The dread that had made her nauseous when she lay in bed knowing that Hereford would be visiting her that night. The trapped and helpless way she had spent the entirety of her engagement and marriage feeling.

She sat up in bed. That's why she had been feeling so morose and bitter ever since Mama and Frederick had arrived. That horrible feeling that she had spent the past two years trying to banish had come back. It was very near a panic that made her feel as if she were slowly suffocating with the way it squeezed her chest and made it difficult to breathe. A part of her still believed that the past might be repeated, that her parents might find a way to make her marry someone she didn't want to marry and that hell would start all over again.

Sitting against the headboard, she forced herself to breathe slowly and deeply. Closing her eyes, however, only made images she didn't want to remember play behind them. Hereford's angry expression as he berated her; his hard grip on her arm as he led her away from some incident that had displeased him; his dispassionate gaze as he reminded her that it was her duty to produce a son for him, even though it was he who frequently had difficulty completing the act. It was all overlaid with the words from Mrs. Woodhull's speech, words that had resonated so deeply that Camille had been afraid to remember them.

Had she suffered abuse at the hands of her husband? He had never physically injured her, but everything else he had done had hurt her in ways that were not visible. Was that the same thing? Tears sprang to her eyes and she didn't bother to wipe them away. Instead, she rose and hurried over to the little writing desk by the window. It was cold, so she wrapped herself in her dressing gown and lit the candle she kept there. Withdrawing a sheet of parchment from the drawer, she picked up her pen and began to write all the things she hadn't been able to earlier. She would write down every way Hereford had hurt her and made her feel hollow and insignificant. She would exorcise herself of Hereford's memory once and for all.

He had taken enough from her.

Chapter 21

❧

Oh dear, Camille, you look tired." Her mother glanced up from the breakfast spread out before her on the little table in her bedroom as soon as Camille walked in the next morning. "Come have a cup of coffee." She poured some from the silver pot on the tray and pushed the cup and saucer across the table to her.

It was midmorning and Camille had slept quite well once she had finished her essay, or letter of accusation, whatever one wanted to call the list of grievances against her dead husband. She was simply in need of more sleep to make up for all that had been lost the past few years.

"Good morning, Mama." The splash of cream she poured into the black coffee spread out like an ink blot on paper. "I hope you slept well."

Her mother nodded and proceeded to smear strawberry jam on a buttered triangle of toast. "Here, darling," she said, placing it on a small plate she set before Camille.

Then she spooned scrambled eggs onto the plate. "Yes, I slept very well. I hope you don't mind that I left you with Frederick last night."

Camille stirred her coffee as she debated on how to begin. Yes, she wanted to discuss Frederick and the reason her mother should not have brought him here, but she wanted to discuss her mother's reasons for coming regardless of Frederick. Deciding that talking about him now would only muddy the waters, she said, "I'd like to discuss why you've come, Mama."

"To see you, of course. You left in a hurry, which I understood, but your father and I worry about you over here by yourself." She cut her off when Camille opened her mouth, anticipating an argument. "I know you have the Crenshaw girls, but they have lives of their own and you are alone."

She couldn't say why an image of Jacob came to mind. They were not a pair in any way that mattered, any way that would give her a claim to him, and yet she had started to think of herself as less alone since she had been spending more time with him. The coffee was too hot yet to drink, but she brought it to her lips anyway to gather the thoughts that memories of him had scattered. It didn't help, however, because as she blew gently on the steam, she remembered how his breath had blown against her ear. Really, she just wanted to be with him rather than dealing with this.

"Thank you for your concern, but I'm doing well. Better than I have been in a long time. I rather thought you might have come for a particular reason."

Mama gave a huff of laughter as she swirled sugar in her own freshly poured cup of coffee. "You know your father was not happy with you joining that men's club."

And here was the first volley. "It's not a men's club. They do accept women."

"I suppose, but it hardly seems decent. Aren't there clubs for women you can join?"

"Yes, and I have joined one . . . of sorts." Though she hardly thought the LSS was the sort of club her mother meant. And come to think of it, several men were members.

"Wonderful. It will do you good to be in the society of other young women."

Camille smiled behind her coffee cup, imagining the demonstration they were planning. Probably not the society her mother meant, either. "But I do not intend to leave Montague Club. It's important that women are seen to do the things that men do, and to be in the places they occupy. We've known we're just as capable as they are for years now. It's time everyone sees that."

Mama raised a brow as she bit into a piece of toast. After a moment, she said, "I suppose I can see your point, darling, but where does that line of thought end? Would you have women in courtrooms? In fishing boats? In mines? Some work should be left to men."

"I disagree. While every woman is not suited to every job, neither is every man. Could you imagine Father down in a mine?"

They both laughed at the imagery. Everyone who knew her father knew that he despised any sort of activity that caused him to break a sweat. Their carriage had broken a wheel one summer many years ago in Newport and he had tossed Camille a penny every minute they had been stranded as long as she had used her fan to keep him cool. She had earned almost fifty cents and had considered herself quite wealthy for a six-year-old.

"Point taken."

"Good, because women *have* been working on fishing boats and in mines for centuries. It's the more lucrative and influential avenues that have been closed off to them."

"I said point taken, Camille. Your father was simply concerned about how it might appear, and I share his apprehension. As I hear it, the proprietor is illegitimate." She whispered the word as if it was a *bad* word. "I understand his father was an earl and that seems to make it excusable here. Before you say it, yes I do know that Leigh and Rothschild are investors of some merit in the venture."

"Mr. Thorne is Christian's brother. Are you suggesting that he should hide away because of the circumstances of his birth?" She hadn't thought ahead to how her parents might perceive her relationship with Jacob, because it didn't seem as if there would be a relationship. Only now she wondered what she thought might happen if they continued to see each other. Did she expect her parents to welcome him into their lives? She realized she hadn't really cared. She had done her duty and given them Hereford as a son-in-law at great cost to herself. She would not let their opinions sway her again.

"No, I'm not suggesting any such thing. I am merely saying that your reputation would be better served elsewhere."

Camille almost opened her mouth to tell her of the notorious bets and goings-on of the other clubs in the city but decided against it. She had only heard rumors, and it was best not to talk about Jacob until she knew for sure where they stood, and currently, it seemed as if *they* were nonexistent.

"My reputation is of little concern to me."

"Yes, that's what I'm afraid of."

"Mama, do you understand how difficult Hereford made my life? He brought me here so that he could have access to the money that came with me, but to his friends he mocked me, and he didn't even have the decency to do it behind my back. They laughed at everything from my mannerisms to the way I speak."

Mama's lips flattened into a thin line. "That was poor of him."

"Poor? Is that all you can say?" She abandoned her cup and grabbed the side of the table to keep herself grounded and her voice modulated. There was no sense in letting her anger get the better of her, but she could feel it slipping away from her.

Her mother's blue-gray eyes reflected a moment of sadness before she said, "He did not treat you as well as I was led to believe that he might." Abandoning her toast, she sat back in her chair, coffee in hand, and smiled. "That whole ordeal is finished, God rest his soul. We must focus on moving forward. You are a widow now and while that comes with some freedom, you must not forget that you are a young woman and subject to the same censure as all the others."

"How can I forget, when I am reminded constantly?"

Mama's jaw tightened. "Is that why you sent the telegram about the contract between your father and Hereford?"

It was such a direct question from a woman who usually did everything but direct her attention to the issue at hand that Camille was momentarily stumped. "Y-yes. Is that why you came?"

She shrugged. "It was a series of things we had heard, but that tipped the scales. Why do you need to know the details? Is there something you need that you aren't being given?"

"I deserve the right to know. It concerns me. I am tired of taking a back seat to my life. I've let you and Father and Hereford control me for long enough. I am a full-grown woman and I deserve to know what has been decided for me. I need to start making decisions for myself."

A tiny furrow appeared between her mother's brows as she took a thoughtful sip of her coffee. When she lowered the cup, she said, "Was it truly that awful with him, child?"

The old need to placate rose up inside her. If she simply said it wasn't that bad, then everything could go back to how it was. There would be no need to take out the dirty truth and examine it in the light. She could be the good girl she was raised to be without any fuss, only doing that had never really helped anything. It had made things more convenient for everyone else while Camille had shouldered the burden of the truth. Her reputation was still questionable because of how Hereford had presented her to his friends, and admittedly, she had not done a thing to change that now that she had found a sort of freedom.

"It was the worst experience of my life, Mama, and I refuse to repeat it. I will refuse to marry anyone if I can't be assured of my own happiness. If you came here with intentions for me and Frederick, then I am sorry to disappoint you. I will not marry him or anyone else who only has an interest in my money."

Mama tutted. "That is not true of Frederick. He has his own money. He cares about you and was crushed when things didn't work out the first time, as was I. I always had a soft spot for him. It was your father who wanted Hereford, you know?"

She had not known that. Her mother had seemed as smitten with the duke as Father. "You wanted him as well," she said, daring her mother to deny it.

Thankfully, she didn't. "I did, but not at first. I didn't like the idea of the age difference, but I allowed your father to convince me it wouldn't matter. He thought you would benefit from having someone older to guide you." She was silent as she looked at Camille before setting her cup and saucer aside. Then she scooted her chair around so that she sat near her. Taking Camille's hand, she said, "Wouldn't Frederick be a nice change? He's younger and handsome. He could give you strong children. You could summer with me in Newport while the men work in the city. It will be fun."

"Frederick would only be more of the same. He doesn't want *me*. He wants what I can bring him."

"Isn't that what marriage is, though? An exchange? Money for status, for business consolidation, for land. It's the way it's always been, even in the Bible."

"What of love and caring, Mama?"

"Love comes with time, darling." When Camille would have spoken, she conceded, "No, probably not with Hereford. You can build affection over time with the right person. Affection that is true and lasting. The passionate love of poetry is only temporary. It fades."

She thought of Jacob and the wicked smile he gave her, of the way she felt that she might die if he wasn't inside her. Perhaps that would fade with time. But then she thought of the way he had held her as she spoke of her past and the way she felt that he understood her as no one else could. How could that understanding fade away? "Why can't I have both?" she whispered. "Why can't I have passion and affection?"

"Because that is being greedy."

"Then I want to be greedy. I don't want to accept anything less."

For the first time her mother's eyes widened as if she was only just seeing her. "What did that man do to you?" It was the first time she had not called him by his title.

"Do you really want to know?"

To her credit, she hesitated. Hurt, fear, and a good deal of confusion washed over her face in waves, one after the next. Finally, she nodded. "Yes, I need to know if you'll share it with me."

Camille reached inside her dressing gown pocket and pulled out the folded pieces of paper. She had put it there to hide away so Ingram wouldn't find it while she was cleaning, but now it seemed perfect that she had brought it with her. A heaviness settled on her chest and pinpricks of warning tickled down her spine. There would be no going back to pretending after this. Still, she handed it over. Her mother accepted it and took a deep breath, as if anticipating the weight of the words within.

"Read it later when you're alone. Tonight."

Mama nodded.

* * *

Despite Jacob's best intentions, thoughts of Camille had consumed him ever since he had sent her home several nights ago. He thought of how good her body felt against him. The sounds she made for those blessed few moments when he'd been inside her. The way her eyes could shine with such joy. The way her trust in him made him feel ten feet tall. Then he'd remember the hurt on her face when he'd pushed her away. Guilt ate at him, but he was dangerously on the edge of a precipice, and holding her again would send him tumbling down. He'd fall headfirst into her and not come up for air until it was too late to breathe anything but her. Christ, perhaps it already was too late.

"Odin's bollocks, man!" Cavell roared at him from the other side of the boxing arena, where he had feinted left away from Jacob's blow and currently nursed a split lip. They had been sparring for sport, not blood, and a small crowd had gathered to watch.

Jacob held up his arms. "If you would pay attention, things like that wouldn't happen."

"We never fight angry," an all-too-familiar voice said from across the room.

Jacob whirled to see Christian standing inside the door to the gymnasium. The men gathered around watching parted to give him a path to the ring. Wonderful. Another person Jacob did not want to see. The day he left for Paris couldn't get here fast enough. His brother was dressed in evening attire, his typical costume when working the club at night. He was supposed to be in the gaming room enticing men to up their bets with his well-placed barbs, not in here bothering Jacob.

"Who says I'm angry?" Jacob forced a drawl, but the tension in his voice was obvious.

Cavell sagged against the ropes. "Pissed on gin," he grumbled.

Jacob glared at him while Christian climbed into the ring.

"Gin, is it?"

"Scotch. *Good* scotch." As if he'd get drunk on gin. Not that he was drunk; he'd only slightly indulged.

His brother gave Cavell a firm pat on the shoulder. "Leave us, will you?"

Cavell nodded, but the men who had gathered for a good fight groaned, as did Jacob. His body was still thrumming with frustration and a strange energy he didn't know how to expend except on a woman. The problem was not just any woman would do.

"Are you quitting now and letting these fine men collect their winnings, or do you need another round before you quit?" Jacob taunted.

Cavell growled and rammed him into the ropes. His blows hurt Jacob's ribs, the cotton batting only marginally softening them. Jacob welcomed the distraction and threw himself into the match. They started trading blows, which were supposed to be light and glancing, but Christian quickly wedged himself between them, effectively ending things. "Let's call it a draw before someone gets hurt even more."

"No one's hurt," Cavell said, though blood dribbled down his chin.

With a hand on each of their chests, Christian raised a brow at Jacob. "Don't fight the boy when you really want to hit me."

He was right in that Jacob was using the fight to make himself feel better. A wave of guilt accompanied that realization. They sparred to improve their speed and reflexes, not to inflict damage. "Sorry, Cavell."

"Sod off." Cavell frowned and left the ring, appearing unhappy the match had been stopped. The crowd that had casually gathered to watch the impromptu sparring session muttered their own disapproval as money was passed around.

"Not everything is about you," Jacob snapped at his brother. "I do occasionally have other frustrations."

Christian watched him with a new understanding dawning in his eyes. Jacob ran a hand over his face. He didn't know why he'd said that. He wasn't about to talk to his brother about Camille.

"What do you want?" he asked to change the subject.

"I came to tell you that I might have overreacted to your announcement." He spoke with particular care, as if every word was pulled from some place deep inside him.

"Did Violet tell you to say that?"

"Perhaps, but she's not wrong."

Jacob let out a huff of laughter as he bent down to exit between the ropes and pull on his dressing gown. It clung unpleasantly to the sweat on his shoulders. "I have to shower."

Mobilized, Christian walked with him to the same door he had led Camille through. Sometimes it was easier to take the back way to his suite of rooms. This time, however, he could think only of how it had felt to walk this corridor with her. Phantom anticipation crackled across his skin.

"Jacob, I apologized."

"No, you said you might have overreacted."

Christian sighed, following him. "Fine, blast you." Through gritted teeth, he said, "I apologize for my behavior. As your brother, I should have tried better to understand."

"What is there to understand?" Jacob knew he should let it go, but he couldn't overcome his bitterness so easily.

Christian sighed again and was silent the few minutes it took them to make it to the private area of the residence. As they opened the door to the wide scarlet hallway, he said, "I understand how you would feel the need to do something on your own. I do. It hurt to not have been included in this and to find out from Turner. To be honest, I still believe you're making a mistake to bring Turner in on this. He's obnoxious, but harmless, I suppose, and it's your decision. I'll honor it."

He hadn't imagined the relief he would feel to hear those words come from his brother. The tightness he'd been carrying in his chest loosened considerably. "Thank you. That is all I wanted."

Christian nodded, then hesitated with his next words. "Did something happen with you and Camille?"

"What do you know about Camille? Did Violet tell you?"

"Yes, but not the extent of things. It's no secret around here with the staff that you two have spent time together."

What did the bloody staff know? He'd been stupid to take her to the room, but his own suite wouldn't have been much better. There would be speculation that they were sleeping together either way.

"Then mind your own business."

Christian held up his hands in a sign for peace. "It's not my business, but you are. Camille is a friend of Violet's and I've grown fond of her. I do not want to see her hurt."

"I wouldn't hurt her."

His brow rose.

Jacob shrugged but he felt terrible. "We had an understanding that came to its rightful end."

Christian was silent for a moment too long. "That explains things, then."

Jacob felt as if he was picking up some gauntlet that had been placed to entice him, but he couldn't help himself. "What does it explain?"

"Violet and I saw her last night at the theater. A man was escorting her. An American from New York."

Jacob swallowed against the bitter taste in his mouth. He should not care. He wanted not to care. She was entitled to be escorted by whomever she chose.

But he did care.

Christian watched him closely, as if seeing far too much. "I admit that I hoped you both might . . ." He shrugged.

"Well, you could be good together, but if your arrangement has come to an end, I suppose I misunderstood."

"That isn't what I want." He started walking toward the door, not prepared to have this conversation.

Christian rolled his eyes before following. "Is this about the Halston men again?"

He wasn't answering that.

"Jacob." His brother took hold of his shoulder to get his attention. "Do you remember what you told me when you found Violet and me in Yorkshire?"

"I knew you were going to bring that up."

Christian continued unfazed. "*Why do you refuse to see what is in front of you?*" he quoted.

"How do you know anything about it? You haven't seen Camille and me together."

"I saw you at the ball, and here at Montague once when you didn't see me. You both were leaving as I came in. I've never seen you look at another woman the way you look at her. I don't know if what you feel is love—I'll grant you that—but it is more than you've had with anyone else. Don't you owe it to both of you to see where it can lead?"

"Let it go, Christian." He walked to the door and put his hand on the knob before he paused, unable to not be bothered by the stranger. "Who is this man from New York?"

Christian shrugged one shoulder. "Something Kip. An heir to a textile manufacturer or some such."

"Heir? Is he young?"

There was a glint in his brother's eye as he said, "Young enough to be competition, you mean? Yes, he's a well-put-together sort. Why do you ask? Jealous?"

"I do not care to discuss this."

But he did care for her. He very much cared.

Chapter 22

✤

The birthday party for Rosie was a small but grand affair that consisted of a few less than twenty guests. The Crenshaw siblings and their families were in attendance, as were Jacob and Lilian and her small family, along with a few other close friends. Rosie had been given her very own pony, which she rode around the garden with her father's assistance. Then her cousin, Lilian's son Jamie, a strapping boy around her age, insisted on showing her how it was done properly, much to the comedic delight of the adults in attendance.

An excellent supper was served after the children had been put to bed, followed by drinks and dessert in the sitting room. The decadent chocolate soufflé might have held Camille's full attention—she loved chocolate and this was the best thing she had tasted in ages—but for the fact that Jacob had held that honor the entire night. From the time he had arrived—late but perfectly charming in his enthusiasm for his niece and nephew—she hadn't been able to concentrate on anything else. Her mother had noticed and kept casting curious glances at Jacob, no doubt wondering about their involvement. Frederick had most certainly taken note and had grown more sullen as the night went on. He was currently in the corner on the far side of the room playing a game of cards with Maxwell Crenshaw. She could feel him eyeing her on occasion, but she honestly couldn't be bothered to care. He hadn't mentioned their night together again, nor had he pressed his suit, but he'd been extra attentive to her. He was due to leave next week for the Continent, where he was meeting a friend, and the day couldn't come soon enough.

"Who is this Mr. Thorne fellow?" Mama asked in a soft voice as she handed off her half-eaten soufflé to a footman.

"You know perfectly well that he is Christian's brother." Camille could barely stop herself from licking the chocolate from the spoon. "This is excellent. I really must ask Violet's cook to give me the recipe." Jacob had encouraged her to indulge her love of baking. Maybe she would give it a try and give her kitchen staff a real shock.

Her mother frowned at the spoon and then glanced back at Jacob, who was standing with a cut-crystal tumbler of scotch talking with Lilian. "Oh yes, the club owner."

"Yes, Mama, the same club that I joined that sent you and Father into a conniption."

"Camille!" She shook her head. "What has gotten into you? We were merely concerned for our only daughter, as any parent would be. We didn't want you to be led astray."

"As you can see, I am fine."

Although, if her mother knew the whole truth of what had happened between her and Jacob, she might think *astray* was a tame word. She still blushed when she remembered watching him in the mirror, how gratified and strangely victorious she had felt when he had found his release with her. A week later and she still remembered it as vividly as if it had happened last night. It was strange being in the same room with him socially knowing how intimate they had been.

"Yes, it would appear so." Her mother continued to watch Jacob, however, making Camille think she herself might have been watching him too much this evening.

A maid appeared at her elbow as if by magic the very second she scraped the final dredges of chocolate from her bowl. "Thank you." She handed her the bowl and then rose to her feet as Mrs. Crenshaw came over to speak to her mother. "If you'll excuse me, I must find Violet and this recipe."

"It was delicious," Mrs. Crenshaw said, taking her vacated seat. The woman had stayed behind for the birthday celebration while her husband had returned home to Monte Carlo. "I'll take a copy as well if you manage to procure it."

Violet had disappeared toward the back of the house with a maid a few minutes ago. Camille made her way there but only found guests in conversation, so she hurried down the stairs to the lower level.

I've always heard the phrase *to stare daggers at someone* but I've never seen it epitomized quite so well." Lilian's voice was low and tinged with amusement as she joined him in the corner of the room.

Even though it only reinforced her statement, Jacob could not stop himself from staring at the American who was engaged in a game of five-card stud with Max Crenshaw. Not that Kip had taken note of his attention; the man was too busy shooting pining glances at Camille. Jacob took a healthy sip of his scotch before he trusted himself to answer. "Whatever do you mean?"

"Jacob." There was a hint of warning in her voice that finally made him look at her. "What has got into you? You're not usually so . . ." She searched for the proper word. "So brooding."

It wasn't *what* had got into him but *whom* he had got into that was the problem. His sister wouldn't appreciate the truth, nor was he ready to share it, so he shrugged instead. "I've things on my mind."

"Mr. Kip is one of those things?"

The very mention of the man's name had Jacob glancing in his direction again to see him glancing at Camille. He hadn't been able to glean any information from Violet about Kip's connection to Camille except for the fact that he was a friend from New York. He wasn't certain, but he strongly suspected he was the same Frederick that Camille had mentioned to him. The one who had left her feeling even more broken.

"He wants her," he found himself saying before he could stop himself.

Standing at his side, Lilian followed his line of sight to Kip and then to where Camille sat on the sofa talking with her mother and eating a chocolate dessert with more relish than was appropriate in mixed company. "And that's a problem for you?"

The betrayal of the query was so shocking that he jerked around to face his sister, but almost immediately he understood it was a perfectly reasonable question. "He is not what she needs."

Her brow arched. "What does she need?"

He took another drink, savoring the warmth on his tongue. How much did she know about his arrangement with Camille? Everyone else seemed to bloody well know more of their affair than they should.

"Not him," he said. "He looks at her as if she is an object. I'd bet Montague on the fact that he's a fortune hunter and isn't as wealthy as everyone believes." There was a calculation in the way Kip looked at her that rubbed him the wrong way.

Settling his shoulder against the wall, this time his attention turned solely to Camille. She was as beautiful as always, but her beauty was even more poignant because he had seen her and held her as she had come undone. He knew how it felt to have her body gripping him as she came. He now knew what it meant to lose himself in her. It had taken a Herculean effort tonight to not touch her. They had exchanged the basest pleasantries and sat at opposite ends of the table. But in passing he had smelled her fragrance and remembered how her scent had lingered on his hands long after he had all but sent her from the room.

"So you, then?" she asked.

"Not me, either."

Lilian clasped his arm. "She would be lucky to have you."

What would that future look like? He couldn't envision it because he had never let himself imagine a wife. "I . . . I . . ."

"You are not our father, Jacob."

He wasn't, but did it matter?

Camille rose before he could reply and started walking toward the back of the house. Alone.

"Excuse me."

A moth drawn to her flame, he followed her.

The lower level housed the kitchen and servants' quarters. If Camille didn't find Violet, she could ask the cook herself. The basement had stone floors and white-washed walls and smelled of lemon oil mixed with the aroma of food. Two maids hurried past her carrying heavy pitchers toward a room that housed a long table. It looked as if the servants were having their meal.

"Excuse me, but have you seen Lady Leigh?" she asked.

"Yes, ma'am. Down that way." The girl nodded toward what Camille assumed was the kitchen.

"Thank you." She hurried in that direction and was almost at the open door when a hand took hers.

"This way," came a whisper near her ear. Any trepidation she might have felt was swept away by the sound of Jacob's voice behind her.

A heavy black curtain was strung on a brass rod across an opening. He pushed it aside and ushered them both into the small room before pulling it closed behind him. The pantry was not lit, but some of the light from the corridor filtered into the space. Bags of flour and meal shared shelves with tins of food.

He released her, leaving her hand tingling from the touch of his fingers. "What are you doing?" she asked to cover the racing of her heart.

His eyes were warm and soft. "I didn't mean to startle you. I wanted to talk to you alone, but there wasn't an opportunity until now."

She couldn't even begin to describe the warmth and feeling of well-being that was spreading throughout her body as he smiled down at her. She wanted to be angry with him for all but dismissing her. What came out instead was, "I've missed you."

"I've missed you as well. How have you been?"

"Good," she said, but that wasn't precisely true. "My mother arrived unexpectedly, so that's been challenging. She and Frederick have been keeping me occupied."

A shadow passed over his face at the mention of Frederick. "Don't marry Kip."

She laughed at the absurdity of that statement. Thankfully, her mother had seemed resigned to accepting her refusal. They hadn't talked about the things Camille had written about Hereford, but she knew her mother had read them. In the days since, her manner had been subdued, and she had not pressed Frederick on her in any way. She hadn't even left them alone together again.

"Why do you believe I might consider marrying him?"

He shrugged. "He wants to marry you."

"How do you know that?"

He shifted and said, "It's obvious from the way he looks at you that's his intention."

"Perhaps I want to, as well." She couldn't resist taunting him just a little. This wasn't any of his business. He had ushered her out of his life.

"You don't want him." His voice was low and searching. He was jealous. Good.

"Is that why you followed me here? To warn me not to marry a man you don't even know? Because if it was, I have other things to attend to." She made a move to walk past him, but he reached for her, though he stopped before he touched her. His hand hovered near her stomach, making her remember all the ways his fingers knew her body.

"No, that's not why I wanted to talk to you." He reached for her again. This time the pad of his thumb brushed the corner of her mouth before he pulled it back. "You have something there."

"Chocolate?" He nodded, and she wiped at her mouth. "Where?"

His gaze had gone hot as he stared at her mouth, and she didn't think it was her imagination that his breathing increased. "My God, Camille." He said the words on an exhale.

"What?"

Before she could find it, he took her lips, licking at the bit of chocolate she had missed. She could taste the bitter and sweet of it on his tongue. Then she was kissing him back, and it was like the days apart had never happened. His hand cupped her neck, and erotic images of all the ways he had touched her played across her mind, making the kiss far more effective than it might have been otherwise.

As if coming to his senses, he pulled back abruptly. "I wanted to speak to you privately before I go to Paris. I'll be leaving tomorrow evening, so there likely won't be another opportunity."

They had run out of time. She felt stricken and momentarily unable to breathe. He was truly leaving. "I hope all goes well for you in Paris," she finally managed. "You deserve it." God, she would miss him.

He didn't look as happy about the trip as he might have. "We've made all the final arrangements. I'll be gone for three months."

Disappointment made her feel weighted. It grounded her after that kiss like nothing else could. "Yes, that makes sense . . . only I had hoped . . ."

"What?" His eyes brightened in an encouraging way she didn't understand. He had pushed her away after all. "What did you hope?"

The words stuck in her throat, but she forced them out. She was tired of not taking what she wanted; that hadn't gotten her anywhere that she'd wanted to go in the past. "I hoped that maybe we might have one more night before you leave." But that wasn't the whole truth. "Actually, I had hoped that we might have more . . ."

His eyes were fathomless as he stared back at her. "I can't, Camille. Not right now."

She knew he didn't mean the sex. He meant *them*. He couldn't do them right now. He *had* felt what she had felt, and he was rejecting it because it didn't fit into his life. The pain was fierce and sharper than she had suspected it would be. "I see."

When she would have looked down, he took her chin. "Camille . . ." he whispered, regret filling the word. Dropping his hand, he said, "Let's talk when I return from Paris."

When he'd had time to steel himself against the things he felt for her, is what he meant. Or maybe he meant to sleep with a lot of other women in Paris before deciding on her. A heady mix of anger and sadness made her voice have an edge. "Maybe. *If* I'm still here."

She pushed past him, but he took her waist in his hands

and pulled her back to him. Before she knew what was happening, his mouth took hers in a deep kiss. She clung to him as he drank from her lips. The world faded away to only Jacob and his arms and mouth. She had no idea how long they had stood in the pantry kissing before someone cleared their throat very forcefully. Startled, they turned to see Violet smiling at them.

"Bloody hell," he whispered against her temple.

As the strength returned to her knees, Camille pushed herself away from him, putting a small amount of space between them. "Violet, I was looking for you."

"As you can see, I was not in the pantry." Her friend smiled.

"No." She felt like a schoolgirl caught being naughty.

"Come along, dear." Violet held out her hand. To Jacob she said, "I'll deal with you later."

They left together with Jacob behind them, but once in the corridor her mother rounded the corner. They must have been in that pantry longer than she'd thought, to have her mother come looking for her. Mama's eyes widened as she saw them, and Camille wanted to melt into the floor. Her lips felt swollen. She was certain it was obvious what they had been doing.

"There you are, Mama," she said, taking control of the situation. She could not handle being chastised when she was so raw. "I'm ready to go home. Let's go collect Frederick, shall we?"

Her mother uttered a few small protests as Camille took her arm and pulled her in the opposite direction of Jacob and Violet. Her mother kept looking behind them until they had turned the corner and were out of sight.

They dropped Frederick off at Claridge's, where he was meeting a friend for drinks. He hadn't appeared very happy when he'd left the carriage, saying he would be home late and would hire a cab. This left Camille and her mother in a very awkward silence as the carriage made its way through the dark streets to her townhome. This would have been fine because Camille needed time to nurse the wound Jacob had given her by refusing what was between them, but her mother was always talkative and the fact that she wasn't meant she suspected something.

"It was a lovely night," Camille said, hoping if she kept up the conversation her mother wouldn't voice the very evident concerns rolling around in her head. She had been able to read every one with every street light they passed.

"Yes." She sounded distracted.

"I'm glad we went. Mrs. Crenshaw was happy to see you. You were such close friends in New York, and you haven't been able to catch up yet properly."

Ever since the morning Camille had given her mother those pages, Mama had kept them busy moving from one activity to another. She knew it was to keep them from talking about what she had written, which hurt, but she also understood. Mama did not like emotional discussions. Camille had never liked the results when she had pushed her to talk about something she wasn't ready to examine.

"Yes, it was good to see her . . . though I suspect we've grown apart for a reason."

"Oh?"

"Camille, is there something between you and Mr. Thorne?"

Steeling herself for the inevitable, she said, "Yes, if you must know. I care for him very much." There was no use denying it. Whether he returned her feelings or not, she could be honest with herself and her mother.

Mama took in a breath. "He owns a gaming hell and is merely the *natural* child of an earl."

Natural, the polite word for illegitimate. Not legal.

"He is kind and very good to me, Mama. Also, he is

successful in his own right. His legitimacy doesn't matter to me."

The other woman processed this, becoming very still at her side. "Do you care for him enough that you might consider marrying this man?"

She did care for him that much, though any discussion of marriage was a bit premature. Camille shook her head. "It hardly matters. He's leaving for Paris tomorrow night, and I won't see him again for a while. He doesn't feel the same affection for me anyway."

"He doesn't? How could he not? Camille, you are an attractive woman and have such a good heart."

"I thought you didn't approve of him?"

Mama huffed. "Well, perhaps I don't, but he should approve of you. This man isn't as special as you think if he doesn't see your value."

She groaned. "I don't wish to discuss this." Not with her mother!

"It's true." Mama fell silent for so long, she thought that perhaps the conversation was mercifully over. "Camille, I have read and reread the words you wrote . . ."

Her muscles tightened, bracing herself.

"Every night before bed, I take them out and . . ." She shook her head. "The things that Hereford did to you were inexcusable." There was a firmness in her voice that Camille had rarely heard. Her mother took her hand and shifted on the cushioned seat to see her better. "I am sorry for that. I had no idea when I agreed to the marriage that he was that way."

Everything inside her stilled. Her mother had never spoken with this level of gravity. "What were you expecting? It was obvious to all that he was not a kind person."

"Yes, I see that now. I thought he was at least fair and charming and that he would take care of you as he had assured us he would. I thought I was sending you to live the life of a princess. That you would attend lavish balls and visit castles. That there would be no advantage beyond your reach." She took in a quivering breath. "I didn't want you or your future children to have the same experiences as me growing up. I grew up in the country, and when I came to New York I had to work very hard to rid myself of the accent. People mocked me. They whispered that your father could have done better. Then they laughed at the grease under his fingernails when he'd come to dinner after visiting one of the factories. Society isn't kind to outsiders."

"But don't you see that I am an outsider here? He made sure they never accepted me. He made sure that I remembered my low birth." Her own voice trembled with unshed tears. "And that he was too good for me."

"Yes." Her mother's voice cracked, and she swallowed audibly. "I despise him for that. He made me think they would accept you because of who he was. Perhaps they did, in a way. You were invited to the parties . . . you weren't excluded, but he still made certain they laughed at you."

A tear that had been trembling on Camille's lashes fell. Her mother let out a sob and pulled her into her arms. "I thought we were doing what was best for you. I understand now that I was wrong. I'm so sorry that I failed you."

Camille cried all the harder. "You didn't know."

Mama shook her head. "I should have known. I let myself be blinded by him. It was a terrible mistake that is unforgivable."

Perhaps her mother was right. She should have known, and Camille could never imagine sending her own daughter halfway across the world to marry a man she didn't know. She also knew that there was no way to make it right. She had tried these past two years to somehow undo her time with Hereford, but it was impossible. Those scars were emblazoned upon her and they always would be. It was enough for now that Mama had acknowledged the mistake and the pain she had caused. It was a start.

Camille squeezed her eyes shut and let the comfort of her mother's arms seep in and lighten all the places that had gone dark inside. Finally, the carriage slowed. Her mother leaned back and produced a handkerchief from somewhere, dabbing it at Camille's cheeks.

"Tomorrow we will go together to the solicitor and untangle all of this contract nonsense. You were right. You deserve to know what has been decided for you and to access your accounts."

Something loosened in her chest, and she took a deep breath. "Thank you, Mama."

"I want you to be happy, Camille. I do. If this Mr. Thorne will make you happy then I approve of him."

Camille laughed with the enthusiasm of someone who had just been relieved of a grievous weight that she had been carrying for far too long. "Thank you, but I'm not sure he's an option." It seemed she had no choice but to wait for him to return from Paris. She was too hurt and angry about that to even guess how she would feel then. "The suffrage fight brings me joy. Perhaps you could come to the demonstration with me tomorrow evening."

"Oh dear, I'm not certain I am up for a demonstration. I could come to a meeting first. I would like to go with you." She cupped Camille's face in her hands. "I am proud of you."

Camille smiled. "Thank you. I would love for you to accompany me to the next one."

They hugged again and she felt that she could finally start to put together the fractured pieces of herself that she thought had been lost years ago.

Chapter 23

❖

Webb had packed Jacob's trunks and sent them on to the train station earlier in the day. It was now dusk and Jacob was to leave soon to catch the train for Dover. From there he would take the boat for France at first light. He had been in a whirlwind all day seeing to the last-minute details so that Montague Club wouldn't suffer in his absence. Christian and Cavell would handle things, with Evan able to step in when needed. He wasn't worried about them. It was simply that he couldn't allow himself any free time or then he'd start thinking too much.

All day he'd been tugging at his collar and feeling uncomfortable in his own skin. That feeling of wrongness was all because of Camille. He hadn't stopped thinking of her for a single moment since last night—no, since he'd been inside her. Her shadow hovered over every decision he made. When he thought of the next months in Paris, those thoughts were tinged with sadness. He already missed the innate gentleness that she tried to hide. Though she had been jaded in the past few years, it was still there lurking in her eyes, in her smile, and in the tender way she touched him with awe, as if she had never considered that what they found together might exist. The fact that he would be an entire country removed from her felt amiss.

It was no surprise his thoughts were still on her when Webb appeared in the doorway of his study with a strange expression on his face. Jacob was working with Cavell, who stood across the desk, running his finger down a column of numbers in a ledger. "Here," Cavell said, pointing to one particular figure. "This is the error."

But Jacob wasn't listening. Webb was so uncharacteristically apprehensive that something in him sharpened in awareness. "Webb?" He didn't know why but his first thought was something terrible had happened. Camille and Lilian were attending the demonstration today. A quick look at the clock confirmed that it would be starting soon.

Cavell whirled to stare at the man.

Webb cleared his throat. "Mrs. Bridwell is here and demanding to speak with you. I told her that you are leaving soon, but she was most insistent."

Camille's mother was here. She had been conducting a rather thorough study of him the night before. Perhaps she had figured out that he had been kissing her daughter in the pantry and had come to give him a piece of her mind. His anxiety shifted from fear to mere dread of what was likely coming.

"Webb, I am in the middle of this. Give her my address in Paris. She can write—"

His words fell off sharply as the woman herself wrenched his door open wider. "Pardon me," she said to Webb. To Jacob she said, "I would have a moment of your time, Mr. Thorne."

Jacob sighed and came to his feet. There was no avoiding this. "If you'll excuse us, Cavell."

The younger man smirked before he managed to hide

his expression from the others by gathering up the ledger. On his way out he greeted Mrs. Bridwell warmly and closed the door behind him, leaving Jacob to face whatever hell fate had in store for him.

"Good evening, Mrs. Bridwell. Would you care to have a seat?" He indicated the chair on the other side of his desk.

She frowned at him and walked with the reticence of a woman being led to her own end. This was awkward.

"Would you care for a drink?" he asked, walking around the desk to lean against it.

She shook her head and sat perched on the edge of the chair. "No, thank you, Mr. Thorne. I do apologize for barging in this way. I wouldn't have come if I didn't think it was important."

The waning fear returned. This might not be a social visit. "Has something happened to Camille?"

A crease formed between her brows and she took in a breath. "I have come to you directly from calling on Scarbury—er, Hereford . . . the new Duke of Hereford." She shook her head as if the words were all jumbled up.

Titles were bloody confusing for the Americans. Camille must have felt so lost and alone when she had first come here. "What did he have to say?"

"He's been threatening Camille by withholding funds she's legally entitled to. We spoke with the solicitor today who went over the marriage contract and dower with us. Scarbury should have no say in her use of the funds. I thought it prudent to talk with him and remind him of his contractual obligations to her."

He gave her a rueful grin. "I am guessing that didn't go over well." He was thankful that someone would be here to support her against Scarbury's interference.

"No, I suppose not. He seemed disinclined to consider my arguments."

"He's too pompous to consider anyone but himself, I'm afraid."

She nodded. "I intend to get my lawyer involved and I'll inform my husband. A review of her statement of accounts is in order. However, that's not what concerns me. He said something that has bothered me since I left."

"What did he say?"

She appeared uneasy, her face lined in concern and her hands clasped tight in her lap. "As we were talking, he expressed his displeasure in some of Camille's actions. Becoming a member of your club was one." She gave him an assessing look to see what he thought of that. He didn't react because of course the man would not like her being independent and stepping out of line with what he thought was socially acceptable. She continued. "I agreed with him that some of her behavior wasn't entirely proper. But then he brought up her involvement in the London Suffrage Society. I pretended to share that concern because I wanted to know what he would say. As it turns out, he had a lot to say on the matter. He railed for a while against the idea of women as equals and the idea of us having political power. Then he went on to talk about the demonstration to protest the defeat of the women's suffrage bill and was very unhappy about it. When I pretended to share his concern, he told me that I needn't worry. Some associates of his would see to the women and their demonstration. At the time I didn't think very much of the comment. I assumed he meant the men would heckle them or some such, but now that I've had time to consider it, I believe he meant something more sinister."

Her accusations were grave, but he couldn't fathom that the man would stoop to anything dangerous. "What do you mean, *sinister*? What do you think he means to do?"

"He had a look in his eye when he spoke of his associates. A gleam. I have the feeling he didn't mean nobles, but rough characters. Perhaps I should have turned back and gone to find Lord Leigh or Rothschild, but I was almost here before I convinced myself that he means to do them harm." A look of desperation came over her. "Will you be able to do something?"

Another glance at the clock confirmed that the demonstration was starting. It also reminded him that he would need to leave soon for his train. "My sister Lilian is on the LSS board. They have hired men for protection when they do events like these. They will be safe."

Mrs. Bridwell leaned forward, and her hands moved to clench the arms of the chair. "I don't think a few men will be enough. I believe they mean to do something terrible."

Jacob kept his voice calm because hers was rising in panic. "The duke would not arrange something dangerous. It would be too easy to trace it back to him."

"Are you so certain of that? He could hire a street gang, and who would believe them over the word of a duke? You forget, sir, not everyone has a pedigree that grants them immunity from doubt."

She was right. The duke and his friends in Parliament would stand together and staunchly deny any such claims brought against them. The hired men would certainly not be believed if they chose to betray those who had hired them. Still, it would be extreme. "Forgive me, madam, but I simply cannot believe that he would stoop to such machinations."

"Then you don't know him. Neither do I, if you want the truth, but I know his type. He would step over my daughter and anyone else who got in his way."

"All right, I'll have my security go over in case something happens," Jacob relented. He still doubted the duke would have arranged anything, but he'd feel better knowing his men were there.

"You're off to Paris tonight. I'd forgotten." She sniffed as if the very idea was disdainful and rose. What exactly had Camille told her about them? "Pardon me, Mr. Thorne, I thought you cared for my daughter."

"I do."

"But not enough to see to her protection for yourself, I suppose? You must think her suitable only for stealing kisses from in closets."

"Mrs. Bridwell, I assure you that I hold your daughter in the highest esteem—"

"She certainly holds great affection for you. I gave her my blessing on this endeavor, but perhaps I was too hasty. If you'll excuse me, Mr. Thorne, I must go and find someone willing to intervene in what might be a terrible tragedy otherwise."

Her blessing? What the hell was happening here? "Mrs. Bridwell—"

She closed the door behind her rather forcefully. He sat back against the desk and remembered the sight of Scarbury's hand on Camille, and the silent flash of anger in his eyes when Jacob had intervened. He didn't know anything about her dower, but he knew that if she died then Scarbury wouldn't have to share any of Hereford's estate with her. He couldn't bring himself to believe that the man would actually plan something so sinister. Perhaps he didn't plan for her death, but he wouldn't mourn her if one of the men he'd hired were careless.

Mrs. Bridwell must have been very worried to come to him, which meant that it was possible the threat was very, very real.

"Bloody hell," he muttered. "Cavell!"

He hurried to the cupboard tucked into one of his bookcases and unlocked it to withdraw two pearl-handled pistols.

Camille had never attended any sort of social demonstration before. She had expected the rhyming chants and the handmade signs that called for women's suffrage. She had not expected the taunts and jeers from passersby.

Men and women would sneer at them as they went about their day, content in their belief that by asking for the right to vote, the women were committing some sort of egregious outrage against God, the very fabric of society, and nature. Perhaps she might have understood the men. After all, they would have to step aside and share roles with women were the vote to pass. She could not, however, understand the women's resistance to suffrage.

If women could vote, then it would only help other women. If the women who disagreed with a woman's right to vote chose not to utilize her right, well then, that was her choice. She could not understand why they would feel threatened or disapprove of such an act. It was the one shock of the evening that she was not prepared for. It helped that Lilian was at her side when the first woman shouted out to them, calling them vulgar names.

"Do not be concerned with her." She spared the woman a glance out of the corner of her eye before giving Camille a sad smile. "We cannot know what motivates such women, but I tell myself she must have a deeply overbearing husband or family who might even punish her if they thought she agreed with us."

"Do you really think so?" Camille asked, distraught by the very idea.

She sighed. "No, not really. People move against their own interests all the time. They are driven by fear and insecurity. All we can do is keep moving forward despite them."

It was true. This was the second bill introduced to Parliament in as many years that had failed. They could only turn their attention to a new bill for women's suffrage, and the current one for women's rights that would be presented as soon as it garnered enough support: the Married Women's Property Act. If it passed, it would go further than the previous act to ensure that women kept freedoms even in marriage. It would be one more chip at the control men kept over the women in their lives.

"I wish there was something more we could do. Something besides marching and demonstrating."

Lilian nodded her agreement. "We have our voices and we'll use them. Your account of your time with Hereford was very powerful and moving. Thank you for being brave enough to write it and share it with me."

It had taken a few days, but Camille had allowed Lilian to read a copy. After some discussion about it, Lilian had helped her craft a speech about her experience. They had culled some of the more intimate parts that Camille wasn't ready to share or talk about publicly and elaborated on others. The only way to reach people would be to share her story.

Camille planned to approach the organizers of the LSS to allow her to give the speech at one of their meetings. Then, hopefully, they would publish it in their monthly newsletter. It would be her first test in front of a crowd of people along with her first time talking about her ordeal publicly. She was excited for this next step and how it would help women.

"I only hope I can deliver the speech with the earnestness it deserves. I've never spoken publicly before, not like that." She had addressed people at a ball, but that was different than pouring your heart out to them. Lilian assured her that other people would want to hear her story as well, so at least her first outing at LSS would be with a sympathetic audience.

"You'll do fine. These people need to hear what happened to you. It's the only way we can change minds. But if you're not ready, we can wait." She touched her shoulder. "You can tell it later, or we could print it first. Whichever you want."

"No, I'm ready whenever they want me to speak." Waiting would only increase her nerves. "I need to do this."

Lilian squeezed her shoulder. "We'll practice together. I'll not heckle you or interrupt, I promise," she teased.

Camille laughed, glad that she had invited this woman to tea so that they could be friends, even if her eyes did remind Camille so much of Jacob's. Tomorrow he would be in another country. She swallowed against the ache thoughts of him evoked. "Thank you. Yes, let's do that. I could use practice."

After a few minutes, Lilian fell back to talk to one of the organizers. Camille tightened her grip on the sign she carried: *Votes for Women* painted in red and blue on a white background. A light snow had been falling all day off and on, which meant the evening was cold. As she continued her march around the green space, the statue of Lord Palmerston looked over the proceedings in disapproval. She shivered and tried to burrow into her coat more. Her enthusiasm for the evening and her pride in taking charge of her life and doing something about the plight of women had kept her warm for the first bit, but the frigid wind was starting to win out.

She could not help but wonder two things. The first was how long they must demonstrate before the men in Parliament noticed them. The second was if Jacob had left for Paris yet. He was supposed to leave tonight, but she had not asked for the specifics of his travel plans. She told herself it was because she didn't want to know. However, she knew it was because she was hurt that she wasn't close enough to him that he would tell her such things. Or perhaps she was hurt that he was leaving. It made no sense to her. He had a life of his own, and a business he planned to start in Paris. She should not want to keep him from that, and she didn't. She simply wanted to share a piece of his life with him. He was pushing her out of his heart, not only his life, and that was the worst of it—the knowing that he was choosing to walk away from what they might have.

A loud pop broke through the normal evening sounds around her. It sounded like a firework or possibly gunfire.

A woman on the other side of the circle screamed and another yelped in surprise. A white pop of light came flying into the middle of the group, and it was quickly followed by several more. White shards of light cut through the gloomy evening dark. A streak of fire touched her cheek but it was gone as quickly as it appeared. All around her trails of fire cascaded from the sky, popping and hissing as they fell into the snow. She realized they were chains of firecrackers tied together right before all hell broke loose. Screams rent through the night air. Panic gripped the crowd and women scattered. She looked for Lilian and saw her helping an older woman to the cover of a nearby tree.

An unholy sound drew her attention back to the street. An entire crate of what she suspected to be fireworks exploded in the middle of the road. A horse screamed and took off, pulling the carriage it towed at a breakneck pace. The dwindling crowds on the sidewalk screeched, fleeing the area. That wasn't the worst of it. A group of at least twenty men, all wearing hoods of burlap, broke from an alleyway and through the evening pedestrians and headed their way. They were yelling and angry and each one carried some sort of baton. For the first time that night she knew real fear. Even the pedestrians were afraid; not knowing who or what was happening, they, too, scattered and it was impossible to know who was a demonstrator and who was a bystander. It was chaos.

She dropped her sign and turned to run, but it was too late. There were masses of people ahead of her and nowhere to go. Someone pushed her into an elderly woman who stumbled. Camille stopped to help her, only to have someone trample on her skirts so that she couldn't get back to her feet as a river of people ran over the wide expanse of fabric. The woman gave her an apologetic look before hurrying away. Camille yanked, ripping her skirt from beneath the heavy boot that held it down but could not get to her feet because someone on her other side tripped into her. Her palm slammed into the cobblestones and she was pushed to her side.

Her hands automatically came up to shield her face, and she caught sight of a hooded man bearing down on her. He raised his baton and she could already imagine the terrible pain as it crushed her rib. An instant before he would have brought it down someone stepped in front of her. The man's forearm came up to stop the blow and his fist punched the man in the stomach, effectively disarming him as he dropped the baton to clatter on the stones. The man didn't even stay to fight. He ran back toward the alley, several of his group running with him.

Her rescuer turned to face her and she couldn't believe her eyes. "Jacob!"

His features were harsh with fear and anger as he looked down at her. She hardly felt him grabbing her arms, but all of a sudden she was standing in front of him and then encircled by his arms. "Are you hurt?" His concerned gaze took in her face as his hands roamed parts of her body she was sure was indecent for public eyes. Not that anyone noticed them in the chaos.

"Yes—No, I'm not hurt. I mean, yes, I'm fine." She couldn't think straight. It didn't make sense that he was here. "Why are you here? Aren't you supposed to be going to Paris?"

"Later," he said and put his arm around her, tucking her against his side as if she were precious and he didn't mean to let her go.

He fought through the crowd, attempting to get them to the relative safety of the tree where Lilian was sheltered with the older woman, but it was like swimming against the tide. Someone rammed into them. She cried out more from shock than pain and Jacob whirled to attack the hooded man. When he reached into his coat to pull out what she suspected would be a weapon, someone intervened. Lord Devonworth, fresh from the halls of Parliament, punched the hooded brute, knocking him down to the ground, where the man groaned and didn't get back up right away. Jacob pushed her toward Lilian, so she hurried the final few yards to reach the small group under the tree. The hooded man rolled, clearly dizzy. Devonworth pulled his arms behind his back and with Jacob's assistance brought him up to his knees.

"Leigh!" he yelled, and Christian hurried over from where he had been with Evan and Cox, whom she recognized from the club. They held another of the culprits as prisoner. With Christian's help, they were able to tie his hands.

The men must have come out from Parliament when the attack had started, which was about the time Jacob must have arrived with Cox and the other men from the club she could see aiding some of the women who had been knocked to the ground. The police and Parliament security had also arrived. The entire episode had probably only lasted a few minutes, but it felt like so much longer.

"The others have run off," Jacob said, stowing the gun back in his coat as he approached.

The green space had cleared considerably. He was right. Only two of the hooded men remained to be arrested, though their burlap sacks had been taken off. Camille didn't recognize the men at all, but from their poor teeth and crooked noses that had been broken more than once in the past, she would have bet they were part of a street gang.

"Are you injured?" Lilian asked, having likely seen Camille get nearly trampled.

"No, I'm not. Are you?" Camille struggled to catch her breath as her heart still raced.

"I'm fine," Lilian said, leaning against the tree as if only now letting herself believe the danger was past.

Anthony, her husband, found them and drew Lilian against him. The embrace lasted only a moment but it conveyed the great affection between them. Lilian touched his face and said something too low for Camille to hear. She was trying to appear uninterested in the exchange as she ascertained whether the elderly woman had any injuries.

"Lilian!" Jacob came up to the group and embraced his sister. "Are you hurt?"

"No," she said, her brow furrowed in concern as her attention was drawn back to the scene. "We were frightened, but it seems as if there are no injuries."

Camille followed her gaze to the criminals. The policemen were leading them away, and some of her fear dissipated, leaving her feeling weak as the tension left.

"They'll be taken to jail," Jacob said. "Is there anything we need to do to get these people home?"

Anthony shook his head. "Our carriages were parked out of the way. We need to get everyone loaded so we can get out of here. They probably won't come back, but I imagine no one wants to linger."

Lilian nodded, and Anthony took the arm of one of the elderly women and led her toward one of the carriages parked down the block. "Camille?"

Before she could answer, Jacob took her hand. "I'll see her home."

Lilian nodded again, an almost-smile touching her lips. Taking the other elderly woman's arm, she led her off.

"What are you doing here, Jacob?" Camille asked as he led her toward the group of noblemen who had run out from Parliament to help.

They were very lucky that Evan and Christian had been there that day. Men in Parliament weren't known for their kindness to protestors.

Devonworth ran a hand through his hair and flinched as he noticed a cut on his brow. One of the men must have hit him. It was a good thing the damage hadn't been worse, she found herself thinking. His face was far too handsome to mar in such a way. Handsome and he had come to the rescue of women's suffragists when he could have stayed inside with most of the other men.

Instead of answering, Jacob squeezed her hand gently, and then put his arm around her. She didn't mind, even though now it was almost certainly indecently close since the chaos had settled and everyone was returning to their senses. She needed his comfort just now. Slight trembles were working their way through her.

To the group, he said, "They used fireworks to startle the crowd and signal chaos." Pointing toward the direction they had come, he added, "Then they ran in. I suspect chaos was the point rather than actual damage and injury."

"There were around a score of them. Maybe twenty-five at most," she clarified. "They ran in from that alley over there."

The group of men looked at the one she indicated. "They couldn't have tossed fireworks from that far. Not with such accuracy." This was from Evan, who joined them holding a chain of exploded fireworks that had been tied together.

"Those were thrown into the crowd first," she said. "I agree it was too far to be accomplished from the alley. There must have been one or two without hoods who blended into the pedestrians and tossed them over. Why would they do this?"

Jacob tightened his arm around her before he said, "I believe Hereford paid them."

"Scarbury? Why?" she asked.

"Because he's a bellend."

The others appeared just as surprised. Jacob relayed the conversation he'd had with her mother, which was almost as surprising as the attack had been. Her mother had gone to see him. She almost couldn't fathom it.

"We need to question Hereford immediately," said Devonworth. The others agreed, and after a moment they headed off to see that accomplished.

Jacob's lips brushed her temple when he said, "We need to get you out of here in case they come back."

"Yes, okay."

They were almost running as he led her down the pavement through the snow, ever vigilant as they passed shops that had closed for the night and only a few pedestrians. The sounds of policemen clearing up the mess disappeared behind them as they turned a corner and Jacob pulled her into the alcove of a closed shop's front door and windows. His hands cupped her face, and he pressed his mouth to her temple.

"I was so afraid when I saw the chaos. I thought I had come too late. Are you certain you aren't hurt?" he whispered.

"I'm not hurt. Surprised, I suppose, a little angry. Do you think Scarbury targeted me?"

He shook his head, sending loose flakes of snow toppling to his shoulders. "Not like you mean. He's said terrible things about the suffragists for a while now. He's still bitter about the Reform Act. He doesn't believe men outside of the gentry should be allowed the vote."

There were still men in the countryside and those who held no property or leases in the city who weren't allowed to vote. It was all because of men like Scarbury, who sought to keep power for themselves, when they were the ones who were too selfish and cruel to hold power responsibly.

"There have been other demonstrations that have been disrupted," he continued. "Now that we know what he's capable of, I bet we can trace some of those disruptions back to him."

She closed her eyes and leaned against his solid strength. His heart beat rapidly beneath her ear, filling her with a sense of well-being completely at odds with the terror of the past few minutes. In her mind she watched him break through the crowd all over again and save her. She relived that single moment of exhilaration and hope that took her over because he had come.

"You came to me," she whispered, looking up at him in awe.

"I couldn't leave you in danger." His fathomless gaze met hers, his eyes black in the night.

She swallowed her foolish disappointment. She had thought he meant to say that he couldn't leave her—end of sentence. "Thank you."

His brow furrowed as he caught something from either her tone or her expression. One hand slid down her back, pulling her tight against him, while the other cupped the nape of her neck, his fingers clenching pleasantly in her hair. "I didn't want to leave you at all," he whispered, an ache in his voice, before he pressed a kiss to the corner of her mouth.

"But you would have." Her head turned of its own volition, seeking him.

His lips brushed hers. "No, I don't think I could have."

His mouth took hers in a soft kiss that quickly became powerful. She held on to his shoulders as if she might lose him forever. His tongue brushed hers, and the taste of him was so familiar and welcome she wanted to cry. How could she have found this only to have him not return everything she felt? It seemed so unfair, and a moment of anger overtook her. Perhaps it was fueled by the chaos from earlier, but she couldn't deny it any longer.

Keeping a firm grasp on his shoulders, she pushed back to see his face. "You meant to leave me, Jacob, and now you think you can kiss me?"

"I was an idiot. Come with me to Paris." His lips traced her jaw and then that spot she was finding she loved just behind her ear. "I can't go without you. I don't want to be without you in my life, Camille." He nipped the fine skin of her neck and lapped at the indentation where her neck met her shoulder. "Come with me."

Her eyes fell closed as she let his words penetrate the fog of arousal that was threatening to consume her. "To Paris? I can't leave. I have to stay and . . ." Why did she need to stay? He cupped her breast through her stiff corset and she longed to feel him against her skin. "I have to give a speech at an LSS meeting."

"We can come back when you're needed here." He rose above her to meet her gaze. "I need you with me. We should be together and I'm tired of fighting it. I cannot fight it anymore. I love you and I want you in my life."

She could barely comprehend what he said and must have stood staring up at him for a full minute. "You love me?"

"I love you, Camille." He took her mouth again in a searing kiss. "Please forgive me for being a fool who thought I could push that aside?"

"I don't understand." She could not bring herself to believe what he was saying to her.

He gave a soft laugh and took her face between his hands. "Camille, you are the single most admirable woman I have ever met aside from my mother. I admire you and how you have overcome your past. More than that, however, I love you. I miss you when you're not with me. I miss your laugh and your soulful eyes and the way you smile at me and I feel as if I can do anything."

"What about the Halston curse?"

He laughed. "Bugger it. It's already got me in its clutches, hasn't it?"

She joined in his laughter because there was nothing else she could do. He loved her and he wanted her. He had come for her. He hauled her against him and half carried her out of the alcove and back to the street.

"What are you doing?" she squealed.

"My carriage is around the corner. We're going home."

His home, not hers. She could think of no complaints about that. A groom awaited, holding the reins of the horse he must have ridden on the way over, and a carriage waited behind them. There was a curious fluttering in her belly as she imagined him riding his horse through the city in a mad dash to get to her. After telling the groom to take his horse home, he ushered her into the carriage like a man possessed and climbed in behind her. She had barely gotten settled before he hauled her onto his lap, and he kissed her the entire way back to Montague Club.

Chapter 24

❦

Webb opened the door to the private area of the house for them as soon as they hurried up the steps. His *good evening* had barely been uttered before Jacob started giving orders. "Send a wire to Blanchet and let him know I'll be a day—" He paused to glance at Camille as she shrugged out of her coat. Her smile was shy and knowing all at the same time after endless kissing in the carriage sent the precious little remaining blood in his head rushing south to his cock. It would take more than a day in bed with her to find his sanity. "Perhaps two days late. I imagine the train has already gone, but please try to retrieve my trunks."

She bit her lip to dampen her smile, her cheeks reddening, and a thrill of excitement at how they might spend those hours rushed in and pushed out the bitter dredges left from what had happened earlier. He would think about it tomorrow. The world had narrowed to only the two of them and their temporary cocoon. Everyone else could be damned until he was ready to face what the future might mean. He was keenly aware that he had confessed his love for her and that she had not said it back to him. Nor had she agreed to come to Paris with him. The hazardous edge of desperate fear loomed that a woman—*this woman*—might not return his feelings. He could be patient with her. He intended to use his time with her showing her exactly how well they fit together. If she intended to refuse him, she would do it whilst in a delirious state from orgasms.

"Have a messenger go to Mrs. Bridwell," he added. "Tell her that Her Grace is well and will be spending the night here."

She had just handed her coat and gloves to Webb, who did not seem particularly surprised by her presence. "Jacob! Staying here is one thing but blatantly stating it to my mother is another."

He grinned and, free of his outerwear, ushered her toward the stairs with his hands on her waist. "She might as well know. It's preferable to her charging over here at an inopportune moment. The woman is prone to barging in," he murmured near her ear.

She giggled, the light and bubbly sound of it washing over him. He loved this side of her, every side of her really, but this side was so new and fresh, he couldn't get enough of it. Near the top of the stairs, she glanced below, sudden doubt crossing her lovely features. Webb had faded away to see to his tasks, but she stiffened in a way that was almost imperceptible. He might not have realized had he not been so in tune with her.

Pausing at the top of the stairs, he turned her to face him, pressing forward until her back came up against the wall. Her eyes were soft and uncertain, piercing his heart. What if he was moving too fast for her again? Kisses in a carriage racing through the streets of London and sex in his bed were two very different things.

He leaned over her, cupping her cheek. "Do I frighten you?"

"No," she whispered, the soft light in the corridor casting shadows that played across her face.

"You do want to stay the night with me?"

She nodded, swallowing thickly as if unable to speak. Her wide-eyed unsophistication was an aphrodisiac that had never appealed to him before her. But when she looked at him that way, God, he wanted to devour her. The light picked up the gold flecks in her eyes.

He traced a path with his forefinger down the slope of her nose to her lips then dropped to the top button of her high bodice. The collar came up almost to her chin. "We don't have to do anything that makes you uncomfortable." Overcome with the need to be closer to her, he leaned down and whispered against her hairline, "I can hold you." His lips brushed her temple, breathing in her scent. Her cheek. "Kiss you." She turned a bit toward him as his fingertip found its way through the space between two buttons in her jacket and touched the linen of her chemise. "Lick you."

She made a soft sound of longing in the back of her throat. Gratification that she was responding favorably to his touch surged through him. "I want you, Jacob. I want to be with you."

His eyes briefly touched on her mouth. Her bottom lip glistened from their recent kisses, and he only barely restrained himself from taking her mouth again. She was on the verge of confessing something and he didn't want to stop her.

Her palm rested on his neck, and her fingers played in his hair. "It's only that . . ." She paused and took a breath before hurrying on as if she could lose her nerve. "I suppose it occurred to me that you might have been with other women lately, and I know I shouldn't mind, we don't—or haven't—discussed exclusivity." He frowned and she closed her eyes tightly before hurrying on. "But I . . . the thought of those others makes me sad and a little angry if I'm being honest. It doesn't matter." She broke off, shaking her head as if she had said too much and any more might humiliate her.

Removing his finger from its play between her buttons, he tipped her chin upward and waited for her to look at him. Whatever fear he felt that she might ultimately reject his heart, it was reflected in her expression. He realized that that may well be why she had not returned the words he so wanted to hear from her. "There hasn't been anyone since that first night with you, Camille."

Her gaze narrowed in suspicion. "But Mrs. Godwin? You were lovers."

"Were, and yes, she wanted to be so again, but I refused her gently."

"What?" Her lips parted at the shock of it.

"Alarming, yes, I know," he said. "There have been opportunities, but I was either too busy or too tired, and then I realized it was neither of those things." He stroked her soft cheek, understanding almost too late how much of an idiot he had been in running from his feelings for her. "It was that I wanted only you. I've thought about you every day, every hour since you came into my life with your delightful proposition."

"Jacob," she whispered, drawing his mouth down to hers.

He kissed her but pulled back because he needed to say this to her, to make certain that she understood. "I was an idiot before when I made you leave. I did it because I thought I could outrun my feelings for you." But that wasn't true. "No, that's not entirely accurate. Even then I knew it was too late to outrun my feelings and I was afraid." He laughed. "I'm not a brave man."

She shook her head. "You are brave. You came and helped us tonight. You saved me."

"Danger to my heart is another matter."

"I wouldn't hurt you." She said it candidly and tenderly, her voice so raw that he wanted to gather her against him.

"It's not a rational fear. I love you and I always will, whether you love me back or not. Running away from that won't stop a damned thing."

She let out a soft laugh and pushed up onto her toes, kissing him again. "I love you, Jacob. I do. I guess I'm afraid of what that means."

"I won't hurt you, Camille."

Her smile widened. "Take me to bed, Jacob Thorne."

He laughed, nearly overcome with the purest joy he had ever felt in his life as he swept her up into his arms.

Camille had never known the blissful contentment of security that she felt in Jacob's arms. It was as if when he held her the world quieted and nothing could penetrate the barrier of his love shielding her. It hadn't always been this way. As he carried her through the front drawing room where they had had their first encounter, she remembered how afraid she had been and how she had left him. She remembered the uncertainty and nausea and all the other bad feelings that had accompanied the first days of their arrangement.

And now she trusted him completely. She knew that he would rather hurt himself than do anything to cause her discomfort, and the sense of well-being that brought with it was damned stimulating. She was already aching between her thighs when he let her slide down the length of his lean muscled body until her feet touched the floor.

"Turn around." His voice was soft but filled with that husky quality she had come to recognize meant he was aroused, as if she didn't already know after sitting on his lap the whole ride here. She loved the way it was always accompanied by a deepening of his eyes that made her feel like he could devour her and she would ask for more.

Her legs trembled as she did as he asked. He tugged at the lacing of her skirts while she unfastened the buttons of her jacket. She gasped when she had barely finished and he was pulling it off her shoulders and down her arms to lie discarded on the floor. Her skirt and petticoat followed and then he was divesting her of her corset. Each tug of the laces sent a thrill running through her. When only her chemise, stockings, and shoes were left, she stepped out of the pile of fabric and turned to face him. There was an almost dangerous dip of his chin as he watched her, as if he were waiting for her to run or thwart him in some way, and she loved the way it made her stomach tumble pleasantly, all because she knew that they could play this game and he would let her keep her power.

Her hands came up to the ribbons at the top of her chemise holding it closed above her breasts, but she didn't tug them open. "Camille," he warned.

She smiled, exhilarated at the power she held over him. The bulge at the front of his trousers let her know exactly how much he wanted her. "You have on entirely too many clothes, Mr. Thorne. It's not fair for you to see me in such a state of undress."

His jaw clenched, the muscle working beneath his smooth skin. His hands came up to work the buttons of his shirtsleeves, and she noticed with not a little bit of awe that his fingers also trembled with his need for her. When he was shirtless, she admired the broad expanse of muscle as he watched her. He raised a brow in question, as if asking if he'd gone far enough.

The only sound in the room was the fire crackling in the hearth, which made the sound of her ribbons coming untied absurdly loud. He followed her movements closely with his eyes as she slowly untied each one until all it took was a little shimmy to make the warm linen fall down her arms to lie in a pool of white at her feet. She still wore her silk stockings, garters, and shoes, and didn't bother to take them off as she climbed onto the large bed. The counterpane had already been pulled back, and she wondered—as she had downstairs and again when she had noticed the fire—how much of this Webb had anticipated.

But then she forgot to think at all because Jacob was furiously unlacing his boots and she refused to miss the sight of those lean muscles working beneath his silken skin. He was, indeed, the most beautiful man she had ever seen. Each boot fell to the floor with a thump, and then his strong hands worked the fastenings of his trousers. She unconsciously held her breath until he finished and pushed them down past his hips, allowing his rather large erection the freedom to arch up toward his navel. She couldn't look away as he stepped out of his trousers, his hand going to his length to caress it, easing the foreskin back to reveal the glistening tip.

She might not have looked away had he not grabbed her ankle and pulled her down the bed to him. She let out a whimper when he put his knee on the bed and crawled toward her. If she ever wanted him more than this, she didn't think she would survive it. Her entire body felt ready to combust, primed for the barest touch of him. Sitting back on his haunches, he unlaced her ankle boots, tossing them off the bed before he took her stocking-clad foot in his hand and brought it to his mouth, where he pressed a kiss to the tender arch. She couldn't believe the tenderness that was contained in this powerful man. An ache formed in her throat, but she swallowed it down before he could think she was afraid.

He kissed a path up her leg to the place where her garter hooked on the silk and he released it, rolling the stocking down her leg. Then he did the same to the other leg until she was completely nude and open before him. He kissed and nipped his way up, pushing her thighs wider with the width of his shoulders sliding between them. She lay back, hardly daring to breathe, as his trail of kisses took him to her damp center. The rough and smooth texture of his tongue worked over her sensitive and swollen flesh, first circling her clitoris before dipping between her inner lips to plunge into her. She gasped at how strange and wonderful it felt. He moved back to her swollen nub and sucked gently, sending spirals of pleasure through her. She tried to hold her composure, to enjoy him without falling apart, but it wasn't long before her fingers found his hair, holding him to her, and her hips rose up, seeking more. His tongue and lips worked together, alternately sucking and licking until she could no longer tell one from the other. Her world narrowed to him between her thighs and the delicious things he was doing to her. Finally, when the coil of pleasure in her belly had tightened almost unbearably, the world came apart at the seams and release crashed over her.

He waited until she lay panting and spent, everything coming back into soft focus, before he let her go and continued his path up her body. He pressed hot, openmouthed kisses to her stomach, his tongue dipping into her navel. Soft kisses covered her ribs and then he settled in at her breast. He teased her nipple with his tongue, laving it before taking it into his mouth and sucking. A tug of longing pulled at her core, surprising her in its ferocity since she had only just come. It didn't seem to matter. She couldn't get enough of him. He moved from one breast to the other, feasting on her as his eyes had promised her he would. When he finally made it to her mouth, she could taste herself on him, and the base intimacy of that had her writhing beneath him, arching toward him with a need she barely recognized.

"Please, Jacob." She hardly recognized her voice.

He knew exactly what she wanted. Levering himself off of her, he pulled open the drawer beside the bed and tossed off the lid of the jar that he kept there. The metal clanged against the glass. He withdrew one of the small round sponges and settled on his knees between her spread thighs, a forearm near her head to hold his weight. She grasped his bicep as he pushed it inside her, marveling at how sensitive she was that even that felt like heaven. He was gentle as he seated it within her and then worked his thick finger slowly in and out, rubbing against a spot inside her that sent her hips arching toward him. He added another finger, priming her for him, causing her hips to move in a seeking rhythm.

"You're so bloody beautiful," he whispered in that honey and whisky voice that sent shivers over her body as he withdrew from her.

He settled over her, moving slowly and with a restraint that left her in awe. His body was taut and rigid, drawn tight with a need that had to be greater than hers since she had so recently found release, but he kept his movements careful and measured. She touched the flat plains of his stomach, drawn by the beauty of his muscular body, her hands settling low on his back to pull him closer. Her thighs widened to accept him.

When he had fully settled over her, his forearms holding the bulk of his weight and his hips cradled between her thighs, he met her gaze. "Is this good?" he whispered.

She couldn't stop the unexpectedly sharp bite of tears. His brow furrowed in concern as he saw them, forcing her to grab hold of his buttocks to keep him in place before he moved away. "Yes," she managed, sucking in a breath. "Yes." How could she explain to him how overcome she was by his tenderness and consideration?

He leaned down and kissed a tear away from the corner of her lashes and then rolled his hips. The hard ridge of his erection pressed against her clitoris. She gasped at the waves of pleasure that sent moving through her. He did it again and once more until she was canting her hips to receive him. "I need you," she whispered.

He took her mouth in a kiss that was made all the more tender by its intensity, and lining his cock up with her entrance, he pressed inside. Releasing her lips, he drew back far enough to study her as he slowly made his way, her narrow passage stretching to receive him. He withdrew twice before he was finally able to fully seat himself inside her. They both stopped breathing at the particular moment when her hips tilted upward and he thrust down, so that he was inside her as deeply as he was able to go. Impossibly deep. They had never done this before. He'd never been so fully a part of her like this. That night in the secret room, he'd only been partially inside her.

"Did I hurt you?" Strain was evident in his voice.

"No." She didn't have a word for how this felt. *Good* seemed too paltry.

"You're tight," he groaned.

"I'm sorry."

He gave a soft laugh. "No, it's a good thing."

She smiled up at him, mildly embarrassed, but not really. "Then is it okay if I say that you're big?" She clenched him intimately.

Mischief lit his eyes. "Yes. As a matter of fact you're required to tell me daily."

She laughed and he rolled his hips and the laugh became a moan. Her fingers tightened on his hips, and she knew her fingernails might be hurting him but she couldn't let him go. He didn't seem to mind as he did it again and again, settling into a gentle rhythm. His demeanor changed as his jaw clenched against the pleasure.

"How is this?" His voice ended on a soft grunt, overcome by what he felt.

She shifted, pressing her hips upward to receive more of him. When she did, it made his cock drag across a sensitive place within her. Her hips jerked and he groaned. "More," she cried, widening her legs to get even closer to him, to possess more of him.

He gave a single hard thrust, testing her as he watched her, gauging her reaction. It was exactly what she wanted, and she responded by grinding against him. She tried to watch him and savor the fact that she had caused the pleasure breaking over his face, but she couldn't. She was too consumed by him. Instead, she tugged him closer, her mouth open against his shoulder, his neck, needing his taste on her tongue.

He muttered something incoherent and took her harder. His hand cupped her bottom, lifting her and showing her how to ride him. Her body didn't need much tutelage; she responded to him instinctively as he rocked inside her. Somewhere in the back of her mind she was aware of how wet she was for him and how the bed squeaked with every thrust and how this was the most amazing thing she had ever experienced. But in her mind she could only think *more, more, more.*

She didn't realize she was chanting it until his hand tangled in her hair and he pulled her head back, just enough to tug in a way that shot directly to her core. His mouth found her neck and he growled, "Like this?"

She nearly came undone. "God, yes, Jacob!" This new position left her clinging to him as he drove into her, each powerful thrust pushing them higher, hurtling toward a breaking point. Nothing mattered but this . . . them.

The coil inside her wound tighter, the tension mounting. Each thrust of his cock against that place inside her pushing her closer and closer until all at once the tension broke and she contracted around him. His breath was harsh in her ear, his soft, masculine grunts filling her with a very different sort of satisfaction. His hips pumped in a fractured rhythm as he found his own release.

There was no sense in talking. There were no words to describe how she felt. Cherished, loved, exhilarated, exhausted. Everything was a jumble in her mind. After a few moments, when they had caught their breath, he moved to the side and held her against his chest. His arms wrapped around her and her leg burrowed between his. He pulled the blanket over them both, and she closed her eyes to savor the beat of his heart against her ear. This is what had been missing from her life. This feeling of well-being surrounded by his woodsy and vetiver scent.

She knew cuddling was acceptable after sex. She had confirmed it with Violet. She meant to tell him, but the warmth of his body on one side and the blanket on the other lured her with promises of the most exquisite sleep she had ever had.

Chapter 25

✤

The sound of the fire blazing higher woke her a short while later. He turned away after having added more coal and shrugged out of the robe he wore. She couldn't stop the smile that tugged at her lips as she watched him come back to bed.

"You left."

"I didn't want you to get cold." He slipped back beneath the covers. He must not have been gone long because the sheets were still warm.

"I haven't been cold since you came to me at the demonstration." Which was true. She hadn't noticed the snow or the biting wind since he had come between her and certain danger.

He smiled down at her, brushing a strand of hair from her face. "How do you feel?"

She stretched beneath the luxury of his devotion. Even her toes felt the happiness of a well-fed cat full on a bowl of warm cream. "Wonderful. Did I sleep long?"

"Only a few minutes."

"Good. I don't want this night to end."

She hadn't meant it any particular way, but a shadow passed over his eyes. "I want you to come to Paris with me."

He had mentioned it earlier, but she had been too caught up in his confession of love to give equal measure to that. "I don't know if I can. I have commitments here."

"Yes, I know. We can come back for that, and the next thing, and the one after that."

She sat up against the headboard and he positioned himself beside her, but it really wasn't fair to have this conversation now. With the sheet pooled at his waist and nothing covering the gorgeous expanse of his chest, she wasn't exactly in a position to think straight. "It's a little more complicated than that. I've had a letter from friends in New York. I've promised to help the Dove sisters find titled husbands. They'll be here this spring, which means I've a house party to plan."

"We can come back for that."

She grinned at the thought. "Yes, imagine that. I'll guide them toward husbands all while my lover's presence scandalizes proper society."

He gave a soft growl and grabbed her hips, lifting her and pulling her astride him in one deft motion. Her breath caught at the sheer strength necessary to carry out the task with such efficiency, as well as the hard erection firmly pressed against her most sensitive parts. Now she really wouldn't be able to think.

"Fiancé," he said, his voice firm. "No one will think twice about the presence of your fiancé."

"Fiancé?"

A single black brow raised in question. "Unless you think we can arrange to be married before spring?"

"Married? Jacob . . . married?"

"I told you." He pressed lazy kisses to her neck and shoulder. "When the Halston men fall in love, they love obsessively and forever. So you might as well come to Paris with me until the club is up and running. We'll come back as often as we need in the meantime, then we'll be married this summer. I'll follow you to London, New York, the wilds of any continent you want." By now he had lifted her a bit so that his lips teased the peak of her breast. His tongue came out to lave her nipple, leaving her breath coming in short rasps. "Say yes."

"There's so much we don't know."

"Such as?" His soft lips brushed across her as he spoke, making it difficult to focus.

"Babies? Do you want them?"

"Do you?" he asked.

"Yes, one day." She had nearly cried in relief every time her courses came during her marriage, but that had only been because a child would have tied her to Hereford even more and been another way he could torment her. But she did want a baby of her own, with Jacob, she realized.

"Then so do I." He said it so matter-of-factly that it was difficult to accept.

"But it wasn't so long ago that you refused to marry me before the age of sixty, far past childbearing years."

He grinned at her. "I'll keep saying it until you understand. I love you and I will do whatever it takes to keep you."

"That's hardly a reason to have a child."

"Children are born every day for terrible reasons. This isn't one of them." Relinquishing his play at her breast, he took in a deep breath. "My life was laid out in two distinct paths. The one I was on was lonely but familiar. It was safe but cold and I had grown accustomed to it. Then you came along. You were the other path. The one that frightened me. The one that required me to live with my heart outside of my body." He gathered her close and she understood that he meant her—she was his heart. "It's too late now to go back to the other path. I have you and I cannot let you go. I love you. Whatever that means, we'll figure it out together. I don't need children to be happy, but I want them if you do. I can devote myself to being a good husband and father."

"Jacob." She didn't know how to refute that. She didn't want to. "You are everything I've ever wanted. I love you."

His eyes shimmered with what she suspected were unshed tears just before his mouth took hers. She curled her fingers in his hair and kissed him back with all the love she felt. He took hold of her hips and lifted her, bringing her forward until she was sliding down onto him. The kiss broke as they both groaned at the exquisite sensation of him stretching her to fit him.

She held him against her as her entire body throbbed, leaving her almost dizzy.

"Marry me?" he whispered, his fingers tightening on her as he rolled his hips beneath her, bringing her down sharply as he bucked upward.

Her breath caught. She couldn't last under this onslaught. Nor did she have to. There would be endless days and nights of him. "Yes," she whispered, gathering herself finally. "I'll marry you."

He smiled as if she had just handed him his heart's desire. "Yes?" he asked.

She laughed. "Yes. Yes. Yes." She kissed him until she could hardly breathe and then she held him, gasping for air as he eventually brought them both to completion.

Camille awoke the next morning delightfully sore in all the best ways. She stretched and smiled as a large male body roused at her back. His hands roamed over her stomach and down her hip as she enjoyed the delicious stretching of her muscles. Last night had seemed endless. After introducing her to the delights of taking a shower bath with him—they lingered so long they outlasted the modest supply of warm water and ran freezing back to bed where cuddling for warmth had meant another long, love-making session—Jacob had ordered a dinner tray for them.

Over beef simmered in wine, pheasant, cheese, orange slices, and jam tarts, they spoke of all the ways they had noticed each other since she had come to London. But their talk wasn't tinged with regret; rather, they marveled over the new openness. Tiny fascinations brought out into the light and savored. By unspoken agreement they talked only of the past and present, as if knowing the future was for tomorrow. Then they had returned to bed, sated and full, whispering their love as they slowly explored each other.

Camille's face heated as she remembered she had finally gotten to taste the salt of his release. In the light of day it seemed wicked, but she didn't care. She would do it again and again in the coming days. She knew it as well as she knew that he would be a part of her from now to forever.

"Good morning." He pressed a kiss to her shoulder before rising up to rest on his elbow and kiss her lips properly.

She smiled up at him, glorying at the look of unabashed love on his face.

"You're blushing," he teased. "Which part of last night has you blushing?"

"All of it."

He grinned and leaned down to flick his tongue over her nipple. She groaned both in pleasure and pain. She really was sore from his thorough attention. His grin turned wicked and he let her go, his thumb coming up to rub over her bottom lip. She felt sore and swollen even there. His eyes deepened and she knew he was remembering how it felt to be pleasured by her mouth. She bit his thumb, but he didn't move it, leaving it there so she could soothe it with her tongue. When she let him go, he stroked his thumb all the way down her body to the curls at the juncture of her thighs.

"Jacob," she pouted with a smile. "I'm tender this

morning." But she was parting her thighs anyway to let him in, because she was now addicted to his touch.

"Shh . . ." he whispered. "I merely need to assure myself that this is real and you're not part of a dream."

The pad of his thumb explored the seam of her lips and then gently delved inside to find her wet and swollen. She gasped at the sensation of wanting him, her body tightening in response despite the soreness of her tender flesh. He brought that thumb to his mouth where he licked her taste from his skin. She wanted him again, instantly, but when she moved to grab him, his grin turned wicked again and he slipped out of bed.

"Beast!" The word didn't hold any bite as she laughed, having started to suspect in the wee hours of the morning that he delighted in teasing her.

He paused to add more coal to the fire since he had given explicit instructions that they not be bothered, so a servant hadn't come to do it. It was cold, so she settled into the folds of the blankets as she admired the view of his nude body walking to the bureau on the other side of the room. Opening the lid of a small wooden chest, he shifted things around before he retrieved something and allowed the lid to fall shut.

The mischief was gone from his face when he joined her beneath the covers, replaced by a solemnity rarely present with him. Keeping a close watch on her face, he held out his palm and she gasped at the ring. It was a perfect, rose-cut solitaire diamond. "It belonged to my mother. Before she died, she gave it to me and told me to give it to the woman I love."

"Jacob . . ." That was all she could get out as she stared at the ring that obviously meant so much to him, overcome. "I love it," she finally whispered when she could draw a breath.

He smiled and slid it onto her finger. The simple gesture somehow solidified the promises they had whispered last night. It made them real and tangible. He kissed her and then gathered her against him. "I love you, Camille."

She nearly cried at how full those words made her heart. Holding him close, she buried her face into his neck and breathed him in. Finally, when she could breathe without trembling, she sat back but didn't leave the circle of his arms. "Tell me about our life in Paris." It hardly seemed real, and they had studiously avoided talk of the future last night except in the most vague terms.

He smiled and stroked her face. "En Soirée is in Montmartre in the 18th arrondissement. We have a flat not very far away. I stayed there last summer. You'll like it. It overlooks a courtyard with a garden so that it's quiet, but there are shops and cafés nearby. From the parlor window you can see the whole city lit up at night."

"It sounds perfectly charming." Particularly since he would be sharing it with her. The idea of living with him felt as decadent as it did naughty, but there was no way she was giving up any part of him now.

"During the day, we'll hold auditions for the acts. Blanchet already has some arranged for next week, but there will be more. You can come help choose the performers. After that our days should be free, and I'll work the club most nights." He brushed his lips against her temple. "Have you given any thought to how you might continue your suffrage work while we're there? I know it's important to you."

"I've volunteered for a letter-writing campaign with LSS. I'm writing to every member of the House of Commons and several landed gentry to campaign for the Married Women's Property Act. I can do that from Paris and send my letters to Lilian to post here."

He smiled in approval. "When you're not busy with that we can go to museums and walk the Seine and Champs-Élysées. I'll make love to you in the early hours of the morning after the cabaret closes, and we'll plan our wedding."

She laughed and blushed. It would take some time to get

used to the casual way he spoke about sex. She liked it, but it was different. Taking a deep breath, she told him the fear that had been nudging at her ever since she opened her eyes this morning. "We have to go see my mother before we leave. Not only do I need to pack a trunk, but I have to tell her what's going on with us."

His eyes clouded only slightly. "Of course. I understand." Then he took a breath and asked what they had both been avoiding. "Will she resist you going with me?"

"I don't know. I don't care. I want to go with you and I want to live with you there. It's likely that she'll insist on coming to Paris herself, so she can pretend to her friends that I am staying there with her."

"Would that bother you?" he asked.

"No, she'll stay at a hotel, while I'll stay in scandal with you."

He brought her hand to his mouth and kissed the finger that wore his ring. "I like this side of you."

She laughed. "I've learned that one perk of being a duchess is that you get to stop caring what people think of you."

"We could marry sooner with a special license."

She brushed back the hair that had fallen over one of his eyes. It still took her breath away every time she remembered that he was hers. "This summer, like we talked about. I want time to plan a real wedding, one that I want this time."

"Whatever you want. I want you to have one that makes you happy."

She couldn't help but smile again. She'd been smiling all morning, it seemed, and she couldn't stop. "I'm happiest with you," she said, kissing him. "Don't you want to have a say in the planning?"

He guided her onto his lap with her legs wrapped tightly around his waist. His arms went around, holding her close. "The wedding is a formality. I'm already your husband in every way that counts."

Epilogue

❧

The months since the night they had declared their love had gone by in a blur. Camille had never dreamed that such happiness could be found on earth. She had given three speeches about the negative impact her marriage had had on her life. Jacob had opened his club in Paris with Blanchet and they sold out every night. The Dove sisters had arrived and one had found a husband. Scarbury had been investigated for instigating several attacks on demonstrators and was currently awaiting a hearing on the matter—it helped that Devonworth, Rothschild, and Leigh were all pushing the investigation. But perhaps the most noteworthy development was that she had married the man she loved at St. George's on Hanover Square a few hours earlier, surrounded by only the people closest to them in their lives.

Camille caught Jacob's eye across the crowded drawing room of Violet and Christian's home on Belgrave Square, where they were hosting their wedding breakfast. They had been set up at the far end of the room to receive the well-wishers who had been arriving in a steady stream, bringing gifts and hoping to get a look at the bride and groom, since the wedding itself had been very limited. He smiled back at her, his gaze full of so much love she had to look away to keep from going to him. Her father stood at his side, looking as severe and unbothered as ever.

The two had met for the first time a few days ago when her father had arrived from New York, and it had gone well. It turned out her father was less concerned about her second marriage than he had been with her first, or perhaps her mother had talked with him. Either way, he had welcomed Jacob as his son-in-law and had gifted them a generous deposit to her bank account. It was the only way the man knew to express his affection. Little did he know that she had earmarked a great deal of it to help fund several women's rights initiatives the LSS supported.

"Darling, Lady Fairhope has come to pay her respects." Mama had posted herself at her side and had taken it upon herself to announce each new guest.

It was a tedious tradition, the wedding breakfast, but she would endure it if it meant she got to spend the rest of her life with her husband in peace. She had been willing to forgo it altogether and celebrate alone with her friends, but her mother had convinced her that receiving everyone instead of avoiding them would go a long way to assuaging curiosity. So she had agreed and greeted Lady Fairhope with genuine happiness. As the older woman moved past her, August hurried over, attempting to hide a smile by pressing her lips together.

"Come with me." August took her hand. "We'll return soon," she promised Mama, and led her through the crowd to the family's private sitting room in the back of the house.

Their progress was slow as they were forced to stop several times to greet people. Finally, August glanced around as if to ensure they were not followed and pushed open the door, ushering her inside and closing it behind her. Violet waited inside, smiling when she saw her and holding out a glass of champagne.

"We thought we could take a moment to have a private celebration."

Nearly overcome with emotion, Camille smiled against the lump in her throat and hugged her friend. August joined in and they laughed at how awkward it was with Violet's protruding belly.

"I can't believe we're sisters now," Camille said, wiping a tear from the corner of her eye. Everything she had ever wanted was coming true, and it felt so good that she wasn't quite certain it wasn't a dream.

"We've always been sisters," Violet said. "This only makes it official."

August squeezed her shoulders. "We're thrilled for you, Camille. You deserve every happiness, and I know that Jacob will spend his days making sure you have it."

"He will or he'll answer to me." Violet was only half teasing.

They laughed and August raised her glass, and Violet followed suit. "To you, Camille."

Camille shook her head and raised her own glass. "To us, the Heiresses. It hasn't been easy, but we have found our way here and I am so happy to call you my family."

"To us," they echoed in unison and took a drink.

A moment later, the door opened and Helena smiled as she walked in, holding her husband's hand. "Found you!"

Max held the door open behind them for Lilian and Anthony to hurry inside, before he closed it and joined the group, drawing Helena back against him. "The wedding was so nice I can't believe I almost forgot that I despise these things. No offense, Camille." He kissed Helena's temple and she smiled up at him.

"None taken. I tend to agree with the sentiment." They

had been among the few guests at the ceremony. The breakfast was a whole other beast.

The door opened again, and Christian hurried in followed by Jacob. She couldn't believe how her heart leaped at merely his presence.

"We saw you leave," Christian explained, his expression slightly accusatory that everyone had escaped and left them behind.

Jacob only had eyes for her and came over, drawing her into his embrace and pressing a quick kiss to the corner of her mouth. "Good afternoon, wife."

That word. Once it had been abhorrent, but he made it sound completely new and different. Butterflies swirled in her belly as his hand went to her nape, his finger stroking the bare skin he found there. The door opened again before she could reply, and this time Evan hurried inside, giving the key a twist to lock it before glowering at them all. "I see the plan was to leave me to the horde."

They all laughed and August hurried to his side, leaning up on her toes to kiss his cheek. He appeared only slightly mollified. "Violet and I wanted a moment with Camille. Sacrifices were made."

He growled playfully and August giggled. "I hope your moment was worth it. You can repay my sacrifice later," he said, drawing a knuckle over her lips. She rolled her eyes and wrapped her arms around him, bringing him into the group.

"With a little luck, they may not even notice we've gone," Jacob said.

Indeed, the sounds of countless conversations had continued uninterrupted in the other parts of the main floor.

"I shall prepare the drinks." Christian walked to the sideboard at the far end of the room and began pouring champagne. Violet hurried over to help hand them out.

As Camille leaned back into the arms of her new husband, she was overcome with happiness. This day was as different from her first wedding as night was to day. She didn't know she was crying silent tears until Jacob looked down at her, wiping a tear away with his thumb.

"What's wrong?"

"I'm just . . . so happy." The people in this room were everything that she held dear, and that didn't even count the children, Jacob's sister Maura, her own mother, and all the other women at LSS who had become so very important to her. "My life is fuller and richer than I ever imagined it could be." Taking his hands, she said, "Thank you, Jacob. I owe it all to you. Thank you for helping me find this wonderful life."

He brought her hands to his mouth and kissed each one. "I love you," he whispered and pulled her into his arms. Then he kissed her fully on the lips.

Camille knew in that moment she had everything she had ever needed or wanted.

Acknowledgments

Camille and Jacob's book was never part of the planned Gilded Age Heiresses series. When I originally conceived of the Crenshaw family, the series was meant to follow the lives of the siblings before coming to an end. I didn't realize that I would get to know Camille so well or that she would suffer quite so much in those books. When readers began reaching out to me to ask about her story, I knew that I had to give her the happily ever after that she deserved. Thank you to everyone who read the first three books and wanted to read hers.

In fact, my thanks go out to everyone who has read my books. When you start writing the first book of what you hope will become a series, you never know how it will be received. Will people want to read the first book? Will they care enough to read the next one? It's because of you and everyone who has shared this series that I have been able to continue writing. A simple thank-you doesn't seem to be enough to express the depths of my gratitude. I will be eternally grateful for every moment I'm able to write more stories for you.

This can't be said enough, but a huge thanks goes out to my agent, Nicole Resciniti, for her enthusiastic support from the first time I told her I *might* have an idea for a series about American heiresses.

And, of course, to Sarah Blumenstock, editor extraordinaire who takes the manuscripts I send her and helps me to turn them into something people might actually want to read.

Thanks to the entire Berkley team for making my books sparkle and getting them into the hands of readers. I am so grateful to have a team of amazing people helping me. So many people are instrumental in getting my books to readers, I know that I can't possibly name them all. These are just a few of the people working so hard behind the scenes to help create my books: Jessica Mangicaro, Stephanie Felty, Rita Frangie, Alison Prince, Megha Jain, Liz Sellers, Jennifer Lynes, Tawanna Sullivan, Emilie Mills.

To my author friends—Nathan, Erin, Tara, Laurie, Elisabeth, Janice, Jenni, Lara, Nicole, Seána, Virginia, Lucy, Melissa, and Terri—every writer needs a support system and I'm so grateful you are mine.

Finally, a big thank-you to my family. I wouldn't be able to do this without you. I love you.

Don't miss

THE STRANGER I WED

*Book one in a new series from
Harper St. George!*

OXFORDSHIRE, ENGLAND
1878

Title hunting was not for the faint of heart. The occupation required a great deal of analysis, focus, and attention to detail, three qualities Cora Dove had no choice but to perfect. One had to be strategic when choosing the ideal candidate for husband. Everyone knew that the perfect groom for a title hunter was a fortune hunter. However, it simply wasn't that easy. Too impoverished and the wealth gained from the marriage would drain away like water through a sieve.

Cora was determined that the man she would marry not be a gambler, at least not to excess. The likelihood of finding an aristocrat who did not gamble at all would be akin to finding a fish that did not swim. There were other considerations, too. In fact, she had made a list. Too young and he'd likely be brash and unruly. Too old and he could hold outdated ideas about a wife's role. Too temperamental or too wicked in his pursuits and he would be difficult to manage. Too attractive and heartache would inevitably ensue—this one had been the last to be put on the list. Cora quite liked good-looking men and wouldn't have minded marrying one. Her older sister, Jenny, however, who knew more than she did about the qualities of handsome men, had been insistent, so the condition had gone on the list. Only a fool would aim for the highest title and leave it at that when there were so many other considerations.

Cora was no fool. Not anymore. She had stepped off the steamer ship from New York with her mother and younger sister last week with her mission at the forefront of her mind. Find a titled husband and marry him by summer. This gave her a couple of months to weigh her options. Thankfully, she would not face the task alone. Camille, Dowager Duchess of Hereford, was a childhood friend from New York who had married a duke a few years ago and agreed to act as a sort of agent to help the sisters find titled husbands.

The duchess wasn't a proponent of the cash-for-class marriages that were becoming so popular between American heiresses and impoverished noblemen. Her own parents had all but auctioned her off to the highest title, and the marriage had been deeply unhappy until the much older duke had died and set her free. Now she was with Jacob Thorne, a man she loved. It had taken several letters and a few telegrams before Cora had convinced Camille that this marriage was what she wanted and that she was not being coerced by her mother. Which was the truth. It was her negligent sire who had made this sort of marriage necessary, but Cora preferred not to dwell on that.

Instead, she devoted every waking moment to finding the perfect husband. She had a journal specifically for the task that she had diligently filled with notes about each man Camille proposed to her. She knew their ages, their immediate family members, and how they spent their days. Perhaps more importantly, she knew how their family had lost their own fortunes. That crucial bit of information could be the difference between a comfortable future and one spent scraping pennies.

Unlike their contemporaries who came from new money families with industrial interests that kept their pockets deep, Cora and her sisters were illegitimate. They weren't marrying for mere social status, though that would be a boon. They were marrying for the very survival of their small family.

"Camille, pardon my disbelief, but there can't possibly be suitors here," Eliza, Cora's younger sister, remarked, her brow furrowed in distinct displeasure.

The three of them descended the steps of the train depot, umbrellas in hand to combat the April drizzle. The train stretched out behind them on the track, belching steam into the cool air. They were in a small village—Cora had already forgotten the name—not far from Camille's country estate in Oxfordshire. The town was little more than a stop along the railroad, but it was quaint and picturesque, as Cora was finding most English villages to be. They possessed a charm lent to them by virtue of age that many of the industrial mill towns that had sprung up back home didn't have. The buildings, made of either stone or wattle and daub, had been standing for centuries longer than Cora's family brownstone back in New York. There was a security in that permanence that she found comforting.

"I quite like it," Cora said.

"Then you can marry any gentleman who might reside here. I'll choose one who lives in London." Eliza nodded her head in finality and Cora hid her grin. If only it were that easy a choice.

"I understand the conditions are not ideal," Camille said, leading them around the muck and mud of the road to the higher packed earth along the edge. They didn't seem to be heading toward the center of town, but in the other direction along a narrow lane that followed the tracks before turning away. "But being able to observe these men outside of normal social conditions will give you rare insight. Since they don't know you yet and don't know that you're watching, they'll be more inclined to be themselves. Once at the house party, they'll all be on their best behavior and you'll only see what they allow you to see."

That was certainly true. Of the ten men Camille had invited to the upcoming house party at Stonebridge Cottage, they had been able to observe five without their being aware. First, they had gone to the Lakes, where they had discreetly assessed two suitors who were participating in an angler tournament. They were two of the most boring individuals Cora had ever encountered. Since boredom hadn't made it onto her list, they had passed the test. Then they had gone to a lecture at the British Museum to locate a third, who had been a bit argumentative with the lecturer. From there, they had quietly observed two others at Hyde Park. Both were a bit snobbish in their bearing, so Cora had put a question mark by their names. Today was their last jaunt before the house party began early next week. They were here to watch a football game.

"I'm afraid the match has already begun, but we'll be able to see enough to judge their sportsmanship. I know that's not on your list, but you can judge a lot from a man by how he treats his teammates and adversaries," Camille continued. "Perhaps after, we can pop over to the public house and watch them, though that might be pushing things."

It wouldn't do to have anyone recognize the duchess. Once any prospective suitors heard the sisters' American accents, their disguises of plain clothing would be quite useless to hide their identities. All objectivity would be gone and they would lose their chance to observe their suitors unaware.

"Perhaps we can watch for a time," Cora said.

They rounded a corner after a row of tiny houses onto a

narrow dirt lane that led to a field. It did appear the game
was already in progress with roughly two dozen men on the
pitch. Half wore green shirtsleeves while the other half
wore yellow. Both wore trousers or pantaloons that would
never be white again with all the mud, along with high
socks and leather boots, and their heads were bare. They
chased a round, leather ball across the field in a match that
was much more physical than Cora had anticipated.

"Careful of your step, dear," Camille said, indicating a
particularly deep puddle, and Cora lithely stepped around
it. When she had righted herself, the duchess and Eliza
were continuing on their way to the left, where a robust
crowd had gathered to cheer on the players.

Cora stood transfixed at the sheer physicality of the
drama playing out on the field. One man hurried to kick the
ball, grunting when another ran into him, nearly sending
him careening onto the soaked ground. The ball had only
been glanced, which sent it several yards toward the far
side. Another man, his golden hair damp with sweat and
falling about his face, cursed and then let out a victorious
yell as he ran through several opponents and managed to
make good contact with the ball, kicking it in an arc, sending it farther downfield toward the goal. The players turned
as one and hurried in that direction. If there was any sort of
coordination among them, Cora couldn't see it. They all
seemed madcap in their zeal to obtain the ball.

For a moment she was struck by the sheer size and athleti-
cism of the men. Without a coat to hide them, their shoulders
appeared extra wide, the muscles working under the thin
material of their shirts as they ran, the rain melding the fabric to them. Their chests seemed thick and strapped with
sinew. It suddenly became apparent why good society insisted on a man wearing his coat at all times. It might prove
too distracting otherwise. Although, most society men she
had met had a bit of soft about them. Not like these men.

She smiled to herself and began to make her way over to

where Camille and Eliza had joined the spectators. However, she couldn't stop herself from looking back at the one who had kicked the ball. He was tall and muscled, his jaw square and firm as his eyes narrowed, watching to see which way the ball would go when it finally broke free of the group. He loped easily toward his teammates, his long legs eating up the distance without making him out of breath. It was probably too much to hope that he would be one of her suitors, though the fact that he was so handsome meant he violated a rule on her list and she shouldn't consider him.

As she stared at him, the ball suddenly broke free of the chaos on the field, hurtling in her direction. A player roughly her own size came rushing toward her, his eyes crazed with ferocity as he screamed with the triumph of a predator about to seize its prey. She barely got a look at him before the man she had been admiring yelled, "Briggs!" drawing her attention back to him. He'd picked up speed, running full-bore in their direction, ostensibly to intercept his teammate before he flattened her.

She sidestepped the ball, somehow managing to avoid Briggs but stepping into the path of the golden-haired man. He tried to stop, but the change in momentum sent him skidding over a patch of mud and directly into her. Her breath rushed out of her at the initial contact, sending her umbrella and journal flying, and her own feet caught the mud and Cora and the man tumbled to the ground together. He twisted, catching the brunt of the fall, but they rolled several more times before coming to a stop in the soggy grass. The players were still following the ball, and as they lumbered closer, sounding like a herd of cattle, she closed her eyes, expecting to be trampled. The anticipated disaster never happened, as they continued running down the field. She opened her eyes to see the man's staring down at her. They were green like emeralds and intense with concern. She had never seen eye color like that on anything but a cat.

"Are you hurt?" he asked.

She took in a breath, surprised to find that nothing was sore. "I don't think so." Her voice came out sounding winded.

He leaned over her as he ran a hand over her ribcage, and up over her breast. She gasped as he pressed, no doubt looking for injury, but her nipple tightened beneath his touch just the same and her blood warmed in a way that was unseemly. She sucked in a hard breath. "Excuse me!"

"You *are* hurt."

"No!" She wrenched his hand away.

His brow furrowed, flummoxed by her outrage. "No?"

Perhaps he hadn't realized that he had all but fondled her breast with his pawing. She took in another breath and managed to speak in a calmer tone. "I am uninjured." She attempted to sit up as embarrassment began to creep in, but she was stuck beneath the weight of his thigh over hers— his very large, very solid thigh. In fact, his entire body seemed very large and very solid. She ought to feel more put out, but suddenly she didn't quite mind lying here like this beneath him.

"Let me help you up," he said just as she was becoming accustomed to his attentions. Removing himself from her, he offered her his hand.

She took it, still too aware of him in a physical sense. Her heart pounded as heat suffused her cheeks. At his full height he stood nearly a head taller than her. His torso might well have been double the width of hers. Aside from a few dances, she had never been this close to a man before, and certainly not one so attractive.

"You might watch where you're going next time." She was struggling to catch her breath, as if she were the one who had run across the field. Her hand shook when she took it back, so she wiped at the blades of grass stuck to her bodice to hide the tremble. His hands followed, helping her wipe them away and sending her nerve endings teetering wildly.

Before she could gather herself to protest—which might have taken a while considering a very real part of her was enjoying the attention—he said, "You might have stayed off the pitch."

His words cut through the havoc within her. "I wasn't on the pitch. I was off to the side. Your friend, Briggs, was outside of the boundary."

"You play association football, do you?" His gaze narrowed in obvious irritation.

"No, but every game has a boundary line. I was outside of yours." She turned to indicate that fact, but there didn't actually seem to be a line designating any boundary.

His brow rose dubiously.

"Are you blaming me for the fact that you ran me over?" she asked.

His lips tightened in what might have been a suppressed grin. "No, of course not."

"Good." She wiped at her skirt.

He walked the few steps necessary to pick up her journal and umbrella and handed them back to her. After she took them, he scraped his hair out of his face, sending rivulets of water running down his cheeks. She couldn't help but watch one make its way to his mouth, where it slid smoothly over his bottom lip.

"Perhaps the next time you see the ball and an entire team of men coming toward you, you might consider removing yourself from the field of play."

There was a spark of humor in his eyes that somehow softened his words. The result was that she felt mildly annoyed but greatly intrigued. "Perhaps you might consider keeping your ball and your men on the pitch."

He smiled, but only for a second before someone called out and his head swiveled in that direction. "Dev!"

He sobered a bit, the spark of mirth dying out as he glanced toward Camille and Eliza, who were hurrying toward them, before asking, "You're an American, are you?"

Damn. She'd forgotten all about not talking to anyone. "Yes, I'm visiting friends."

He seemed to size up Camille and then glanced at Cora once more. With a tip of his head, he ran back out onto the field to rejoin the fray.

"Cora!" Eliza ran up and held her umbrella over them both to block the sprinkle of rain.

"That looked horrific. Are you hurt?" Camille wiped at the grass and mud on Cora's skirt with a handkerchief, nearly losing her hat and veil in the process.

"Not unless you count my bruised pride." Cora smiled and led them away from the field.

"He might have broken your ribs," Eliza said, somewhat indignant on her behalf.

"But he didn't."

"Thank goodness for that," Camille added, standing to her full height, her attention back on the game still in play. "He still hasn't confirmed his attendance at the house party. If he broke your rib, I suspect he wouldn't come at all."

Cora whipped around to look at her friend before finding the man called Dev among his teammates. He whooped and raised his hands above his head in triumph as his teammate scored a goal. "Dev," she whispered. Then louder, "Devonworth?"

"Yes, that was the Earl of Devonworth," Camille confirmed for her.

That name was in her journal. She had written down his family members, his family history, and the fact that he was passionate about his seat in Parliament. She had thought he might be an ideal candidate for husband because he met all the requirements. Except now she knew he was handsome. Too handsome, really. He completely violated the last rule.

For the first time, Cora understood why Jenny had insisted on that rule. It would be terribly difficult to divorce a man so tempting.

Ready to find
your next great read?

Let us help.

Visit prh.com/nextread

Penguin
Random
House